THE LOCK AND KEY LIBRARY

CLASSIC MYSTERY AND DETECTIVE STORIES OF ALL NATIONS

TEN VOLUMES

North Europe   Mediterranean   German   Classic French
Modern French   French Novels   Old Time English
Modern English   American   Real Life

TRANSLATORS

whose work is represented in this collection of "CLASSIC MYSTERY *and* DETECTIVE STORIES," many here rendered into English for the first time

Arthur Arrivet	*Japanese*
John P. Brown	*Turkish*
United States Legation, Constantinople	
Jonathan Sturges	*French*
Sir Richard Francis Burton	*Arabic*
Lady Isabel Burton	*Arabic*
Grace I. Colbron	*German-Scandinavian*
Frederick Taber Cooper, Ph.D.	*Romance Languages*
George F. Duysters	*Spanish*
Herbert A. Giles	*Chinese*
British Consular Service	
Glanvill Gill	*French*
D. F. Hannigan, LL.B.	*French*
Louis Hoffmann	*French*
Florence Irwin	*French*
Charles Johnston	*Russian-Oriental*
Royal Asiatic Society, Indian Civil Service	
Eugene Lucas	*Hungarian*
R. Shelton MacKenzie	*French*
Ellen Marriage	*French*
John A. Pierce	*French*
W. R. S. Ralston, M.A.	*Tibetan*
Edward Rehatsek	*Persian*
Royal Asiatic Society, Examiner Bombay University	
George Rawlinson, M.A. (Oxon.)	*Greek*
Mary J. Safford	*French*
Franz Anton von Schiefner	*Tibetan*
Librarian, St. Petersburg Academy of Sciences	
Charles Henry Tawney, M.A., C.I.E. . . .	*Hindoo*
Librarian, India Office	
R. Whittling, M.A. (Oxon.)	*French*
Edward Ziegler	*German*

How the Second Sharper Knew the Horse's Pedigree

Drawing by S. L. Wood. To illustrate
"The Craft of the Three Sharpers"

THE LOCK AND KEY LIBRARY

CLASSIC MYSTERY AND DETECTIVE STORIES

EDITED BY

JULIAN HAWTHORNE

MEDITERRANEAN

Italian Spanish Oriental

Ancient Latin and Greek

NEW YORK
THE REVIEW OF REVIEWS CO.
1909

THE QUINN & BODEN CO. PRESS
RAHWAY, N. J.

Table of Contents

PART I.—ITALIAN AND SPANISH MYSTERY STORIES

PART II.—ORIENTAL MYSTERY STORIES

PART I

Italian and Spanish Mystery Stories

Italian Mystery Stories

I. M. Palmarini

Shadows

This story won the prize of five hundred lire offered in the competition held by the Italian newspaper, the *Marzocco*, in the issue of April 16, 1896. The committee of judges were the members of the editorial staff, including Angiolo Orvieto, Enrico Corradini, Ugo Ojetti, and others.

I

ON the deck of the bathing floats few persons were still lingering. The hour was late, the night black and threatening. Along the dim line of the horizon, at equal intervals, flashed dazzling tongues of fire; then after a heavy silence, came a dull, prolonged booming, that made the planking tremble. The sea lay motionless, somber, ominous. The flashes and the thunder drew steadily nearer; at times the mighty outpour of light rent asunder the solemn darkness. A sullen north wind blustered in fitful gusts around the great awning stretched above the spacious promenade; and forcing its way within the sparse night-lamps, tormented the flickering flames.

Mario Ravaschieri and Teodora Alvise were seated upon the bench nearest the sea, at the right-hand corner. He, with elbows resting on knees, had buried his face in his hands; she, leaning back against the back of the bench, her hands lying idly on the seat, was staring wide-eyed upward, through the black humidity of the night.

"What are you thinking of?" Teodora asked presently, without changing her position. A silence followed; then the young man said slowly:

"I am thinking, Teodora, that the sea is black and profound, that in its depths there is peace, that in its depths there is no more desire, no more suffering, no more hope——"

"And I, on the contrary, am thinking how to-morrow the sun will flood both sky and sea with light!"

"How many to-morrows have already passed!" he rejoined, with a sigh.

"But what glorious sunshine it will be, when the day comes!"

"Oh, Dora mine!" exclaimed the man, impetuously clasping her slender waist, and speaking with his lips almost resting on her face, "when you revive my hopes, when you call up the vision of that day, I feel the strength to wait a thousand years!"

She sealed his mouth with her slender hand: "Hush!" she murmured, without raising her head from its rest against the curving wood, "I also must be strong!"

"What a strange speech! Tell me at least your secret thoughts; you are hiding something!"

"Say no more, if you don't believe!" interrupted the woman.

"What am I to believe?" demanded the young man desperately.

"Believe in me, and in my love! Why will you urge me to steps that I cannot take? Does it not show that your love is founded upon sand?"

"I do not know what it shows——" interrupted the lover, ardently pressing her chill fingers. "I know only that I love you utterly. Perhaps I am to blame for too much eagerness, but day by day it grows harder for me to resist the longing to clasp you to my heart, to bind you to me wholly, to feel that you are mine, body, mind, and soul; to——"

"Oh, hush! hush!" she interrupted impetuously, again closing his lips with her hand.

"No, you do not love me," resumed Mario despairingly as soon as he was freed from the tender restraint; "you do not love me; your thoughts are serene and prudent, your heart——"

"Not love you! Ah, but I do!" The confession broke violently from her lips, and she clung to his arm with a vice-like grip of nervous fingers. A blaze of lightning flared above the sea, followed shortly by the prolonged echo of a heavy thunder peal.

"I repeat that I do not understand you," resumed the young man, when the dead silence had again fallen. "How am I to understand you, when you have never opened your thoughts to me?"

Under cover of the heavy darkness, the waters had become troubled. After a deceptive calm, that had lasted during the battle of opposing winds, the sea, which had awaited impassively the outcome of the struggle, now surrendered itself to the victor. Already it was breaking with muffled force against the wooden piles.

"Look!" said Teodora Alvise, rising and stretching out her arm in the obscurity. "You can see nothing? Well, that is like my own thoughts; they are all darkness, even to me. I should have to make a tremendous effort, to gather together all the little sparks of light that glimmer in that darkness. I know only that he is hateful to me; that I loathe him; that my repulsion is so great that my greatest defense against you is the fear that I might need to blush before such a man!"

"What an extraordinary idea!" sighed Ravaschieri.

"Extraordinary to you, because you cannot feel as I do. We women are far finer than you, in our inner feelings. By what right do you claim that you can fathom a woman's soul and understand its secret subtleties? Have you ever been an inexperienced girl, married by her parents to a vicious old man? What do you know of the feelings of such a girl, who after having every one of her most treasured illusions destroyed, finds the man ever at her side, tormenting her with base suspicions, with every form of vulgar jealousy, and at the same time giving daily proof of his own cowardice and vileness? Do you not know that he is almost certain that we love each other, that he turns pale with hatred every time you meet, and yet he lacks the courage to brave you, to insult you, to challenge you; on the contrary, he treats you with exaggerated politeness! But no sooner are we alone than he hurts me bitterly with his evil-minded sneers. Can't you understand now that it is only my own sense of blamelessness that gives me the courage to endure, the proud right to despise him?"

"But, Dora," observed the young man, "according to your code, you have already transgressed, in owning that you love me!"

"No!" answered the woman emphatically. "That is not so! I know little of ethics, but my own good sense tells me that so long as I am strong against you, I need not lower my eyes before him. Think what it would mean to me if I had cause to blush before him; to confess that his malignant shots had hit their mark, that he was justified! Never, never! I would kill myself sooner!"

Another flash quivered over the sea, already lashed to a foam, and Mario was deeply moved by the momentary sight of the tall, graceful, somber figure of the woman he loved, standing erect with arms outstretched towards the distant storm. There followed a long pause. The waves had augmented in volume and in violence, the water could be heard beating against the hatchways, the bridge, the pier. From time to time, the dashing spray was flung upward into their faces. A sullen muttering arose from the sea, the flashes had become more vivid and more frequent.

"Leave him and come with me, somewhere far away!" Ravaschieri suggested impetuously.

"Leave him and come with you!" she echoed in sarcasm. "Would not that prove him to have been right?"

"Then divorce him!" persisted the young man.

"How could I? What reason could I give? According to our social code, he is a model husband!"

Another silence followed. The sea was still rising; many of the lamps had been blown out; the roar of the surf augmented, the crash of breaking waves became more and more frequent. The deck of the bathing float was quite deserted; now and then a servant hurried past, on his way below to close doors and windows. On the left, the gleaming eye of a lighthouse threw a far-reaching jet of blood-red light athwart the darkness, barely touching the surface of the sea, whose waves looked like an innumerable herd of dusky horses, galloping with unequal stride.

"Well, then," questioned Ravaschieri, breaking the gloomy silence, "there is only the one hope for me?" His voice trembled with a shiver of horror.

"Don't ask it of me!" answered Teodora.

"That one terrible hope!"

"Who can read the future?" Her words were drowned in the rumbling of the thunder, while a great wave, breaking over the deck, wrapped her in its dusky spray.

"Come along!" exclaimed Mario, suddenly springing up and nervously drawing her dear form towards him. But Teodora would not move; sitting undaunted at the very end of the bench, with hands still clasped behind her neck, she seemed to be fathoming the blackness of the tempest.

"Come, Dora, we must be going," he repeated, almost dragging her away.

"How beautiful it is, how beautiful!" she exclaimed, the salt water dripping from her, and her arms outstretched towards the storm. The sea was moaning; the furious and unexpected summer tempest was churning up the water with increasing violence. The billows dashed against the pier with dull, sullen, insistent thuds, like a school of dolphins hurling themselves against the bulwarks. Along the abandoned shore, the surf sounded like a herd of a thousand lowing cattle; the wind, steadily gathering force, filled the black air with strange voices; hisses, howls, groans, wails, and shrieks.

"Do come, Dora!" the man said once again, with a suggestion of anguish in his voice.

"Why, you are trembling!" she exclaimed, seizing his hands and trying to see his face through the darkness.

"No, I am not!"

"Yes, you are trembling!" Teodora insisted.

"It is the chill of the night, I am shivering a little,"

Ravaschieri rejoined defensively. For a few moments the woman held her lover's hands clasped tightly, studying his face through the black night. Then, letting them fall, she murmured:

"Well, yes, let us be going."

Close-pressed together, like Paolo and Francesca, they passed back through the gusty night, along the deserted pier, lashed by the water, beaten by the wind; from a clock tower came the strokes of half-past eleven.

"When will he be back?" questioned Mario, shuddering.

"Perhaps within an hour."

They returned to the hotel. Ravaschieri accompanied his companion to the second floor, pressed his lips upon her fingers, and then descended to his own room on the floor below. Why had such piercing cold invaded his entire being? A torturing trembling had seized upon every fiber; in his breast he felt a sensation of ice, ponderous, depressing; he had to labor hard and deep to draw his breath, as though really all within his breast was one congealed mass. He lit a candle, let himself fall into an armchair at the foot of his bed, and remained there with his eyes for a long time fixed upon the flame.

Little by little his eyes closed, his limbs relaxed; Mario Ravaschieri had gone to sleep.

II

Mario roused himself with a start, as though someone had shaken him violently. For an instant he fixed his staring eyes upon the flame of the almost consumed candle, then sprang to his feet, trembling all over, with hair rising in horror and a strangling sensation at his throat. He cast a hopeless glance around, then gazed at his hands, the fingers of which were cramping and twisting convulsively. The night wind, entering through the half-closed window, swelled out the folds of the curtain on the right, and floated it halfway across the room; the lower hem of it flapped upon the young man's head, so that he sprang aside into one corner, and stood there cowering.

Then once more he fell to gazing at his hands. A low, choking cry came from his contracted throat, in a vain effort to speak. "How could I, how could I have done it?" he wanted to cry aloud.

Even now, he had the frightful scene before his eyes: the Baron Alvise lying on his back, diagonally across the bed, his legs spread apart, his head dangling over the opposite edge, his hands raised to his throat,—those hands of which Mario could even now feel the spasmodic grip around his wrists; and that face! Oh, the memory of that face! Mario felt a convulsion run through his entire person.

The cadaverous features were swollen and empurpled, the eyeballs starting from their sockets, the mouth widely opened, showing the blackened and defective teeth; and the tongue, that hideous tongue! black, swollen, glutinous, lolling from the mouth almost its entire length; the dilated nostrils, owing to the pendent position of the head, appeared like two mere holes. The features were all distorted, the bald head had turned livid, the scant gray hair bristled stiffly above the temples where the veins had congested.

Ravaschieri could see all this, and the bedroom, and the candle in its porcelain candlestick, ringed around with figures of children in relief; he could see the Baron's clothes upon a chair at the foot of the bed, and among them he noted a rose in the buttonhole of the coat. But just as a blast of wind sweeps away the cloud that has veiled the outlines of a landscape, and suddenly renders every detail clear; the thing which suddenly brought everything before him with unmistakable vividness was the memory of a button that lay glistening, between the bureau and the sofa.

"It was I! It was I!" he found himself murmuring at last. "But how could I? How could I? Oh, if it would only turn out to be a dream!" was his next thought.

The mere doubt shook him; it was just a vague hope, of which at heart he was quite convinced of the fallacy; yet it sufficed to spur him to action. He took a few steps towards the bed, then stopped, then continued on his way stealthily, on the tips of his toes. He paused once more at the door, pressed his ear to the keyhole, and stood listening. At that hour before dawn the hotel lay in profound silence.

An irresistible need to see, and to assure himself, spurred him on. He must have gone up those stairs, to the second floor, he must have opened the door——

Opened the door——? And why had he left the door open? And how had he opened it? He sought in vain to answer his own questions; the whole matter was in utter darkness. Very softly he laid his hand upon the white porcelain handle; then paused. Who could have so badly damaged that handle? The question flashed through his mind simultaneously with a vision of the number of happy, innocent times that same handle had been turned. He pushed upon it; a faint creaking assailed his ears. He suddenly turned faint, recoiled a step, and remained for some moments motionless, staring at that closed door that inexorably prolonged his anguish.

But why had that handle creaked just now, when it had never made a sound before? Then he realized that it was his stealthy, trembling hand that had made it creak. No sooner had he grasped this idea than he flung himself upon the handle with impetuous wrath, seized and turned it. The door turned upon its hinges without the faintest sound, the young man paused to listen, then made his way on tiptoe towards the stairs that, at the end of the corridor, ascended to the floor above.

"Where can that light come from?" he asked himself, halting after a few steps. All the lights were extinguished, and yet he could see around him quite distinctly; but he saw red, as though it were all in flames. He pressed his hands over his eyes; he could see it all, just the same! He was filled with terror, but the dominant thought spurred him on. He reached the foot of the stairs, ascended, made his way along the upper hall, and turned ashy pale. The door of the

Baron's room was ajar, and a thin band of light cleft the darkness of the corridor.

"Then it is true, really true," he gasped, his teeth chattering as in a fever. Yet even then he hoped. He went forward, supporting himself with his hands against the wall, with his eyes fixed upon that band of light.

Suddenly he recoiled, as if mortally stricken. He saw again, in all the ghastly distinctness of reality, the horrible object of his vision; the Baron, strangled to death, lying flat upon his back, diagonally across the bed, the candle still burning on the little night-stand, the Baron's clothes upon a chair, and among them in the buttonhole of the coat he beheld the rose.

Mario Ravaschieri could not wrench himself away from the sight; it seemed as though the very intensity with which he strained his eyes must dispel the malevolent enchantment that made him behold this scene; because, surely, it must be the work of enchantment. It was impossible that he himself should have done this thing!

But all at once a paroxysm of fear took possession of him; he turned and fled desperately, down to his own room, closing the door. The expiring candle still shed a feeble ray of livid light; with one breath he blew it out, then cowered into bed, dressed as he was, and covered himself with the sheet, drawing it even over his head. He was trembling in every fiber, and his teeth continued to chatter; while his heart was beating with such violence as almost to interrupt his breathing. He lacked the strength to shape a definite thought; he knew only that his brain was all awhirl with disconnected, mad ideas, in the midst of which he could see, more definite than ideas, two words written in giant characters, floating towards him, out of a crimson mist: *Teodora . . . assassin.* They were floating towards him, because little by little he discerned a black tempestuous sea; the howling of the wind and the waves tortured his ears; he was being swept away, whither and by what he did not know; he knew only that from time to time there appeared upon the blackness of the water two tablets of fire, on which was written in giant characters: *Teodora . . . assassin.* Instinctively he closed his eyes, as though it were a real vision which he could shut out. It seemed as if the touch of his hands burned his skin. Oh, those hands, those hands! his own hands, against which he could still feel pulsing, in a final convulsive contraction, the throat muscles and arteries of her husband! Mario Ravaschieri flung out his arms, spasmodically brandishing his hands, as though he would gladly have cast them from him.

When the first crisis had passed, he began again to ask himself miserably: "But how, how could I have done this thing? I, Mario Ravaschieri, who have always been kind-hearted to the point of weakness? I, who have never willingly harmed a living soul?" At this moment, a sudden, overwhelming self-pity took possession of him; his staring eyes became suffused with tears; and at the same time he recalled a multitude of occasions on which he had laughed at himself for his own soft-heartedness. His mind seemed to be searching eagerly in the remotest and most secret repositories of memory for incontrovertible proofs of his natural goodness, as if he must already prepare a defense against the crime committed. And little by little, as these memories returned, the tears flowed freely, and it seemed to him that part of his anguish was poured out with them; at least his thoughts were diverted from the enormity of what had occurred. But a sudden flash of visual memory brought before him something that lay glistening, not far from the bureau. It needed only this to bring on a fresh access of dispair, recalling every detail to his mind. He sprang up in bed, to a sitting posture, panting, stretching out his arms towards the darkness; and, shaking with horror, gasped between dry sobs:

"My God! My God! how could I have done this thing?"

III

When all the usual formalities had been complied with, following the assassination, and the authorities had finished their first investigation, and the body had been placed in a temporary coffin, preparatory to sending it to Rome for burial; when the Baroness Teodora Alvise, who had personally overseen all those sad duties that accompany death, "with vigilant mind and devoted heart,"—so said the mayor of the city, when he called to condole with her upon the sad occurrence,—had at last rid herself of all callers and disturbances, she bade the servant to request Mario Ravaschieri to be so kind as to come upstairs for a few moments to see her.

Mario had not had a chance to speak to Teodora since that night, except in the presence of others. A number of ladies had volunteered their kind offices to the Baroness, so suddenly stricken with this great misfortune, and had been constantly on hand to aid her. Yet Mario, whose invincible consternation appeared to others to be keen sorrow for the friend so brutally murdered, had been the Baroness's greatest help. He had been sustained by a feverish excitation. He found himself in a sort of somnambulistic trance, in which his consciousness thought and acted by force of habit. The voice and the glance of Teodora, unwearying in her melancholy duty, were his guidance; and everyone united in praising the activity and devotion of such a friend. It was only when the magistrate, during the hasty formalities of justice, summoned and examined him in the presence of the corpse, that Mario Ravaschieri fainted away. But it was easy to understand this final moment of weakness in a tender-hearted man, when asked to testify beside the friend he had so tragically lost.

The apartments which Teodora occupied after her husband's death—a bedroom, opening off of a small parlor—overlooked the sea, which was not so far distant that a pair of good eyes could not recognize a person down on the shore. The two rooms were on the upper floor, on the quietest side of the hotel, for an extensive kitchen-garden lay on that side of the building.

Teodora waited impatiently. It was ten o'clock in the morning; at half-past eleven the Marchesa Di Santorsola was coming to keep her company. She passed out of her bedroom, crossed the parlor, and glanced into the hall. She heard her lover's steps ascending the stairs, and withdrew again to the inner room.

Mario paused in the doorway, with his eyes resting upon her own.

"Did you close the parlor door?" she questioned, in hushed and agitated tones.

He started violently: "Close it?" he said, almost as though dazed. "Close it? And why should I?"

The woman looked at him a moment, intently, then methodically went and shut it herself, returned, and bolted the door of the bedroom door also. She was very pale, her beautiful blond hair seemed to have grown darker and full of shadows; on each side of her narrow, short, assertive nose, there descended from the green opalescence of her eyes, two purplish lines. Teodora paused beneath the portière; for a long time they gazed at each other, without speaking; then she came nearer to him, grasped his arm, and questioned:

"Did he know that it was you?"

The man gave a start, from head to foot.

"I don't know!" he gasped through his contracted throat. They remained there, silent and motionless, Teodora still grasping his arm mechanically.

"How did you do it?" the woman at last resumed, studying her lover's face.

Mario Ravaschieri raised his dark, bewildered eyes to hers, as if marveling at such a question.

"Tell me!" she urged, slightly shaking his arm.

"But I don't know!" again gasped the young man with a desperate air.

Teodora Alvise raised her lover's arm, took his hand between her own, and gazed with somber curiosity at the long, white, almost girlish fingers. Then, as if to herself, she murmured:

"To think they were so strong!"

For a few moments Ravaschieri also gazed at his hands,

then shrank backward with a sob of repulsion, still unable to turn his eyes from those clenching fingers.

Teodora watched him, with frowning brow. Then she smiled, approached him, drew him down upon the sofa, and wound both arms around his neck.

"How much you must have loved me!" she whispered, and her lips pressed lingeringly upon his.

Despite his love, he shivered beneath the kiss, and rose to his feet, with a sense of suffocation.

"Mario!" cried the woman, "what is it?"

Ravaschieri crossed over to the window and, with wide-open mouth, drank in the morning breeze to the full depths of his lungs.

"I feel as though I were choking!" he managed to say; then held himself there, his eyes staring out upon the measureless azure of sea and sky. Suddenly he quivered, as if assailed by an unforeseen idea, and turning to Teodora, who had again drawn near him, said in stifled tones, stretching out his hand towards the far-off horizon:

"Dora—think,—he will never see that again. Never, do you understand?—never, never again!" He threw himself upon the sofa in an agonized outburst of grief.

The woman sank upon her knees beside him, encircled him with tender arms, and overwhelmed him with a tempest of caresses.

"You must cease at once to think of anything but my love," she commanded, rendering him breathless with the ardor of her words. "I will make up to you for everything. I will make you forget these dreadful days! If my beauty is to blame for what you have done, it is yours, utterly yours. Listen," added the woman, resting her cheek against the young man's face, "feel how my heart is beating, my heart that has only room for you!" She was looking at him with passionate eyes; and Mario Ravaschieri, controlling his grief, gazed upon her delicate beauty as if fascinated; yet even in his fascination, he remained bewildered, almost terrified.

"Mario, my own Mario," continued Teodora, with growing intensity of feeling, and seating herself upon his knee. "Of what are you thinking? Not of me, no, you are not thinking of me, although you have removed the last obstacle that stood between us!" And she continued to press her lips to his forehead, his neck, his lips, clasping him in her eager arms, and caressing his cheek with her own.

But unexpectedly Mario Ravaschieri uttered a tortured cry, sprang to his feet with a livid face, with wide eyes staring at an object lying on the floor, near the window, that inspired him with horror. Teodora, who had also risen, followed his glance and turned pale; a tremor ran through all her limbs.

Near the corner of the sofa, towards the window, lay a fragment of pasteboard, on which could be seen half the forehead, one eye, and part of the mouth of a man. That single eye on that scrap of torn photograph seemed to be returning their glance with menacing fixity.

"Now you're gone!" cried the woman in a violent reaction of anger, snatching up the bit of cardboard and tearing it again and again, and flinging the particles out of the window. Mario Ravaschieri still remained as if stunned, his eyes focused upon that part of the carpet where he had first seen the fragment of the portrait. The woman turned towards him.

"Calm yourself, Mario! Don't be so alarmed over nothing!" She encircled his neck once more, murmuring words of tempestuous ardor in his ear; but the young man freed himself, gazing uncertainly at her; then murmured, as he put aside her arms:

"No, I can't, I can't! Not now, not here!" A long silence followed. "Why did you tear it up? Supposing," he suggested in shaking tones, "supposing someone should——?"

"Don't be afraid!" replied Teodora, smiling. "Come here; look!" She drew him to the window and showed him, directly below, a wide-mouthed, unused well, whose margin was overgrown with green.

"Let us go away, Dora, let us go away!" entreated the

young man, suddenly clinging to her. "You don't know what I am suffering! It seems to me——" he was forced to pause, on account of the stricture in his throat. "It seems to me," he resumed, "that here, in this place, everyone is spying upon me; that on all sides they are seeking for me; that from every single thing about us a sign is raised, a voice, a cry. . . . Oh, the pain that I endure here, that you don't know!" and in despair he covered his face with both his hands.

IV

TEODORA ALVISE had satisfactorily arranged everything. Having persuaded him to relinquish his idea of a voyage to distant lands,—for that might well have aroused suspicion, —she and her lover returned to Rome. Having assumed most rigorous mourning, she received visits from her women friends, with features adjusted to a reasonable degree of grief, since any extreme demonstration would have been a palpable pretense.

"You must wait," she told Mario, "for me to come to you. Meanwhile remain secluded in your studio, do some work, free your thoughts of all anxiety, live in me and for me. Forget that there is such a thing as death. Just now life is smiling on us; sky and earth are both on our side,—on the side of our love and our youth."

Mario Ravaschieri had listened to these words and had felt all their magic charm. It had seemed to him as though at that moment a mysterious breath had banished from his soul the last shadow of remorse, and that simultaneously there had begun for him a new life made up wholly of love. It even seemed to him that the whole night of the assassination had been a ghastly dream, whose details had already begun to fade from his memory, in the dawn of this new life.

When he entered his studio, beyond the Porta del Popolo, and found himself, after his long absence, in the midst of all his familiar possessions; when he saw again the old sofa, still enveloped in a Venetian coverlid, his paintings of landscapes, figures, portraits, his studies and sketches, his boxes of colors, his suit of old armor in the right-hand corner, beneath the big window; when he found himself at last in his bedroom, adjoining the studio, it seemed to him really that it had all been a dream. An unforeseen thrill of joyousness filled his heart with a renewed faith in life. Since the sunshine gladdened his studio with color, and Dora would soon become his own, what had death to do with them? He even dared to hope that he was going to sleep, just as in former days, the deep, dreamless sleep of boyhood.

He busied himself with rearranging his belongings, went out to dinner, came in again; he prepared a large canvas for a painting, which he had for some time past been planning, and for which he had already made the rough draft; then he set to work. His spirit had apparently become tranquilized, but could not yet endure quiet, inaction, silence. He sang aloud as he worked, sang with uplifted voice, at the same time seeking to distract his thoughts in the pursuit of his artistic ideals.

But little by little the sun was slanting towards the west; he raised the shade to the very top. And still the sun sank lower, the light gradually faded, everything was shrouded in shadow, evening had come. Mario Ravaschieri arose impulsively from his stool, hastily washed, dressed, and went out. He had intended to go to the Art Club, but changed his mind; it was only too likely that everyone would expect to learn from him the particulars of the Baron's murder! He wandered aimlessly along the principal and most crowded streets of the city, observing everything, attentively studying everything, and everybody; his mind, wearied with its long struggle and loss of sleep, seemed to find relief in the restfulness of merely objective reflection.

Leaning against the parapet of the Sistine Bridge, he saw by the flare of a street lamp a dwarf pass by, with eyes loathsomely diseased. Mario Ravaschieri was seized with an instinctive repulsion.

"And yet," he thought a moment later, "that man is innocent!" This recurrence of remorse came upon him unexpectedly, like a relapse of chills and fever. He was all at once conscious that the flattering hopes of tranquillity and of love were shattered; and since his spirit was hounded onward, his body obeyed the impulse. He hastened his steps; these narrow, sparsely lighted streets stifled him. In the distance he perceived a spot ablaze with light; he moved faster and faster, until at last he arrived, almost running, before the entrance of a popular restaurant. The bright, cold radiance of the electric light calmed him somewhat; he moved uncertainly, here and there, among the tables set for guests beneath the wide veranda, and took his place at the first one that he found vacant.

While he absently trifled with the food that the waiter had suggested and served, his attention was drawn by a conversation between a group of young men seated near him. They were chatting over their cigars, around the table at which they had just had dinner; from their neat but unassuming dress, and their intelligent faces, he conjectured them to be young artists or students.

"My dear fellow," said one of them, tall, dark, restless, "to be a materialist to-day means to be thirty years behind the progress of science. Materialism was merely an ethical crisis in human history!"

"Accordingly you are ready to accept the old-fashioned theories of spiritualism?" demanded one of his companions.

"No, for science never goes back to what she has destroyed. Now I, for example, admit that existence may have far more complex gradations than those of which we can conceive; I admit that what we call the mind may be not merely a function of the brain, but something apart from matter, which through successive transformations is rising towards a progressive development, the goal of which is the Unknowable."

Mario Ravaschieri was listening with absorbed attention.

"Accordingly," questioned the first disputant ironically, "the mind is a spirit which at death is separated from the body to go to taste the joys of Paradise or the pains of the Inferno?"

"Don't be idiotic!" exclaimed the tall young man, rising to take his leave. "I was not talking of Paradise or Inferno, but of a revolution of the spirit; for that matter, neither you nor I know what the soul is, or how it lives; but beyond a doubt, there are hovering, all around us, superior beings, whose nature we cannot, with our present limitations, even conceive. . . ."

These words were uttered with such profound earnestness that Mario Ravaschieri was stirred to terror by them. For his own part, he had, since his college days, lived solely for art, feeding his mind with abundant but unsystematic reading, and had continued to suppose, without taking the trouble to investigate, that the last word of science was materialism. And when he had read some review of French positivism or Spencerian positivism, he had thought that these were simply disguised forms of materialism. Whether that which produces life be called material force or energy, or whether all the complex movement of cosmos be produced by an unknown force, was in his eyes one and the same thing; human life was but a moment in the transformation of matter.

But now the hypotheses of those young strangers, uttered with the accent of intimate conviction, had burst upon Ravaschieri's consciousness, just when it was already passing through a serious crisis, and inevitably he continued to brood upon them. He had been profoundly impressed by this unexpected revelation of an invisible world; it seemed to him that he could feel new sensations and perceive new and unknown phenomena. With his fantastic temperament, his artistic sense of form, Mario little by little came to see, rather than to feel, a shadowy movement all around his being; every simple fact of life now seemed to him an eloquent manifestation of a mysterious superhuman handiwork.

He made his way homeward in a state of extreme agitation. The silence of the slumbering city filled him with dread; as he walked, he hugged the walls, so that the unseen existences might have room to move through the air, just as though, like night moths, they might strike him in the face. He strained his ear for every sound, he searched the cause of every shadow, he studied the source of every movement, as though he dreaded at every instant to discover the palpable evidence of unseen life—of the life that is not of this world—if we really know.

Where was the soul of *the other man?* This was a question that he dared not brood upon, because it seemed to him that suddenly he felt upon his face a burning, pungent, acrid breath; he was even impelled to cover his face with his hands, so vivid was the anguish of the sensation. Gradually he could see and hear the whole surrounding space become more and more crowded with forms and with sounds; the shadows themselves had sound and movement, almost imperceptible sounds, that he alone could hear. He imagined that he could even hear the inaudible friction that his own shadow made upon the pavement; the heavy shadows along the street, cast by the lamps, seemed to him full of movement, of color, of strange rustlings.

He reached his home in a state of over-excitement that was almost spasmodic; the gloom of the studio seemed funereal and threatening, and he lit every candle he could find, and set them here and there, wherever the shadows lay heaviest. When the entire studio was thus illuminated, Mario Ravaschieri flung himself down, nerveless, exhausted, upon his sofa, so utterly wearied that he hoped to sleep. Ever since *that night,* when sleep fled from his eyes, he had had moments of prostration, of lethargy, far more terrible than his waking hours, because they were a series of nightmares, peopled with horrid visions. He had dreamed on one occasion that his hands were amputated, and that as they fell away there fell with them the whole of his atrocious remorse; and another time he had dreamed of painting a picture, the center of which was a bed, that bed, and across it the body of the strangled Baron. And so vividly had the horrid scene impressed itself that he could have flung the colors upon the canvas as unerringly as if from life.

Suddenly he started up, spurred by a new impulse, by the echo deep within him, of forgotten words of his childhood days, fell upon his knees, clasped his hands, and sobbed out in the extremity of his anguish:

"My God, my God, help me to sleep, one hour only, just one hour!"

V

WHAT new form of obsession was this?

"My God, my God, help me to sleep, one hour only, just as in a garden certain plants germinate from the very nature of the soil. His whole being was absorbed by a new form of mental torture; the fearful vision attacked him now through the medium of his art. Little by little he had lost his power to see anything else than *that room, with that bed, with the body of the strangled man.* It seemed as though his creative power had exhausted itself, wasted itself in the particularized reproduction of that scene. He saw it so definitely, in a pictorial sense, that many a time he felt himself driven to placing it on canvas. But just so often as, by an instinctive movement, his hand went to his brush, as though he could lay on the colors without need of outline, he shrank back in an access of shuddering.

And yet he was able to see nothing else. Wherever he turned his glance, straightway there appeared the forms of that horrible vision. Frequently, at night, when the whole bedroom was alight from the four-branched candlestick, and Mario had momentarily sunk into a doze, he would see every surrounding object change, little by little, into those of the Baron's room; the carpets and hangings take on the color of red, the chair at the foot of the bed become heaped with a pile of black clothing, in the midst of which he could discern a rose; and on his bed, his own bed, it seemed to him that over one side hung pendent the head and ghastly face of *the other man!* And he would lie there motionless, cowering, fearing that if he did move, he would inadvertently touch the corpse.

And Dora had not yet come. He felt himself alone, terribly alone. Notwithstanding that every morning he received a note, in which were written the same tender words, "I am yours with all my soul," nevertheless this new obsession bade fair to undermine his small remaining courage.

One dismal, rainy night, he found himself so invaded by terror that he decided, at any cost, to try to see Teodora. He set forth. It was the first of the rainy days of September. The Via Flaminia was a stream of sluggish mud; over which the street lamps, flaring dimly in the gray twilight, shed only a feeble ray. Mario Ravaschieri sprang into the first passing carriage.

He found Teodora in hat and wrap, on the point of going out. When she saw her lover appear, she gave a start of alarm.

"Why have you come?" she demanded, as soon as the servant who had ushered Ravaschieri in, withdrew.

"Oh, Dora, Dora!" broke forth the young man helplessly. "I can no longer bear it! I fear that I am going mad! I am ready to kill myself!" In the presence of this outburst of grief, Teodora Alvise removed her hat, sat down beside her lover, and encircled him tenderly, almost maternally, with her arms.

"Mario, my own Mario, tell me what ails you, tell me everything!"

"What ails me? What ails me? I no longer live! I can find no peace! All my efforts to control myself are in vain. Since that night I have been unable to sleep, do you understand? I pass the whole night with my eyes wide open; there are times when weariness overcomes me . . . and then, oh! then," added the young man, flinging up his arms in desperation, "then I am tortured by the most horrible nightmares, and I wake up panting, bathed in cold perspiration, with my hands clenching! Oh, those hands! those hands!" sobbed Ravaschieri, brandishing his arms above his head, " it seems as though his flesh still clung to them ! "

The young man came nearer and seized her by the wrist: " You don't know," he said, " what it means to kill a man, to press your fingers into his throbbing flesh, to cut short his days at one stroke, to usurp the privilege of God! Do you realize, to kill a man is a thing that even justice itself hesitates to do? And how about his spirit? Where has that gone? May it not still be near us, perhaps even in this room, now?" Nerveless and exhausted, Mario Ravaschieri sank into an armchair. The woman continued to gaze at him, for a long time.

The fading afterglow of twilight fell faintly on the young man's pallid, kindly features; his long, black hair fell in heavy, disordered locks over his temples and high, white forehead. These terrible days of anguish had left haggard and sunken the features once ruddy with health. Teodora flung herself into his arms, seeking his lips with eager kisses, and whispering softly:

" Oh, my poor, dear, cowardly boy! Away with such dismal phantoms! Away with them!" She drew him down again beside her on the sofa.

" Listen," she told him. " I want to talk to you about our marriage. If you wish it, and it can be done secretly, it shall be much sooner than we planned,—a week from next Sunday. And you must have the whole studio a bower of flowers. But until then you must paint, paint, paint! for work will keep away bad dreams. Now what is the matter?"

" But I cannot work!" groaned Mario.

" And why not?" she demanded.

" Why not? Ah, you don't see what I see, you don't know that I have before my eyes constantly that room, and that bed. . . . Many a time I have tried to work, to think, but it was no use; it seems as though my imagination could see nothing else than that. . . . I have tried to paint landscapes, to make sketches; but no, my mind is empty, my hand is disobedient and weary. And that horrible vision is so vivid that at times my hand involuntarily grasps the brush."

For an instant both were silent.

"Very well!" exclaimed the woman suddenly, "then make a painting of it!"

"Make a painting of it?" repeated the artist, as if unable to grasp the meaning of her suggestion.

"Yes, paint what you see. Perhaps that is your only road to freedom."

From the moment that Teodora suggested the possibility of yielding to the invincible temptation by which her lover was possessed, he experienced a sudden reversal in the current of his sufferings. That horrible vision, which had become a poisoned sting in his life, was suddenly transmuted into an artistic conception. And so completely did the artistic temperament triumph that the very next morning Ravaschieri set himself to work. The canvas which, after his return, he had prepared for very different work, was still unsullied. And he applied himself to the tremendous experiment with the agonized trepidation of a man who voluntarily submits himself to the torture of a surgical operation.

Within a few hours he had, in a paroxysm of work, outlined with obedient pencil the entire scene. When he began to mix the colors his hand was shaking, his face was deathly white; when he dipped the brush in that dull red, to lay on the first strokes, his hand was shaking still; but little by little the work absorbed him, carried him away; he was no longer the assassin; he was the artist.

And, strange phenomenon, little by little as the vision assumed concrete form, as the scene took life upon the canvas, it seemed as though his mind and his imagination threw off their burden. And this sense of liberation was so keen that Ravaschieri found himself working with steadily growing eagerness and courage.

That night he slept. The next morning, on waking with the sunshine full in his eyes, he sprang out of bed, in an access of lightheartedness. He felt refreshed, strong, almost serene. He resumed his work; the Baron's empurpled face no longer caused him horror; indeed he concentrated his mind several times in an effort to recall it in all its details.

In a few days the picture, half life-size, was practically finished. Mario was as though born again. From his sight and memory that scene had been materially transferred to the canvas, and there it remained.

VI

FLOWERS were strewn around the old divan, which Ravaschieri had covered with a magnificent antique mantle of blue velour, a Venetian mantle which had served him in one of his pictures. Flowers had been scattered in that corner, in profuse handfuls; there was an inebriating symphony of color. Amid the faint bluish-white of the azaleas, the carnations, the camellias, the jessamines, was the glowing yellow of the Indian rose, the languid green of the reseda, the vivid flame color of the geranium, the carnal richness of the orchid. Mario looked upon these flowers, his heart pulsing with impatience. They formed an appropriate setting for the dark beauty of the woman he loved. Nature, laboring in the moist warmth of the hothouse, had done no more than was due to this woman, whom he regarded as Nature's choicest and most complex creation.

The picture was practically finished, and Ravaschieri decided to put it aside, in a closet, so that its repulsive presence should not, even though covered, mar the gladness of this day. But he remembered that a waiter from the Café Roma would come presently to take orders for what would be their wedding supper, and he decided to ask him to help in moving it. Besides, if he should try to move that picture alone, he felt as though the weight of it would be enormous.

When Ravaschieri heard the tinkle of the door-bell, it made him jump. He hurried to the door and admitted a man, respectably dressed, very pale and dark, who looked at him with scared eyes. The face seemed not wholly unfamiliar to Ravaschieri, who inquired:

"Are you the waiter from the Café Roma?"

"Yes, sir, I am," replied the other, in trembling tones.

Mario studied the man attentively, whose countenance aroused in him a sense of uneasiness and repulsion. Why should it? the young man asked himself; and his uneasiness increased, as he became aware that his questioning glance threw the waiter into visible agitation.

Mario decided that this was merely a freak of his imagination, and proceeded to give the order for supper. While the servant was writing, Mario's eyes rested upon the man's hands, and he felt a shudder run all through him. Those hands Ravaschieri had seen before, but where and when? He even seemed to discern a scratch across the right-hand thumb.

At last the servant, whose hand had trembled as he wrote, turned to bow himself out, when Mario made him a sign to wait.

"Do me the favor to help me carry this picture into my closet."

The servant put down his cap and approached the easel on which the canvas rested, covered with a green cloth.

"We had better take the cloth off," said Ravaschieri, suddenly unveiling the painting.

A howl of abject fear issued from the throat of the waiter, who with trembling limbs, chalky face, and hair rising on his head, staggered backward from before the easel. Mario stood for an instant in stunned amazement; but suddenly a lightning flash of understanding burst upon him. He sprang upon the servant, seized him by both arms, and fairly screamed at him:

"Tell the truth, man; tell the truth!"

The waiter fell upon his knees, helpless with terror, and seemed hardly to have breath enough to gasp: "Yes, I will tell, I will tell! But save me! save me!" For a few moments he could not speak, struggling for breath as though he feared to suffocate; then, with starting eyes fixed upon the picture, he stammered:

"I didn't mean to do it! No, that I swear!"

"To do what? Go on, speak out!" commanded Ravaschieri, in whose brain so strange a hope had been born that he feared he was losing his reason.

"Oh, I will speak, I will speak!" resumed the servant, in a paroxysm of terror, still on his knees, bent over, supporting himself on his left arm. "I had entered the room to get his money—only for that, I swear! The week before, when he paid me his dinner check he opened a pocketbook that bulged with hundred-franc notes. Give me some water!"

He drank eagerly, then continued tremblingly:

"I had never seen so much money. It drove me mad. When he left for Rome, a few days later, I fitted an old key, and oiled the springs of the lock, . . . and the night he came back, the moment I saw that the door to the back stairs was open, I made up my mind to go up. I was alone, every servant in the house was asleep; for a moment——" It seemed as though his voice would die out utterly.

"Go on!" commanded Mario, raging with impatience.

"I let myself in . . . he was asleep, with the candle burning. I crept over to put it out, when——"

"When what? Go on, quicker!"

"He awoke, I saw that I was ruined,—and before he could cry out—he was dead!"

A tense silence followed. Mario Ravaschieri raised his hands to his hair, and tore violently at it, to convince himself that he was alive and awake. He stared first at the man and then at the picture, and it dawned upon him that a very strange and mysterious thing had happened, to give reality to his hope.

"But did he see you?" Mario asked the waiter, in a quiver of excitement.

"No, I don't think so, I don't think so,—when he woke up, the candle was going out——"

"And you didn't hear him say a word?"

"Yes, a few," replied the servant, with a convulsive shudder.

"And what did you hear?"

"What did I hear! It seemed to me that he gasped out '*schiei, vaschiei, assassin, Teodoa,*'" pronounced the man, omitting all the r's from the words, just as he had heard them issue from the compressed and strangled throat. Now everything was becoming clear; the mad hope had been changed to a certainty; Mario Ravaschieri was frightened at his own joy. He flung himself into the nearest seat, and in his turn drank eagerly.

"Oh, please, sir, please!" begged the waiter, "don't betray me! It was the fear of being found out; I didn't mean to——"

Mario stared at the man, without grasping the meaning of his words.

"What is that you said?" he demanded, as if in a dream.

"Don't betray me, please, sir! Don't denounce me! I have three children!" repeated the waiter, sobbing in his desperation.

Mario Ravaschieri continued to gaze at him; then rose to his feet, and seizing the man by his arm, drew him up also, studied his face keenly, and then fairly shouted at him:

"Tell me, you are not mad, are you? Is what you have said true? Speak out! I have nothing to do with law and justice! Tell me that you are not mad!"

When the man found his arms free again, he silently showed the other a short, deep scratch upon his right-hand thumb. At the sight of that scratch, Mario Ravaschieri, in an access of joy, seized the servant by the shoulders, and gently pushed him through the door.

"There, go! Off with you! Don't worry, poor wretch! I am the last one in the world to betray you!"

Left alone, Mario seized a chair and flung it so violently against the picture that the canvas was rent into shreds. Jubilant cries, bursts of laughter, snatches of song issued from his lips. He felt himself a boy again! He put on his hat to go out, changed his mind, and flung his hat aside again,—Teodora might arrive at any moment. But how could he have the patience to await her?

He strode up and down the studio, in his excitement, gesticulating, singing, when suddenly his glance fell upon his hands. He raised them up before his eyes, as though he now beheld them for the first time; an unaccustomed tenderness assailed him, for these gentle, innocent hands, and between sobs and laughter he raised them to his lips.

The door-bell sounded. Before the woman he loved had taken one step into the room, Mario sprang upon her, encircling her with his arms, showering her with kisses, stammering incoherently through tears and laughter:

"It wasn't I! No, no, I tell you, it wasn't I! I am innocent! It was all a dreadful dream!"

The woman gazed at her lover in bewilderment.

"No, no, I have not gone mad, Dora mine!" cried the young man, laughing from pure joy. "I have not gone mad!" and in broken, confused words, he related the tragic scene with the waiter. Teodora Alvise's face became transfigured.

"Now," she cried, "will you forget death? Will you grasp life and love?"

Camillo Boito

The Gray Spot

By Frederick Taber Cooper

THIS gray spot, that I see inside my eyes, may be the most commonplace occurrence known to the science of you oculists; but it causes me great annoyance, and I should like to be cured. You shall make examination with your most improved instruments, when I come to you a fortnight from now, of cornea, pupil, retina, and the rest. Meanwhile, since you ask it in the name of friendship, I will describe to you as best I can my new affliction.

In the midst of abundant light I have the eyesight of a lynx. In the streets by day, in the theater at night, I can distinguished a hundred paces off a mole on the cheek of a pretty woman. I can read without fatigue, ten hours at a stretch, the finest English type. I have never needed to wear glasses; indeed, I may enroll myself among those "animals of such unflinching gaze," as, in the words of Petrarch, "even bid defiance to the sun." But never have I so intensely loved the sun as for the last two months; no sooner does dawn begin than I fling my shutters wide open and thank God for it.

I hate the darkness. At night, in proportion as the obscurity deepens, there appears before me, with growing intensity, at the very point where I fix my gaze, a spot the color of ashes, changeable, shapeless. During the twilight, or while the moon is shining, it is exceedingly faint, almost imperceptible; but in the darkness it becomes enormous. At one time it is motionless, so that, as I look up at the black sky, it appears to be a patch of gray light, showing through an irregular rent, like the paper of circus hoops, after the body of the clown has passed through; and I fancy that I can see, beyond the opening, still another somber sky, behind the stars. At other times it becomes restless, rising, sinking, widening, lengthening, throwing out tentacles like a devil-fish, horns like a snail, feet like a toad; it becomes monstrous, whirls around to the right, then whirls back to the left, and keeps on revolving like this, for hours together, furiously, before my eyes.

I have made these comparisons merely for the purpose of trying to make myself understood; but to tell the truth, it does not possess the shadow of a form. During the month that I have been obliged to indulge myself in such a spectacle, I have never once been able to seize upon a definite figure. Whenever it seems as though I had discovered a certain analogy with some living creature, or some object, perhaps even fantastical, something in short capable of being defined, lo and behold! in the next instant the outline was twisted and altered beyond the power of deciphering.

I do not say that I see it always. I see it every night, but for a longer or shorter time according to the condition of my mind or my body, I know not which. Frequently, thank Heaven, it comes and goes aagin, almost immediately.

The terrible part of it is that it comes before me without warning, when I am thinking of something utterly foreign to it. I was holding the hand of a young woman who is dear to me, by the flickering ray of an expiring lamp, and telling her things that are not to be repeated, even to you doctors, when all of a sudden that spot befouled the whiteness of her throat. I felt myself seized with shudderings.

Even in the daytime if I enter, let us say, a dimly lit church, I run the risk of discovering the same polluting spot below the heavy shadow of the organ, or on the ancient, smoke-stained paintings, or before the dark little window of the confessional. The fear of seeing it makes me discover it all the sooner.

At night I can never look with impunity at the water of a river or the sea. I went a few days ago to Genoa.

It was a beautiful evening, a lingering touch of summer. The vault of heaven was one serene expanse, one unbroken tint, barely distinguished from west to east by a tinge of yellow, a tinge of green, a tinge of purplish blue; nevertheless, it showed, almost on the horizon, one isolated zone of dense clouds. The narrowest, most limpid band of clear atmosphere glowed between clouds and sea. The sun, which had remained for some time hidden behind those clouds, descended past their lower margin, preparing to sink beneath the tranquil waves. At first its golden orb, while only the under segment could be seen, appeared like a vast lamp suspended from the clouds; then the fiery circle touched with its circumference for a minute both clouds and sea; then it hid itself very, very slowly in the water, its upper segment suggesting the blazing incandescence from the mouth of some vast furnace. I had dined well with a certain old friend of mine. We hired a rowboat and turned our course towards open water. After the splendors of the sunset, the twilight was ineffably soothing. We sang in softened tones, dreamily. The night shut down. The water, of a somber green, gleamed and sparkled. All of a sudden, far off in the distance, I saw floating that gray spot of mine; fearfully I averted my eyes to within the boat, and the spot followed me between oars and rowlocks, and its livid presence accompanied me, chilled with horror, back to land.

It must be (my good doctor, do not laugh) that the retina is injured; there is in it a certain blind point, a small paralyzed space, a *scotoma* in short. I have read that in the eyes of criminals sentenced to death there has been found, after execution, upon the retina a picture of the last objects upon which the poor wretches had fixed their gaze. Accordingly the retina not only receives transitory impressions; in certain cases they remain actually engraved upon it.

Observe furthermore that, when I close my eyes to sleep, I become aware that this spot of mine is inside of me. And then begins a different form of torture. The spot no longer whirls round and round upon itself, but moves about with a rush. It rushes upward and, as it goes, drags my pupils with it; so that it seems as though the whole eyeball must turn wrong side out, turning completely over in its socket. Then it rushes downward, then sideways; and the eyeballs follow it, and the muscles seem ready to snap, and in a little while I feel my eyes actually throbbing with the pain. The next morning, even after I have slept, they remain painful and slightly swollen.

You doctors have the virtue of curiosity; you wish to penetrate to the causes, to remount to the source of things. For this reason I shall tell you under what circumstances this malady of mine, which you must cure, first manifested itself. And, if you will hear me patiently, I will tell it all, down to the most insignificant particulars, because I know that from some one trifle, such as escapes the notice of the common herd, you men of science can strike a spark that will shed a beacon light over the most hidden truths.

On the 24th of last October, just at nightfall, I crossed over the Bridge of Kings adjoining Garbe, intending to go as far as Vestone, my customary walk after dinner, just as that of the morning was towards Vobarno, excepting when I preferred to clamber up the shoulder of some mountain, or make an excursion, on foot in any case, to Bagolino, or Gardone, or into the Tyrol. Of the two months and a half that I passed in the Val Sabbia, the first two weeks were an unbroken calm, the next two unbroken fire, and the remainder sadness and terror. In place of the beauties of nature, which everyone rushes to see and which everyone admires, I had chosen that modest and lowly valley, where the mountains already take on a certain aspect of wildness, and where there is no danger of ever seeing the gaunt-limbed figure of an Englishman, or even the black beard of an Italian Alpinist. I feasted upon fine, rosy trout from the Lake of Idro, savory crawfish, mushrooms, game birds, goat's milk cheese, and an abundance of eggs and polenta.

There is at Idro a diminutive inn with two small chambers, as airy as they are neat. He who is without remorse may live there in the quiet of Paradise, without daily papers, without cafés, without gossip, gazing at the mirror of the lake, the young girls in rowboats, the Rocca d' Anfo on the opposite shore, exercising his legs rather than his brain, and degenerating little by little into the sweet and blessed liberty of not thinking of anything, and of doing absolutely nothing at all.

When the sky is thickly strewn with clouds, swept forward by a driving wind, the aspect of the landscape becomes infinitely variable. The mountains rising one above another, the cliffs that bear the walls of ruined castles, or little churches with their white spires, the low-lying hills with coronets of pine trees, change from minute to minute in appearance. Now the clouds throw into shadow the foreground of the picture, while the sun shines brilliantly in the distance; now again the sun shines in the foreground, while the distance is all in shadow; and still again, this part or that of the central view shows blackly in the midst of light, or luminous in the midst of shadow; and all the while, innumerable bursts of varied and resplendent color blaze forth and then die down again.

One should make the ascent of the rocky height, that rises opposite the little church of St. Gothard, on the other side of the Chiese River. Towards the river, the mountain slopes down almost perpendicularly. To the right, on an odd little hill, can be seen the church of Sabbio, tall and slender; to the left, far off, appears the Rocca di Nozza, of which nothing remains save some fragments of crumbling wall; beneath your feet yawns a profound void. You cling with your hands to the shrubbery, and you look downward. The Chiese flows in a semicircle, its headlong waves breaking against the enormous rocks with which its bed is strewn.

Garbe lies far below, a little to the right; and further off, but well up the mountainside, is the belfry of Provaglio. Almost on a level with you, but clear across the narrow valley, which contracts at this point until there is scarcely room for the passage of the river and the post road, you can see from top to bottom the little church of St. Gothard, the tower of which is so foreshortened as to appear dwarfed, and the arches of the little portico have a flattened look. On my first ascent, I was very nearly overcome with giddiness. I was trying to climb higher still, where the bare rock, almost perpendicular, hardly afforded a foothold in its narrow crevices. I glanced behind me. Below my feet the mountain lay in dense shadow; above me it towered upward into the light of heaven.

It must have been about five o'clock in the afternoon, a fortnight after my arrival at Garbe. The sun had begun to sink behind the mountain crest; a freshening breeze was blowing down the length of the narrow valley, and I had to keep a hold upon my hat, to save it from plunging over the precipice, when an impetuous puff, coming at a moment when both hands were clinging to the foliage of some strange plant, sent it rolling for a space, and then descending in great leaps, from point to point of the jutting crags. I bid it good-by, and continued my devout attention to the botany of that spot. And then, within less than ten minutes, there appeared before me quite unexpectedly a mountaineer's daughter, who, with some embarrassment and a certain rustic grace, handed me my luckless hat. I thanked her heartily, studying her face as I did so. She was probably between sixteen and seventeen years old; bronzed as she was by exposure, it was easy to divine the fairness of the flesh beneath the tint of the sun. In her small mouth gleamed teeth of admirable whiteness and regularity; in her eyes lurked a suggestion of wildness and of wonderment, a timidity that had just a touch of impertinence.

"Are you from Garbe, my pretty maid?"

"No, sir, I am from Idro."

"And you are staying here?"

"I leave to-morrow, with my father. He is down there, among those bushes, with our goats. Can't you see him? Take a good look, as far in as you can see——" and she indicated the spot; but at that distance I could make out only that there was a man, and that his beard was gray.

"And when you are in Idro, where do you live?"

"Outside the town, about two miles, on the road to Mount Pinello."

"And what is your name, my pretty maid?"

"Teresa, at your service, sir."

So the conversation ran on. I showered questions upon her, gazing into her eyes, which part of the time strayed here and there, as if embarrassed by my glance; and then again looked me straight in the face,—indeed, it almost seemed, straight into my heart. Of marriage she had never so much as thought; she did not know,—and this she swore with a laugh, and a wider opening of her honest eyes,—she did not know even the meaning of love. There was no one in the world belonging to her, except her father, whom she adored, of course, and whom she had never left for a day, since she was born; but the kind old man had to go away precisely at this time, for a fortnight, to Gardegno, in order to establish his claim as heir to his brother, who had died, leaving many possessions and no children. The old man, once a corporal under Austrian rule, could read and write like a notary, was highly respected, and besides that was more agile, more vigorous, more courageous than many a young man of twenty. The girl was to remain at Idro, during her father's absence, in the care of a good old soul of seventy.

You will readily understand, doctor, how I came to spend a couple of weeks in that well-kept, remote little inn at Idro. Every morning and every evening I ascended that narrow little lane, steep, crooked, strewn with sharp-edged stones, that leads to Mount Pinello, and halted at the home of my charming mountain maid. For two days she would have none of me; after that, there was not a grassy corner on all that rugged slope where we did not linger, talking,—searching by day the densest shade, beside some mountain stream, within some natural grotto, in the wide interstices of the enormous masses, flung down, Heaven knows when, from the mountain crest.

During the early days, Teresa loved three objects: her

father, her goats, and me; after a week, she ceased to speak of her father, she no longer tended her goats, but would stand watching for me, in the doorway of her little cottage, from the first dawn of day; often she would come to meet me, all the way down to Idro, and seize and drag me along with a rude violence, as though she would have torn me in pieces. The madness of such an attachment was plain; I struggled to leave; I could not; I prayed inwardly for the old father's return.

The day before his arrival, I summoned courage to announce my own departure. I told Teresa I was obliged to go to Brescia and to Milan, but added hastily that I should soon be back, in two weeks at most, perhaps in one. She shed no tears; she only began to tremble all over, while her face became the color of lead. She kept repeating, in choking tones, "I know that you will not come back; I know that you will never come back again!" I promised to come, I swore to come, yet she continued to gaze at me, with those wide, tearless eyes, and, made clear-sighted by her passion, kept insisting,—"You are never coming back; I feel in my heart that you are never coming back!" I could win from her no other words.

Instead of going to Brescia or to Milan, I returned to Garbe. My soul was torn with remorse; many a time I felt my conscience urging me to hasten back to Idro, to Teresa's cabin; then the memory of her tempestuous greetings would fill me with fear; but none the less, I could think of nothing else than of her. I could not tell whether I loved her, and yet her image was ever before me, as though graven there. To seek her again was to ruin both our lives; to flee was to sadden the little girl's existence.

At length, tortured, I made my escape; I fled to Brescia, but found the uproar of the city had become unendurable; I returned to Garbe, and there, by constantly repeating to myself that time remedies all things, even the anguish of passion and abandonment, I found some minutes of peace. Nevertheless, I slept but little, tormented as I was by horrible dreams and feverish anxiety; I ate but little; I walked a great deal, finding that weariness brought relief.

I began by telling you, Doctor, that on the 24th of last October I was passing at nightfall over the Bridge of Kings, not far from Garbe. A man with elbows on the parapet of the bridge, and chin in his hands, was staring intently down into the water of the river. From between his fingers projected the strands of a snow-white beard; his face, half-hidden by the hat drawn low upon his forehead, was not easy to distinguish. His dress was not properly that of a peasant nor of a workingman; he wore a jacket and loose trousers of a light gray color. I passed close to the old man; he made no movement, but continued to gaze fixedly at the water near the piles that support the bridge, where the current boils with gathered impetus, as it narrows to pass beneath the twofold arch. I, too, gazed downward, thinking that there might be something curious to see; I discovered nothing unusual, but the sport of the waves, to which I had never before given attention, amused me.

It is a formidable struggle between the flowing water and the colossal rocks that strive to bar its way. The waves, spurred on by those that follow after, and those again urged forward by others in pursuit, beginning in the cloud-born rivulets, expend who knows what labor and what craftiness! and how they strain themselves to force the bridge to follow in their course! The spectacle of the fatal conflict between motion and immobility, eternal and uninterrupted, fills the mind with a faint-hearted discouragement, yet at the same time makes one smile at such a blind impetus of effort and such blind obstinacy of resistance. There are moments when the opposing forces of nature resemble ill-mannered children, one of whom cries "I will," and the other, stamping his feet, rejoins "I won't!"

The old man continued to gaze downward, impassively.

I went on my way, thinking no more of him, strolling slowly as far as Nozza. The cloud-laden and threatening sky was beginning to darken, and a cold wind was sweeping down from the high mountains. I turned back from my projected walk, and retraced my steps. On the Bridge of Kings, the old man was still standing, in the selfsame position, the same attitude as before. He was still gazing down at the pier of the bridge.

The circumstance struck me as odd; I approached the old man and asked him:

"Excuse me, my good man——" He made no motion. I repeated: "Excuse me for disturbing you; but the sky is black, a storm is threatening, and night is not far off. If your home is not near by, you ought to be moving on."

The old man straightened himself, very, very slowly, and gazed into my face as if in a dream; then, without opening his lips, resumed his post, leaning over the parapet and staring down upon the river. But I was insistent:

"Is there anything you want?"

"No," he replied, without turning.

I bade him good-night, and went on my way towards Garbe. A hundred paces further on, I turned back. I do not know whether it was curiosity or compassion; in the face of that white old man, I seemed to have read a profound sorrow, a sinister melancholy. His pallor, his deep-sunken eyes, his bloodless lips had filled me with pity and alarm. I found myself at his side again, borne back by an almost involuntary force, and I asked him breathlessly, awaiting a reply which did not come:

"Excuse me once more. Tell me if there is any way in which I can help you. Are you not feeling well? I can offer you a room at Garbe, for the night. You seem to be a stranger here. I too have known what it is to find myself in a strange land, without money. May I loan you some?"

At these last words, the old man turned gravely, trying to force his lips into a smile. "Thank you, I need nothing at all," he answered. Then, putting his hand into his trouser pocket, he drew it forth again tightly closed, and extending it above the parapet, opened his fingers. The wind caught and sent flying above the river, scattered at random, a score or more of small banknotes.

In my irritation, I was on the point of remonstrating with him, when he stammered, in choking tones, "I am thirsty."

"Then go down to the river and drink!" I answered harshly. The old man made his way to the rough path that descended from one end of the bridge; but reaching it, he tottered on his trembling limbs. I ran to help him, and with one hand beneath his arm, led him down to the river bank. Of my own accord, I filled his hat with water. He drank slowly, a little at a time.

"Do not put on your hat while it is wet, or it will do you harm. Do you live far from here?"

"No."

"But you do not belong in this town?"

"No."

"Then where do you live? I will see you home."

"You need not. I live nearby."

"I will see you home in any case."

The old man looked me straight in the eyes, and said in tones of decision: "I do not wish you to." Then he added, more gently, but as if against his will: "I am waiting for someone."

"Your son, perhaps?"

"I have no son."

"A relative?"

"I have no relatives?"

"A friend?"

"I have no friends."

"Whom, then?"

He thought for a time and then answered, "Destiny."

He leaned once more over the parapet of the bridge, and resumed his watch upon the waters below.

"Forgive my insistence. What place do you come from?"

"From a place where people die of sorrow."

"And where are you going?"

"To a place that I know nothing of."

These mysterious answers roused in my mind a ridiculous suspicion, and I exclaimed impulsively: "If you are seeking concealment, if the authorities are in search of you, I promise not to betray you."

The old man suddenly held himself erect and answered proudly: "I have nothing to hide from the eyes of men!" then, murmuring half to himself, "My own conscience is clear."

"Other men, perhaps, have deceived you, and done you harm? You have found that the world is full of enemies."

"Enemies? I have never had but one!"

These last words were spoken by the old man in so wild a tone, and his eyes showed so strange a stare, that I felt myself suddenly chilled. I said, "Then I will leave you, and God bless you!"

"God, God!" I heard him repeat, several times; and the sepulchral tones of the old man's voice died away beneath the murmur of the river.

I did not intend to abandon the poor man. In a dozen strides I had reached Garbe, fully intending to speak to the mayor, who is a skillful physician and a heart of gold, and to take back with me a couple of peasants, to keep watch, all night if necessary, over the strange old man. I found the mayor on the threshold of his dwelling, an ancient dwelling, erected by one of his ancestors, a French gentleman who had escaped the massacre of St. Bartholomew.

The mayor was talking with the secretary of the commune, and with the innkeeper from Sabbio. These gentlemen, and three peasants, whom I had routed out from a neighboring wine-shop, returned with me to the bridge. We passed before the church of St. Gotthard; but at this point I could no longer restrain myself, and leaving the aged mayor to follow at his accustomed gait, which he tried his best, poor fellow, to hasten, but which still seemed to me far too slow, I rushed on ahead. I crossed and recrossed the bridge, I flung myself down to the river's bank, I searched on this side and on that, in the blind darkness of that foul night, which had already shut down: there was not a living soul to be seen. The others joined me, out of breath. In the twinkling of an eye, my instructions were given: The mayor was to keep watch upon the bridge; mine host was to patrol a mile or so of the road to Nozza; the secretary was to follow up the course of the Chiese, by the narrow path on its left bank; the three peasants were to ascend the more accessible paths up the mountain. As for the more precipitous routes, it was impossible to imagine that the unfortunate old man had even attempted them. General headquarters, the bridge.

I had reserved for myself the cabins of the charcoal-burners, on the other side of the Chiese. In fifteen minutes I had reached the first of their little huts. All were sound asleep. I knocked loudly; no one answered; I continued to knock, with such violence that the blows reverberated down the valley, and at last I heard voices and imprecations. After a short delay, a small window opened and a blackened face appeared, in the midst of which shone two eyes, like the eyes of a cat.

"Do you know anything of an old man with a long, white beard, who seemed half-sick, and is dressed in light gray clothes, a stranger who was wandering to-night in the neighborhood of the Bridge of Kings?"

"Go to the devil!"

"Won't you please ask your comrades if they know?"

"Go to the devil, you and your old man with you!" and the window shut again.

After another fifteen minutes, I had climbed up another path, to another cabin. My walking stick, falling upon the panels of the small door, awoke four or five distinct echoes from the mountainside.

"Who is there?"

"A friend."

"What name?"

"A friend."

"You can't come in."

"Open the window."

"Not much, I won't."

"Have you seen an old man?"

"I haven't seen anyone."

"An old man, dressed in light gray, a sick man, with a long white beard?"

"I haven't seen anyone."

"He was wandering to-night on the Bridge of Kings and the adjoining roads."

"I haven't seen anyone, I tell you," and straightway he was snoring again.

Within an hour, we were all back upon the bridge. Not one of us had seen anything, not one had learned anything. Even the two carbineers, from Vestone, whom the innkeeper had met by the way, and brought back with him, were unable to give us any help. The mayor decided that it was time for us to go home and get some sleep. And in fact that was the only sensible thing that remained for us to do.

It is time for me to enter at last into the heart of my story. You have observed how I shrink from it; in fact, as I run over the wasted ink upon these pages, I realize that I have acted like a man with a toothache, who is going to have the tooth out. He starts out briskly, almost on a run; but little by little, as he approaches the dentist's office, he goes more and more slowly, until at last, on reaching the door, he stops perplexed, asking himself, "Is my tooth aching now, or isn't it?" And accordingly he turns back, quite a good bit of the way; and every trifle serves him for delay, an advertisement on the street corner, a dog that barks at him. Then he becomes ashamed, and returns, straight up to the door, and resolutely puts his hand upon the bell, when suddenly he stops again to ask himself: "Shall I have it out, or shan't I?"

Accordingly, now for a bold start. That evening, after giving the three peasants a few pennies, with which to drink a bottle or two; after bidding good-night to the mayor, who started homeward; to the secretary, who was on his way for a last drink at the wine-shop; and to the innkeeper, who was returning to Sabbio, caroling a song with his deep bass voice; I found myself without the slightest desire to sleep, and quite as little for writing, reading, or conversing. I had a great weight on my mind, and I felt the need of breathing forth the oppression, of expelling it from the inmost pores of my lungs.

There had been, for several evenings past, an interminable discussion at the little inn upon this point; whether, between Vestone and Vobarno, trout are more easily caught after sunset, in the early morning, by moonlight, or on a night of darkness. One fisherman swore that he had made a marvelous catch in the most profound obscurity.

Taking a rod and a small lantern, I installed myself on the further bank of the Chiese, where certain enormous rocks form a species of dike. It seemed to me, from time to time, that I felt a nibble at the hook; I pulled in, but there was nothing there. Becoming tired, I seated myself upon a stone and looked around me. There was not a blessed thing to be seen. The sky was black, the earth was black; not a star, not a light. Garbe, hidden by a clump of trees, at that hour was slumbering. High up on the mountainside, in the direction where Provaglio should lie, appeared a faint glimmer, perhaps a candle burning by the bedside of a dying man. The darkness was that of a tomb, but a tomb full of discordant sounds. The Chiese, beating against its rocks, produced a music that was deafening, a mingling of all the tones and all the chords, while the wind added the shrill notes of the upper scale. After a while the eyes became accustomed to the obscurity and began to distinguish certain objects: the big, repulsive toads, for example, which would suddenly hop across in front of me; the white foam, and also the somber green of the water.

I had just taken up my rod, in order to try my luck once more, when I discerned a large, grayish object, borne headlong onward by the current, and coming to a pause before the dike. I could not understand what manner of thing it was; yet none the less a shudder ran over me from head to foot. I went back for the little lantern, which I had left in the pathway; but while I was returning with my light to that gray object, the water, which had been making a great hubbub round about it, raised it up and bore it some twenty paces further downstream, until it struck with a heavy thud against a big stone that rose high out of the river. Concentrated attention sharpened my sight. Aided by the feeble rays of my lantern, I tried to wade across the narrow space, placing my feet upon the surface of the stones; but I did not succeed. The waves beat upon the shapeless mass, scattering foam as though in furious wrath, and whirled it round and round, forming a vortex of incredible rapidity. The Chiese was savagely insistent in its purpose of bearing off its prey, and drove it onward. The strange object made a circuit of the rock, and resumed its journey, whirled over and over by the river.

Then there began a terrible struggle between the river and myself; for I was determined to solve the mystery of that gray object, and the river was determined to hide it from me. I knew the path along the bank, step by step. At one point alone the cliff, rising almost vertically for a hundred yards or more, makes it necessary to climb up and down again. The rest of the path, all the way to Sabbio, is level. But that upward climb, and above all the descent were not without peril in the nighttime, and on that narrow path, flanked as it was by a deep ravine. The rains of the preceding week had at one point washed away the path, and there was nothing else to do than take a flying leap midway down the precipice. I sprang without stopping to think, not knowing where my feet would land, and found myself across the gap, safe and sound, but with my lamp extinguished. I continued along my goat-path in the dark, blundering over roots, entangled by thorny bushes, stumbling downwards upon smooth round pebbles that went rolling on ahead of me, to the bottom. Finally I once more reached the river bank. But what had become of that mass of gray? Had it swept by without hindrance, or had some of the obstacles, with which the river is strewn, held it back? I watched for a time, with strained, unwinking eyes, so hot and dry that they seemed to burn me. At last it swept past, in the current, in an instant of time.

Then I too began once more to rush onward, along the river margin, amid the growth of slender willows and broad-leaved menuphars. The mass of shapeless gray had gone aground upon a shoal of gravel near the bank. I removed my shoes and stockings, rolled up my trousers above the knee, and waded out into the current. I found it impossible to keep my footing. The river dragged me downward with invincible violence. I realized the impotence of man when opposing the will of inanimate things. At that instant, the Chiese must have invoked all the powers of its depths; it covered that shoal of gravel with an impetuous wave, and rolling over and over that ghastly gray-white object, bore it inexorably away. I felt that I was vanquished.

Returning to my lodging at Garbe, I found myself dripping with water and perspiration, as well as utterly exhausted. My eyes were inflamed; my head was on fire; my pulse was beating like a hammer. Sleep proved to be impossible. At dawn of day, I arose unsteadily, and following the post road along the left bank of the Chiese, made my way to Sabbio. At one time my limbs would be cold as ice, at another I was forced to wipe my forehead.

At Sabbio, where I had often gone for breakfast, the innkeeper and his wife received me with a world of courtesy, asking a score of times if I felt ill. "It is nothing," I answered. "The fresh air, the exercise, and your breakfast will restore me." "But you are eating nothing!" I gazed, as if in a dream, at the wide portico festooned with spiderwebs, at the hens that came to gather crumbs of polenta, to carry to their chickens, at the Church of the Madonna that, placed as it is high up on the hills and directly opposite, looked as if planted squarely on the roof of the hostelry.

As I sat there, immersed in these visions, one of my hostess's sons, Pierino, a handsome little lad of seven, came bounding in, at the same time shouting out: "Say, mamma, I have seen him!"

"Who?"

"The man they found in the river this morning."

"Was he good-looking?"

"No, horrid! Ask Nina if he wasn't!"

Nina had come in together with her brother, but had immediately crept into a corner of the portico, and with clasped hands was murmuring something to herself. At intervals, one caught the word *Requiem,* in tearful, choking tones.

"Is he young or old?" resumed the mother. Nina made no reply, but Pierino announced, "It's an old man, with a white beard, very, very long. His eyes are staring wide open."

"Where is he? I want to see him!" I cried, springing to my feet. The innkeeper's wife gave me a strange look, and muttering, "Heavens, what a queer taste!" told Pierino to show me the way.

In four strides I had reached the church, where they had placed the body of the drowned man, in a damp little room adjoining the sacristy. The room was crowded to overflowing with the peasantry. One of them was saying:

"Who is going to know him? It is plain to see, from his clothes, that he doesn't come from here."

And another rejoined: "I tell you, he is a German."

"No, he comes from Milan."

"Did they find nothing in his clothes?" asked a young man.

"No, not a paper, nor a penny."

"He must have drowned himself because he had no money."

"I tell you, he fell into the river accidentally!"

"I tell you, he was thrown in!"

"He looks as if he had the evil eye!"

"With that wide-open mouth, he looks as though he wanted to eat us alive!"

A little girl took refuge behind her father's legs, and kept repeating, over and over: "I'm afraid! I'm afraid! Take me away! Take me away!"

The father meanwhile was closely examining the dead man's clothing, feeling of it, and expressing his opinion: "Good stuff that! It must have cost him a pretty penny!"

I was carried forward with the crowd. The old man of the Bridge of Kings stared me in the face, with eyes that were sinister and menacing. I felt, in that motionless regard, a supreme reproval. In my ears there droned a breath from the tombs, that seemed to say: "You have let me die; may you be accursed. You might have saved me, you have let me die; may you be accursed. You had guessed what I had planned to do, and you let me die; may you be accursed!"

The ceiling seemed to be shutting down upon my head; the crowd was slowly rending me asunder. I fancied that I was in hell, surrounded by devils, receiving judgment from a gray corpse, with a cavernous voice, and eyes that were implacable.

There entered a peasant, one whom I remembered having seen at Idro. Gazing at the drowned man, he exclaimed:

"Poor old man! how much I always liked him! Two days were all that he could live, after the death of his daughter, Teresa!"

They put me to bed with a raging fever. The impressions of that morning, the fatigue of the preceding evening, my remorse, produced their effect; I had hallucinations of a frightful sort. My inflamed eyes pained me exceedingly. The good mayor of Garbe came to see me twice a day, and sat beside me hours at a time, measuring out my medicine with his own hands, and telling me in low tones, at such times as I seemed somewhat rational, some droll story, that could not win a smile from me.

From that time on the fever abated, but in defiance of quinine, it refuses to leave me. My physicians say that it is of the periodic sort, such as are easily contracted from exposure and dissipation. I bear it patiently; but I cannot on any condition bear this accursed spot that hovers before my eyes. I had no sooner recovered from delirium than I saw it plainly before me; and I continue to see it, just as I have described it to you,—that obstinate, abominable, gray spot!

Why, at this very moment, a pale, undefined specter dances before my sight; it seems to soil the whiteness of the paper on which I write. The sun has begun to set, and my writing-desk is left half in shadow, though there is still light enough for me to fling these words hastily upon the page,—yet not enough to allow me to reread them. I wanted to finish before lighting the lamp; and the gray spot takes advantage of the partial obscurity to lacerate my brain.

The spot is spreading. The spot—a new departure!—is taking on the form of a man! It is throwing out arms, it is throwing out legs, it is putting forth a head! It is that old man of mine, that terrible, gray old man!

I start to-night! To-morrow, I shall hand you this manuscript in person. Either you will cure me, or I shall put out my eyes.

Giovanni Verga

The Stories of the Castle of Trezza

I

THE Signora Matilde was seated upon the crumbling parapet, with her shoulders resting against the ivy-grown tower, her thoughtful glance fathoming the black and impenetrable abyss. Her husband, with cigar in mouth and hands in pockets, his gaze idly following the faint blue wreaths of smoke, was listening with an air of boredom. Luciano, standing beside the lady, was trying, so it seemed, to read the thoughts mirrored in her eyes, that were as impenetrable as the abyss they contemplated. The rest of the party were scattered here and there about the terrace cumbered with stones and brambles, chatting, laughing, exchanging witticisms. The sea was slowly turning to a livid azure, its surface slightly ruffled and dotted with flecks of foam. The sun was sinking behind a bank of fantastic clouds, and the shadow of the castle continued to lengthen, melancholy and gigantic, over the sea-washed crags.

"Was it here?" suddenly asked the Signora Matilde, brusquely raising her head.

"Precisely here."

She gave another glance around her, lingering and meditative. Then she demanded, with a burst of gay, mocking laughter:

"And how do you know that?"

"Reconstruct in imagination the vaults of these high, gloomy corridors, in which the remnants of the gold decorations still glitter; that vast, smoke-blackened fireplace, surmounted by the jealous coat-of-arms that never suffered a stain without exacting payment in blood; that alcove, profound as a cavern, draped with somber tapestries, and with sword suspended above the pillow of the proud nobleman who never had drawn it from its sheath in vain, and who slept on the *qui vive,* with ear strained like a brigand,—who held his honor a little higher than his God, and his wife a little lower than his battle-horse! Imagine the wife, weak, timid, alone, shrinking before the lowering frown of her lord and master; disowned by her own family from the day that she had been intrusted with the exacting and implacable honor of another name;—and behind that alcove, separated only by a frail partition, and covered by a treacherous plank, that lurking chasm, which to-day reveals, without hypocrisy, its yawning jaws! the death-trap of that huge, dark, hairy brute who snored between his lady and his sword;—imagine the rays of the night-lamp flickering over the immense surface of those walls, and forming frightful and fantastic shapes; with the wind howling like a malignant spirit down the throat of the chimney, and wrathfully shaking the time-worn shutters;—and from time to time, from behind that partition, rising from the depths of that pit-fall, where the sea moaned around its base, a groan muffled by the abyss, delirious with agony, a groan that makes the woman start upright from her pillow, with hair erect from horror and moist with the sweat of anguish more terrible than that of the man slowly expiring at the bottom of the shaft; a groan that makes her turn her staring, half-crazed eyes upon the husband who hears nothing and who snores."

The Signora Matilde listened in silence, her eyes fixed, intent, gleaming with interest. She did not say "That is how it was!" but she nodded her head. Her husband shrugged his shoulders, and arose to withdraw. From the surrounding depths of ruined walls and precipice the shadows of night were rising.

"If this is all true," she said, speaking rapidly, "if it happened as you have described, they must sometimes have leaned upon this very stone, which is all that is left of the window-ledge, to look down upon the water, as we are doing now," and she placed a feverish hand upon it, "this very stone!"

His glance rested upon her hand, then upon the sea, then once more upon her hand. She made no motion, but remained silent, gazing off into the distance. "Let us be going," she said suddenly; "the legend is interesting, but at this hour my husband much prefers to hear the sound of the dinner-bell. Let us go back."

The young man offered his arm, and she rested her weight upon it, gathering up the folds of her skirts and springing lightly from stone to stone. As they passed a moldering beam, she noticed that fragments of the plastering still adhered to it.

"If they could only tell what they have seen!" she said, laughingly.

"They would tell you that at the very point where your own hand rested the Baroness's hand clung convulsively, as she strained her ear in anguish, down the passage from which there no longer came the sound of his footsteps, nor his voice, nor even a groan, but only the echoing ring of the Baron's blood-stained spurs."

The lady drew back with a start, as though she had been touching fire; then again she replaced her hand, intentionally, nervously, shrinkingly; she seemed avid of emotion; on her lips she wore a strange smile; her cheeks were flaming, her eyes brilliant.

"You see," she said, "there isn't a sound from it now!"

"How lucky!" exclaimed the Signor Giordano. "In that case we can go to dinner!"

His wife threw him a preoccupied glance, then added:

"Oh, please, just a moment longer!"

The sun's rays, just on the point of setting, had found their way through a crevice at the water's level, and unexpectedly illuminated the bottom of the well-like shaft which constituted the death-trap, revealing the jagged points of its black walls, the white pebbles gleaming in the mold and dampness of the bottom, the struggling lichens which the autumn had already tinged with purple. The smile had vanished from the merry lady's face, and turning towards her husband, timidly, caressingly, hesitantly she asked him:

"Won't you look too?"

"Be careful," answered the Signor Giordano, with his ironical smile. "You will see the bones of that fine cavalier down there, and you will dream bad dreams to-night."

She neither answered nor moved, but remained leaning above the opening, with her elbow on the surrounding coping of stones; finally, in uncertain tones:

"Why, really, there is something white, down there at the bottom!" And without waiting for an answer: "If that man fell in here, he must have clung instinctively to that point of rock, . . . don't you see? One would say there was blood on it even yet!"

Her husband flung the butt of his cigar into the shaft; she shivered, as though she had seen a tomb profaned, flushed vividly, and rose to go. She was a graceful brunette, rather too pale, delicate and nervous, with large, beautiful eyes, black and profound. Her foot stumbled for a moment on a loosened stone, she wavered and had to cling for support to Luciano's hand.

"Thanks!" she said to him, with an enigmatic smile. "One would think that the abyss was calling to me!"

II

THE dinner had proved excellent; not without cause had the Signor Giordano preferred the dinner-bell to the legends of the castle. As eleven o'clock approached, the piano was still resounding through the villa, the dancing still went gayly on in the great parlor, and cards were in progress in the other rooms. The Signora Matilde had slipped out into the garden for a breath of air, forgetful of the polka that she had promised to the Signor Luciano, who had been seeking her for the past half-hour.

"At last!" he exclaimed, discovering her. "And now about our polka?"

"You really cared about it?"

"Immensely!"

"Suppose we let it go at that?"

"Poor polka!"

"Why, frankly,—you are so successful in telling a certain kind of story that I never would have suspected you of being such an enthusiastic dancer!"

"Then you take such stories seriously?"

"Oh, that depends on what the hour is!"

The silence was profound. The wind was sweeping the clouds rapidly onward, and from time to time rustled through the trees in the garden; the sky was overstrewn with tattered silver; the shadows seemed to chase each other across the moonlit earth; and the murmur of the sea and that occasional hushed whispering of the leaves possessed, at this hour, an indefinable mystery. The Signora Matilde turned her gaze hither and thither, absent-mindedly, letting it rest at last upon the black, gigantic mass of the castle that was outlined in fantastic profile against the constantly changing background of the sky. The light and shadow alternated rapidly upon the ruins, and a shrub which had found a root-hold on the highest rampart, bent back and forth from time to time, like a grotesque phantom stooping towards the abyss.

"Do you see?" she said with her uncertain smile, and in a voice that was not quite steady. "There is something alive and moving, up there!"

"The specters of the legend!"

"Who knows?"

"This is surely the hour for stories!"

"Or else——"

"Or else what?"

"Who knows?—What is my husband doing?"

"He is playing cards."

"And the Signora Olani?"

"She is looking on."

" Oh!—You may tell me that story," she added a moment later, with a curious vivacity, " if you are not still mourning for that polka!"

The story which Luciano related was indeed a strange one.

The second wife of the Baron d' Arvelo was a Monforte, noble as the King and as poor as Job, strong as a man-at-arms and of a build to hold her own against the heavy-handed gallantry of Don Garzia. Before the wedding, she had been told that spirits were known to walk the castle, and that at night there was great disturbance in corridors and chambers, and that doors were found wide open and windows yawning, one knew not how nor through whom,—doors and windows that the night before had been securely fastened;—that groans from another world were heard, and peals of laughter such as to make the flesh creep on the boldest scoundrel who ever bore halberd and coat of mail. Donna Isabella had answered that, between herself and a husband such as, to all appearances, Don Garzia promised to be, she would have no fear of all the witches of Spain and Sicily, nor of all the devils of hell. And she was a woman to keep her word.

The first morning that she awoke in the bed where poor Donna Violante had slept her last, to find that her maid Grazia, who had also served the Baron's first wife, was bringing in her chocolate and opening the windows, she asked contemptuously:

" Well, how comes it that the spirits cut no special capers last night, in honor of the new chatelaine?"

" Then your ladyship heard nothing——?" stammered poor Grazia, who had a great dread even to speak of such things.

" Oh, yes, I heard Don Garzia snoring; and I can tell you that he snores as loud as a dozen troopers!"

" It must be that the chaplain's benediction worked better this time than it did before."

" Ah, possibly! Or else the devil and his imps are afraid of me!"

"Or else they waited over a day."

"Indeed? Their infernal lordships stand on ceremony, do they, like his Majesty the King? Come, tell me about it!"

"I really don't know, my lady."

"Then who does know the story?"

"Old Mamma Lucia, Brigida, Maso the cook, Anselmo and Rosso, the two valets of my lord the Baron, and Master Bruno, the head huntsman."

"And what have they all seen?"

"Nothing."

"Nothing! Well, what have they heard, then?"

"They have heard all sorts of things, from which Heaven protect us!"

"And when did they begin to hear these things from which Heaven is to protect us?"

"After the death of the poor Lady Violante, my lord's first wife."

"They heard them here?"

"Yes, my lady, that is to say, on this side of the castle; but they heard them from the highest battlement clear down to the kitchens, where the windows open on the court."

The Baroness began to laugh and that evening she related to her husband what had been told her. But Don Garzia, instead of joining in her laughter, flew into a greater rage than ever before, and began to blaspheme God and all the saints, as Donna Isabella had never heard them blasphemed by the foulest-mouthed grooms at her brothers' home, and to threaten that if he could learn who had dared to spread such preposterous lies, he would have them flung from the loftiest turret of the castle. The Baroness was extremely surprised that a man of his make, who ought not to fear even the devil himself, should attach so much weight to silly gossip; and in her secret heart she was rather pleased to feel herself better fitted than her husband to take the upper hand, and play the part of chatelaine as she meant to play it.

"Sleep in holy peace, my lady," Don Garzia bade her, "for here, within this castle and without, for ten leagues around, to the full reach of my good title and my good sword, there is no other thing to fear except my anger."

Now whether it was that her husband's words had left their imprint, or that something of the idle tale she had heard still lingered in her mind, the fact remains that somewhere near the hour of midnight the Baroness awoke with a great start, thinking that she had heard, or had dreamed of hearing, an indistinct sound close at hand, and directly behind the wall of the alcove. She remained listening, with a slightly quickened heart-beat; but there was nothing further to hear—the night-lamp was still burning, and the Baron still snoring his loudest. She dared not awaken him, but for her own part could not again fall asleep. The next morning her maid found her pale and somber; and while she dressed her hair before the mirror, the Baroness, resting her feet on the andirons and closely wrapped in her brocaded dressing-gown, asked her, after considerable hesitation:

"Come, tell me all that you know about the castle being haunted!"

"I know nothing more than what I have heard told by Rosso and Brigida. Do you wish me to ask Brigida to come here?"

"No!" answered Donna Isabella with some emphasis. "What is more, you are not to tell a living soul that I have talked to you of it. Let me hear just what Brigida and Rosso have told you."

"When Brigida was sleeping in the little room that opens off the corridor just beyond here, she heard every night, a little before or a little after the twelve strokes of the big bell, the sound of someone opening first the window that looks out upon the balcony, and then the door of the corridor. The first time that Brigida heard this sound was the second Sunday after Easter. She had been sick with fever and could not sleep. The next day everyone whom she told about it thought that the fever had played her a trick. But as evening came on again the poor girl showed such great fear and began to talk so strangely about the dreadful hubbub the night before, that they were all sure she was delirious, and Mamma Lucia stayed to sleep with her. But the next day Mamma Lucia herself said that she would not spend another night in that room for all the gold in the world. And then the very ones who had been the most incredulous began to ask questions, and Maso the cook told what he had not been willing to tell before, for fear of being made the laughing-stock of those who were braver than he. For more than a month he had been hearing noises in the servants' dining-hall, and had convinced himself that the spirits had been helping themselves in the pantry. And finally he told us, little by little, what he had seen."

"What he had seen?"

"Yes, my lady. He suspected that some of the under-servants were playing a trick upon him; so he hid in the passage, outside the servants' hall, with his big knife in his belt, and waited there until midnight, the time when the noises were usually heard. Then, all of a sudden,—there was not a sound, not so much as the buzzing of a fly,—a tall white phantom appeared in sight and came straight towards him, never saying a word, and brushed past him with no more noise than a mouse would make that was on the trail of an old cheese. The poor cook did not wait to learn more, and very nearly took to his bed from fright."

"Well, what did he do next?" asked the Baroness, laughing.

"Nothing at all, my lady. He turned pious, and went to confession and to communion; and every night before going to bed he never failed to say all his prayers and to commend himself very, very carefully to all the souls in purgatory that are in the habit of roaming at night, in search of *requiems* and relief."

"If I were Master Maso and had to deal with the sort of spirits that rob larders like starving cats or thieving knaves,

I should waste no time over *paternosters,* but trust to my sharpest blade, and try to find out who the rascal is who dares to play the part of ghost!"

"Ho, my lady, that is the very thing that Rosso said, and he is the kind of man that would not be afraid of the devil, the real, true devil himself; and he began to laugh very loud, and told Maso that all he needed was the courage to take the spirit, the phantom, the devil by his own horns, and make him cough up all the good things on which, by all accounts, he had made such a fine meal in the kitchen,—but that that was a thing he never would have dared to do! The very next night Rosso took his turn, hiding in the passage, just as the cook had done, with his good, stout truncheon in his hand, and he waited an hour, two hours, three hours. At last he began to think that Maso had been playing a trick on him, or that too much wine had made him talk nonsense, and he was on the point of falling asleep, sitting there on a bench, with his shoulders against the wall. When, all of a sudden, between waking and sleeping, he saw before him a figure in white, that touched the ceiling with its head, and stood straight in front of him, without moving, without having made the slightest sound in coming, without his knowing from what direction it had come. A faint gleam of light came from the lamp in the guardroom, through an open archway high up in the wall, and Rosso swears that he saw the two eyes of the phantom staring down at him, and that they shone like the eyes of a cat. Either because he was not quite awake, or because he was a bit frightened at the sudden apparition, Rosso did not stop to count one, two, three, but laid hold of his truncheon and dealt such a blow as should have cleft in two even a bull cast in bronze; but the weapon broke in his hands, as if it were made of glass or had struck against the wall; there was a shower of sparks, like the rockets they shoot off on holidays, and the phantom disappeared, just like a puff of wind, neither more nor less, leaving Rosso shaking with fear, still holding the broken truncheon in his hand, and pale enough to frighten anyone seeing him for the first time. And since then instead of calling him Rosso the Ruddy, they call him White-face."

The Baroness continued to laugh, with an incredulous air; but her brows were knit from time to time, and although she kept her eyes upon the mirror, she gave no heed to the manner in which Grazia dressed her hair and arranged the ruffs of her embroidered collar. Either the maid's conviction was so sincere as to be contagious, or else the dream of the night before had made a deep impression upon her, for in spite of herself she kept thinking that she must pass the coming night in that selfsame alcove.

"And what do they say in the castle about these apparitions?" she demanded after a short silence.

"My lady——"

"Well, go on!"

"My lady, . . . they say many foolish things——"

"Let me hear them."

"My lord, the Baron, would fly into every sort of a rage if he should know."

"So much the better! Let me hear them."

"My lady,—I am only a poor girl,—an ignorant girl,—I have been talking without knowing what I was saying,—my lord, the Baron, would have me flung out of the window more easily than I could fling away this worn-out comb. In charity, my lady, do not expose me to the anger of his lordship!"

"Would you prefer to expose yourself to mine?" exclaimed the Baroness, with frowning brow.

"For pity's sake! My lady——"

"Come, come! Speak out! I mean to know all that is being said, I tell you, and remember that if the Baron's anger is dangerous, my own is no jesting matter."

"They say that it is the ghost of poor Donna Violante, the Baron's first wife," answered Grazia desperately, and trembling from head to foot.

"In what way did Donna Violante die?"

"She flung herself into the sea."

"Donna Violante?"

"Yes, my lady, from the half-ruined balcony, that runs outside the windows of the main corridor, down upon the rocks below. They found her white veil at the foot of the precipice. It was the night of the second Thursday after Easter."

"And why did she kill herself?"

"Who can tell? My lord had been sleeping quietly beside her, when he was awakened by a loud cry, no longer found her by him, and before he was fully awake he saw a white figure fleeing from him. There was a great commotion throughout the castle, the whole household was on foot in less time than it takes to say an *ave Maria,* the doors and windows of the main corridor were found wide open, and the Baron running back and forth upon the balcony like a crazy cat! If it had not been for the head huntsman, who seized him just in time, the Baron would have fallen from the ruined parapet, at the point where the stairs began that used to lead to the watchtower. But now there is nothing left of them except the projecting stones on which the steps used to rest. It was just there that the phantom disappeared."

The Baroness had become very thoughtful. "It is certainly strange!" she said.

"Nothing remained of the poor lady, and nothing was ever found, except that veil; in the castle chapel and in the village church, masses were said, for three days, for the dead woman's soul, and a great crowd attended on their knees at the funeral, because everyone wanted her to rest in peace, on account of her great charity while she lived. And yet, although my lord had given orders that the services should be such as were due to so rich and powerful a lady, and the bier with the family arms embroidered on the four corners of the pall stood three days and three nights in the chapel, with more than forty candles burning constantly, and the grand standard at the foot of the altar, and the flags and shields all around, so that there never was seen greater pomp,—the Baron departed immediately after; and he was not seen again at the castle until now."

" Heaven forfend! " murmured Donna Isabella. " Don Garzia never told me any of this, but it is well that I should know it! "

" And then there were some fishermen who put to sea earlier in the morning than the others; and they told how they had seen the spirit of the Baroness, dressed all in white, like the saint she was, up yonder in the doorway of the watchtower, and moving tranquilly up and down the broken stairway, where even a gull would fear to perch, just as though she were walking on a fine Turkish carpet, in the grandest room in all the castle! "

" Indeed! " exclaimed the Baroness, then said nothing more, but rose and crossed over to the window. The day was warm and clear, and the joyous sunshine, entering through the window, seemed to bring gladness into the gloomy chamber. But Donna Isabella seemed unconscious of this and completely absorbed in her own thoughts. Suddenly she turned again to Grazia.

" Show me just where it was that Donna Violante fell," she said.

" There, at the place where the wall has crumbled and the steps used to lead up to the sentinel's tower, in the time when they kept a sentinel there."

" And why is there no sentinel now? " demanded the Baroness, with singular interest.

" He would need wings, to make his way up there; now that the steps are in ruins the boldest bricklayer would not venture to set foot on what remains of them."

" Ah, that is true! " And she remained for a long time, gazing up at the little tower that in its isolation had the appearance of clinging to the massive rampart, in terror of the abyss that yawned beneath, while the remnants of the stairway, crumbling, dismantled, without parapet, suspended in the air above four hundred feet of precipice, looked like the cogs of some fantastic mechanism.

" Really," she murmured, as if to herself, " it would be impossible! It makes one giddy, even to look up there." She drew back brusquely, and closed the window. Grazia beholding her light-hearted mistress so downcast, and realizing what an unexpected impression her story had produced, felt a sudden thrill of fear as great as though she herself had to pass the night in the haunted room.

"Alas, my lady, I have told everything in obedience to you, and without thinking that it was as much as my life was worth if the Baron should know of it. Have pity on me, my lady!"

"Don't be afraid!" replied Donna Isabella, with a singular smile, "matters like these, whether true or false, are not of a kind to tell my lord and husband. But tell me further what they say of the motive that drove Donna Violante to kill herself,—for there must have been a motive of some kind. Whatever they say, whether right or wrong, tell me."

"I swear by the five wounds of our Lord, and by the holy Friday, which is to-day, that they say nothing at all, or at least nothing that I know of. At first, when groans began to be heard at night, excepting on church days, and soon any night from Sunday to Saturday, and every time that the moon shone, and that any misfortune threatened the castle or the neighborhood, they thought that the Baroness had died in mortal sin, and that was why her soul was calling for help from the other world, while demons tortured her. But then Beppo, the fisherman, told of the vision that had appeared to him from way up in the guard tower; and a few days afterwards his honest old uncle, Gaspare, confirmed it; and everyone felt sure that the blessed soul of the Baroness had found salvation, and they thought instead of Corrado, the page, poor fellow—God have mercy on his soul!"

"And how did the page die? Did he also kill himself?"

"He didn't die; he disappeared!"

"When did he disappear?"

"Two days before the death of Donna Violante."

"And who caused him to disappear?"

"Who?" stammered the girl, turning very pale. "Why, who can make a soul, that belongs to God, disappear, and carry it off to his own abode, as a wolf carries off a sheep? Who but the devil?"

"Oh, then this Master Corrado was a great sinner?"

"No, my lady, he was the handsomest and best-mannered lad in all the castle."

The Baroness began to laugh again: "Oh, my poor Grazia, those are the sinners that the devil usually takes off, in that sort of fashion!" Then becoming thoughtful again, she cast a long and searching glance upon the bed where the previous night she had been suddenly awakened by that frightful groan.

"When does one hear those groans from the other world?" she inquired.

"On the nights when the phantom is not seen walking."

"That is strange! Where are they heard?"

"Here, my lady, in this alcove, and in the passage alongside; in the corridor that goes by this chamber, and in the dressing-room behind the alcove."

"In short, all around us here?"

Instead of replying, Grazia made the sign of the cross. Suddenly the Baroness compressed her lips.

"That will do!" she said brusquely, "you may go now. Have no fear; I shall repeat nothing of what you have told me."

III

DONNA ISABELLA passed the day examining minutely all the rooms, passages, and corridors in the vicinity of her chamber; and Don Garzia asked her in vain the motive of her preoccupation. That night she slept little and uneasily, but she heard nothing, except that the wind which sprang up towards morning kept slamming one of the windows which opened on the balcony. The next morning the Baroness was still in bed when, from behind the bed-curtains, she heard the following dialogue between her husband and Rosso, who was helping him draw on his heavy boots:

"Tell me, you rascal, what was the meaning of all the racket my windows made last night?"

Rosso scratched his head and replied:

"That was because the sirocco began to blow an hour before daylight."

"That is all very fine! But if the windows had been properly closed, the sirocco would not have set them dancing like a girl with Saint Vitus' dance! Now, see that you do your duty, you loafer, for in this castle I mean that everything shall go as regularly as the clock in the church tower, now that I am home again."

"My lord, you are the master," replied Rosso hesitatingly, "but there are reasons why that window has to be left open."

"And what are these reasons?"

"Because when the window is shut, one hears things!"

"What!"

"One hears things, my lord!"

"Curses on your soul!" howled the Baron, snatching up a boot, to hurl it in the other's face.

"My lord, you can murder me, if you wish, but I have told you the truth."

"And who has been filling your ears with such fine truth, you confounded idiot?"

"I have seen things and heard things, as plainly as I see and hear now that you are angry, to my misfortune and without my fault."

"You have seen and heard things?"

"Yes, my lord."

"You have been stealing wine out of my cellar, you jailbird!"

"I have drunk nothing, my lord!"

"Then you have turned coward! A lovelorn cat has scared you! You are growing old, my Rosso, rubbish for the junkman! It is time I flung you out of the castle, with an extra kick or two for good measure."

"My lord, I am still good for something, if you put me face to face with a dozen devils in flesh and bone, that can be reached with a good sword-thrust, or can strike me down, like a dog! But against an enemy that has neither flesh nor bone, and breaks the blade in your hand, like a wisp of straw, by my soul! I do not know what you yourself could do, even though you are known as the most daredevil Baron in all Sicily!"

This time it was the Baron's turn to scratch his head and frown, but without anger, or at least without anger towards Rosso.

"All the same," he said, "fasten all the windows securely to-night, go to bed, and think no further of it."

Donna Isabella arose, paler and more silent than usual.

"Are you afraid?" Don Garzia asked her.

"There is nothing I am afraid of!" the Baroness answered very dryly. Yet when night came, she was unable to close her eyes; and while her husband snored like a bass viol, she turned and turned again upon the bed; and all of a sudden she shook him roughly by the arm, and sprang up into a sitting posture, with pallid face and wide, staring eyes: "Listen!" she said.

Don Garzia also stared, wide-eyed, in his turn, and seeing the state she was in, he also sprang up in bed and laid his hand upon his sword.

"No," said she, "your sword will not avail you now!"

"What did you hear?"

"Listen!" Both of them remained motionless, speechless, with straining ears. Finally Don Garzia flung his sword scornfully into the middle of the chamber, and lay down again, muttering curses.

"This time it is you that are going crazy!" he grumbled. "That worthless Rosso has addled your brain with his nonsense! I will slice the rascal's ears off!"

"Hush!" exclaimed the woman once more, and this time in such a tone and with such a look that the Baron dared not answer a single word. "Did you hear that?"

"Nothing, on my soul!"

But all of a sudden he too sprang up, a second time, if not as pallid and perturbed as his wife, at least curious and attentive, and began to dress himself. As he drew on his boots, he trembled visibly.

"Do you hear?" repeated Donna Isabella, making the sign of the cross. Her husband took refuge in a good, round oath, instead of the cross; he sprang upon the sword that he had thrown into the middle of the chamber, and half-dressed as he was, with the bare blade in his hand, flung himself through the darkness into the passage, behind the alcove.

Shortly afterwards he returned. "Nothing there!" he said. "The windows are closed; I have looked through the corridor, the passage, and the dressing-room. We are crazy, you and I! Let me sleep in peace, now, for if Rosso should find out in the morning what I have done to-night, and what a fool I have made of myself, I should be ashamed to look him in the face!"

No further sound was heard; the Baroness remained awake; and although Don Garzia, from time to time, emitted one or two sonorous snores, he could not continue to sleep as usual. At dawn he arose, with face so pallid that Rosso, alertly hurrying through his usual ministrations, prepared to beat a retreat.

"Tell Bruno that I want him," said the Baron, and resumed his striding up and down the room, while the Baroness continued combing her hair. Donna Isabella anxiously watched him out of the corner of her eye, and saw him turn down the passageway, and heard him moving about in the dressing-room; then he returned, shaking his head and murmuring to himself: "No! It is impossible!"

Bruno and Rosso appeared together.

"Old comrade," said the Baron, "do you feel like earning a bright gold ducat, and passing the night in the corridor, outside here, without trembling like a silly girl who has been hearing ghost stories?"

"My lord, I am ready to do whatever you command," replied Bruno, but not without visible hesitation. The Baron, who had long looked upon Bruno as a case-hardened scoundrel, was much surprised at his hesitation, and at the discovery that Bruno, contrary to all expectation, had grown very serious.

"By the infernal!" he cried, striking a mighty blow upon the table, "are you all turning into a brood of cowards?"

"My lord, in order to prove that we are not all of us cowards, I will do what you command!"

"And I too," added Rosso, ashamed that he had not been put to the test, in place of the head huntsman. "In this way, you will no longer have reason to doubt our word!"

"Very well, then! Since you have all had the advantage of seeing it and hearing it and laying your hands on it, keep good guard for me to-night! Take your posts on the path usually followed by this rascally spirit that has set my whole household in a tremble. Where does it generally make its appearance?"

"In the corridor, alongside, usually. . . . But no one saw it during the time that this wing of the castle was unused."

"You, Bruno, will stand guard behind the door leading into the great hall; and Rosso by the window at the upper end of the corridor. Then, when this ill-begotten spirit is caught within, and you have your trusty blades beside you, and neither your hands nor your hearts fail you, the rascal will have no way of escape but through my room, . . . and then, by the help of God, or of the devil! he will have to deal with me! Go now, and see that you keep good guard!"

"I think that you would do better to order extra masses for the soul of your Donna Violante!" the Baroness told him, very seriously, when they were once more alone. The Baron was on the point of flying into a rage, but succeeded in controlling himself, and answered with a sneer:

"How long is it since my wife has become as credulous as a hysterical girl?"

"Ever since I have been seeing and hearing things that I never before either heard or saw!"

"Will you kindly tell me what sort of things you have heard?"

"The same that you yourself heard!" she retorted, without discomposure. Don Garzia frowned.

"I have neither heard nor seen anything!" he exclaimed contemptuously.

"And I saw you as clearly as I see you at this moment, and you would be greatly surprised if you could see the way you looked!"

"Ah!" exclaimed the Baron, with a laugh that showed his teeth, white and pointed like those of a wolf, "the fact is that you have even made me lose my nerve and feel frightened, myself!"

"Did you think that I was frightened, my lord?"

My lord had no answer ready, but crossed over to the window in a mood far blacker than the big black clouds that the wind was driving at a gallop along the horizon.

IV

THE Baron was unwontedly abstemious at dinner that evening. Donna Isabella withdrew to retire, without uttering a word, but pale and serious. After Don Garzia had assured himself that Rosso and Bruno were already at their posts, he also went to bed, jestingly telling his wife:

"To-night we are going to see whether the devil will leave his tail in our hands!"

Midnight had struck some time before, the Baron had raised his head and listened to the twelve strokes, then had turned and turned again two or three times in bed, had yawned, and at last fallen asleep in good earnest. Everything was tranquil; even the wind had died down. Donna Isabella, who had been wakeful until now, was just beginning to doze off.

Suddenly a terrible cry reverberated down the immense corridor; it was a cry so delirious, so terror-stricken, that it was impossible to recognize the voice that uttered it; there was nothing in the sound that was human. At the same time there came a deafening din, the door and window of the chamber were flung violently open, and in the flickering lamplight a white form seemed to flash across the room and vanish through the window.

The Baroness, congealed with terror beneath the coverlets, saw her husband plunge in pursuit of the phantom, sword in hand, and leap from the window out upon the balcony. He ran like one possessed, followed by Bruno, in the wake of the phantom, that fled like a bird, along the brink of the ruined parapet; both of them, with hair rising on their heads, saw beyond a doubt—there was no delusion—that white figure lightly pick its way along the stones that still projected from the rampart, to the point where the stairway used to be, and there vanish into the darkness.

"By the Madonna!" exclaimed the Baron, after some moments of stupefaction. "I will run it through with my sword, or it may carry off my soul, be it the devil himself, in flesh and bone!" Don Garzia believed in neither God nor the devil, although he had a great respect for them both; but without knowing why, he recalled the words spoken that morning by Donna Isabella, and shuddered.

Donna Isabella had until now not made the slightest request, whether because she had feared to do so, or because she judged it useless. The Baron, for that matter, was in such a humor that he would not have tolerated any. The next day, however, she told him with decision that she did not intend to sleep any longer in that chamber.

"Wait just one more night," replied her husband. "I myself will stand guard to-night, and if to-morrow you do not laugh at your own fears, I will leave you free to do whatever you judge best."

She dared not add further words, excepting after a few moments to ask him:

"Of what manner of sickness did your first wife die, my lord?"

He cast a grim look at her and replied:

"Of the falling sickness, my lady!"

"That is a sickness I shall never have, I promise you!" she told him, with a singular accent.

Together with all the vices that belong to the soldier of fortune and the gentleman-brigand, Don Garzia possessed their single virtue, an invincible courage. He did what was now beyond the daring even of Bruno, the redoubtable Bruno, and what had almost caused the death of Rosso, a hardy knave if there ever was one,—for he passed three nights in succession, in the corridor, without closing an eye, without making a movement, any more than the pilaster against which he leaned, his hand on the hilt of his sword, his ear tensely strained. The wind rattled the framework of the window, which had been left open by his order; owls came wheeling and flitting around the balcony; bats chased each other, whirling through the passageway; the rays of the lamp shone through the archway high up in the wall of the guardroom, and flickered as if dying out. Aside from this, all remained quiet, and Don Garzia would have grown tired of passing his nights as a sentinel, like a man-at-arms, if the memory of what he had seen with his own eyes had not made a profound impression on his mind, and if the words spoken by his wife had not become one of those obsessions which banish sleep from body and mind, one of those doubts which imperiously demand enlightenment. His conscience was still slumbering, but certain recollections, certain circumstances that had passed at the time unheeded, suddenly awoke and arose before him, in the form of such a suspicion that Don Garzia, boorish, brutal, despotic noble though he was, skeptical and superstitious at the same time, but at heart sincerely a baron—that is to say, one that does homage to his king and to the Church, that between them had made him what he was—felt himself mastered by it, and felt the imperious need of freeing himself from it, either by persuasion or by the sword.

This was the fourth night that Don Garzia had been waiting. The sea was in a tempest; thunder shook the castle to its foundation; the hail rattled impetuously against the panes, and the weather-vanes upon the pinnacles creaked and groaned at intervals. From time to time, a lightning flash cleft the darkness of the corridor from end to end, and seemed to flood it with specters. All of a sudden the light in the guardroom died out.

Don Garzia was left in darkness. The shadows that surrounded him seemed to contract and oppress him on all sides, to stifle the breathing in his breast, the voice in his throat, to clinch his sword in its sheath. Without warning, the daredevil soldier felt a shudder penetrating his very marrow. Enveloped in darkness, in the midst of all these varied and confused noises, which still possessed an indefinable dread, he seemed to hear another sound nearer at hand and far more frightful,—a sound that set his pulse beating feverishly. The darkness was riven by a lightning flash, and he found himself face to face with a rigid, motionless figure in white,—the same figure that he had once before seen fleeing before him, and which, from that time onward, had haunted his conscience and his thoughts. And now it gazed at him, with glowing, terrible eyes. All this was the vision of an instant; with hair rising on his head, he dealt a formidable thrust; he felt the hilt strike against some substance, he heard a cry of mortal anguish, that froze the blood in his veins and caused him, in a delirium of terror, to wrench his sword free and leap backward, cowering with fear, and calling for help with all the voice he had in his body.

Two or three terrible minutes passed, in which not a sound was heard. He remained in the midst of that darkness, close beside that *thing* through which his sword had passed. Throughout the castle was heard a great confusion, people hastening here and there, and along the walls came the reflected glimmer of torches which the pages bore. Don Garzia flung himself into the doorway, roaring:

"Let no one but Bruno enter here, if you value your lives!"

They had all stopped, amazed to see the Baron so ghastly white, with eyes starting from their sockets, and the sword in his hand still dripping with blood. Bruno entered and beheld a horrible spectacle.

Close to the wall lay the body of Donna Violante, clad in

her white gown, just as she had fled from her husband's bed, on the night when it was supposed that she had flung herself into the sea. Her face was pale as wax and fearfully emaciated, her hair disordered and unkempt, her eyes wide open, in a fixed and frightful stare. The wound had been mortal and had scarcely bled; only a few drops of blood had issued from her mouth, and flowed down the chin.

"You were right, Bruno!" said the Baron, in a stifled voice. "I was not willing to believe in phantoms; I thought they were the folly of hysterical women. But now I too believe in them. We shall have to throw into the sea this semblance of my poor wife, which some malignant spirit has assumed,—and no one within the castle nor without must know anything about it, because there is no knowing what sort of absurd story they would be capable of inventing."

Bruno quite understood and had no need of further explanation. His master, however, did not forget to add in a low tone:

"Listen, old comrade, you know quite well that if this matter should become known exactly as it seems to have happened, I should be made out a bigamist, or worse; and your own head would be none too firm upon your shoulders, take my word for it!"

On the anniversary of Donna Violante's death, imposing and costly services were held for her in the church. And yet, in some unknown way, it began to be whispered around, within the castle and without, that things had really happened just as they seemed to have happened, and just as Don Garzia did not wish that they should seem to have happened. And since Bruno was now beginning to have his doubts whether his head really was quite firm upon his shoulders, one fine day while out hunting, he absent-mindedly lodged a bullet between his lord's first and second vertebræ.

Donna Isabella, who was greatly afraid of the falling sickness, had gone to spend the summer with her own family; and since the air seemed to benefit her, she never returned.

V

This was the legend of the Castle of Trezza, which everyone in the neighborhood knew, and which everyone related in a different way, with a liberal intermingling of demons and souls in purgatory. Earthquakes, time, and human agency had reduced to a pile of ruins the splendid stronghold of those Barons who in bygone days had defied with impunity the anger of their king, and seemed to have left upon it an accursed stigma that added a mysterious attraction to the legend, and held the fascinated gaze of the Signora Matilde, all the while that she listened in silence.

"And how about the other man?" she demanded unexpectedly. "How about the young page who was not killed, poor fellow, when he fell into the shaft, but lingered there in agony? What became of him?"

"Who knows? Perhaps the Baron continued to hear his stifled groans, his desperate cries imploring death,—perhaps he chose to hasten the inevitable, and threw down quicklime to consume the body."

"It is a frightful story!" murmured the Signora Matilde. "Even leaving out the phantoms, the midnight dream, the wind slamming doors and windows, the weather-vanes that creak and groan, it is still a frightful story!"

"A story such as would no longer be possible to-day, now that husbands resort to the law courts, or at the worst fight duels," responded Luciano, laughing.

But she froze the laughter on his lips by the strangeness of her glance. "Do you think so?" she demanded. He found himself silenced by that glance, by her tone, by the detachment and formality of her whole manner. They were joined by the Signor Giordano.

"Talk of something else," she said under her breath, with singular vivacity. "Do not let us talk of this again. . . ."

VI

THE Signor Luciano and the Signora Matilde saw each other almost every day, in the little gathering of friends who met together regularly for evening dances and day-time excursions around the neighborhood. But for two or three days the lady was indisposed and did not join the others. The first time after this that they met she seemed so altered that Luciano made anxious inquiries about her health; but her manner and her answers showed such embarrassment that the young man himself was embarrassed, without knowing exactly why.

Evidently she was avoiding him. She was as gay, witty, and charming as ever with the others; but towards him she had changed. Her husband's manner also had changed,—and yet nothing had happened; not a word had been spoken, nor did Luciano himself as yet realize why he was so perturbed, why her embarrassment made him embarrassed also, and why he was so sensitive to the change in the Signor Giordano. One beautiful evening, when the moon was full, the entire party started for a stroll, and Luciano boldly offered his arm to the Signora Matilde. She hesitated slightly, but did not venture to refuse. They walked slowly and in silence, while all the others chatted and laughed gayly. All at once, she pressed his arm and said, in a mere whisper:

"Do you see?"

Signor Giordano was close beside them, offering his arm to the Signora Olani. The hand that rested on Luciano's arm trembled convulsively, and her voice had an unaccustomed vibration.

When the Signor Giordano had parted from the Signora Olani at the villa gateway, he seemed at the same time to have let fall a mask that he had worn up to that moment, and revealed himself somber, taciturn, menacing.

"I am afraid; oh, I am afraid of him!" murmured Matilde, under her breath. Luciano pressed the delicate arm that rested so lightly on his own, and that responded tremblingly and yielded itself confidingly to him, who for all his love had not the power to protect her, though he should give the last drop of blood in his viens. They exchanged a glance, a single eloquent glance, under the moonlight,—that of the woman full of helplessness,—then lowered their eyes. On the threshold of the house they parted. He dared not even clasp her hand.

She went away, not knowing what nights of ardent visions he had spent, what fevers had consumed him on account of her, all the while that he had seemed so calm and indifferent; how many times he had feasted his eyes upon her, unobserved; and what a crisis had passed within him, when forced to bid her a smiling good-by, in the presence of the rest; and when he saw her pass by, shrinking back in the corner of her carriage, with pallid cheeks and unseeing eyes; and what a knot of bitterness had gathered at his heart, when he beheld the window tightly closed, where he had so often seen her face. Did she divine all this? Did he himself divine what she in her turn had suffered? When they met again, after a long interval, they seemed not to know each other, not to see each other, but turned pale and passed without bowing.

Finally they met again, at a dance, in church, or at the theater, under the guidance of God or of fate. He said to her, "When can I see you?" She turned first white, then crimson; lowered her eyes, then met his ardent gaze, and said: "To-morrow."

And on the morrow they met, their pulses trembling with fever, their eyes suffused with tears. "Why did you tell me that story?" she murmured, over and over again, as if in a dream.

Was it repentance, reproach, or presentiment?

Some months later, in the autumn, the same gathering of friends met once more at Aci Castello. The two lovers had either kept their secret well, or the husband had concealed his jealousy, or the Signora Olani had been more than usually absorbing. They met as formerly, they planned excursions as formerly, they were as light-hearted, or so appeared to be, as formerly. A fitful flush the more upon their cheeks, an occasional gleam in their eyes,—but nothing more. They took part in the usual outings, the usual dances; they even talked of the usual dinner up on the old castle tower. To this the Signora Matilde raised every possible objection. Her husband looked at her in a peculiar way and asked the reason of her unusual repugnance.

Accordingly she went with the rest.

The meal passed off as gayly as that of the preceding year. They spread the table on the grass; they danced upon the grass; and they flung the bottles on the grass, as fast as the corks were drawn. They gossiped of the castle, of its storied memories, of Normans and Saracens, and the age of chivalry; and finally they reverted to the old-time legends, and told again, in a fragmentary way, the story that Luciano had told on the former occasion, in that self-same spot, and that some of the newcomers listened to with avidity, in the peace that follows a good dinner, and while savoring the sparkling wine of Syracuse.

Luciano and Matilde remained for a long time silent, and evaded each other's glance.

VII

At the age of fifty, Don Garzia d' Arvelo had become unexpectedly lord of numerous fiefs dependent upon the baronetcy of Trezza; his nephew, the Baron, had been found in a deep ravine, one fine day or one foul night, interrupted in his chase of some fair quarry. The Knight of Arvelo, now that he was Baron, held a preliminary hanging of two or three vassals, who had the misfortune of possessing attractive game at home, and a sad reputation of valuing their honor as though they were gentlemen. Then he had mounted his horse, and since he suspected that the lord of

Gravia had settled in a similar hasty way certain old family accounts, he went to await him at a crossroad, and without stopping to waste words over the correctness of the rumor, had wound up his account also.

Having thus fulfilled his obligations as a d' Arvelo and a noble unaccustomed to submit quietly to insults, he had gone tranquilly to occupy his baronial seat, had hung his sword upon the nail where the sword of his predecessor had hung; and merely to show that he was master, had let the weight of an iron hand be felt by all the poor devils who lived within the limits of his jurisdiction,—and even beyond the limits, because something of a freebooter remained in him, along with his old habits of soldier-of-fortune. At the *requiem* ordered at the service for the young Baron, as many as intermingled, under their breath, certain words not contained in the liturgy, had reason to repent of it. As between wolf and wolf, the old one who succeeded the young one showed such jaws and such an appetite, that by comparison the deceased had become a lamb. As the younger son of a noble family, Don Garzia had spent so long a time sharpening his tusks and begging for a bone out of the abundance in which his nephew reveled, that despite all sorts of foraging, to which the nephew closed his eyes, it might be fairly said that he had been famished for fifty years; so that it was only natural that, when he could gorge himself on all the luxuries of unrestrained power, he should have shown himself a glutton, with the stomach of an ostrich.

Furthermore, the King, his sovereign next to God, was far away, and the house of d' Arvelo was an illustrious one, grandees of Spain, of the kind that uncover their heads neither before their King nor before God. Don Garzia went to court; fought with a gentleman who dared to laugh at his hirsute mustache and his tarnished braid, and ran six inches of iron between his ribs; then made his homage to the King, who received him at his table, and over the cheese and the dried figs told him that, since the house of Arvelo had no other heirs, it was his good pleasure that Don Garzia should wed a young Castilian lady, who was waiting for a husband in the convent of Monte Vergine. Don Garzia, as befitted a loyal subject and the head of a great house, espoused the lady without needing to be asked twice, and without having once seen her before leading her to the altar, but after having carefully inspected his bride's family records and the quarterings of her coat-of-arms. He placed her in a new litter, with an imposing retinue of troopers in front, on each side, and behind; mounted his own steed, and led her back to Trezza.

On the evening that the bridal pair arrived, there was a grand illumination at the castle, in the village, and throughout the country round about; the bell of the little church was rung to the point of cracking; there was dancing all night, down upon the shore, and the wine of Bosco and of Terreforti from the Baron's cellars flowed like the waters of the sea. None the less, when the bride had entered the wretched chamber, dark and gloomy, in the deep alcove of which the bed loomed up like a scaffold, she could not overcome a sense of repugnance, almost of fear, and inquired of her husband:

"How is it, my lord, that with all your wealth, you have so mean a sleeping chamber?"

Don Garzia, mindful of his duty to be gallant for the time being, replied: "The chamber will be fine enough, now that you are in it, my lady!"

Nevertheless, the first time that Donna Violante awoke in that ugly chamber, and found herself beside her ugly lord, it must have been an extremely ugly awakening. But she was the daughter of a noble race, well-trained in passive obedience, proud only of her family name and of that other newly intrusted to her. She had been snatched brusquely from the peace of her convent, the tranquil delights and vaguely troubled dreams of youth, and flung—she who had the blood of kings in her veins—into the power of a vulgar brute on whose brow chance had placed a baron's coronet; she had accepted this brute because the King, the head of her house, the laws of her caste, had ordered it; and she had stifled her repugnance when the old man's black and callous hand rested upon her proud, white shoulder, because he was her husband. She even tried, with mild and gentle ways, to tame the old wolf who snarled beside her and showed his pointed teeth when trying hardest to be amiable. For he was not the sort of a wolf whom the holy water of marriage could cause to change his skin. That delicate, white-handed wife, who spoke with lowered voice, who blushed at his joyous songs and jovial exclamations, who fled from him in alarm when his lordship was in his best humor; who did not know how to season his favorite dishes; who had not even served to give him an heir, impressed him as a mere luxurious toy, something to be kept under lock and key, like the family diamonds. Accordingly, far from abandoning his trooper's habits, he held to his own joyous way, without even taking the trouble to keep his wife in ignorance. For she was so timid, and trembled so visibly whenever he flew into a rage, that she had impressed him as stupid. He hunted, he drank, he spent his time where and how he would; and when he returned home drunk, or in bad humor, woe to the flies who allowed themselves to buzz!

One last escapade of Don Garzia, however, had wounded his resigned victim to the quick. The pride of race, the self-esteem of the woman, the jealousy of the wife, all rebelled at last in Donna Violante, and gave her for the first time a fictitious energy.

"My lord," she said, with shaking voice, but without lowering her eyes before her husband's frown, "send me back to the convent from which you took me, since I have so far fallen in your esteem!"

"What is all this nonsense?" grumbled Don Garzia, "and who has told you that you have so far fallen?"

"How is it then that you respect yourself so little as to stoop to the level of a girl like Mena?"

The Baron was preparing to pour forth a round half-dozen of those blasphemies that used to shake the castle to its foundations, but contented himself with an ugly sneer:

"How long since, my lady, have the hens of the Castle of Trezza permitted themselves to do the crowing!"

The Baroness arose next morning, pale and suffering, but her eyes shone with an unwonted splendor. She seemed resigned, but it was an ominous resignation that from time to time flashed forth rebellion and revenge.

VIII

ONE night the Baron lingered late abroad. The moon mirrored itself in the storied panes of the lofty window; the sea undulated tranquilly. The Baroness remained for a long time silent, her chin in her hand, her thoughts far away. Corrado, the Baron's handsome page, had twice asked her in vain if she would have him mount his horse and go in search of his lord.

At last Donna Violante fixed her absent gaze upon his face. He was a handsome lad, was Corrado, with dark velvety eyes and fresh, brown cheeks, like those of some slender girl of Trezza; and so timid that those same olive cheeks were tinged with a faint purple under the preoccupied glance of his lady. She looked at him for a long time without seeing him.

"No," she said finally, "why should you?"

She rose, flung open the window, and leaned her elbows on the sill. The sea was mirror-like and gleaming; fishermen scattered along the shore, or standing in groups before the doors of their huts, were gossiping of the day's catch of fish; far away, lost in the dim distance, some sailor could be heard at intervals, singing a monotonous eastern song; the waves died like a sigh at the foot of the lofty wall; the foam gleamed white for an instant, and the acrid odor of the sea rose in puffs, that also followed each other wave-like. The Baroness stood gazing absently at all this, and found herself marveling that she from the height of her gilded chamber could listen with such singular interest to the talk of these folk so far below her, at the tower's base.

Finally she turned brusquely, surprised to find the page still waiting for her orders. And this time she looked at Corrado longer and more attentively. Suddenly she blushed, and, for the sake of saying something, demanded carelessly:

"What time is it, Corrado?"

"It is two o'clock, my lady."

Her brow gathered in another frown, and in a tone of indescribable bitterness she said:

"The Baron returns very late to-night!"

"Have no fear, my lady, the neighborhood is safe, the night is clear, the moon without a cloud."

"That is true," she said, with a strange smile, "it is really a night for lovers." And she continued to gaze at the lad, seemingly unaware of the trouble that her glance caused him.

"Are you acquainted with Mena?" she demanded suddenly.

"The miller's daughter of Capo dei Molini?"

"Yes, the miller's daughter of Capo dei Molini," she repeated, with her singular smile.

"I am acquainted with her, my lady."

"And so am I!" she exclaimed in stifled tones. "I made her acquaintance through my husband!"

To the proud Castilian Corrado was nothing more than a servant, a young lad who wore her arms embroidered on the velvet of his jacket, a lad who was good to look at, and whose curling hair was blonde. Accordingly she spoke as if to herself, because her heart was too full, because its bitterness had found no outlet in tears; and she asked him a strange question, in a strange tone, and with eyes fixed upon the ground:

"Why are not you also one of Mena's lovers?"

"I, my lady?"

"Yes, all the men go mad over that miller's daughter!"

"I am only a poor page, my lady!"

She fixed her frowning glance upon his once again, and little by little her brow cleared. "Poor or not, you are a handsome page! Did you not know it?"

Their eyes met for an instant, and at the same time sought to avoid each other. Had the youth's vanity been stirred by these words, her patrician pride would have flamed up at the page's audacity, and her woman's heart would have closed forever against him. But instead, the young man sighed, and answered, with downcast eyes:

"Alas, my lady!"

And his sigh possessed an immense attraction.

A thousand confused and violent emotions swelled up in the heart of the Baroness, like clouds above a tempestuous sea. Pure and white and proud as she was, a descendant of royal princes and Castilian kings, she could not help comparing this handsome, ingenuous youth, who had a knightly heart beneath a servant's livery, with that coarse, ill-mannered brute who wore a Baron's coronet and to whom she had been given.

"Corrado!" she exclaimed unexpectedly, and in broken tones, as though losing self-control, "since you know her,—since you are a man,—tell me if that miller's daughter is beautiful,—more beautiful than I! Tell me,—don't be afraid——"

The lad gazed in fascination at the wrathful, unnerved, jealous woman, flushed with shame and mortification, beautiful enough to cause the fall of an angel. He turned pale and remained silent; then, with trembling voice, clasped-handed, and in a tone that thrilled the lady from head to foot, exclaimed:

"Oh, have some pity for me, my lady!"

She cast upon him one blind, unseeing glance, and withdrew hurriedly, almost as if fleeing from him.

IX

DONNA VIOLANTE passed a sleepless night. In the morning, with feverish cheeks and a nervous smile, she said to her husband:

"Do you not think it time to find me another page, Don Garzia?"

"Why so?"

"Corrado is no longer a boy, and you leave your wife alone far too often for him to be always by my side, without giving your enemies a chance to gossip."

The Baron knit his brows and answered: "Friends and enemies both know me far too well for either the occurrence or the gossip to be possible. And further," he added, "I esteem you far too highly to fear that you, with your rank and pride, would stoop to share your favors with a page!"

Nonetheless, in spite of his baronial arrogance and confident power, Don Garzia was too old a sinner himself to sleep in peace after this idea had once been put into his head. Accordingly, he sought out Corrado.

"See here, my fine lad," he said, "here is a purse for traveling expenses, and a recommendation of faithful service,—and off you go to seek your fortune elsewhere!"

The lad was completely dumfounded; and never suspecting the quarter from which his dismissal came, he feared that his secret passion had become known, and trembled, not for himself, but for her of whom he had dreamed all night, with glowing eyes.

"At least, my lord," he stammered, "have the goodness to tell me why I am banished."

"Because you are old enough to be earning your bread, with the work of your hands, instead of hanging around, strumming a guitar; and it is time to think of bearing arms, rather than a velvet doublet."

"Ah, my lord, let me as a favor remain in your service, if I have in no way displeased you; and in whatever capacity you choose to use me."

The Baron scratched his nose, as was his habit when anyone ventured to oppose him.

"Be off with you!" he said, with a look that made it clear that he did not mean to cover the same ground twice. "Get out from under my feet, you nuisance! I want no more of your services! And remember this, that if I still find you in the castle to-morrow night, you shall not leave it through the door!"

The poor page had lost his head, and in spite of his great awe of his lord, he tried every means to see once again the lady who for an instant had made his life luminous, and whom he loved more than life. But the Baroness avoided him, almost as though she were trying to avoid herself and her memories. The most absurd projects and fears crowded into the young lover's excited brain. And, imagining that the life of Donna Violante was threatened by the Baron, he decided to go to any length to save her.

Finally, as he drew aside a curtain, beneath which she was passing, proud, calm, and impenetrable, he whispered in her ear:

"If my blood could aid you in any way, it is yours to take, my lady!"

She passed onward, neither turning nor replying, and he remained as if thunderstruck.

X

The evening on which Corrado must no longer be found within the castle approached rapidly; yet he did not even remember the terrible threat of the master who had never threatened in vain. He was mad with love; he would have paid with his head the chance to speak for fifteen minutes with his lady. Before retiring for the night, the Baron was accustomed to make a round of inspection through the castle. Corrado counted on this moment to have a last explanation, or take a last farewell of the Baroness. When night had fallen he found his way unseen to the balcony, and reached the window of Donna Violante's room. Don Garzia was seated with his back to the window, finishing his evening meal. His wife sat facing him, with her chin resting on her hand, and her eyes fixed in a stony stare. All at once, whether through presentiment, or some mysterious magnetic flow, or some slight noise made by the youth as he pressed his face against the pane, she trembled, raised her head suddenly, and her eyes met those of the page, like live electric currents.

"What is the matter?" asked the Baron.

"Nothing," she answered, white and impassive as a statue.

The Baron turned toward the window; "What is that noise?"

Donna Violante summoned her maid, and ordered her to close the fastenings. "It must have been the wind," she suggested, "or the window is not properly closed."

Corrado had barely time to conceal himself in an angle of the wall. The Baron from time to time stole a strange glance at his wife; and what was stranger still, he remained sober. "Won't you drink with me?" he asked, pouring out some wine. She dared not refuse, but slowly raised the goblet, and her teeth could be heard clicking several times against the glass.

"I must find you another page, now that Corrado is gone," said the Baron, looking her straight in the face. Donna Violante did not answer, but in her turn raised her eyes, and their glances met. The Baron drained another glass of sparkling wine, then rose to make his usual evening round.

Left alone, the woman rose also, as if impelled by a hidden spring, and began to stride up and down the chamber in great agitation. Suddenly she went boldly to the window, and flung it open. They found themselves face to face, and their eyes met in silence.

"Well, what are you doing here?" demanded Donna Violante, in feverish tones.

"I have come to die," replied the page, with terrible calmness.

"Ah!" she exclaimed, with a bitter smile, "you know it was I who sent you away?"

"It was you?"

"Yes."

"Why did you have me sent away?"

"Because I could not arrange to be sent away myself!"

"What harm have I done you?" he exclaimed, with tears in his eyes.

"What harm have you done me?" replied the woman, staring at him with haggard eyes. "What harm have you done me? Well, what further do you want? What have you come here for?"

"I came to tell you that I love you," said he, without enthusiasm, yet without bitterness.

"You?" exclaimed the Baroness, hiding her face in her hands.

"Forgive me, my lady!" continued the page, with a mournful smile, "this love that offends you will be paid for at a terrible price!"

"No!" she answered, wildly, "I don't want you to die! But I don't want to love you; I don't want ever to see you again! Never again! Begone!"

He shook his head resignedly. "Begone?" he said. "It is too late! The drawbridge has been raised; and the Baron told me that I must not be found here after nightfall. It was worth risking something to see you one last time, as beautiful as I always see you in my thoughts; it was worth paying something very precious for the chance of uttering the terrible word that I have uttered here!"

"So be it!" answered Donna Violante, as pale and trembling as her companion. "I too will pay the price, . . . it is only just!"

At that moment they heard the footsteps of the Baron returning, in company with an attendant.

"So be it!" repeated the Baroness convulsively. "I too love you, and we will die together!" She encircled his neck with her arms, and pressed her feverish lips to his. Don Garzia's voice was heard saying to Bruno: "Go out upon the balcony, and stand guard there."

Corrado broke away from her desperate embrace, and clasped her hand resolutely: "No! Not you! Keep me in your memory, Violante, and have no fear for yourself. A poor page may know how to die like a gentleman!"

And while the footsteps of the Baron were heard approaching the door, and Bruno was patrolling the balcony, Corrado flung himself down the passage that led behind the alcove and at the further end of which was the yawning chasm.

Don Garzia entered with rapid stride, ignoring his wife, who looked more like a corpse than a living woman, cast one glance at the closed window, and entered the passage, without speaking a word.

No further sound was heard. Shortly afterwards Don Garzia reappeared, calm and impenetrable as usual.

"All is tranquil," he said. "Let us retire for the night, my lady!"

XI

THE night had grown tempestuous; the wind seemed laden with voices and human moans, and the waves beat upon the rocks with the sound of a heavy fall, such as would drown a groan of agony. The Baron was asleep.

She watched him sleeping, motionless, despairing, half-dead with anguish, stilling the tempest in her heart, not daring to move for fear of rousing him. Her eyes were ringed with black, her lips half parted, her heart beating as though it would burst its bounds. She was prey to inexplicable impulses, mad temptations, screams that rose up in her throat, visions that froze her blood, horrors that urged her on to madness. It seemed from time to time that the ceiling of the alcove was sinking to suffocate her, or that the sea had risen and dashed against the window, or that the shutters were violently shaken by a hand desperately clutching for support, or that the roar of the sea was drowning out a cry that was delirious with agony. The moaning of the wind penetrated to her very bones, whispering mysterious words that she alone could understand, telling her hidden secrets that caused each separate hair to rise upon her head. And all the while she kept her straining, fascinated gaze upon her sleeping husband, who seemed to be watching her from under his closed lids, and reading clearly all the terrors that were threatening her reason. From time to time she wiped away the icy sweat that bathed her brow, and rearranged mechanically the hair that she could feel forming itself into ringlets like a thing alive. When the hurricane subsided, she felt a fear of a still stranger sort, and with an instinctive movement buried her head beneath the coverlets. All of a sudden, the sound that she had imagined that she heard in the midst of the howling tempest, a groan of agony, whether fancied or real, arose again, clearer and more distinct. Hereupon, she too uttered a cry that bore no semblance to a human voice, and hurled herself out of the bed.

The Baron, awakened violently, beheld her like a white phantom, fleeing through the window, sprang in pursuit, leaped upon the balcony, and found—nothing. The tempest was raging once more. The only trace of her was the handkerchief that had wiped away the moisture of her terrible anguish.

XII

THE story had entertained them all, even those who had already heard it, and who enlarged upon it for the benefit of the newcomers, with legends of the ghosts who had haunted the castle. Evening had come, and both the hour and the topic promoted the idle flights of fancy born of a good dinner. But Luciano and the Signora Matilde had turned pale more than once, in the course of the story that they knew so well.

"Be careful!" he warned her, beneath his breath. "Your husband is watching you!"

She turned first red, then white again, gazed out upon the sea that lay in dusk, and was the first to rise and start for home. They made their way slowly down the crumbling steps, and it was already quite dark when they reached the platform. The long, flat stone that served as bridge across the fearful chasm that yawned below the cliff, offered at that hour a dangerous crossing. The more prudent hesitated before venturing upon it, and suggested sending to the village for lamps.

"Are you afraid?" exclaimed the Signor Giordano, with a slight sardonic smile. And he sprang daringly upon the narrow bridge. His wife followed him quietly, though slightly pale. Luciano kept close behind her, and closely clasped her hand.

At such a time, above a precipice of five hundred feet, beside a husband whose suspicions were awakened, that furtive hand-clasp, under cover of the dark, reached the limits of audacity. It may be that the other saw them, dark as it was; perhaps he only guessed, perhaps he had calculated on that very thing. He turned suddenly, and called his wife by name. A cry was heard, a despairing cry; she wavered, clinging to the hand which in trying to aid her had been her ruin, and fell, dragging him with her into the abyss.

At Trezza it is said that on all but holy nights groans are once more heard, and phantoms are seen wandering among the ruins of the castle.

Antonio Fogazzaro

The Imp in the Mirror

A FABLE FOR MARY

ONCE upon a time there lived in Milan, but a few steps from the De Cristoforis Gallery, an elderly lady, the Countess X., who was very rich and very homely and found great pleasure in entertaining her friends; and since she had an excellent cook, her friends never failed her. One evening eleven guests were gathered together in her parlor: a young widow, an English lady, a judge of the Appellate Division, a portly general, a spruce young lieutenant, a long-haired composer, and a threadbare poet, all of them celebrities, and four young men of fashion, whose time was fully occupied in doing nothing at all.

The discussion having turned upon the eternal comparison between the vanity of men and the vanity of women, the majority were of the opinion that the vainer sex was the masculine. But when the hostess declared, by way of example, that there was not a man living, no matter how old or sedate, capable of passing before a mirror without giving at least one approving glance at his own seductive image, two of her distinguished guests, the judge and the portly general, protested that this was not so, and that masculine vanity revealed itself in other ways. Straightway, a short, shrill peal of laughter echoed through the room. Each of the guests thought that it was the widow who had laughed, while the widow thought that the one who had laughed was the other lady, the Englishwoman. As a matter of fact, the laughter had come from a little imp, one of the sort that are always lying in wait, to tempt people to tell lies and commit sins of vanity. Thereupon the discussion was dropped, partly because midnight was just striking. The two ladies arose, and the hostess with great cordiality invited the entire company to dine with her on the morrow, at six o'clock.

The morrow chancing to be a joyous, balmy April day, the guests all kept their dinner engagement, the ladies arriving by carriage, the gentlemen on foot, and each by himself. The judge and the general resided in the Via Alessandro Mazzoni; of the others, one came from the Via del Monte, another from the Via San Andrea, another from the Borgo Spesso, another from the Borgo Nuovo. In short, the route of everyone lay through the De Cristoforis Gallery, and in spite of the fact that they all passed through there between five forty-five and six o'clock, chance willed it that none of them should encounter any of the others on his way. The De Cristoforis Gallery, you know, has two branches, forming a right angle, with a mirror fitted into the corner, which everyone must pass in turning from one branch into the other, opposite the Trenk beer hall. Behind this mirror the malicious little imp had installed himself, and lay in wait for the guests, in order to put into effect his diabolical little jest. There passed, first of all, the general; and he glanced at himself in the mirror, out of one corner of his eye, and discovered, with a violent start, an ink-stain upon his left cheek. It lacked but five minutes to six; there was no longer time to return home. The general hastened his steps, holding a handkerchief against his face, and no sooner was he within the vestibule of the countess than he asked the butler for a towel and a little water. The butler ushered him into a bedchamber and was in the act of pouring water into a basin, when again there came a ring at the front door. This time it was the judge who entered, holding a handkerchief over his left cheek.

"Quick, for goodness' sake! get me a towel and some water!"

The butler led him into another bedchamber and poured him out some water. Another ring. This time it was the lieutenant, who said, holding one hand over his face:

"I am very sorry, but I have a pair of gloves the color of which rubs off. Is there any water?"

The servant, marveling greatly, led him into a third bedchamber. The bell sounded for the fourth time. It proved to be the musician, who said brusquely:

"Some water! Show me into a private room."

"Excuse me, sir," replied the butler stiffly, "but there are already three gentlemen washing themselves in three different rooms, and there is not another one vacant excepting the countess' own bedchamber. With your permission, I shall bring the water and towel out here."

"Bring them," replied the composer. The butler went and returned with the water and a towel. The other scrubbed his face and then examined the towel, to see if it was soiled; and since the towel still remained quite clean, he scrubbed and looked, scrubbed and looked, and scrubbed again, with desperate energy. Still another pull at the door-bell. It was the famous poet, who entered in time to see his friend still violently scrubbing, and he said, "Bravo! Splendid! Just what I need myself!"

"Is my face clean?" demanded the other, turning his cheek for inspection.

"Perfectly."

The composer, delighted, passed in, to greet the countess, and there found the other ladies and the general. Next the bell was rung three successive times, by three of the young men of fashion, each of whom desired water, towels, and soap besides. The butler, with a great effort, refrained from laughing, and knew not where to turn next; his supply of towels having given out, he must needs obtain some from the housekeeper, and he hurried off to find her. The housekeeper lost her temper; and meanwhile, the front door-bell rang again, and no one opened the door. The countess also rang for someone to open it. Presently she rang again, and still no one answered. At last she arose and went out herself, to call her servants. Meanwhile the fourth of the fashionable young men, who was waiting outside the entrance, absorbed in the thought of a stain upon his cheek, heard the voice of his hostess; and fearing that he should meet her in the vestibule, he moistened his handkerchief with his tongue, and making sure that there was no one to see him commit the impropriety, scrubbed his left cheek as energetically as all the others had done. At last all the guests were assembled in the parlor; and the countess, who meanwhile had gathered some of the facts from her butler, said with a smile:

"My dear general, what have you been doing to your cheek, to make it so red?"

Immediately, all the other guests of the male sex, remembering that they also must have one red cheek, each instinctively raised a hand to his face. The countess laughed; then one of the young men laughed, then another, then a third; then followed a general burst of merriment. Now that the ice was broken, the countess laid the facts before the other two ladies, and all three wished to know the wherefore of this extraordinary epidemic.

"For my part," replied the poet, "I need only tell you that a friend of my childhood, the Duchess Y., who has been like a sister to me, must have been biting the point of her pencil to-day; for, just before I came here, I met her at the railway station, and she kissed me, precisely where the spot was, on my cheek."

"I, on the contrary," said the judge, "think that I must have been stained with the hair dye of the Cabinet Minister R. He was in Milan to-day, and sent for me on a matter of the greatest importance. We are old friends; and he, in his familiar way, pinched my cheek between his thumb and forefinger. Since he uses hair-dye, it is most likely that his fingers were soiled with it."

"As for me," said the lieutenant, quite forgetting the story that he had already told of the gloves that shed their color, "I had promised an aquarelle to Sarah Bernhardt, and I worked upon it up to the last moment, because she was in a hurry for it. Of course I must have spattered my face with the India ink."

"I," said the composer in his turn, "was just setting

forth, when an idea came to me for the prelude to my fourth act—a lightning flash, you know, really and truly. I may say so, because I claim no credit for it; good ideas come to me just like that, mysteriously. I ran back, to jot down half a dozen bars, and undoubtedly in the excitement of writing them out, I must have daubed my face."

"It was like this," said the general, who was past his sixtieth year, "I take a great deal of exercise every day. At five o'clock this morning, I pulled myself up to the chin a number of times on the flying rings. It is quite likely that one of those rings was not clean and that I rubbed my face against it."

"I really do not understand how such a thing could have happened to me," said one of the young men of fashion. "It was this very day, not half an hour ago, that I used Shetland soap, an English toilet novelty, imported from London expressly for me, and which probably no one else in Milan knows about."

"Oh, I say! I say!" exclaimed two of his companions, "Didn't I get a cake yesterday? Didn't I get one the day before?"

"In that case," replied the first speaker, "there must have been some impurity in the Shetland soap!"

"That couldn't be!" exclaimed the fourth, the one who had made his toilet outside the door, "because I also use Shetland soap, and I have no reason to believe that there is any stain on my face. Look and see!"

"But, gentlemen," interrupted the countess, "you have explained to me that it must have been the soap, it must have been the ink, it must have been this, it must have been that! But now I should very much like to hear how you all happened to discover those stains on your faces, and why you did not discover them until after you left home."

There followed a rather lengthy silence.

"A friend——" began the poet, with some embarrassment. But at this moment, the general made up his mind to explain frankly.

"Let us own up! For my part, countess, I confess that

I looked at myself in the mirror, in the De Cristoforis Gallery!"

"Well, I never!"—"Oh, the deuce!"—"Why, by Jove!" were the involuntary exclamations of the composer, the lieutenant, and one of the young men of fashion. "Aha!" exclaimed the ladies in their turn, as the truth dawned upon them; and they compelled these three to confess that they also had looked at themselves in the mirror. Then the ladies and the four acknowledged culprits joined in a vociferous attack upon the others, to force them also to make confession; and everyone, excepting the poet, who obstinately adhered to his story of a friend, ended by owning up to that confounded mirror in the gallery.

"Say, rather, gentlemen, that *blessed* mirror!" observed the countess, with a laugh. "Because I understand that without it you would all have cut a pretty figure before me to-night!"

"Much too pretty!" rejoined the general, "as Frederico will bear witness."

Frederico, the butler, entered at that moment to announce dinner.

"Isn't it true, Frederico," the general asked him, "that I had my face badly smirched? And all the others, too, didn't we?"

"To tell the truth," replied Frederico, "as for their excellencies, the general, the judge, and the lieutenant, I cannot say, since they kept their faces covered. But as for the other gentlemen, I saw quite plainly that they had not a spot upon them!"

All the men protested, but the butler adhered to his statement, and let it be plainly seen that he suspected the same to be true of the general and the lieutenant.

"Why, how is this?" exclaimed the countess. "There is magic at work! We shall not go in to dinner until we have solved this mystery!"

"The planchette, countess!" said the English lady, who was a spiritualist, and had often made experiments, together with her hostess. "We must question the planchette!"

No sooner said than done. The little board was brought in, and straightway started in to spin around, scratching and squeaking as though shaking with laughter; and upon being questioned as to the when, the how, and the wherefore of those enigmatic stains, it gave answer in due form:

> Behind each mirror I may dwell;
> Those stains,—the sort of lies I tell.
> But all the lies you've heard since then
> Were uttered by these gentlemen.
>
> *The Imp of the Gallery.*

The gentlemen scarcely waited for the planchette to finish, before they broke forth in a hilarious uproar. "Come to dinner! Come to dinner! Hurry up! Hurry up! Fiddlesticks! Stuff and nonsense! Come to dinner! Come to dinner!" And bearing off with them the ladies, who were convulsed with laughter at their expense, and chiefly at the poet, his duchess, and his friend, they flung themselves into the dining-room like a hurricane.

NOTE.—Although this tale, in form, is a fairy story, in substance it holds so much familiar, easily recognized truth, that its inclusion seemed appropriate.—EDITOR.

Luigi Capuana

The Deposition

"I KNOW nothing at all about it, your honor!"

"Nothing at all? How can that be? It all happened within fifty yards of your shop."

"'Nothing at all,' I said, . . . in an off-hand way; but really, next to nothing. I am a barber, your honor, and Heaven be praised! I have custom enough to keep me busy from morning till night. There are three of us in the shop, and what with shaving and combing and hair-cutting, not one of the three has the time to stop and scratch his head, and I least of all. Many of my customers are so kind as to prefer my services to those of my two young men; perhaps because I amuse them with my little jokes. And, what with lathering and shaving this face and that, and combing the hair on so many heads—how does your honor expect me to pay attention to other people's affairs? And the morning that I read about it in the paper, why, I stood there with my mouth wide open, and I said, 'Well, that was the way it was bound to end!'"

"Why did you say, 'That was the way it was bound to end'?"

"Why—because it had ended that way! You see—on the instant, I called to mind the ugly face of the husband. Every time I saw him pass up or down the street—one of those impressions that no one can account for—I used to think, 'That fellow has the face of a convict!' But of course that proves nothing. There are plenty who have the bad luck to be uglier than mortal sin, but very worthy people all the same. But in this case I didn't think that I was mistaken."

"But you were friends. He used to come very often and sit down at the entrance to your barber shop."

"Very often? Only once in a while, your honor! 'By your leave, neighbor,' he would say. He always called me 'neighbor'; that was his name for everyone. And I would say, 'Why, certainly.' The chair stood there, empty. Your honor understands that I could hardly be so uncivil as to say to him, 'No, you can't sit down.' A barber shop is a public place, like a café or a beer saloon. At all events, one may sit down without paying for it, and no need to have a shave or hair-cut, either! 'By your leave, neighbor,' and there he would sit, in silence, smoking and scowling, with his eyes half shut. He would loaf there for half an hour, an hour, sometimes longer. He annoyed me, I don't deny it, from the very start. There was a good deal of talk."

"What sort of talk?"

"A good deal of talk. Your honor knows, better than I, how evil-minded people are. I make it a practice not to believe a syllable of what I am told about anyone, good or evil; that is the way to keep out of trouble."

"Come, come, what sort of talk? Keep to the point."

"What sort of talk? Why, one day they would say this, and the next day they would say that, and by harping on it long enough, they made themselves believe that the wife— Well, your honor knows that a pretty wife is a chastisement of God. And after all, there are some things that you can't help seeing unless you won't see!"

"Then it was he, the husband——"

"I know nothing about it, your honor, nothing at all! But it is quite true that every time he came and sat down by my doorway or inside the shop, I used to say to myself, 'If that man can't see, he certainly must be blind! and if he won't see, he certainly must be— Your honor knows what I mean. There was certainly no getting out of that—out of that— Perhaps your honor can help me to the right word?"

"Dilemma?"

"Dilemma, yes, your honor. And Biasi, the notary, who comes to me to be shaved, uses another word that just fits the case, begging your honor's pardon."

"Then, according to you, this Don Nicasio——"

"Oh, I won't put my finger in the pie! Let him answer for himself. Everyone has a conscience of his own; and Jesus Christ has said, 'Judge not, lest ye be judged.' Well, one morning—or was it in the evening? I don't exactly remember—yes, now it comes back to me that it was in the morning—I saw him pass by, scowling and with his head bent down; I was in my doorway, sharpening a razor. Out of curiosity I gave him a passing word as well as a nod, adding a gesture that was as good as a question. He came up to me, looked me straight in the face, and answered: 'Haven't I told you that, sooner or later, I should do something crazy? And I shall, neighbor, yes, I shall! They are dragging me by the hair!' 'Let me cut it off, then!' I answered jokingly, to make him forget himself."

"So, he had told you before, had he? How did he happen to tell you before?"

"Oh, your honor knows how words slip out of the mouth at certain moments. Who pays attention to them? For my part, I have too many other things in my head——"

"Come, come—what had he been talking about, when he told you before?"

"Great heavens, give me time to think, your honor! What had he been talking about? Why, about his wife, of course. Who knows? Some one must have put a flea in his ear. It needs only half a word to ruin a poor devil's peace of mind. And that is how a man lets such words slip out of his mouth as 'Sooner or later I shall do something crazy!' That is all. I know nothing else about it, your honor!"

"And the only answer you made him was a joke?"

"I could not say to him, 'Go ahead and do it,' could I? As it was he went off, shaking his head. And what idea he kept brooding over, after that, who knows? One can't see inside of another man's brain. But sometimes, when I heard him freeing his mind——"

"Then he used to free his mind to you?"

"Why, yes, to me, and maybe to others besides. You see, one bears things and bears things and bears things; and at last, rather than burst with them, one frees one's mind to the first man who comes along."

"But you were not the first man who came along. You used to call at his house——"

"Only as a barber, your honor! Only when Don Nicasio used to send for me. And very often I would get there too late, though I tried my best."

"And very likely you sometimes went there when you knew that he was not at home?"

"On purpose, your honor? No, never!"

"And when you found his wife alone, you allowed yourself——"

"Calumnies, your honor! Who dares say such a thing? Does she say so? It may be that once or twice a few words escaped me in jest. You know how it is—when I found myself face to face with a pretty woman—you know how it is—if only not to cut a foolish figure!"

"But it was very far from a joke! You ended by threatening her!"

"What calumnies! Threaten her? What for? A woman of her stamp doesn't need to be threatened! I would never have stooped so low! I am no schoolboy!"

"Passion leads men into all sorts of folly."

"That woman is capable of anything! She would slander our Lord himself to His face! Passion? I? At my age? I am well on in the forties, your honor, and many a gray hair besides. Many a folly I committed in my youth, like everyone else. But now— Besides, with a woman like that! I was no blind man, even if Don Nicasio was. I knew that that young fellow—poor fool, he paid dearly for her—I knew that he had turned her head. That's the way with some women—they go their own gait, they're off with one and on with another, and then they end by becoming the slave of some scalawag who robs and abuses them! He used to beat her, your honor, many and many a time, your honor! And I, for the sake of the poor husband, whom I pitied— Yes, that is why she says that I threatened her. She says so, because I was foolish enough to go and give her a talking to, the day that Don Nicasio said to me, 'I shall do something crazy!' She knew what I meant, at least she pretended that she did."

"No; this was what you said——"

"Yes, your honor, I remember now exactly what I said. 'I'll spoil your sport,' I told her, 'if it sends me to the galleys!' but I was speaking in the name of the husband. In the heat of the moment one falls into a part——"

"The husband knew nothing of all this."

"Was I to boast to him of what I had done? A friend either gives his services or else he doesn't. That is how I understand it."

"Why were you so much concerned about it?"

"I ought not to have been, your honor. I have too soft a heart."

"Your threats became troublesome. And not threats alone, but promise after promise! And gifts besides, a ring and a pair of earrings——"

"That is true. I won't deny it. I found them in my pocket, quite by chance. They belonged to my wife. It was an extravagance, but I did it, to keep poor Don Nicasio from doing something crazy. If I could only win my point, I told myself, if I could only get that young fellow out of the way, then it would be time enough to say to Don Nicasio, 'My friend, give me back my ring and my earrings!' He would not have needed to be told twice. He is an honorable man, Don Nicasio!"

"But when she answered you, 'Keep them yourself, I don't want them!' you began to beg her, almost in tears——"

"Ah, your honor! since you must be told—I don't know how I managed to control myself—I had so completely put myself in the place of the husband! I could have strangled her with my own hands! I could have done that very same crazy thing that Don Nicasio thought of doing!"

"Yet you were very prudent, that is evident. You said to yourself: 'If not for me, then not for him!' The lover, I mean, not Don Nicasio. And you began to work upon the husband, who, up to that time, had let things slide, either because he did not believe, or else because he preferred to bear the lesser evil——"

"It may be that some chance word escaped me. There are times when a man of honor loses his head—but beyond that, nothing, your honor. Don Nicasio himself will bear me witness."

"But Don Nicasio says——"

"He, too? Has he failed me? Has he turned against me? A fine way to show his gratitude!"

"He has nothing to be grateful for. Don't excite yourself! Sit down again. You began by protesting that you knew nothing at all about it. And yet you knew so many things. You must know quite a number more. Don't excite yourself."

"You want to drag me over a precipice, your honor! I begin to understand!"

"Men who are blinded by passion walk over precipices on their own feet."

"But—then your honor imagines that I, myself——"

"I imagine nothing. It is evident that you were the instigator, and something more than the instigator, too."

"Calumny, calumny, your honor!"

"That same evening you were seen talking with the husband until quite late."

"I was trying to persuade him not to. I said to him, 'Let things alone! Since it is your misfortune to have it so, what difference does it make whether he is the one, or somebody else?' And he kept repeating, 'Somebody else, yes, but not that rotten beast!' His very words, your honor."

"You stood at the corner of the adjoining street, lying in wait."

"Who saw me there? Who saw us, your honor?"

"You were seen. Come, make up your mind to tell all you know. It will be better for you. The woman testifies, 'There were two of them,' but in the dark she could not recognize the other one."

"Just because I wanted to do a kind act! This is what I have brought on myself by trying to do a kind act!"

"You stood at the street corner——"

"It was like this, your honor. I had gone with him as far as that. But when I saw that it was no use to try to stop him—it was striking eleven—the streets were deserted—I started to leave him indignantly, without a parting word——"

"Well, what next? Do I need tongs to drag the words out of your mouth?"

"What next? Why, your honor knows how it is at night, under the lamplight. You see and then you don't see—that's the way it is. I turned around—Don Nicasio had plunged through the doorway of his home—just by the entrance to the little lane. A cry!—then nothing more!"

"You ran forward? That was quite natural."

"I hesitated on the threshold—the hallway was so dark."

"You couldn't have done that. The woman would have recognized you by the light of the street lamp."

"The lamp is some distance off."

"You went in one after the other. Which of you shut the door? Because the door was shut immediately."

"In the confusion of the moment—two men struggling together—I could hear them gasping—I wanted to call for help—then a fall! And then I felt myself seized by the arm: 'Run, neighbor, run! This is no business of yours!' It didn't sound like the voice of a human being. And that was how—that was how I happened to be there, a helpless witness. I think that Don Nicasio meant to kill his wife, too; but the wretched woman escaped. She ran and shut herself up in her room. That is—I read so afterwards, in the papers. The husband would have been wiser to have killed her first. Evil weeds had better be torn up by the roots. What are you having that man write, your honor?"

"Nothing at all, as you call it. Just your deposition. The clerk will read it to you now, and you will sign it."

"Can any harm come to me from it? I am innocent! I have only said what you wanted to make me say. You have tangled me up in a fine net, like a little fresh-water fish!"

"Wait a moment. And this is the most important thing of all. How did it happen that the mortal wounds on the dead man's body were made with a razor?"

"Oh, the treachery of Don Nicasio! My God! My God! Yes, your honor. Two days before—no one can think of everything, no one can foresee everything—he came to the shop and said to me, 'Neighbor, lend me a razor; I have a corn that is troubling me.' He was so matter-of-fact about it that I did not hesitate for an instant. I even warned him, 'Be careful! you can't joke with corns! A little blood, and you may start a cancer!' 'Don't borrow trouble, neighbor,' he answered."

"But the razor could not be found. You must have brought it away."

"I? Who would remember a little thing like that? I was more dead than alive, your honor. Where are you trying to lead me, with your questions? I tell you, I am innocent!"

"Do not deny so obstinately. A frank confession will help you far more than to protest your innocence. The facts speak clearly enough. It is well known how passion maddens the heart and the brain. A man in that state is no longer himself."

"That is the truth, your honor! That wretched woman bewitched me! She is sending me to the galleys! The more she said 'No, no, no!' the more I felt myself going mad, from head to foot, as if she were pouring fire over me, with her 'No, no, no!' But now—I do not want another man to suffer in my place. Yes, I was the one, I was the one who killed him! I was bewitched, your honor! I am willing to go to the galleys. But I am coming back here, if I have the good luck to live through my term. Oh, the justice of this world! To think that she goes scot free, the real and only cause of all the harm! But I will see that she gets justice, that I solemnly swear—with these two hands of mine, your honor! In prison I shall think of nothing else. And if I come back and find her alive—grown old and ugly, it makes no difference—she will have to pay for it, she will have to make good! Ah, 'no, no, no!' But I will say, 'Yes, yes, yes!' And I will drain her last drop of blood, if I have to end my days in the galleys. And the sooner, the better!"

Pedro de Alarçon

The Nail

I

THE thing which is most ardently desired by a man who steps into a stagecoach, bent upon a long journey, is that his companions may be agreeable, that they may have the same tastes, possibly the same vices, be well educated and know enough not to be too familiar.

When I opened the door of the coach I felt fearful of encountering an old woman suffering with the asthma, an ugly one who could not bear the smell of tobacco smoke, one who gets seasick every time she rides in a carriage, and little angels who are continually yelling and screaming for God knows what.

Sometimes you may have hoped to have a beautiful woman for a traveling companion; for instance, a widow of twenty or thirty years of age (let us say, thirty-six), whose delightful conversation will help you pass away the time. But if you ever had this idea, as a reasonable man you would quickly dismiss it, for you know that such good fortune does not fall to the lot of the ordinary mortal. These thoughts were in my mind when I opened the door of the stagecoach at exactly eleven o'clock on a stormy night of the Autumn of 1844. I had ticket No. 2, and I was wondering who No. 1 might be. The ticket agent had assured me that No. 3 had not been sold.

It was pitch dark within. When I entered I said, "Good evening," but no answer came. "The devil!" I said to myself. "Is my traveling companion deaf, dumb, or asleep?" Then I said in a louder tone: "Good evening," but no answer came.

All this time the stagecoach was whirling along, drawn by ten horses.

I was puzzled. Who was my companion? Was it a man? Was it a woman? Who was the silent No. 1, and, whoever it might be, why did he or she not reply to my courteous salutation? It would have been well to have lit a match, but I was not smoking then and had none with me. What should I do? I concluded to rely upon my sense of feeling, and stretched out my hand to the place where No. 1 should have been, wondering whether I would touch a silk dress or an overcoat, but there was nothing there. At that moment a flash of lightning, herald of a quickly approaching storm, lit up the night, and I perceived that there was no one in the coach excepting myself. I burst out into a roar of laughter, and yet a moment later I could not help wondering what had become of No. 1.

A half hour later we arrived at the first stop, and I was just about to ask the guard who flashed his lantern into the compartment why there was no No. 1, when she entered. In the yellow rays I thought it was a vision: a pale, graceful, beautiful woman, dressed in deep mourning.

Here was the fulfillment of my dream, the widow I had hoped for.

I extended my hand to the unknown to assist her into the coach, and she sat down beside me, murmuring: "Thank you, sir. Good evening," but in a tone that was so sad that it went to my very heart.

"How unfortunate," I thought. "There are only fifty miles between here and Malaga. I wish to heaven this coach were going to Kamschatka." The guard slammed the door, and we were in darkness. I wished that the storm would continue and that we might have a few more flashes of lightning. But the storm didn't. It fled away, leaving only a few pallid stars, whose light practically amounted to nothing. I made a brave effort to start a conversation.

"Do you feel well?"

"Are you going to Malaga?"
"Did you like the Alhambra?"
"You come from Granada?"
"Isn't the night damp?"

To which questions she respectively responded:

"Thanks, very well."
"Yes."
"No, sir."
"Yes!"
"Awful!"

It was quite certain that my traveling companion was not inclined to conversation. I tried to think up something original to say to her, but nothing occurred to me, so I lost myself for the moment in meditation. Why had this woman gotten on the stage at the first stop instead of at Granada? Why was she alone? Was she married? Was she really a widow? Why was she so sad? I certainly had no right to ask her any of these questions, and yet she interested me. How I wished the sun would rise. In the daytime one may talk freely, but in the pitch darkness one feels a certain oppression, it seems like taking an unfair advantage.

My unknown did not sleep a moment during the night. I could tell this by her breathing and by her sighing. It is probably unnecessary to add that I did not sleep either. Once I asked her: "Do you feel ill?" and she replied: "No, sir, thank you. I beg pardon if I have disturbed your sleep."

"Sleep!" I exclaimed disdainfully. "I do not care to sleep. I feared you were suffering."

"Oh, no," she exclaimed, in a voice that contradicted her words, "I am not suffering."

At last the sun rose. How beautiful she was! I mean the woman, not the sun. What deep suffering had lined her face and lurked in the depths of her beautiful eyes!

She was elegantly dressed and evidently belonged to a good family. Every gesture bore the imprint of distinction. She was the kind of a woman you expect to see in the principal box at the opera, resplendent with jewels, surrounded by admirers.

We breakfasted at Colmenar. After that my companion became more confidential, and I said to myself when we again entered the coach: "Philip, you have met your fate. It's now or never."

II

I REGRETTED the very first word I mentioned to her regarding my feelings. She became a block of ice, and I lost at once all that I might have gained in her good graces. Still she answered me very kindly: "It is not because it is you, sir, who speak to me of love, but love itself is something which I hold in horror."

"But why, dear lady?" I inquired.

"Because my heart is dead. Because I have loved to the point of delirium, and I have been deceived."

I felt that I should talk to her in a philosophic way and there were a lot of platitudes on the tip of my tongue, but I refrained. I knew that she meant what she said. When we arrived at Malaga, she said to me in a tone I shall never forget as long as I live: "I thank you a thousand times for your kind attention during the trip, and hope you will forgive me if I do not tell you my name and address."

"Do you mean then that we shall not meet again?"

"Never! And you, especially, should not regret it." And then with a smile that was utterly without joy she extended her exquisite hand to me and said: "Pray to God for me."

I pressed her hand and made a low bow. She entered a handsome victoria which was awaiting her, and as it moved away she bowed to me again.

Two months later I met her again.

At two o'clock in the afternoon I was jogging along in an old cart on the road that leads to Cordoba. The object of my journey was to examine some land which I owned in that neighborhood and pass three or four weeks with one of the judges of the Supreme Court, who was an intimate friend of mine and had been my schoolmate at the University of Granada.

He received me with open arms. As I entered his handsome house I could but note the perfect taste and elegance of the furniture and decorations.

"Ah, Zarto," I said, "you have married, and you have never told me about it. Surely this was not the way to treat a man who loved you as much as I do!"

"I am not married, and what is more I never will marry," answered the judge sadly.

"I believe that you are not married, dear boy, since you say so, but I cannot understand the declaration that you never will. You must be joking."

"I swear that I am telling you the truth," he replied.

"But what a metamorphosis!" I exclaimed. "You were always a partisan of marriage, and for the past two years you have been writing to me and advising me to take a life partner. Whence this wonderful change, dear friend? Something must have happened to you, something unfortunate, I fear?"

"To me?" answered the judge somewhat embarrassed.

"Yes, to you. Something has happened, and you are going to tell me all about it. You live here alone, have practically buried yourself in this great house. Come, tell me everything."

The judge pressed my hand. "Yes, yes, you shall know all. There is no man more unfortunate than I am. But listen, this is the day upon which all the inhabitants go to the cemetery, and I must be there, if only for form's sake. Come with me. It is a pleasant afternoon and the walk will do you good, after riding so long in that old cart. The location of the cemetery is a beautiful one, and I am quite sure you will enjoy the walk. On our way, I will tell you the incident that ruined my life, and you shall judge yourself whether I am justified in my hatred of women."

As together we walked along the flower-bordered road, my friend told me the following story:

Two years ago when I was Assistant District Attorney in ———, I obtained permission from my chief to spend a month in Sevilla. In the hotel where I lodged there was a beautiful young woman who passed for a widow but whose origin, as well as her reasons for staying in that town, were a mystery to all. Her installation, her wealth, her total lack of friends or acquaintances and the sadness of her expression, together with her incomparable beauty, gave rise to a thousand conjectures.

Her rooms were directly opposite mine, and I frequently met her in the hall or on the stairway, only too glad to have the chance of bowing to her. She was unapproachable, however, and it was impossible for me to secure an introduction. Two weeks later, fate was to afford me the opportunity of entering her apartment. I had been to the theater that night, and when I returned to my room I thoughtlessly opened the door of her apartment instead of that of my own. The beautiful woman was reading by the light of the lamp and started when she saw me. I was so embarrassed by my mistake that for a moment I could only stammer unintelligible words. My confusion was so evident that she could not doubt for a moment that I had made a mistake. I turned to the door, intent upon relieving her of my presence as quickly as possible, when she said with the most exquisite courtesy: "In order to show you that I do not doubt your good faith and that I'm not at all offended, I beg that you will call upon me again, *intentionally.*"

Three days passed before I got up sufficient courage to accept her invitation. Yes, I was madly in love with her; accustomed as I am to analyze my own sensations, I knew that my passion could only end in the greatest happiness or the deepest suffering. However, at the end of the three days I went to her apartment and spent the evening there. She told me that her name was Blanca, that she was born in Madrid, and that she was a widow. She played and sang for me and asked me a thousand questions about myself, my profession, my family, and every word she said increased my love for her. From that night my soul was the slave of her soul; yes, and it *will be forever*.

I called on her again the following night, and thereafter every afternoon and evening I was with her. We loved each other, but not a word of love had ever been spoken between us.

One evening she said to me: "I married a man without loving him. Shortly after marriage I hated him. Now he is dead. Only God knows what I suffered. Now I understand what love means; it is either heaven or it is hell. For me, up to the present time, it has been hell."

I could not sleep that night. I lay awake thinking over these last words of Blanca's. Somehow this woman frightened me. Would I be her heaven and she my hell?

My leave of absence expired. I could have asked for an extension, pretending illness, but the question was, should I do it? I consulted Blanca.

"Why do you ask me?" she said, taking my hand.

"Because I love you. Am I doing wrong in loving you?"

"No," she said, becoming very pale, and then she put both arms about my neck and her beautiful lips touched mine.

Well, I asked for another month and, thanks to you, dear friend, it was granted. Never would they have given it to me without your influence.

My relations with Blanca were more than love; they were delirium, madness, fanaticism, call it what you will. Every day my passion for her increased, and the morrow seemed to open up vistas of new happiness. And yet I could not avoid feeling at times a mysterious, indefinable fear. And this I knew she felt as well as I did. We both feared to lose one another. One day I said to Blanca:

"We must marry, as quickly as possible."

She gave me a strange look. "You wish to marry me?"

"Yes, Blanca," I said, "I am proud of you. I want to show you to the whole world. I love you and I want you, pure, noble, and saintly as you are."

"I cannot marry you," answered this incomprehensible woman. She would never give a reason.

Finally my leave of absence expired, and I told her that on the following day we must separate.

"Separate? It is impossible!" she exclaimed. "I love you too much for that."

"But you know, Blanca, that I worship you."

"Then give up your profession. I am rich. We will live our lives out together," she said, putting her soft hand over my mouth to prevent my answer.

I kissed the hand and then, gently removing it, I answered: "I would accept this offer from my wife, although it would be a sacrifice for me to give up my career; but I will not accept it from a woman who refuses to marry me."

Blanca remained thoughtful for several minutes; then, raising her head, she looked at me and said very quietly, but with a determination which could not be misunderstood: "I will be your wife, and I do not ask you to give up your profession. Go back to your office. How long will it take you to arrange your business matters and secure from the government another leave of absence to return to Sevilla?"

"A month."

"A month? Well, here I will await you. Return within a month, and I will be your wife. To-day is the fifteenth of April. You will be here on the fifteenth of May?"

"You may rest assured of that."

"You swear it?"

"I swear it."

"You love me?"

"More than my life."

"Go, then, and return. Farewell."

I left on the same day. The moment I arrived home I began to arrange my house to receive my bride. As you know I solicited another leave of absence, and so quickly did I arrange my business affairs that at the end of two weeks I was ready to return to Sevilla.

I must tell you that during this fortnight I did not receive a single letter from Blanca, though I wrote her six. I started at once for Sevilla, arriving in that city on the thirtieth of April, and went at once to the hotel where we had first met.

I learned that Blanca had left there two days after my departure without telling anyone her destination.

Imagine my indignation, my disappointment, my suffering. She went away without even leaving a line for me, without telling me whither she was going. It never occurred to me to remain in Sevilla until the fifteenth of May to ascertain whether she would return on that date. Three days later I took up my court work and strove to forget her.

A few moments after my friend Zarco finished the story, we arrived at the cemetery.

This is only a small plot of ground covered with a veritable forest of crosses and surrounded by a low stone wall. As often happens in Spain, when the cemeteries are very small, it is necessary to dig up one coffin in order to lower another. Those thus disinterred are thrown in a heap in a corner of the cemetery, where skulls and bones are piled up like a haystack. As we were passing, Zarco and I looked at the skulls, wondering to whom they could have belonged, to rich or poor, noble or plebeian.

Suddenly the judge bent down, and picking up a skull, exclaimed in astonishment:

"Look here, my friend, what is this? It is surely a nail!"

Yes, a long nail had been driven in the top of the skull which he held in his hand. The nail had been driven into the head, and the point had penetrated what had been the roof of the mouth.

What could this mean? He began to conjecture, and soon both of us felt filled with horror.

"I recognize the hand of Providence!" exclaimed the judge. "A terrible crime has evidently been committed, and would never have come to light had it not been for this accident. I shall do my duty, and will not rest until I have brought the assassin to the scaffold."

III

My friend Zarco was one of the keenest criminal judges in Spain. Within a very few days he discovered that the corpse to which this skull belonged had been buried in a rough wooden coffin which the grave digger had taken home with him, intending to use it for firewood. Fortunately, the man had not yet burned it up, and on the lid the judge managed to decipher the initials: "A. G. R." together with the date of interment. He had at once searched the parochial books of every church in the neighborhood, and a week later found the following entry:

"In the parochial church of San Sebastian of the village of ——, on the 4th of May, 1843, the funeral rites as prescribed by our holy religion were performed over the body of Don Alfonso Gutierrez Romeral, and he was buried in the cemetery. He was a native of this village and did not receive the holy sacrament, nor did he confess, for he died suddenly of apoplexy at the age of thirty-one. He was married to Doña Gabriela Zahura del Valle, a native of Madrid, and left no issue him surviving."

The judge handed me the above certificate, duly certified to by the parish priest, and exclaimed: "Now everything is as clear as day, and I am positive that within a week the assassin will be arrested. The apoplexy in this case happens to be an iron nail driven into the man's head, which brought quick and sudden death to A. G. R. I have the nail, and I shall soon find the hammer."

According to the testimony of the neighbors, Señor Romeral was a young and rich landowner who originally came from Madrid, where he had married a beautiful wife; four months before the death of the husband, his wife had gone to Madrid to pass a few months with her family; the young woman returned home about the last day of April, that is, about three months and a half after she had left her husband's residence to go to Madrid; the death of Señor Romeral occurred about a week after her return. The shock caused to the widow by the sudden death of her husband was so great that she became ill and informed her friends that she could not continue to live in the same place where everything recalled to her the man she had lost, and just before the middle of May she had left for Madrid, ten or twelve days after the death of her husband.

The servants of the deceased had testified that the couple did not live amicably together and had frequent quarrels; that the absence of three months and a half which preceded the last eight days the couple had lived together was practically an understanding that they were to be ultimately separated on account of mysterious disagreements which had existed between them from the date of their marriage; that on the date of the death of the deceased, both husband and wife were together in the former's bedroom; that at midnight the bell was rung violently and they heard the cries of the wife; that they rushed to the room and were met at the door by the wife, who was very pale and greatly perturbed, and she cried out: "An apoplexy! Run for a doctor! My poor husband is dying!" That when they entered the room they found their master lying upon a couch, and he was dead. The doctor who was called certified that Señor Romeral had died of cerebral congestion.

Three medical experts testified that death brought about as this one had been could not be distinguished from apoplexy. The physician who had been called in had not thought to look for the head of the nail, which was concealed by the hair of the victim, nor was he in any sense to blame for this oversight.

The judge immediately issued a warrant for the arrest of Doña Gabriela Zahara del Valle, widow of Señor Romeral.

"Tell me," I asked the judge one day, "do you think you will ever capture this woman?"

"I'm positive of it."

"Why?"

"Because in the midst of all these routine criminal affairs there occurs now and then what may be termed a dramatic fatality which never fails. To put it in another way: when the bones come out of the tomb to testify, there is very little left for the judge to do."

In spite of the hopes of my friend, Gabriela was not found, and three months later she was, according to the laws of Spain, tried, found guilty, and condemned to death in her absence.

I returned home, not without promising to be with Zarco the following year.

IV

THAT winter I passed in Granada. One evening I had been invited to a great ball given by a prominent Spanish lady. As I was mounting the stairs of the magnificent residence, I was startled by the sight of a face which was easily distinguishable even in this crowd of southern beauties. It was she, my unknown, the mysterious woman of the stagecoach, in fact, No. 1, of whom I spoke at the beginning of this narrative.

I made my way toward her, extending my hand in greeting. She recognized me at once.

"Señora," I said, "I have kept my promise not to search for you. I did not know I would meet you here. Had I suspected it I would have refrained from coming, for fear of annoying you. Now that I am here, tell me whether I may recognize you and talk to you."

"I see that you are vindictive," she answered graciously, putting her little hand in mine. "But I forgive you. How are you?"

"In truth, I don't know. My health—that is, the health of my soul, for you would not ask me about anything else in a ballroom—depends upon the health of yours. What I mean is that I could only be happy if you are happy. May I ask if that wound of the heart which you told me about when I met you in the stagecoach has healed?"

"You know as well as I do that there are wounds which never heal."

With a graceful bow she turned away to speak to an acquaintance, and I asked a friend of mine who was passing: "Can you tell me who that woman is?"

"A South American whose name is Mercedes de Meridanueva."

On the following day I paid a visit to the lady, who was residing at that time at the Hotel of the Seven Planets. The charming Mercedes received me as if I were an intimate friend, and invited me to walk with her through the wonderful Alhambra and subsequently to dine with her. During the six hours we were together she spoke of many things, and as we always returned to the subject of disappointed love, I felt impelled to tell her the experience of my friend, Judge Zarco.

She listened to me very attentively and when I concluded she laughed and said: "Let this be a lesson to you not to fall in love with women whom you do not know."

"Do not think for a moment," I answered, "that I've invented this story."

"Oh, I don't doubt the truth of it. Perhaps there may be a mysterious woman in the Hotel of the Seven Planets of Granada, and perhaps she doesn't resemble the one your friend fell in love with in Sevilla. So far as I am concerned, there is no risk of my falling in love with anyone, for I never speak three times to the same man."

"Señora! That is equivalent to telling me that you refuse to see me again!"

"No, I only wish to inform you that I leave Granada tomorrow, and it is probable that we will never meet again."

"Never? You told me that during our memorable ride in the stagecoach, and you see that you are not a good prophet."

I noticed that she had become very pale. She rose from the table abruptly, saying: "Well, let us leave that to Fate. For my part I repeat that I am bidding you an eternal farewell."

She said these last words very solemnly, and then with a graceful bow, turned and ascended the stairway which led to the upper story of the hotel.

I confess that I was somewhat annoyed at the disdainful way in which she seemed to have terminated our acquaintance, yet this feeling was lost in the pity I felt for her when I noted her expression of suffering.

We had met for the last time. Would to God that it had been for the last time! Man proposes, but God disposes.

V

A FEW days later business affairs brought me to the town wherein resided my friend Judge Zarco. I found him as lonely and as sad as at the time of my last visit. He had been able to find out nothing about Blanca, but he could not forget her for a moment. Unquestionably this woman was his fate; his heaven or his hell, as the unfortunate man was accustomed to saying.

We were soon to learn that his judicial superstition was to be fully justified.

The evening of the day of my arrival we were seated in his office, reading the last reports of the police, who had been vainly attempting to trace Gabriela, when an officer entered and handed the judge a note which read as follows:

"In the Hotel of the Lion there is a lady who wishes to speak to Judge Zarco."

"Who brought this?" asked the judge.

"A servant."

"Who sent him?"

"He gave no name."

The judge looked thoughtfully at the smoke of his cigar for a few moments, and then said: "A woman! To see me? I don't know why, but this thing frightens me. What do you think of it, Philip?"

"That it is your duty as a judge to answer the call, of course. Perhaps she may be able to give you some information in regard to Gabriela."

"You are right," answered Zarco, rising. He put a revolver in his pocket, threw his cloak over his shoulders and went out.

Two hours later he returned.

I saw at once by his face that some great happiness must have come to him. He put his arms about me and embraced me convulsively, exclaiming: "Oh, dear friend, if you only knew, if you only knew!"

"But I don't know anything," I answered. "What on earth has happened to you?"

"I'm simply the happiest man in the world!"

"But what is it?"

"The note that called me to the hotel was from *her*."

"But from whom? From Gabriela Zahara?"

"Oh, stop such nonsense! Who is thinking of those things now? It was she, I tell you, the other one!"

"In the name of heaven, be calm and tell me whom you are talking about."

"Who could it be but Blanca, my love, my life?"

"Blanca?" I answered with astonishment. "But the woman deceived you."

"Oh, no; that was all a foolish mistake on my part."

"Explain yourself."

"Listen: Blanca adores me!"

"Oh, you think she does? Well, go on."

"When Blanca and I separated on the fifteenth of April, it was understood that we were to meet again on the fifteenth of May. Shortly after I left she received a letter calling her to Madrid on urgent family business, and she did not expect me back until the fifteenth of May, so she remained in Madrid until the first. But, as you know, I, in my impatience could not wait, and returned fifteen days before I had agreed, and not finding her at the hotel I jumped to the conclusion that she had deceived me, and I did not wait. I have gone through two years of torment and suffering, all due to my own stupidity."

"But she could have written you a letter."

"She said that she had forgotten the address."

"Ah, my poor friend," I exclaimed, "I see that you are striving to convince yourself. Well, so much the better. Now, when does the marriage take place? I suppose that after so long and dark a night the sun of matrimony will rise radiant."

"Don't laugh," exclaimed Zarco; "you shall be my best man."

"With much pleasure."

Man proposes, but God disposes. We were still seated in the library, chatting together, when there came a knock at the door. It was about two o'clock in the morning. The judge and I were both startled, but we could not have told why. The servant opened the door, and a moment later a man dashed into the library so breathless from hard running that he could scarcely speak.

"Good news, judge, grand news!" he said when he recovered breath. "We have won!"

The man was the prosecuting attorney.

"Explain yourself, my dear friend," said the judge, motioning him to a chair. "What remarkable occurrence could have brought you hither in such haste and at this hour of the morning?"

"We have arrested Gabriela Zahara."

"Arrested her?" exclaimed the judge joyfully.

"Yes, sir, we have her. One of our detectives has been following her for a month. He has caught her, and she is now locked up in a cell of the prison."

"Then let us go there at once!" exclaimed the judge. "We will interrogate her to-night. Do me the favor to notify my secretary. Owing to the gravity of the case, you yourself must be present. Also notify the guard who has charge of the head of Señor Romeral. It has been my opinion from the beginning that this criminal woman would not dare deny the horrible murder when she was confronted with the evidence of her crime. So far as you are concerned," said the judge, turning to me, "I will appoint you assistant secretary, so that you can be present without violating the law."

I did not answer. A horrible suspicion had been growing within me, a suspicion which, like some infernal animal, was tearing at my heart with claws of steel. Could Gabriela and Blanca be one and the same? I turned to the assistant district attorney.

"By the way," I asked, "where was Gabriela when she was arrested?"

"In the Hotel of the Lion."

My suffering was frightful, but I could say nothing, do nothing without compromising the judge; besides, I was not sure. Even if I were positive that Gabriela and Blanca were the same person, what could my unfortunate friend do? Feign a sudden illness? Flee the country? My only way was to keep silent and let God work it out in His own way. The orders of the judge had already been communicated to the chief of police and the warden of the prison. Even at this hour the news had spread throughout the city and idlers were gathering to see the rich and beautiful woman who would ascend the scaffold. I still clung to the slender hope that Gabriela and Blanca were not the same person. But when I went toward the prison I staggered like a drunken man and was compelled to lean upon the shoulder of one of the officials, who asked me anxiously if I were ill.

VI

We arrived at the prison at four o'clock in the morning. The large reception room was brilliantly lighted. The guard, holding a black box in which was the skull of Señor Romeral, was awaiting us.

The judge took his seat at the head of the long table; the prosecuting attorney sat on his right, and the chief of police stood by with his arms folded. I and the secretary sat on the left of the judge. A number of police officers and detectives were standing near the door.

The judge touched his bell and said to the warden:

"Bring in Doña Gabriela Zahara!"

I felt as if I were dying, and instead of looking at the door, I looked at the judge to see if I could read in his face the solution of this frightful problem.

I saw him turn livid and clutch his throat with both hands, as if to stop a cry of agony, and then he turned to me with a look of infinite supplication.

"Keep quiet!" I whispered, putting my finger on my lips, and then I added: "I knew it."

The unfortunate man arose from his chair.

"Judge!" I exclaimed, and in that one word I conveyed to him the full sense of his duty and of the dangers which surrounded him. He controlled himself and resumed his seat, but were it not for the light in his eyes, he might have been taken for a dead man. Yes, the man was dead; only the judge lived.

When I had convinced myself of this, I turned and looked at the accused. Good God! Gabriela Zahara was not only Blanca, the woman my friend so deeply loved, but she was also the woman I had met in the stagecoach and subsequently at Granada, the beautiful South American, Mercedes!

All these fantastic women had now merged into one, the real one who stood before us, accused of the murder of her husband and who had been condemned to die.

There was still a chance to prove herself innocent. Could she do it? This was my one supreme hope, as it was that of my poor friend.

Gabriela (we will call her now by her real name) was deathly pale, but apparently calm. Was she trusting to her innocence or to the weakness of the judge? Our doubts were soon solved. Up to that moment the accused had looked at no one but the judge. I did not know whether she desired to encourage him or menace him, or to tell him that his Blanca could not be an assassin. But, noting the impassibility of the magistrate and that his face was as expressionless as that of a corpse, she turned to the others, as if seeking help from them. Then her eyes fell upon me, and she blushed slightly.

The judge now seemed to awaken from his stupor and asked in a harsh voice:

"What is your name?"

"Gabriela Zahara, widow of Romeral," answered the accused in a soft voice.

Zarco trembled. He had just learned that his Blanca had never existed; she told him so herself—she who only three hours before had consented to become his wife!

Fortunately, no one was looking at the judge, all eyes being fixed upon Gabriela, whose marvelous beauty and quiet demeanor carried to all an almost irresistible conviction of her innocence.

The judge recovered himself, and then, like a man who is staking more than life upon the cast of a die, he ordered the guard to open the black box.

"Madame!" said the judge sternly, his eyes seeming to dart flames, "approach and tell me whether you recognize this head?"

At a signal from the judge the guard opened the black box and lifted out the skull.

A cry of mortal agony rang through that room; one could not tell whether it was of fear or of madness. The woman shrank back, her eyes dilating with terror, and screamed: "Alfonzo, Alfonzo!"

Then she seemed to fall into a stupor. All turned to the judge, murmuring: "She is guilty beyond a doubt."

"Do you recognize the nail which deprived your husband of life?" said the judge, arising from his chair, looking like a corpse rising from the grave.

"Yes, sir," answered Gabriela mechanically.

"That is to say, you admit that you assassinated your husband?" asked the judge, in a voice that trembled with his great suffering.

"Sir," answered the accused, "I do not care to live any more, but before I die I would like to make a statement."

The judge fell back in his chair and then asked me by a look: "What is she going to say?"

I, myself, was almost stupefied by fear.

Gabriela stood before them, her hands clasped and a far-away look in her large, dark eyes.

"I am going to confess," she said, "and my confession will be my defense, although it will not be sufficient to save me from the scaffold. Listen to me, all of you! Why deny that which is self-evident? I was alone with my husband when he died. The servants and the doctor have testified to this. Hence, only I could have killed him. Yes, I committed the crime, but another man forced me to do it."

The judge trembled when he heard these words, but, dominating his emotion, he asked courageously:

"The name of that man, madame? Tell us at once the name of the scoundrel!"

Gabriela looked at the judge with an expression of infinite love, as a mother would look at the child she worshiped, and answered: "By a single word I could drag this man into the depths with me. But I will not. No one shall ever know his name, for he has loved me and I love him. Yes, I love him, although I know he will do nothing to save me!"

The judge half rose from his chair and extended his hands beseechingly, but she looked at him as if to say: "Be careful! You will betray yourself, and it will do no good."

He sank back into his chair, and Gabriela continued her story in a quiet, firm voice:

"I was forced to marry a man I hated. I hated him more after I married him than I did before. I lived three years in martyrdom. One day there came into my life a man whom I loved. He demanded that I should marry him, he asked me to fly with him to a heaven of happiness and love. He was a man of exceptional character, high and noble, whose only fault was that he loved me too much. Had I told him: 'I have deceived you, I am not a widow; my husband is living,' he would have left me at once. I invented a thousand excuses, but he always answered: 'Be my wife!' What could I do? I was bound to a man of the vilest character and habits, whom I loathed. Well, I killed this man, believing that I was committing an act of justice, and God punished me, for my lover abandoned me. And now I am very, very tired of life, and all I ask of you is that death may come as quickly as possible."

Gabriela stopped speaking. The judge had buried his face in his hands, as if he were thinking, but I could see he was shaking like an epileptic.

"Your honor," repeated Gabriela, "grant my request that I may die soon."

The judge made a sign to the guards to remove the prisoner.

Before she followed them, she gave me a terrible look in which there was more of pride than of repentance.

I do not wish to enter into details of the condition of the judge during the following day. In the great emotional struggle which took place, the officer of the law conquered the man, and he confirmed the sentence of death.

On the following day the papers were sent to the Court of Appeals, and then Zarco came to me and said: "Wait here until I return. Take care of this unfortunate woman, but do not visit her, for your presence would humiliate instead of consoling her. Do not ask me whither I am going, and do not think that I am going to commit the very foolish act of taking my own life. Farewell, and forgive me all the worry I have caused you."

Twenty days later the Court of Appeals confirmed the sentence, and Gabriela Zahara was placed in the death cell.

The morning of the day fixed for the execution came, and still the judge had not returned. The scaffold had been erected in the center of the square, and an enormous crowd had gathered. I stood by the door of the prison, for, while I had obeyed the wish of my friend that I should not call on Gabriela in her prison, I believed it my duty to represent him in that supreme moment and accompany the woman he had loved to the foot of the scaffold.

When she appeared, surrounded by her guards, I hardly recognized her. She had grown very thin and seemed hardly to have the strength to lift to her lips the small crucifix she carried in her hand.

"I am here, señora. Can I be of service to you?" I asked her as she passed by me.

She raised her deep, sunken eyes to mine, and, when she recognized me, she exclaimed:

"Oh, thanks, thanks! This is a great consolation for me, in my last hour of life. Father," she added, turning to the priest who stood beside her, "may I speak a few words to this generous friend?"

"Yes, my daughter," answered the venerable minister.

Then Gabriela asked me: "Where is he?"

"He is absent——"

"May God bless him and make him happy! When you see him, ask him to forgive me even as I believe God has already forgiven me. Tell him I love him yet, although this love is the cause of my death."

We had arrived at the foot of the scaffold stairway, where I was compelled to leave her. A tear, perhaps the last one there was in that suffering heart, rolled down her cheek. Once more she said: "Tell him that I died blessing him."

Suddenly there came a roar like that of thunder. The mass of people swayed, shouted, danced, laughed like maniacs, and above all this tumult one word rang out clearly:

"Pardoned! Pardoned!"

At the entrance to the square appeared a man on horseback, galloping madly toward the scaffold. In his hand he waved a white handkerchief, and his voice rang high above the clamor of the crowd: "Pardoned! Pardoned!"

It was the judge. Reining up his foaming horse at the foot of the scaffold, he extended a paper to the chief of police.

Gabriela, who had already mounted some of the steps, turned and gave the judge a look of infinite love and gratitude.

"God bless you!" she exclaimed, and then fell senseless.

As soon as the signatures and seals upon the document had been verified by the authorities, the priest and the judge rushed to the accused to undo the cords which bound her hands and arms and to revive her.

All their efforts were useless, however. Gabriela Zahara was dead.

Alfredo Oriani

(ADAPTED)

The Moscow Theater Plot

I

"I WILL begin by telling you my name. I am Prince Vladimir Gregorovitch Tevscheff."

"The Senator?"

"Yes."

There was a slight pause before the Prince continued: "Now we know each other. I have come to make terms with you."

"In the name of the Inner Circle?"

"No, in my own name."

"Wait. You say that we know each other; but all I know is that I have heard your name spoken a few times. And what do you know of me? Your president told me, in your presence, that I was the abandoned son of a Russian priest, a student, poor and friendless, until I made a fortune in foreign countries, cheating at cards. Have you yourself a better knowledge of me?"

"Since the Executive Committee consented to receive you at a secret session, it must have been well-informed as to your character. I do not know the small vicissitudes of your life, but I do know enough to feel justified in entering into a compact with you. Yesterday, at a meeting of students at the house of Count Ogareff, you revealed your plan, and it was rejected."

"Just as it had been by the Executive Committee."

"What do you mean to do next?"

"What have you come to suggest?"

"You have need of powerful aid, to carry out your plans. I have come to offer it to you."

"What are your conditions?"

"I make no conditions. I only set forth the situation. Alexander III must die as his father died. That is not merely a debt of honor that we owe to Russia, but without it the fate of Alexander II would lose all significance. To-day the Government makes a greater show of repressing the revolutionists than in the past. To submit is to recognize its omnipotence. If Alexander III perishes, faith in the invincibility of Czarism is destroyed."

"Then whoever kills the Czar could make himself master of all the forces of nihilism?"

"Yes."

"It is not enough to kill the Czar. It is necessary that he should die with as many others as it is possible to gather around him!" The Prince examined his companion intently; they were talking with the greatest calmness; had anyone been able to overhear them, he would have thought himself in the presence of two madmen.

"If it were a matter merely of killing the Czar," resumed Loris, "nothing would be simpler. You might have done it yourself, since you are received at court. A man is never anything more than one man against another. But this time it is quite a different question. We must do something bigger; we must blow up an entire theater on a gala night, Czar, court, and aristocracy all at once!"

"Impossible! Remember the attempt upon the Winter Palace!"

"Who said that we should need to *tunnel?* Sixty pounds of melinite would be enough to wreck a theater, without a single soul escaping. The Czar must perish in Moscow, in the city that is sacred to Czarism. The attempt may be extremely dangerous, but not at all difficult for anyone who looks upon himself as already dead—as I do. The regicides in the past who have failed have done so because they had not really renounced their lives. If nihilistic proclamations can be placed in the Czar's own bed-chamber, why has he not been killed by those who placed them there?"

Loris suddenly checked himself:

"You yourself, Prince, sometimes take part in the Czar's councils; the papers often cite your name among those invited to the court balls!"

The Prince, who had been expecting this objection, replied promptly:

"That is for my wife's sake. She does not know that I belong to the cause."

"It is plain," said Loris, "that we must come to a better understanding. Why are you taking part in the revolutionary movement? What reason have you for wanting to kill the Czar? My own reasons are easy to give; my father was condemned unjustly, and died on his way to Siberia; my mother killed herself. I was born in injustice, I have suffered every misery, I have hated all my life. That is why I want to destroy this world, which for thousands of years has strangled untold millions of men for the benefit of the few. But what is there in common between those who suffer, and you who do your share in making them suffer, selfishly spending your wealth for your own pleasure?"

"Do you not admit that we can love the people without belonging to them?"

"No, I do not believe in revolutions that are born of love. What is it that has made you a nihilist? In what way has the Czar injured you?"

The Prince's face became livid; an expression of feverish hatred distorted his features. It was evident that he had suffered deeply.

"Your wife is young?" Loris inquired, with significant irony.

The Prince sprang to his feet; Loris followed his example.

"I understand," said Loris, "it is nothing but male jealousy, in place of a noble enthusiasm! Without it you would not have espoused our cause. The love of a woman, whose vanity has been flattered by the Czar, and whom you love all the more for that reason,—that is your revolution!"

"What man are you, to read one's secret thoughts?" exclaimed the Prince, recoiling in amazement.

"A man who has never known what love is. Sit down again, we have much to say to each other. One cannot give oneself to a woman and a revolution, at the same time. For remember this: a revolution is like a woman to this extent, that it insists upon a man's exclusive devotion!"

. . . .

Once in Moscow, Loris's thoughts turned to a small Hebrew friend, Sergius Nicolaivitch Lemm, and to the girl revolutionist, Olga Petrovna, in whom he was aware that he had inspired a sentiment not far removed from love. In fact, the young woman, meeting him recently in the street, had flushed such a vivid red that a far less observant person than Loris would have been aware of her partiality. He was quite ready to avail himself of this for his own purposes.

He called upon Olga at her home; but if she expected him to pay court to her, she was quickly disillusioned. With a directness that was almost brutal, he explained to her the purpose of his visit. Olga turned white, but Loris did not even leave her time to be afraid. He outlined his plans with a cold eloquence; yet no book in the whole range of revolutionary literature had ever had for her such a horrible fascination. She did not even try to resist it. Impressed in spite of himself by her mute surrender, Loris asked her:

"Then you are willing to aid me?"

"What has my will to do with it? You would crush my will, as you do that of everyone else."

Lemm he sought out in a neighboring village, on the road to St. Petersburg. "Sergius Nicolaivitch," he said to him, "I am glad to see that you remember me. I need you at once. You must drive back with me to Moscow. I will explain on the way."

The little Hebrew was in an even more dilapidated condition than usual. Although longing for an explanation, he curbed his curiosity, and hurried away to make his preparations, while Loris waited, walking his horses up and down the street. Before night, Lemm was no longer recognizable; Loris had sent him to a big furnishing store, which effected such a transformation that, with no slight assistance from the barber, he might have passed for a model of fashionable elegance.

Loris's first business in Moscow was to search for an apartment, facing on the same square as the great theater. He could not obtain possession of one until the end of the week, the day on which Olga, who was to play the part of his wife, arrived from St. Petersburg by train. Loris met her at the station.

"Do I satisfy you?" she asked him, glancing down at her new frock, which she had bought to sustain her rôle.

"Those flowers are much too loud. No real lady would have put them on a traveling hat. Otherwise you are all right."

II

THE great imperial box was empty, its lights turned out. In its midst, the massive golden crown above the royal seat looked not unlike a miniature dome. Olga had not shown herself at the front of her box. A calm of inertia had come over her, after the first terror at becoming a conspirator, so that Loris had to remind her to remove her cloak, and to go forward, to avoid the appearance of trying to hide. As she obeyed, Olga felt around her waist the pressure of the coiled wire, hidden there, like a mysterious clutch tightening to suffocate her. In the darkest corner, Loris had hidden the muff, containing the dismounted pieces of the auger, and under shadow of the portière he emptied his pockets; he had managed to secrete ten tubes of melinite that the Prince had furnished. Lemm was due to arrive shortly, after the concert had begun, with ten more tubes; and during the intermission they were to return to the house together, and bring the remainder.

The theater continued to fill up slowly. Most of the ladies appeared in the boxes in hat and walking costume; a majority of the men, on the contrary, wore the conventional evening clothes. In the orchestra, the musicians were already tuning their instruments. Suddenly the flames of gas redoubled their brilliance, and all the white and gold of that vast chamber flung back the light, while the countenances and the gay apparel of the audience, leaping, as it were, from out the shadow, seemed like the beginning of the spectacle.

Lemm entered, ahead of time. Olga was startled by his exceeding pallor.

"If I were a detective," Loris told him, "I should have discovered you already!"

Lemm, who was turning down the high coat collar, behind which he had sought to hide his face, felt that he merited the reproof; but his whole stock of courage had not sufficed to keep him from trembling while passing through the body of the theater. In the box, he recovered himself, for there were three of them.

The music seemed to continue endlessly, reaching their ears like an indistinct murmur of water or of leaves, across the noonday brilliancy of the gaslight, evoking in their minds the rival brilliancy of snow; they thought of that other night, when at even greater risk they must stretch the connecting wire all the way to their apartment, across the public square before the theater, and under the watchful eyes of the police; and all the while, the snow would keep on falling fast and silently. And they three, hidden in the remote depths of their apartment, would await the signal from the Prince, to fling that white theater into the air of heaven, and bring it down in unimaginable ruin about the heads of that joyous throng. It was a disordered and atrocious vision, that made their brains reel in anticipation.

It seemed an eternity before Lemm took the last tubes of melinite from under his coat, and said good-by—then the finale—the hum of departure—the anxiety of hearing the attendants lock up and pass, oblivious of the two forms crouching behind the curtains.

At last alone, their first task was to adjust the tubes of melinite beneath the seat of the sofa. After inserting the necessary number of metal hooks, Loris asked Olga for the coil of wire concealed around her waist, and she passed it to him from beneath her cloak. He rapidly wove a network of the wire through the hooks, arranging the thirty tubes in three rows; the most delicate part of the task was to connect the wires with the explosive caps; Loris satisfied himself with establishing electric connection with the first row only. If these exploded, they would inevitably set off the other two rows. All this operation was carried out in complete silence.

Next came the second problem, that of leading the wire from the rear leg of the sofa, beneath the carpet, through box and corridor, all the way to the window, near which Loris had assured himself, earlier in the evening, that the drainpipe descended. Loris glanced at his watch; it was on the stroke of two. Obviously, they must hasten. Olga suggested that it would be better to pierce the drainpipe first, and drop the whole length of wire into it, and then draw back what they needed to reach the box, passing it along the wall, where the carpet was attached by almost invisible little hooks. Nothing could be easier than to place it underneath. The only difficulty would be to bring it across the corridor in front of the box; but since the metal offered a certain rigidity, they could undoubtedly, with patience, eventually work it across.

The work finished at last, with infinite calm Loris threw himself down, closely wrapped in his fur coat, with collar raised and knees drawn up, in order to keep his feet tucked in. After twisting and turning several times, in search of a comfortable position,

"Go to sleep," he said to Olga.

Yet even he found sleep no easy matter. After the accomplishment of his herculean task, his mind was agitated with a savage joy. Blunted by long years of contact with revolutionary movements, his brain saw nothing in the coming carnage save a maneuver of war. He, the unknown general, had been self-sufficient. Hannibal, upon the Alps, straining his eyes for a sight of distant Rome; Moltke, re-reading in the silence of his cabinet the plan of campaign against the second Napoleonic empire, must, he thought, have shared his emotion of the present moment. Then a flood of images followed each other through his brain,—the roar of the explosion, sending the theater hurtling through the air; while the entire city wailed in terror, and throughout Russia and beyond Russia, all people, roused by the tremendous news, would demand who had done it! The Czar dead! The aristocracy dead! And he alone, master of the secret, would advance from across the steppes, at the head of a host of peasants, mounted on their lean horses, not speaking to them, save in one of those curt commands that change the physiognomy of people and of things!

Little by little, he sank to sleep. Olga, crouching in one corner of the opposite sofa, warmed her hands upon the chimney of the lantern, hidden beneath her cloak. From time to time she shuddered, besieged with fears of the cold and the dark, besides remorse for the atrocious crime, disproportionate to even the worst of human sufferings. Her woman's heart, too tender to understand Loris's savage passion, turned to her love for him as to a refuge,—and meanwhile, he was able to sleep tranquilly above the mine that he had laid!

III

From that day forward, everything worked in their favor; but the relations between Olga and Loris became more and more strained. Three days later, the azure of the sky had turned to white, and the cold had perceptibly diminished. These were the first symptoms of snow, which, driven by an impetuous wind, began that evening to fall over houses and streets, like a storm of fine dust. Loris was in readiness. As he left the house, at half-past ten, the storm-swept square was empty.

Lemm saw Loris move off in the direction of the theater, which could hardly be distinguished through the cloud of snowflakes. The street lamps glimmered faintly, as if seen through a thick fog. The cold was increasing; the whole square was already white, and it remained white, in spite of passing carriages and people. It was time for Lemm to do his part. Gathering his courage, he made his way back to the corner where Loris's house stood, twirling his stick with assumed carelessness, but slackened his pace, as he noticed an approaching carriage. That would be the best moment to give the blow. As the horses passed noisily, their steel-shod hoofs striking the pavement through the light covering of snow, he pretended to stumble and struck a powerful blow upon the pipe, that resounded dully. To Lemm it sounded like a formidable explosion; his ears buzzed painfully, his head whirled, and he instinctively threw himself prostrate, in order to escape the notice of the policeman, who must infallibly be coming. But no policeman came, no one seemed to have heard. Becoming calmer, he inserted three fingers through the puncture, found the wire, drew it forth, and stretched it a few yards along the wall. His part of the work was done and he was safe.

Brushing the snow from his coat, he turned back to a point from which he could watch for Loris. But growing anxiety made it impossible for him to stand still. What could have happened to Loris? Madly he hurried on, almost running, meaning to pass close to his friend and tell him to make haste; then checked himself. If Loris saw him approaching he might mistake him for an enemy. Shortly after, he perceived a white mass looming up from the direction of the square. Loris was approaching with methodical slowness. Lemm divined that he had the coil in his hand, and that he was treading on the wire as it unrolled, in order to bury it more effectually in the snow; immediately he set himself to do likewise. This was the most perilous moment of all; any passer-by crossing their line might catch his toe in the wire, and stop to investigate.

When they met, Loris flung him the end of the coil, saying, "Take the pliers out of my pocket and make the connection, my fingers are numb." Lemm, who had already snatched off his gloves, rapidly made the joint, hiding the rest of the wire in his pocket.

"Now Russia is in our hands!" As he spoke, Loris's voice trembled from the cold. Yet they must remain at least two hours longer waiting for the snow to become deep enough to hide the wire beyond possible discovery.

Three hours later Loris was asleep; Olga still stood before the window, her burning forehead pressed against the glass; Lemm, sitting by the stove, drank and drank.

IV

The Emperor arrived in Moscow on the morning of January 6th. The evening of the 8th would be the gala night at the theater. Those last two days seemed an eternity. The imminence of the catastrophe oppressed them like an unforeseen fatality. Loris and Olga had ceased even to speak to each other, and Lemm avoided coming to their apartment. Meanwhile Loris had been undergoing the worst strain of all, because the city authorities had kept workmen busy digging a number of holes in the snow throughout the square, to make place for the bonfires that were to keep the coachmen warm while waiting for the close of the performance. He had forgotten this custom, which might easily defeat his whole attempt, if by chance a single pile should be placed along the line of the wire. But as luck would have it, they came nowhere near.

The sight of the Square, with its tumult of people and carriages, fascinated him. The gay mood of the public was steadily augmenting; the massing throngs would be content to remain for long hours, unconscious of the cold, consumed with curiosity regarding this festival from which they were excluded, worshiping from without, as if before a mysterious temple. The great woodpiles were all ablaze, sending up spirals of ruddy flame, that drowned the light of the street lamps, and seemed to impart an eddying motion to all the surrounding buildings. Carriages found difficulty in cleaving a furrow through the compact mass of humanity, even when the dragoons, posted there to keep order, spurred forward their horses into the thick of the crowd. From every window lights were shining; from every doorway came a joyous glow; while the roar of the rising tide of men and women continued to gain volume, mingling in the air with the whirling smoke of the bonfires. And the theater, whiter than ever in the midst of the incandescence, flung back the light from all its dazzling walls, as wave after wave of illumination ran over their surface as over the gleaming surface of water.

Loris summoned Olga and Lemm, bidding the former stand guard at the window and give notice if any suspicious person should enter the house; while the latter was to go to the theater, and wait in the entrance for the Prince.

The performance had already begun, when Lemm, working blindly with shoulders and elbows, reached the front row, before the massive portico of the main entrance. The lobby of the theater emitted the blinding glow of a furnace, within which the arriving guests were, one after another, successively engulfed, still enveloped in their costly furs.

The people around him were shouting and struggling and wasting their efforts in vain attempts to break through the lines and obtain a nearer view of that other crowd of aristocratic guests.

Suddenly the Prince appeared in the entrance, flung himself down the two outside steps, his coat unbuttoned and flying open, revealing his decorations. Lemm sprang forward, slipping behind the dragoon's horse. "Prince!" he exclaimed.

The dragoon was about to drive him back again, when the Prince turned and waved the soldier aside. "Oh, hurry, hurry!" he said, dragging Lemm along.

"What has happened?" questioned Lemm, whose numbed limbs found difficulty in keeping up with him.

The other replied with a gesture of despair. They were halfway across the Square; carriages impeded their progress, while the snow, crushed by all those trampling feet, had become perilously slippery. Two or three times, in trying to dodge the passing wheels, they were on the point of falling. As they passed one of the bonfires, Lemm got a good view of his companion's face; it looked ghastly. The Prince plunged ahead, in furious haste, towards Loris's house.

When they entered the cabinet, Olga, who had recognized them from the window, was already there, waiting at the door. The cabinet was almost in darkness. The single flame of a kerosene lamp that stood near the electric battery was shielded by a green shade, that seemed to concentrate all its rays upon the gleaming nickel of the electric key.

Loris arose, pushing back his chair, but the altered expression of their faces arrested him. Lemm had entered close upon the Prince, whose labored breathing seemed steadily growing more painful. Suddenly the Prince staggered and grasped at a chair for support. Loris gazed in his face with piercing eyes.

"The Emperor?" he questioned. But the other, staggering forward another step, answered precipitately, in strangling tones:

"My daughter is there!"

Loris, imagining that he was about to fling himself upon the electric transmitter, turned swiftly and laid his hand upon it. But the Prince recoiled in horror; his face was livid, his eyes staring wildly.

"No! no!" he cried pantingly. "Wait! oh, wait!"

Olga and Lemm came nearer. Loris, foreseeing a startling explanation, had turned even whiter than his wont, wearing that sinister expression of a face carved in marble, which Olga knew only too well. One and all, they scarcely dared to breathe.

"My daughter is there!" repeated the Prince, as though

in these simple words he had with one supreme effort condensed his final argument.

Loris made no answer.

Then the Prince made a gesture of hopeless impotence, as if now for the first time he realized that he was face to face with the impossible. His face had become the color of clay, his eyes shot forth flame. He drew himself to his full height; an unavailing struggle was about to begin. Loris turned upon him a glacial glance, and grasped the key of the transmitter in the hollow of his hand.

"Wait!" cried the Prince once more. "Grant me just a word. My daughter,—can't you understand?—she entered the theater just a minute ago——" His lips were trembling convulsively. "I was in my box with the Minister of the Navy; I had noticed that one of the boxes opposite was empty; suddenly she came in, ahead of the rest of her party. She had not intended to go to-night. For God's sake wait!" he cried, seeing a movement of the hand upon the key. "She is my only child, the one being in the world who loves me. I did not dare to stop, to warn her, to invent some excuse to bring her away. I was afraid, horribly afraid, that you might not wait my signal before touching the key." Pausing, he gazed anxiously at Loris. The latter remained silent, impassively examining the batteries.

"What!" cried the Prince, "will you not even answer me?" He glanced around, as if invoking aid from Lemm and Olga; the latter left the room, apparently unable to endure the painful scene.

"What is the use of discussing?" replied Loris.

The Prince advanced a few steps, but something in Loris's glance warned him that the least attempt at violence would be the signal for pressing the key.

"You place your daughter's welfare above that of Russia?"

"We can wait, and mine the theater at St. Petersburg!"

"Revolutions cannot be countermanded."

"But I won't have it! I won't have it!" cried the Prince in accents of desperate grief. "I will kill the Czar with my own hands! I am ready to go back now and kill him openly in the theater!"

"Prince," said Louis, "let us not discuss it. Because of your wife, you precipitate a revolution; because of your daughter, you would bring it to a halt. That is an impossibility, you must see for yourself. The sacrifice of a daughter is nothing unusual; recall the names of conspirators who have sacrificed themselves and their entire families to the cause of the revolution."

"Is there then no one in the world whose presence tonight in the theater would stop you from firing the mine?"

Loris did not even deign to answer.

The Prince seemed upon the point of falling, but Lemm sprang forward and caught him by the arm. He also looked at Loris with pleading eyes, not venturing to speak.

"Be merciful," murmured the Prince once more. But Loris resolutely averted his head, and with nervous haste pressed the electric key. It was the work of an instant. Neither Lemm nor the Prince had time to utter a cry; they seemed to feel the tremendous explosion in their very hearts, it seemed to them that the house itself was crumbling in ruins. Instead—nothing happened!

Loris glanced up in amazement; then, scarcely crediting his senses, struck the key furiously, several times in succession.

At this moment Olga reappeared in the doorway.

"Ah!" roared Loris. "You have cut the wire!"

Olga fell upon her knees, with clasped hands, but before the Prince or Lemm could make a movement to intervene, Loris had drawn a revolver and fired.

Olga fell forward upon her face.

The Prince flung himself upon Loris. "Unhappy man, what have you done?"

Loris stood, as if in a trance, the smoking pistol still in his grasp. He saw the girl lying motionless; the fury left his face. But through its ghastly pallor the marble fixity remained.

"Come," said the Prince.

PART II

Oriental Mystery Stories

From the *Japanese* of KIKUCHI JUN. From the *Chinese* of PU SUNG LING (17th Century). From the *Tibetan MSS.* called KAH-GYUR. From *Persian* sources. From the *Turkish* of AHMED IBN HEMDEM SHE KETK-HODA, called "Sohailee." From the *Arabian* BOOK OF A THOUSAND NIGHTS AND A NIGHT. From the *Sanskrit* of SOMADEVA (about 1070), as narrated in the "Katha Sarit Sagara," or "Ocean of Rivers of Stories."

A Web of World-Old Oriental Tales

Introduction by Charles Johnston

British India Civil Service: Royal Asiatic Society

HUCKLEBERRY FINN insisted that Indiana is pink because it is so on the map. We have much the same view of Eastern lands. We think that Arabia is pink, that Egypt is green, that Persia is blue, that India is yellow. And we imagine them as ruled off from each other by sharply marked lines, which, whosoever crosses, promptly has his head cut off.

In reality, there are no such lines. The East is the East, and it is much the same in many things from Morocco to far Timor and the Spice Islands; the same gleam and glow, the same rainbow colors, the same stir and surge of bronzed men and veiled women. And that has been so for ages. Long before the days of Solomon, proud ships plowed the Eastern main, trading between the Red Sea coasts and distant India, bringing thence the gold and ivory, the apes and peacocks, and the algum trees which, even in the story of Solomon, bear Indian names. And wherever they went, the sailors of those sapphire seas carried with them the sailor's open-eyed curiosity, his love of adventure, his romance that blossomed in every port. And some dusk sweetheart in the Camphor Isles, or by the pearl banks of Sulu, or in that miraculous land where dwell the paradise birds, told him old tales of love and death and witchcraft; and in the long night watches on the homeward way, he told them over again to his shipmates. So the tales went to and fro, weaving the many-colored garment of fantasy.

It was so in Solomon's time. It was so before they built the Pyramids. It was so through all the long centuries that have since slipped by and fallen into Time's treasury. It is so to-day. There is but one vast treasure-house of Eastern lore, and from its miraculous riches every bard and rhymer, every recounter of things marvelous and glad and sad, has drawn to his heart's content since the days of Babylon—Babylon long ago. No one can say how old these stories are. They are primeval. Some of them are as old as man. Some of them go back to those days when kindly spirits walked the earth among mortals, wondering gently at the new creature, with his fancies and his whims, and now and then touching man's work to unravel some knot of fate or to bring an unexpected blessing to some simple, good person. Of these tales of fairyland and its ministering visitants there is a web all round the world, and every wise child should believe them until he grows old and hard and incredulous.

So with tales of mysteries and wonders, of crafty robbers, and quick-witted women who out-tricked them. No interest is more universal than that which listens wide-eyed to a tale of dark deeds and their subtle unraveling. Sir Arthur Conan Doyle, that skilled knight who in quite recent years has enthralled the world with his tales of thrice-hidden mysteries, of invisible clews, of preternatural acumen, is but delving in a mine that was worked before they quarried for the Pyramids; he is but appealing once again to the world-old interest in the mystery tale that has held spellbound auditors through long centuries in every land lapped by the Seven Seas. The very word clew goes back to Ariadne, and that thread of hers that led Theseus safe through the Cretan labyrinth.

Take the story in this collection, "The Clever Thief" (page 169). As it stands here it comes from the Tibetan, from an ancient Buddhist book that goes back nearly a thousand years. But even then it was not new. Missionaries carried it thither from India in an odd corner of their bags, or in some chamber of the memory not filled with the riddles of being. Where did they get it? Who can say? It was old when Herodotus wandered through sunlit Egypt twenty-four centuries ago, gleaning tales from the priests of Amen and of Ptah. He tells it, point for point, as did those Buddhist missionaries, but lays it in the days of

Rameses, nigh four thousand years ago. Everything is there—the cutting off of the head to elude detection, the tricks by which the relatives mourn over the headless trunk, the snare set for the thief and his outwitting it. And that same tale, like good merchandise, was carried both east and west. It found its way to India, over the vast Himalayas, to the gray roof of the world. It came with equal charm to the Mediterranean isles, up the Adriatic coasts, and as far as Venice, bride of the sea. There Ser Giovanni told it, transmogrifying Pharaoh of the Nile into a worshipful Doge, as he had already been made over into a Buddhist magnate, but in no way altering the motive, the suspense, the artfulness of the tale. What is this story then? Is it Venetian? Is it Pharaonic? Is it Greek? Is it Tibetan? It is all these, and perhaps something more, vastly older than them all. Its craft, mayhap, goes back to that primal serpent who, more subtle than all the beasts of the field, has ever inspired darkling feints and strategies. Stories whose motive is a subtly discerned clew are not less primordial. Take that tale of the treasure stolen from the foot of the medicinal nàgabala tree, where the thief was recognized because he used the roots of the tree to cure his headaches. The tale is here (page 178) taken from the Sanskrit, from that wonderful book of books called the "Ocean of the Rivers of Stories." And it was written in that book some eight centuries ago. Are we to say, then, that the tale is Indian? But there is a Persian tale with exactly the same motive; but there the tree is a jujube tree, and its root is used as a cure for asthma. And almost the same story is told in Italian by Sacchetti, who was born a few years after Dante died.

The most vivid of these tales of deduction are, perhaps, those which come to us through the Arabs, in their treasure store, "The Thousand and One Nights." The Arabs gleaned them from every land in southern Asia, and from most ancient Egypt, in those days when Moslem power overshadowed half the world. And then they retold them with a charm, a vivid freshness, a roguishness, and a dash of golden light through it all that make them the finest story tellers in the world. So in this volume we have taken many stories from the Arabs, to get that fine touch of genius in the telling which gives them their perfection.

Can we fix the dates of these Arabian stories? Only in a very general way. Some of them came from Cairo, some from Syria, some from the Euphrates and Tigris valleys, some from Persia and India and China; and they were gathered together, it would appear, in the century before Shakespeare was born, by some big-hearted, humorous fellow, among the great anonymous benefactors of mankind. But he made no claim of inventing them. If he had he would have been laughed at for his pains. For old men had heard them from their grandfathers, generation after generation, and the gray grandsires always began to tell them, saying: " So 'twas told to me when I was such a tiny child as thou art."

Many of these Arabic tales take us back to the golden time of good Harun al Raschid, who used to disguise himself of an evening and go forth in Bagdad's streets with his Wazir Ja'afar, descendant of the Barmecide fire worshipers, and Ishak the cupbearer and Masrur the Eunuch, the Sworder of his vengeance, going out by the postern gate and taking boat on the river Tigris. That was eleven hundred years ago and more, before the eventful Christmas day when Charlemagne was crowned emperor. A man of vigor and valor, of an alert and subtle spirit, worker of justice and protector of the weak was that same caliph; he has won the hearts of all story tellers and story hearers through a thousand years.

So these tales have surged to and fro, under many moons, in ceaseless tide since the world was young. Flying on the wings of night from one to another of those Eastern lands where the sun bronzes all faces that are not veiled, they have rested now in some Himalayan fastness, now in some pillared temple by the Ganges, now in a lane in Bagdad, now under the shadow of Turkish minarets. They are of no one land, but are part of the common riches of mankind.

Oriental Mystery Stories

The Power of Eloquence

From the Japanese of Kikuchi Jun

UWOZUMI SEZAEMON, a rich inhabitant of the province of Etchigo, had a daughter of sixteen summers, by name Yuki-no, "the field of snow." Her marvelous beauty equaled her sparkling wit. She was a skillful musician, sang most charmingly, and excelled in making verses. The hearts of her parents exulted when they saw her perfections, and many were the suitors who demanded her hand in marriage. But Sezaemon, who deemed no youth a match for his fair girl, would not come to a decision, and ever put off the moment of separation, so that folks began to liken her to beautiful Komatchi, pledged to maidenhood.

Alas! how fickle is fortune! A grave sickness overtook the maiden; for many moons she lay pining on her couch, till at last she faded and sank to sleep, at the very moment when she should have burst forth in all the brightness of her beauty, like a sweet flower whose petals are strewn by the tempest. Her parents were in despair, and would not be comforted.

Yet needs must that they busy themselves about their daughter's burial. They brought her body in state to the monastery of Gokuraku, where the tombs of her ancestors were.

Some three months after the sad ceremony there was a knocking, long after midnight, at the monastery door. The porter peered through the wicket, and beheld a young man in rich vestments, whose twin swords with richly carved hilts of ivory declared him to be of noble birth. The porter hastened to open the door to him, and asked what he desired. The young man, announcing his titles and degree, said that he wished to see the master of the monastery, and slipped some pieces of money into the hands of the porter, who was delighted with this good fortune, and led him into the presence of the chief Bonze, prior of the monastery.

The young man seemed to be eighteen or nineteen years old; his eyes were bright, his hair black and shining, his face full of charm, noble and sweet.

He first saluted the worthy priest most honorably, kneeling, and advancing toward him on his knees, and then addressed him thus:

"I am the son of a noble of Kyoto; disaster overtook my family, bringing us to poverty, so that I had to leave Kyoto and migrate hither. And now I have a pressing desire to make known to you. This is the cause of my coming at so late an hour, though I am unknown to you. I know not how you will receive my prayer, for it concerns a matter of profound secrecy, and if ever it should come to be known——"

His voice broke, and he could not complete his sentence. Drawing from his purse five pieces of gold, he laid them on his fan, presenting it point forward to the reverend prior.

"Deign," he said, "to accept this modest present, which I offer, not to buy your favor, but only as a token of my humble obedience. You will make me happy, if you will have the kindness to employ it for the needs of worship."

The Bonze, who was fond of money, could not conceal his joy at receiving so rich a present. His face, which had been overcast and stern, burst into a beaming smile, and he said, with unctuous sweetness: "It is not common to find young people of your age animated by such a fervent religious spirit, for to-day few have any devotion. You are certain to receive pardon for all the sins of your past life, and to be received by our Lord Buddha into the abode of the blest, where you will enjoy eternal bliss and everlasting joy. But what is it you desire of me? Speak without fear, speak openly, for I keep all secrets that are intrusted to me."

But the young man still hesitated. He opened his mouth to speak, but his voice died away on his trembling lips. At last he seemed to make up his mind, and said: "So be it! Since it is useless to delay any longer, I will reveal to you the secret of my heart, whatever shame it may bring me. But I beg of you, make certain that none may remain within earshot, lest we be overheard."

"It is past midnight," said the Bonze. "Listen! every-one is already snoring. Who, then, could overhear what you have to tell me?"

Then the young man, his eyes downcast, and a blush of shame, which suffused his cheeks, but adding to his charms, began thus to speak:

"One day, a year ago, when I had gone into the country to admire the pretty flowers of sweet spring time, I met an adorable maiden, whose beauty put even the flowers to shame. My eyes were dazzled, my heart was perturbed. I followed her footsteps at a distance, and learned from the maid servant who accompanied her, walking a few paces behind her, that she was Uwozumi's daughter. From that moment, I was so deeply in love with her that I could think of naught else from morn till eve; and every night I dreamed of her ravishing beauty. Unable to withstand the force of my passion, I employed all possible means to win over the servant maid, and after difficulties without number I at last was able to declare my burning love to her whose radiant image possessed my heart. Mutual trust sprang up between us, and we swore to love each other to the end of our days.

"Alas! Heaven mocked at our design! What is more inconstant than human life? It is compared to the dew of the morning, but the dew ever lasts a certain space. Farewell, my beloved, farewell for ay. The door of death opened for thee in the flower of thy springtide. Can it be true, or is it but an evil dream? But why give way to my sorrows before you, reverend sir? She whom I loved so desperately is no more; nor can aught console me for my irremediable loss. As the days flit by my sorrow increases; naught in life attracts me; I long only for death. I would fain join in the other world her who has all my love. My own desire in this world is to open her grave, once more to embrace her upon this earth. O venerable priest, have pity on my grief! Grant me this last request, after which death will seem to me infinitely sweeter than life."

Greatly perturbed by so strange a request, the Bonze tried to console the youth, and to ween him from his plan. But the despairing young man's plan seemed only the more firmly fixed in his heart. "I know well," he said, "that a grave cannot be opened without the magistrate's order duly sealed; I know that you will oppose reasons to my entreaties; but my determination is only the firmer, and my grief is stronger than the whole world. Little do I reck of the heavy punishment that may overtake me.

"If you finally refuse me this last wish which I have revealed to you—well, my resolution is taken. I shall die on the spot!" And seizing his dagger, he was about to plunge it in his throat. The priest in terror stopped him, and consented to his request, but first he made him swear an oath. The young man drew a little blood from his finger to seal the bond, and promised to reveal nothing.

The girl's tomb was on the hillside, behind the monastery. The Bonze led his strange visitor thither. The hour was very late; there was a dampness in the air that bedewed their faces; a light breeze stirred through the darkness. In silence they went forward. Soon the tombs in regular rows began to show through the veil of mist, and the Bonze stopped. Pointing to a newly made grave he said "It is hers."

"At last!" cried the young man, attaining his desire, and, seizing the gravestone, he raised it from the tomb without visible effort. Then he opened the coffin, and rained kisses on the lifeless form of the maiden. The

Bonze withdrew in grief and horror, and watched his strange visitor from afar.

The sorrow-stricken youth, altogether given up to his grief and his love, remained there, uttering bitter complaints and filled with a preternatural joy, which was terrible and incomprehensible. A half hour passed thus, and still he could not tear himself away from the lifeless form of his beloved. At last he laid the sad vestiges of his charmer once more in the tomb, arranging them with tender care, covering them with earth, and putting back the tombstone as before. Thereafter he rejoined the priest, and poured out to him his unbounded gratitude.

A year after the death of Yuki-no, "the field of snow," the whole family had come together in Uwozumi's house, for the anniversary service to her spirit. Her father and mother wept at the memory of the happy days of their beloved child; they beheld her once more in memory; charming, frank, delighting them with her countless fancies and pretty jests, amusing herself by weaving flower wreaths for her brow, singing sweet ditties, and dancing lightly with her companions. They laid on the family altar all the little things that she had loved best. And meanwhile the Bonzes repeated their prayers, and the whole family, ranged in a circle around them, shed tears.

Just as the sun was setting behind the mountain, a pilgrim Bonze presented himself at the door, ringing his little bell and uttering prayers. They took him in, offering him hospitality for the night, and set pure food before him. After a short time, he addressed the master of the house and his wife, saying: "I have come from afar solely in order to communicate to you something of great moment concerning your daughter. I beg you to send to a distance all your servants, so that I may speak freely to you, after which I shall not regret all the pain and weariness of my coming." They led him immediately to a remote apartment, and begged him to begin at once what he had to tell, because it was already late.

The Bonze drew himself together, took his rosary in both

hands and passed it between his fingers, then several times repeating the invocation to Amida Buddha, he began as follows:

" While I was traveling through the province of Etchigo, I ascended Mount Tateyama, and passed through a valley called Jigoku Dani. Not a living creature was in sight; not a hut was visible that could serve as a shelter. The sun had already set, darkness had begun to envelope the earth, and I was obliged to take shelter under the branches of an ancient tree. The wind whistled, and the cold, damp air pierced me to the bone, so that my eyelids, though heavy with sleep, refused to close. The night descended in thick darkness. All at once a slender flame, half reddish, half bluish, passed flickering before my eyes, now growing dim, now glowing brightly, now fading and then lighting up again; in a word, something mysterious, strange, indefinable, like everything that comes from the other world. At the same time I heard what seemed to be a plaintive voice approaching me. It was in vain that I lent all my attention, for I could distinguish nothing clearly. I thought that I must be the sport of some illusion, such as the fox witches and badger wizards impose on human beings. Then at last I went to sleep, my head leaning on my arm for a pillow. But while I slept I saw arise before me the specter of a young girl, who might have been about sixteen. Her pale, haggard face peered through her long black hair, which fell in disorder to the ground. Red blood flowed from a wound in her body and stained her white raiment. At last she began to speak to me in trembling tones, giving me three objects which she held in her hands: 'Sadly taking my own life,' she said, 'at the moment when my youth was about to burst into bloom, and when I should have been a joy to my parents' hearts, I left them in inconsolable sorrow. All my regrets have not been enough to expiate this crime, and I am now condemned to suffer night and day in a lake of blood. But I have been told that I may be set free, and may enter the abodes of the blessed, if some one will make an offering for my soul of a thousand copies of the holy texts, and will bury on a holy mountain or in some sacred stream these three objects which I give to you. If this be not done, my soul will return to the earth, to be imprisoned in the body of some animal, and I shall never regain a human form. Ah! how happy would I be if I could change my wretched state for the happiness of eternal paradise. Therefore I beg you to journey to my native province, and to tell to my parents all that I have said to you.'

"Hardly had she uttered these words when her image disappeared like a wreath of mist which vanishes away in the sky. Only the murmur of a nearby spring broke the silence of that solitude. I noted it then, hearing it distinctly. I was awake, lying stretched at the root of the tree where I had lain down to rest. I had awakened indeed from a dream, but how could I explain this wonder? I really held in my hands the three objects which the specter had given to me! I lighted a fire of withered leaves, and examined them in the glow of the flame. They were a little bag filled with sacred objects, a linen sleeve, and a cord tied round a few locks of hair, the first cut from a baby's head. They were wrapped together in a piece of paper, on which was written her name, her abode, and the day of her birth. Here are the three objects!" said the Bonze, and ceased speaking.

The father and mother examined them attentively, and, to their great astonishment, recognized the inscription which they themselves had traced and placed in the tomb of their beloved. Unable to check their feelings, they burst into sobs, and knew not what to do or say. Finally wiping away the tears which trickled over his cheeks, Uwozumi said:

"To-day is the very anniversary of the death of our dear child, and I cannot for a moment doubt that she came to you to implore your protection, to save her from the place of punishment. We pray you, therefore, venerable priest, to visit for her all the holy places of the west, and to bury these three objects, as she instructed you. As for the thousand copies of the holy texts, we will pay you for them twice, four times their value. Have pity on our tears, and grant us what we beg of you." Then they offered five hundred gold pieces to the pilgrim Bonze, as the price of the holy texts, and a hundred more for the cost of his journey.

But the Bonze shook his head, and replied: "We Bonze pilgrims pass our lives in traveling from place to place. What use, then, would money be to me? Our home is in every mountain, every river, every place where our footsteps rest." Saying this, he rose and made ready to take leave of his sorrow-stricken hosts. But they held him by the sleeve, and begged him to accept their money. Resisting until they forced him to comply, he at last accepted it, and said, as he departed: "Remember that, despite my age, despite the weariness of my long journey, I consent to do what you demand, in favor of your daughter and all your family."

"Oh, venerable saint!" they cried, falling down before him, their hands joined in entreaty. All the family accompanied him far on his way, and at last the Bonze departed, his pilgrim's staff in his hands.

The bystanders watched him depart, and disappear gradually from view, and even after he was out of sight their eyes remained fixed on the spot where he had disappeared, and they thought they still could see him, so deeply was his image graven on their minds.

After he had traveled seven or eight leagues, the Bonze plunged into a forest, and directed his steps toward an old ruined temple, which was in the depths of the forest. At the sound of his steps the door opened, and a young man ran to meet him.

The Bonze pulled off his wig and false beard, and showed his real form, young and vigorous. The two looked at each other and exchanged a smile. "Well played!" cried the young man. "It could not have been better planned," replied the other. "Now to Niigata to taste the sweets of life." So dividing their plunder, they set out. The false

Bonze was the young man who had visited Yuki-no's tomb, whence he had taken the three objects which served to confirm his story.

The Dishonest Goldsmith and the Ingenious Painter

From the Turkish

IT is narrated by a person of veracity that once in the land of Adjem (Persia) a master goldsmith and a painter of talent for a time formed an association together, and lived on terms of brotherly intimacy. After this, being disposed to travel, they entered into a covenant to remain faithful to each other, and not to go one step beyond their association—that one should not act without the consent of the other, nor in any manner be treacherous to the other's interests.

Having made this agreement, they set out upon their journey. Their means being rather limited, on coming to a great convent, they put up there as guests. The monks of that convent, being pleased with them, showed them respect and tokens of esteem. They, particularly the painter, covered the walls of the convent with curious paintings; and the monks paid him much attention, and begged them to remain awhile with them. Having assented to this, they spent some time in the convent; and the monks placed so much confidence in them as to disclose to them the places containing the gold and silver idols of the convent. So one day they collected all these idols, and at night they made their escape with them. On reaching a city in a country of Islamites, they took up their abode there; when, according to their agreement, they put the gold and silver into a box, and spent only as much of it as their necessities required.

It so happened that the goldsmith married a parson's daughter, and the expenses of the association were thus increased. In the course of time the wife bore her husband two children; and one day, when the other was absent, the goldsmith opened the box containing the treasures, and, stealing away one half of the gold and silver, carried it to his own dwelling. On the painter's return he remarked that the box had been opened, and a portion of the contents taken out. When he questioned the goldsmith about it, the latter said that he had not touched it, and denied the theft.

Now the painter was a cunning fellow, and he immediately saw that the matter required good management. In the vicinity of their residence lived a huntsman, to whom he applied to procure him two bear cubs, for which he promised to pay him handsomely. The hunter consenting, he was soon furnished with the cubs, which the painter took and tamed. There was in that city also a carpenter; and, going to his shop, he bought of him the figure of a man made out of wood, and returned home. He then painted the figure, so that it was quite impossible to tell it from the goldsmith. This he put in a place by itself; and when the bear cubs were to be fed, he always had it done from the hand of the figure, until they became in time so accustomed to the sight of it as to treat it like their father or mother.

One day the painter invited the goldsmith to his house; and he accordingly came, bringing his two young sons with him. He treated them hospitably, and they passed the night there. On the following day he put the sons of the goldsmith in a secret part of his house; and when the father asked permission to take his leave he inquired for his sons. The painter replied, "An occurrence has happened which may serve as an example to others; I am really ashamed to relate it to you." "What is it?" asked the goldsmith with surprise. The painter added, "Whilst your sons were at play, and running about, they both became suddenly metamorphosed into the form of two bear cubs; and the affliction which has befallen these two innocent children must have been sent on account of some great sin." The goldsmith became excessively grieved. "What does this mean?" exclaimed he; "and why have you done this to my sons?" They quarreled, and finally both went before the cadi of the place. The cadi and his associates were greatly surprised at the strangeness of the case. "What can this mean?" exclaimed they all. "Never has such a thing happened before since the coming of Mohammed. What are the evidences of this remarkable occurrence?" I am quite as much astonished at it as yourselves," answered the painter; "but if you will allow me, I will bring the two metamorphosed children into your presence. The case will then be clear, and we will see whether or not they recognize their father."

The cadi and his company at once agreed to have the cubs brought before them. "Let us see," said they, "and judge for ourselves." The painter had cunningly kept the cubs hungry from the preceding night; and he now brought them from his house to the Mehkemeh of the judge, and placed them opposite the goldsmith. The cubs, as soon as they saw the latter, supposing him to be the same figure which the painter had made, rushed toward him, licked his feet, and began caressing him. The cadi and those with him were much affected at the sight, and exclaimed that if the cubs had not recognized their father in the goldsmith, they certainly would not act as they did. The goldsmith was bewildered between doubt and conviction; and so taking the two cubs with him, he returned to the house of the painter, where he begged pardon for his fault, and avowed it. He also returned the gold and silver effects which he had stolen from the box, and placed them all before the painter; at the same time he acknowledged his fault, and repented of what he had done. He likewise begged that the painter would pray to God to restore his sons to man's form again. The painter now led away the cubs, and putting them into the same house in which he had confined the goldsmith's children, he sat up all the following night apparently engaged in prayer. Early the next morning he went for the boys, and taking them by the hand, brought them to their father, exclaiming, "God be praised! our prayers have been accepted"; and delivered them up to their parent. The goldsmith was very much rejoiced, and offered many thanks to the painter, after which he carried his sons home.

Now news of this occurrence became spread about in the city, and it was told how the two sons of the goldsmith, after becoming metamorphosed, were again restored to human shape. Upon this the cadi had the painter cited before him, and required him to relate the truth about the matter. The painter informed him that such and such a compact had been made between himself and the goldsmith; that the latter had acted so and so toward him, but that he was unable to prove the charge. "So I got up a ruse," said he, "to make him acknowledge the theft of the gold and silver, and succeeded by my skill in the art of painting." "Barik Allah!" exclaimed all those who heard the recital; "a person's talents should be such as these." They added also many compliments and praises to the painter on the ingenuity of his thought, and his success in laying so wise a plan.

The Craft of the Three Sharpers

From the Arabic

THERE were in time of yore three Sharpers who were wont every day in early morning to prowl forth and to prey, rummaging among the mounds which outlay the city. Therein each would find a silver bit of five parahs or its equivalent, after which the trio would foregather and buy whatso sufficed them for supper: they would also expend two half-dirhams upon Bast, which is Bhang (Hashish), and purchase a waxen taper with the other silver bit. They had hired a cell in the flank of a Wakalah, a caravansary without the walls, where they could sit at ease to solace themselves and eat their Hashish after lighting the candle, and enjoy their intoxication and consequent merriment till the noon o' night. Then they would sleep, again awaking at day-dawn when they would arise and seek for spoil, according to their custom, and ransack the heaps where at times they would hit upon a silvering of five dirhams and at other times a piece of four; and at eventide they would meet to spend together the dark hours, and they would expend everything they came by every day. For a length of time they pursued this path until, one day of the days, they made for the mounds as was their wont and went round searching the heaps from morning to evening without finding even a half-parah; wherefore they were troubled and they went away and nighted in their cell without meat or drink. When the next day broke they arose and repaired for booty, changing the places wherein they were wont to forage; but none of them found aught; and their breasts were straitened for lack of a find of dirhams wherewith to buy them supper. This lasted for three full-told and following days until hunger waxed hard upon them and vexation; so they said one to other, "Go we to the Sultan and let us serve him with a sleight, and each of us three shall claim to be a past master of some craft: haply Allah Almighty may incline his heart usward and he may largesse us with something to expend upon our necessities." Accordingly all three agreed to do on this wise and they sought the Sultan whom they found in the palace-garden. They asked leave to go in to him, but the Chamberlains refused admission: so they stood afar off unable to approach the presence. Then quoth they one to other, "'Twere better we fall to and each smite his comrade and cry aloud and make a clamor, and as soon as he shall hear us he will send to summon us." Accordingly they jostled one another and each took to frapping his fellow, making the while loud outcries. The Sultan hearing this turmoil said, "Bring me yonder wights"; and the Chamberlains and Eunuchs ran out to them and seized them and set them between the hands of the Sovereign. As soon as they stood in the presence he asked them, "What be the cause of your wrath one against other?" They answered, "O King of the Age, we are past masters of crafts, each of us weeting an especial art." Quoth the Sultan, "What be your crafts?" and quoth one of the trio, "O our Lord, as for my art I am a jeweler by trade." The King exclaimed, "Passing strange! a sharper and a jeweler: this is a wondrous matter." And he questioned the second Sharper saying, "And thou, the other, what may be thy craft?" He answered, "I am a genealogist of the horse-kind." So the King glanced at him in surprise and said to himself, "A sharper, yet he claimeth an astounding knowledge!" Then he left him and put the same question to the third who said to him, "O King of the Age, verily my art is more wondrous and marvelous than aught thou hast heard from these twain: their craft is easy, but mine is such that none save I can discover the right direction thereto or know the first of it from the last of it." The Sultan inquired of him, "And what be thy craft?" Whereto he replied, "My craft is the genealogy of the sons of Adam." Hearing these words the Sovereign wondered with extreme wonderment and said in himself, "Verily He informeth with His secrets the humblest of His creatures! Assuredly these men, an they speak truth in all they say and it prove soothfast, are fit for naught except kingship. But I will keep them by me until the occurrence of some nice contingency wherein I may test them; then, if they approve themselves good men and trustworthy of word, I will leave them on life; but if their speech be lying I will do them die." Upon this he set apart for them apartments and rationed them with three cakes of bread and a dish of roast meat and set over them his sentinels dreading lest they fly. This case continued for a while till behold, there came to the Sultan from the land of 'Ajam a present of rarities, among which were two gems whereof one was clear of water and the other was clouded of color. The Sultan hent them in hand for a time and fell to considering them straitly for the space of an hour; after which he called to mind the first of the three Sharpers, the self-styled jeweler, and cried,

"Bring me the jeweler-man." Accordingly they went and brought him and set him before the Sovereign who asked him, "O man, art thou a lapidary?" And when the Sharper answered "Yes" he gave him the clear-watered stone, saying, "What may be the price of this gem?" Then the Sharper took the jewel in hand and turned it rightward and leftward and considered the outside and pried into the inside; after which he said to the Sultan, "O my lord, verily this gem containeth a worm bred within the heart thereof." Now when the King heard these words he waxed wroth with exceeding wrath and commanded the man's head to be stricken off, saying, "This jewel is clear of color and free of flaw or other default; yet thou chargest it falsely with containing a worm!" Then he summoned the Linkman who laid hands on the Sharper and pinioned his elbows and trussed up his legs like a camel's and was about to smite his neck when behold, the Wazir entered the presence and, seeing the Sovereign in high dudgeon and the Sharper under the scimiter, asked what was to do. The Sultan related to him what had happened, when he drew near to him and said, "O my lord, act not after this fashion! An thou determine upon the killing of yonder man, first break the gem and, if thou find therein a worm, thou wilt know the wight's word to have been veridical; but an thou find it sound then strike off his head." "Right is thy rede," quoth the King: then he took in hand the gem and smote it with his mace and when it brake behold, he found therein the worm amiddlemost thereof. So he marveled at the sight and asked the man, "What proved to thee that it harbored a worm?" "The sharpness of my sight," answered the Sharper. Then the Sultan pardoned him and, admiring his power of vision, addressed his attendants saying, "Bear him back to his comrades and ration him with a dish of roast meat and two cakes of bread." And they did as he bade them. After some time, on a day of the days, there came to the King the tribute of 'Ajam-land accompanied with presents, among which was a colt whose robe black as night showed one shade in the sun and another in the shadow. When the animal was displayed to the Sultan he fell in love with it and set apart for it a stall and solaced himself at all times by gazing at it, and was wholly occupied with it and sang its praises till they filled the whole country side. Presently he remembered the Sharper who claimed to be a genealogist of the horse-kind and bade him be summoned. So they fared forth and brought him and set him between the hands of the Sovereign who said to him, "Art thou he who knoweth the breed and descent of horses?" "Yea verily," said the man. Then cried the King, "By the truth of Him who set me upon the necks of His servants and who sayeth to a thing 'Be' and it becometh, an I find aught of error or confusion in thy words, I will strike off thy head." "Hearkening and obedience," quoth the Sharper. Then they led him to the colt that he might consider its genealogy. He called aloud to the groom, and when they brought him he bade the man back the colt for his inspection. So he mounted the animal and made it pace to the right and to the left, causing it now to prance and curvet and then to step leisurely, while the connoisseur looked on and after a time quoth he to the groom, "'Tis enough!" Then he went in to the presence and stood between the hands of the King who inquired, "What hast thou seen in the colt, O Kashmar?" Replied the Sharper, "By Allah, O King of the Age, this colt is of pure and noble blood on the side of the sire: its action is excellent and all its qualities are praiseworthy save one; and but for this one it had been perfect in blood and breed nor had there been on earth's face its fellow in horseflesh. But its blemish remaineth a secret." The Sultan asked, "And what is the quality which thou blamest?" and the Sharper answered, "Its sire was noble, but its dam was of other strain: she it was that brought the blemish and if thou, O my lord, allow me I will notify it to thee." "'Tis well, and needs must thou declare it," quoth the Sultan. Then said the Sharper, "Its dam is a buffalo-cow." When the King heard these words he was wroth with wrath exceeding and he bade the Linkman take the Sharper and behead him, crying, "O dog! O accursed!

How can a buffalo-cow bear a horse?" The Sharper replied, "O my lord, the Linkman is in the presence; but send and fetch him who brought thee the colt and of him make inquiry. If my words prove true and rightly placed, my skill shall be stablished; but an they be lies let my head pay forfeit for my tongue. Here standeth the Linkman and I am between thy hands: thou hast but to bid him strike off my head!" Thereupon the King sent for the owner and breeder of the colt and they brought him to the presence. And the Sultan asked him saying, "Tell me the truth anent the blood of this colt. Didst thou buy it or breed it so that it was a rearling of thy homestead?" Said he, "By Allah, O King of the Age, I will speak naught which is not sooth, for indeed there hangeth by this colt the strangest story: were it graven with graver-needles upon the eye-corners it had been a warning to whoso would be warned. And this it is. I had a stallion of purest strain whose sire was of the steeds of the sea; and he was stabled in a stall apart for fear of the evil eye, his service being intrusted to trusty servants. But one day in springtide the Syce took the horse into the open and allowed him to mate with a buffalo-cow. She conceived by him and when her days were completed and her throwing-time came she suffered sore pains and bare yonder colt. And all who have seen it or have heard of it were astounded," said he, presently adding, "By Allah, O King of the Age, had its dam been of the mare-kind the colt would have had no equal on earth's surface or aught approaching it." Hereat the Sultan took thought and marveled; then, summoning the Sharper he said to him when present, "O man, thy speech is true and thou art indeed a genealogist in horseflesh and thou wottest it well. But I would know what proved to thee that the dam of this colt was a buffalo-cow?" Said he, "O King, my proof thereof was palpable nor can it be concealed from any wight of right wits and intelligence and special knowledge; for the horse's hoof is round while the hooves of buffaloes are elongated and duck-shaped, and hereby I kenned that this colt was a jumart, the issue of a cow-buffalo." The Sultan was pleased with his words and said, "Ration him with a plate of roast meat and two cakes of bread"; and they did as they were bidden. Now for a length of time the third Sharper was forgotten till one day the Sultan bethought him of the man who could explain the genealogy of Adam's sons. So he bade fetch him and when they brought him into the presence he said, "Thou art he that knowest the caste and descent of men and women?" and the other said, "Yes." Then he commanded the Eunuchs take him to his wife and place him before her and cause him declare her genealogy. So they led him in and set him standing in her presence, and the Sharper considered her for a while, looking from right to left; then he fared forth to the Sultan who asked him, "What hast thou seen in the Queen?" Answered he, "O my lord, I saw a somewhat adorned with loveliness and beauty and perfect grace, with fair stature of symmetrical trace and with modesty and fine manners and skillful case; and she is one in whom all good qualities appear on every side, nor is aught of accomplishments or knowledge concealed from her, and haply in her center all desirable attributes. Natheless, O King of the Age, there is a curious point that dishonoreth her, from the which were she free none would outshine her of all the women of her generation." Now when the Sultan heard the words of the Sharper, he sprang hastily to his feet and clapping hand upon hilt bared his brand and fell upon the man, purposing to slay him; but the Chamberlains and the Eunuchs prevented him saying, "O our lord, kill him not until his falsehood or his fact shall have been made manifest to thee." The Sultan said to him, "What then appeared to thee in my Queen?" "She is ferly fair," said the man, "but her mother is a dancing-girl, a gypsy." The fury of the King increased hereat and he sent to summon the inmates of his Harem and cried to his father-in-law, "Unless thou speak me sooth concerning thy daughter and her descent and her mother I"— He replied, "By Allah, O King of the Age, naught saveth a man save soothfastness! Her mother indeed was a Ghaziyah: in past time a party of the tribe was passing by my abode when a young maid strayed from her fellows and was lost. They asked no questions concerning her; so I lodged her and bred her in my homestead till she grew up to be a great girl and the fairest of her time. My heart would not brook her wiving with any other; so I wedded her and she bare me this daughter whom thou, O King, hast espoused." When the Sultan heard these words the flame in his heart was quenched and he wondered at the subtlety of the Sharper man; so he summoned him and asked him saying, "O wily one, tell me what certified to thee that my Queen had a dancing-girl, a gypsy, to mother?" He answered, "O King of the Age, verily the Ghaziyah race hath eye-balls intensely black and bushy brows, whereas other women than the Ghaziyah have the reverse of this." On such wise the King was convinced of the man's skill and he cried, "Ration him with a dish of roast meat and two scones." They did as he bade and the three Sharpers tarried with the Sultan a long time till one day when the King said to himself, "Verily these three men have by their skill solved every question of genealogy which I proposed to them: first the jeweler proved his perfect knowledge of gems; secondly the genealogist of the horse-kind showed himself as skillful, and the same was the case with the genealogist of mankind, for he discovered the origin of my Queen and the truth of his words appeared from all quarters. Now 'tis my desire that he do the same with me that I also may know my provenance." Accordingly they set the man between his hands and he said to him, "O fellow, hast thou the power to tell me mine origin?" Said the Sharper, "Yes, O my lord, I can trace thy descent, but I will so do only upon a condition; to wit, that thou promise me safety after what I shall have told thee; for the saw saith, 'Whilst Sultan sitteth on throne 'ware his despite, inasmuch as none may be contumacious when he saith 'Smite.'" Thereupon the Sultan told him, "Thou hast a promise of immunity, a promise which shall never be falsed." And the man said, "O King of the Age, when as I acquaint thee with thy root and branch, let it be between us twain lest these present hear us." "Wherefore O man?" asked the Sultan, and the Sharper answered, "O my lord, Allah of Allmight hath among His names 'The Veiler'"; wherefore the King bade his Chamberlains and Eunuchs retire so that none remained in the place save those two. Then the Sharper came forward and said, "O my lord, thou art not the son of a king." As soon as the King heard these words his case changed and his color waxed wan and his limbs fell loose: he foamed at the mouth; he lost hearing and sight; he became as one drunken without wine and he fell fainting to the ground. After a while he recovered and said to the Sharper, "Now by the truth of Him who hath set me upon the necks of His servants, and thy words be veridical and I ascertain their sooth by proof positive, I will assuredly abdicate my Kingdom and resign my realm to thee, because none deserveth it save thou and it becometh us least of all and every. But an I find thy speech lying I will slay thee. He replied, "Hearing and obeying"; and the Sovereign, rising up without stay or delay, went inside to his mother with grip on glaive, and said to her, "By the truth of Him who uplifted the sky above the earth, an thou answer me not with the whole truth in whatso I ask thee, I will cut thee to little bits with this blade." She inquired, "What dost thou want with me?" and he replied, "Whose son am I, and what may be my descent?" She rejoined, "Although falsehood be an excuse, fact and truth are superior and more saving. Thou art indeed the very son of a cook. The Sultan that was before thee took me to wife but we had no issue; and he would mourn and groan from the core of his heart for that he had no seed, nor girl nor boy; neither could he enjoy aught of sweet food or sleep. Now it chanced that the wife of the Kitchener bare him a boy, and I prevailed upon her to keep the birth secret; and my women brought the child to me, and spread abroad that at last an heir was come. Now at that time the Sultan was hunting and birding and enjoying himself about the gardens; and when the bearer of good news went to him and announced the birth of a man-child he hurried back to me and forthright bade them decorate the capital and he found the report true; so the city adorned itself for forty days in honor of its King. Such is my case and my tale." Thereupon the King went forth from her to the Sharper and bade him doff his dress, and when this had been done he doffed his own raiment and habited the man in royal gear and hooded him with the Taylasan and asked him saying, "What proof hast thou of my being base born?" The Sharper answered, "O my lord, my proof was thy bidding our being rationed, after showing the perfection of our skill, with a dish of roast meat and two scones of bread; whereby I knew thee to be of cook's breed, for the Kings be wont in such case to make presents of money and valuables, not of meat and bread as thou didst, and this evidenced thee to be no king's son, but a cook's son." He replied, "Sooth thou sayest," and then robed him with the rest of his robes including the Kalansuwah or royal head-dress under the hood, and seating him upon the throne of his estate, went forth from him after abandoning all his women to him and assumed the garb of a Darwaysh who wandereth about the world and formally abdicated his dominion to his successor. But when the Sharper-king saw himself in this condition, he reflected and said to himself, "Summon thy whilom comrades and see whether they recognize thee or not." So he caused them be set before him and conversed with them; then, perceiving that none knew him he gifted them and sent them to gang their gait. And he ruled his realm and bade and forbade and gave and took away and was gracious and generous to each and every of his lieges; so that the people of that region who were his subjects blessed him and prayed for him.

The Cheerful Workman

From the Arabic

IT is mentioned in the celebrated Arabic work entitled the "Mirror of the Age," that one of the caliphs of the house of Abbass, Mutâsid Billah, besides being a very brave and courageous person, was also possessed of keen observation, and the faculty of knowing men by their physiognomy. One day as he was inspecting the erection of a palace on the banks of the Tigris, which he was wont to do once a week, and encourage the builders with presents and other acts of favor, he observed that each of the men employed carrying stones to the edifice bore but one at a time, and that with great gravity and slowness. Among them, however, he perceived one, with black hands and dark complexion, who invariably lifted two at a time, put them on his back, and with evident joy and elasticity carried them from the wharf to the masons. On seeing this, the caliph pointed him out to Hussian, one of his attendants, and asked the cause of this man's unnatural gayety. The attendant answered that the caliph was more competent to form an opinion of the case than himself. The caliph then added that the man was probably possessed of a large sum of money, and was therefore happy from the consciousness of his wealth; or, that he was a thief, who had only sought employment among the workmen for the purpose of concealment. "I do not like his appearance," continued the Prince of the Faithful; "have him brought into my presence."

So, when the man was come, the caliph asked him what his occupation was, and he answered that he was a common laborer. "Have you any money laid by?" demanded the caliph. "None," replied the man. "Tell me the truth," again asked the caliph, repeating the question, and again the man answered in the negative.

Then the caliph ordered an officer to strike the man,

which being done, he immediately cried out for pity and pardon. "Speak the truth," said the officer, "or the caliph will punish you as long as you live." So the man avowed that his trade was that of a tilemaker; and one day, added he, "when I had prepared my kiln, and lit the fire, a man approached me, mounted on an ass, who, dismounting before my kiln, let the ass go, and beginning to undress himself, took from around his waist a girdle, which he placed by his side and began fleaing himself. I, seeing that the man was quite alone, caught him, and throwing him into the furnace of my kiln, closed it down. I then took his girdle, and after killing the ass threw it also into the fire. See, here is the girdle." The caliph took it, and on examining it found it contained some thousands of gold pieces, and, moreover, had its owner's name written upon it. On this discovery the caliph sent criers out, to ask in the streets whether any family had lost a member, or a friend, and if so, to come before him. Soon an aged woman approached, and exclaimed, "My son left me with some thousands of pieces of gold, with which to buy merchandise, and is lost." They showed her the girdle, which she immediately recognized as her son's, and said that it had his name upon it.

The caliph now gave the girdle into the old woman's hands, saying, "See before you the murderer of your son." She demanded the right of retaliation, and the man was forthwith hung upon the door of him whom he had murdered.

All the world admired the caliph's sagacity and commended his justice.

The Robber and the Woman

From the Arabic

A CERTAIN Robber was a cunning workman and used not to steal aught, till he had wasted all that was with him; moreover, he stole not from his neighbors, neither companied with any of the thieves, for fear lest some one should betray him, and his case become public. After this fashion he abode a great while, in flourishing condition, and his secret was concealed, till Almighty Allah decreed that he broke in upon a beggar, a poor man whom he deemed rich. When he gained access to the house, he found naught, whereat he was wroth, and necessity prompted him to wake that man, who lay asleep alongside of his wife. So he aroused him and said to him, "Show me thy treasure." Now he had no treasure to show; but the Robber believed him not and was instant upon him with threats and blows. When he saw that he got no profit of him, he said to him, "Swear by the oath of divorce from thy wife that thou hast nothing." So he swore and his wife said to him, "Fie on thee! Wilt thou divorce me? Is not the hoard buried in yonder chamber?" Then she turned to the Robber and conjured him to be weightier of blows upon her husband, till he should deliver to him the treasure, anent which he had forsworn himself. So he drubbed him with a grievous drubbing, till he carried him to a certain chamber, wherein she signed to him that the hoard was and that he should take it up. So the Robber entered, he and the husband; and when they were both in the chamber, she locked on them the door, which was a stout and strong, and said to the Robber, "Woe to thee, O fool! Thou hast fallen into the trap and now I have but to cry out and the officers of police will come and take thee and thou wilt lose thy life, O Satan!" Quoth he, "Let me go forth"; and quoth she, "Thou art a man and I am a woman; and in thy hand is a knife, and I am afraid of thee." He cried, "Take the knife from me." So she took it and said to her husband, "Art thou a woman and he a man? Pain his necknape with flogging, even as he flogged thee; and if he put out his hand to thee, I will cry out a single cry and the policemen will come and take him and hew him in two." So the husband said to him, "O thousand-horned, O dog, O dodger, I owe thee a deposit wherefore thou hast dunned me." And he fell to bashing him grievously with a stick of holm-oak, while he called out to the woman for help and prayed her to deliver him: but she said, "Keep thy place till the morning, and thou shalt see queer things." And her husband beat him within the chamber, till he overcame him and he swooned away. Then he left beating him and when the Robber came to himself, the woman said to her husband, "O man, this house is on hire and we owe its owners much money, and we have naught; so how wilt thou do?" And she went on to bespeak him thus. The Robber asked, "And what is the amount of the rent?" The husband answered, "'Twill be eighty dirhams"; and the thief said, "I will pay this for thee and do thou let me go my way." Then the wife inquired, "O man, how much do we owe the baker and the greengrocer?" Quoth the Robber, "What is the sum of this?" And the husband said, "Sixty dirhams." Rejoined the other, "That makes two hundred dirhams; let me go my way and I will pay them." But the wife said, "O my dear, and the girl groweth up and needs must we marry her and equip her and do what else is needful." So the Robber said to the husband, "How much dost thou want?" and he rejoined, "An hundred dirhams in a modest way." Quoth the Robber, "That maketh three hundred dirhams." Then the woman said, "O my dear, when the girl is married, thou wilt need money for winter expenses, charcoal and firewood and other necessaries." The Robber asked, "What wouldst thou have?" And she answered, "An hundred dirhams." He rejoined, "Be it four hundred dirhams." And she continued, "O my dear and O coolth of mine eyes, needs must my husband have capital in hand, wherewith he may buy goods and open him a shop." Said he, "How much will that be?" And she, "An hundred dirhams." Quoth the Robber, "That maketh five hundred dirhams; I will pay it; but may I be triply divorced from my wife if all my possessions amount to more than this, and they be the savings of twenty years! Let me go my way, so I may deliver them to thee." Cried she, "O fool, how shall I let thee go thy way? Utterly impossible! Be pleased to give me a right token." So he gave her a token for his wife and she cried out to her young daughter and said to her, "Keep this door." Then she charged her husband to watch over the Robber till she should return, and repairing to his wife, acquainted her with his case and told her that her husband the thief had been taken and had compounded for his release, at the price of seven hundred dirhams, and named to her the token. Accordingly, she gave her the money and she took it and returned to her house. By this time, the dawn had dawned; so she let the thief go his way, and when he went out, she said to him, "O my dear, when shall I see thee come and take the treasure?" And he, "O indebted one, when thou needest other seven hundred dirhams, wherewith to amend thy case and that of thy children and to pay thy debts." And he went out, hardly believing in his deliverance from her.

The Wonderful Stone

From the Chinese

IN the prefecture of Shun-t'ien[1] there lived a man named Hsing Yün-fei, who was an amateur mineralogist and would pay any price for a good specimen. One day as he was fishing in the river something caught his net, and diving down he brought up a stone about a foot in diameter, beautifully carved on all sides to resemble clustering hills and peaks.

[1] In which Peking is situated.

He was quite as pleased with this as if he had found some precious stone; and having had an elegant sandal-wood stand made for it, he set his prize upon the table. Whenever it was about to rain, clouds, which from a distance looked like new cottonwool, would come forth from each of the holes or grottoes on the stone, and appear to close them up. By-and-by an influential personage called at the house and begged to see the stone, immediately seizing it and handing it over to a lusty servant, at the same time whipping his horse and riding away. Hsing was in despair; but all he could do was to mourn the loss of his stone, and indulge his anger against the thief. Meanwhile, the servant, who had carried off the stone on his back, stopped to rest at a bridge, when all of a sudden his hand slipped and the stone fell into the water. His master was extremely put out at this, and gave him a sound beating; subsequently hiring several divers, who tried every means in their power to recover the stone, but were quite unable to find it. He then went away, having first published a notice of reward, and by these means many were tempted to seek for the stone. Soon after, Hsing himself came to the spot, and as he mournfully approached the bank, lo! the water became clear, and he could see the stone lying at the bottom. Taking off his clothes he quickly jumped in and brought it out, together with the sandal-wood stand which was still with it. He carried it off home, but being no longer desirous of showing it to people, he had an inner room cleaned and put it in there. Some time afterwards an old man knocked at the door and asked to be allowed to see the stone; whereupon Hsing replied that he had lost it a long time ago. "Isn't that it in the inner room?" said the old man, smiling. "Oh, walk in and see for yourself if you don't believe me," answered Hsing; and the old man did walk in, and there was the stone on the table. This took Hsing very much aback; and the old man then laid his hand upon the stone and said, "This is an old family relic of mine: I lost it many months since. How does it come to be here? I pray you now restore it to me." Hsing didn't know what to say, but declared he was the owner of the stone; upon which the old man remarked, "If it is really yours, what evidence can you bring to prove it?" Hsing made no reply; and the old man continued, "To show you that I know this stone, I may mention that it has altogether ninety-two grottoes, and that in the largest of these are five words:

'A stone from Heaven above.'"

Hsing looked and found that there were actually some small characters, no larger than grains of rice, which by straining his eyes a little he managed to read; also that the number of grottoes was as the old man had said. However, he would not give him the stone; and the old man laughed, and asked, "Pray, what right have you to keep other people's things?" He then bowed and went away, Hsing escorting him as far as the door; but when he returned to the room the stone had disappeared. In a great fright, he ran after the old man, who had walked slowly and was not far off, and seizing his sleeve entreated him to give back the stone. "Do you think," said the latter, "that I could conceal a stone a foot in diameter in my sleeve?" But Hsing knew that he must be superhuman, and led him back to the house, where he threw himself on his knees and begged that he might have the stone. "Is it yours or mine?" asked the old man. "Of course it is yours," replied Hsing, "though I hope you will consent to deny yourself the pleasure of keeping it." "In that case," said the old man, "it is back again"; and going into the inner room they found the stone in its old place. "The jewels of this world," observed Hsing's visitor, "should be given to those who know how to take care of them. This stone can choose its own master, and I am very pleased that it should remain with you; at the same time I must inform you that it was in too great a hurry to come into the world of mortals, and has not yet been freed from all contingent calamities. I had better take it away with me, and three years hence you shall have it again. If, however, you insist on keeping it, then your span of life will be shortened by three years, that your terms of existence may harmonize together. Are you willing?" Hsing said he was; whereupon the old man with his fingers closed up three of the stone's grottoes, which yielded to his touch like mud. When this was done, he turned to Hsing and told him that the grottoes on that stone represented the years of his life; and then he took his leave, firmly refusing to remain any longer, and not disclosing his name.

More than a year after this, Hsing had occasion to go away on business, and in the night a thief broke in and carried off the stone, taking nothing else at all. When Hsing came home, he was dreadfully grieved, as if his whole object in life was gone; and made all possible inquiries and efforts to get it back, but without the slightest result. Some time passed away, when one day going into a temple Hsing noticed a man selling stones, and among the rest he saw his old friend. Of course he immediately wanted to regain possession of it; but as the stone-seller would not consent, he shouldered the stone and went off to the nearest mandarin. The stone-seller was then asked what proof he could give that the stone was his; and he replied that the number of grottoes was eighty-nine. Hsing inquired if that was all he had to say, and when the other acknowledged that it was, he himself told the magistrate what were the characters inscribed within, also calling attention to the finger marks at the closed-up grottoes. He therefore gained his case, and the mandarin would have bambooed the stone-seller, had he not declared that he bought it in the market for twenty ounces of silver,—whereupon he was dismissed.

A high official next offered Hsing one hundred ounces of silver for it; but he refused to sell it even for ten thousand, which so enraged the would-be purchaser that he worked up a case against Hsing[1] and got him put in prison. Hsing

[1] A common form of revenge in China, and one which is easily carried through when the prosecutor is a man of wealth and influence.

was thereby compelled to pawn a great deal of his property; and then the official sent some one to try if the affair could not be managed through his son, to which Hsing, on hearing of the attempt, steadily refused to consent, saying that he and the stone could not be parted even in death. His wife, however, and his son, laid their heads together, and sent the stone to the high official, and Hsing only heard of it when he arrived home from the prison. He cursed his wife and beat his son, and frequently tried to make away with himself, though luckily his servants always managed to prevent him from succeeding.[1] At night he dreamed that a noble-looking personage appeared to him, and said, "My name is Shih Ch'ing-hsü (Stone from Heaven). Do not grieve. I purposely quitted you for a year and more; but next year on the 20th of the eighth moon, at dawn, come to the Hai-tai Gate and buy me back for two strings of cash." Hsing was overjoyed at this dream, and carefully took down the day mentioned. Meanwhile the stone was at the official's private house; but as the cloud manifestations ceased, the stone was less and less prized; and the following year when the official was disgraced for maladministration and subsequently died, Hsing met some of his servants at the Hai-tai Gate going off to sell the stone, and purchased it back from them for two strings of cash.

Hsing lived till he was eighty-nine; and then having prepared the necessaries for his interment, bade his son bury the stone with him,[2] which was accordingly done. Six months later robbers broke into the vault[3] and made off with the stone, and his son tried in vain to secure their capture; however, a few days afterwards, he was trav-

[1] Another favorite method of revenging oneself upon an enemy, who is in many cases held responsible for the death thus occasioned.

[2] Valuables of some kind or other are often placed in the coffins of wealthy Chinese; and women are almost always provided with a certain quantity of jewels with which to adorn themselves in the realms below.

[3] One of the most heinous offenses in the Chinese Penal Code.

eling with his servants, when suddenly two men rushed forth dripping with perspiration, and looking up into the air, acknowledged their crime, saying, " Mr. Hsing, please don't torment us thus! We took the stone, and sold it for only four ounces of silver." Hsing's son and his servants then seized these men, and took them before the magistrate, where they at once acknowledged their guilt. Asking what had become of the stone, they said they had sold it to a member of the magistrate's family; and when it was produced, that official took such a fancy to it that he gave it to one of his servants and bade him place it in the treasury. Thereupon the stone slipped out of the servant's hand and broke into a hundred pieces, to the great astonishment of all present. The magistrate now had the thieves bambooed and sent them away; but Hsing's son picked up the broken pieces of the stone and buried them in his father's grave.

The Weaver Who Became a Leach

From the Arabic

THERE was once, in the land of Fars (Persia), a man who wedded a woman higher than himself in rank and nobler of lineage, but she had no guardian to preserve her from want. She loathed to marry one who was beneath her; yet she wived with him because of need, and took of him a bond in writing to the effect that he would ever be under her order to bid and forbid and would never thwart her in word or in deed. Now the man was a Weaver and he bound himself in writing to pay his wife ten thousand dirhams in case of default. After such fashion they abode a long while till one day the wife went out to fetch water, of which she had need, and saw a leach who had spread a carpet hard by the road, whereon he had set out great store of simples and implements of medicine and he was speaking and muttering charms, whilst the folk flocked to him from all quarters and girt him about on every side. The Weaver's wife marveled at the largeness of the physician's fortune and said in herself, "Were my husband thus, he would lead an easy life and that wherein we are of straitness and poverty would be widened to him." Then she returned home, cark-full and care-full; and when her husband saw her in this condition, he questioned her of her case and she said to him, "Verily, my breast is narrowed by reason of thee and of the very goodness of thine intent," presently adding, "Narrow means suit me not and thou in thy present craft gainest naught; so either do thou seek out a business other than this or pay me my rightful due and let me wend my ways." Her husband chid her for this and advised her to take patience; but she would not be turned from her design and said to him, "Go forth and watch yonder physician how he doth and learn from him what he saith." Said he, "Let not thy heart be troubled," and added, "I will go every day to the session of the leach." So he began resorting daily to the physician and committing to memory his answers and that which he spoke of jargon, till he had gotten a great matter by rote, and all this he learned and thoroughly digested it. Then he returned to his wife and said to her, "I have stored up the physician's sayings in memory and have mastered his manner of muttering and diagnoses and prescribing remedies, and I wot by heart the names of the medicines and of all the diseases, and there abideth of thy bidding naught undone: so what dost thou command me now to do?" Quoth she, "Leave the loom and open thyself a leach's shop"; but quoth he, "My fellow-townsmen know me and this affair will not profit me, save in a land of strangerhood; so come, let us go out from this city and get us to a foreign land and there live." And she said, "Do whatso thou willest." Accordingly, he arose and taking his weaving gear, sold it and bought with the price drugs and simples and wrought himself a carpet, with which they set out and journeyed to a certain village, where they took up their abode. Then the man fell to going round about the hamlets and villages and outskirts of towns, after donning leach's dress; and he began to earn his livelihood and make much gain. Their affairs prospered and their circumstances were bettered; wherefore they praised Allah for their present ease and the village became to them a home. In this way he lived for a long time, but at length he wandered anew, and the days and the nights ceased not to transport him from country to country, till he came to the land of the Roum (Greeks) and lighted down in a city thereof, wherein was Jalinus (Galen) the sage; but the Weaver knew him not, nor was aware who he was. So he fared forth, as was his wont, in quest of a place where the folk might be gathered together, and hired the courtyard of Jalinus. There he spread his carpet and setting out on it his simples and instruments of medicine, praised himself and his skill and claimed a cleverness such as none but he might claim. Jalinus heard that which he affirmed of his understanding, and it was certified unto him and established in his mind that the man was a skilled leach of the leaches of the Persians and he said in himself, "Unless he had confidence in his knowledge and were minded to confront me and contend with me, he had not sought the door of my house, neither had he spoken that which he hath spoken." And care and doubt got hold upon Jalinus: so he drew near the Weaver and addressed himself to see how his doings should end, whilst the folk began to flock to him and describe to him their ailments, and he would answer them thereof, hitting the mark one while and missing it another while, so that naught appeared to Jalinus of his fashion whereby his mind might be assured that he had justly estimated his skill. Presently, up came a woman, and when the Weaver saw her afar off, he said to her, "Is not your husband a Jew and is not his ailment flatulence?" "Yes," replied the woman, and the folk marveled at this; wherefore the man was magnified in the eyes of Jalinus, for that he heard speech such as was not of the usage of doctors. Then the woman asked, "What is the remedy?" and the Weaver answered, "Bring the honorarium." So she paid him a dirham and he gave her medicines contrary to that ailment and such as would only aggravate the complaint. When Jalinus saw what appeared to him of the man's incapacity, he turned to his disciples and pupils and bade them fetch the mock doctor, with all his gear and drugs. Accordingly they brought him into his presence without stay or delay, and when Jalinus saw him before him, he asked him, "Knowest thou me?" and the other answered, "No, nor did I ever set eyes on thee before this day." Quoth the sage, "Dost thou know Jalinus?" and quoth the Weaver, "No." Then said Jalinus, "What drove thee to do that which thou dost?" So he acquainted him with his adventure, especially with the dowry and the obligation by which he was bound with regard to his wife, whereat the sage marveled and certified himself anent the matter of the marriage-settlement. Then he bade lodge him near himself and entreated him with kindness and took him apart and said to him, "Expound to me whence thou knewest that the woman was from a man, and he a stranger and a Jew, and that his ailment was flatulence?" The Weaver replied, "'Tis well. Thou must know that we people of Persia are skilled in physiognomy, and I saw the woman to be rosy-cheeked, blue-eyed, and tall-statured. These qualities belong not to the women of Roum; moreover, I saw her burning with anxiety; so I knew that the patient was her husband. As for his strangerhood, I noted that the dress of the woman differed from that of the townsfolk, wherefore I knew that she was a foreigner; and in her hand I saw a yellow rag, which garred me wot that the sick man was a Jew and she a Jewess. Moreover, she came to me on First Day; and 'tis the Jew's custom to take meat-puddings and food that hath passed the night and eat them on the Saturday their Sabbath, hot and cold, and they exceed in eating; wherefore flatulence and indigestion betide them. Thus I was directed and guessed that which thou hast heard." Now when Jalinus heard this, he ordered the Weaver the amount of his wife's dowry and bade him pay it to her and said to him, "Divorce her." Furthermore, he forbade him from returning to the practice of physic and warned him never again to take to wife a woman of rank higher than his own; and he gave him his spending-money and charged him to return to his proper craft.

Viśākhā

From the Tibetan

MṚGADHARA, the first minister of King Prasenajit of Kośala, after he had married a wife of birth like unto his own, had seven sons. To six of these he gave names at his pleasure, but the youngest one he called Viśākha.

After his wife's death he arranged marriages for his six elder sons, but they and their wives gave themselves up to dress, and troubled themselves in no wise with household affairs.

The householder Mṛgadhara was sitting one day absorbed in thought, resting his cheek upon his arm. A Brahman, who was on friendly terms with him, saw him sitting thus absorbed in thought, and asked him what was the cause of his behavior. He replied, "My sons and their wives have given themselves up to dress, and do not trouble themselves about household affairs, so that the property is going to ruin."

"Why do you not arrange a marriage for Viśākha?"

"Who can tell whether he will make things better, or bring them to still greater ruin?"

"If you will trust to me, I will look for a maiden for him."

The minister consented, and the Brahman went his way. In the course of his researches he came to the land of Champā. In it there lived a householder named Balamitra, whose daughter Viśākhā was fair to see, well proportioned, in the bloom of youth, intelligent and clever. Just as the Brahman arrived, she and some other girls who were in quest of amusement were setting out for a park. On seeing the girls, he thought that he would like to look at them a little. So he followed slowly after them, occupied in regarding them. The girls, who were for the most part of a frivolous nature, sometimes ran, sometimes skipped, sometimes rolled about, sometimes laughed, sometimes spun round, sometimes sang, and did other undignified things. But Viśākhā, with the utmost decorum, at an even pace walked slowly along with them. When they came to the park, the other girls undressed at the edge of the tank, entered into it, and began to sport. But Viśākhā lifted up her clothes by degrees as she went into the water, and by degrees let them down again as she came out of the water, so circumspect was she in her behavior. After their bath, when the girls had assembled at a certain spot, they first partook of food themselves, and then gave to their attendants to eat; but Viśākhā first of all gave food to the persons in attendance, and then herself began to eat.

When the girls had finished their eating and drinking and had enjoyed the charm of the park, they went away. As there was water to be waded through on the road, the girls took off their boots and walked through it, but Viśākhā kept her boots on. They went a little farther and came to a wood. Into this Amra wood she entered, keeping her parasol up, though the others had discarded theirs. Presently a wind arose together with rain, and the other girls took shelter in a temple, but Viśākhā remained in the open air. The Brahman, who had followed her, and had noted her characteristics and her behavior, marveled greatly and began to question her, saying:

"O maiden, whose daughter are you?"

"I am Balamitra's daughter."

"O maiden, be not angry if I ask you a few questions."

She smiled at first, and then said, "O uncle, why should I be angry? Please to ask them."

"While these girls, as they went, were all running, skipping, rolling, turning round, singing, and doing other undignified things, you wended your way slowly, decorously, and in a seemly manner, reaching the park together with them."

Viśākhā replied, " All girls are a merchandise which their parents vend. If in leaping or rolling I were to break an arm or a leg, who then would woo me? I should certainly have to be kept by my parents as long as I lived."

" Good, O maiden; I understand."

He said to her next, " These girls took off their clothes at a certain place, and went into the water and sported in it unclothed, but you lifted up your clothes by degrees as you went deeper into the water."

" O uncle, it is necessary that women should be shamefaced and shy, and so it would not be well that anyone should look upon me unclothed."

" O maiden, who would see you there? "

" O uncle, you would have seen me there yourself."

" Good, O maiden; that also I comprehend."

He said to her further, " These girls first took food themselves and then gave to the persons in attendance; but you first gave food to the persons in attendance, and then took your own."

" O uncle, that was for this reason: we, reaping the fruits of our merits, constantly have feast-days; but they, reaping the fruits of their trouble, very seldom obtain great things."

" Good, O maiden; I comprehend this also."

He asked her, moreover, " While all the world wears boots on dry land, why did you keep yours on in the water? "

" O uncle, the world is foolish. It is precisely when one is in water that one should wear boots."

" For what reason? "

" On dry land one can see tree-stems, thorns, stones, prickles, fragments of fish scales or shells of reptiles, but in the water none of these things can be seen. Therefore we ought to wear boots in the water and not upon dry land."

" Good, O maiden; this also I understand."

Then he asked her this question: " These girls kept their parasols up in the sun; you kept yours up in the wood under the shade of the trees. What was the meaning of that?"

" O uncle, the world is foolish. It is precisely when in a wood that one must keep a parasol up."

" For what reason?"

" Because a wood is always full of birds and monkeys. The birds let fall their droppings and pieces of bones, and the monkeys their muck and scraps of the fruit they eat. Besides, as they are of a wild nature, they go springing from bough to bough, and bits of wood come falling down. When one is in the open this does not happen, or, if it takes place, it is but seldom. Therefore a parasol must be kept open in a wood; in the open it is not necessary to do so."

" Good, O maiden; this also I comprehend."

Presently he said, " These girls took refuge in a temple when the wind arose with rain, but you remained in the open air."

" O uncle, one certainly ought to remain in the open air and not take refuge in a temple."

" O maiden, what is the reason for that?"

" O uncle, such empty temples are never free from orphans, the low-born, and sharpers. If one of them were to touch me on a limb or joint as I entered such a temple, would not that be unpleasant to my parents? Moreover, it is better to lose one's life in the open than to enter an empty temple."

Full of delight at the demeanor of the maiden, the Brahman betook himself to the dwelling of the householder Balamitra and said, desiring to obtain the maiden:

" May it be well! May it be good!"

The people of the house said, " O Brahman, it is not yet the time for asking; but what do you ask for?"

" I ask for your daughter."

" On whose behalf?"

" On behalf of the son, Viśākha by name, of Mṛgadhara, the first minister of Śrāvastī."

They replied, " It is true that we and he are of the same caste, but his country lies too far away."

The Brahman said, " It is precisely in a far-away country that a man should choose a husband for his daughter."

" How so? "

" If she is married in the neighborhood, joy increases when news comes that she is prosperous; but if a misfortune occurs, a man's property may be brought to naught, he being exhausted by gifts, sacrifices, and tokens of reverence."

They said, " This being so, we will give our daughter."

After Viśākhā's marriage, on one occasion some country folks came bringing a mare and her foal. As they could not tell which was the mare and which the foal, the king ordered the ministers to examine them closely, and to report to him on the matter. The ministers examined them both for a whole day, became weary, and arrived at no conclusion after all. When Mṛgadhara went home in the evening, Viśākhā touched his feet and said, " O master, wherefore do ye return so late? " He told her everything that had occurred. Then Viśākhā said, " O master, what is there to investigate in that? Fodder should be laid before them in equal parts. The foal, after rapidly eating up its own share, will begin to devour its mother's also; but the mother, without eating, will hold up her head like this. That is the proper test."

Mṛgadhara told this to the ministers, who applied the test according to these instructions, and after daybreak they reported to the king, " This is the mother, O king, and that is the foal." The king asked how they knew that.

" O king, the case is so and so."

" How was it you did not know that yesterday? "

" O king, how could we know it? Viśākhā has instructed us since."

Said the king, " The Champā maiden is wise."

It happened that a man who was bathing had left his boots on the bank. Another man came up, tied the boots round his head, and began to bathe likewise. When the first man had done bathing and came out of the water, he missed the boots. The other man said, " Hey, man, what are you looking for? "

" My boots."

" Where are your boots? When you have boots, you should tie them round your head, as I do, before going into the water."

As a dispute arose between the two men as to whom the boots belonged to, they both had recourse to the king. The king told the ministers to investigate the case thoroughly, and to give the boots to the proper owner. The ministers began to investigate the case, and examined first the one man and then the other. Each of the men affirmed that he was the owner. While these assertions were being made, the day came to an end, and in the evening the ministers returned home wearied out, without having brought the matter to a satisfactory conclusion. Viśākhā questioned Mṛgadhara, and he told her all about it, whereupon she said, " O master, what is there to investigate? Say to one of them, 'Take one of the boots,' and to the other man, 'Take the other boot.' The real owner will say in that case, 'Why should my two boots be separated? ' But the other, the man to whom they do not really belong, will say, 'What good do I gain by this if I only get one boot? ' That is the proper test to apply."

Mṛgadhara went and told this to the ministers, and so forth, as is written above, down to the words, " The king said, 'The Champā maiden is wise.' "

It happened that some merchants brought a stem of sandal-wood to the king as a present, but no one knew which was the upper end of it and which the lower. So the king ordered his ministers to settle the question. They spent a whole day in examining the stem, but they could make nothing of it. In the evening they returned to their homes. Mṛgadhara again told Viśākhā all about the matter, and she said, " O master, what is there to investigate? Place the stem in water. The root end will then sink, but the upper end will float upward. That is the proper test."

Mṛgadhara communicated this to the ministers, and so forth, as written above, down to the words, "The king said, 'The Champā maiden is wise.'"

There was a householder in a hill-village who, after he had married in his own rank, remained without either son or daughter. As he longed earnestly for a child, he took unto himself a concubine. Thereupon his wife, who was of a jealous disposition, had recourse to a spell for the purpose of rendering that woman barren. But as that woman was quite pure, she became with child, and at the end of nine months bare a son. Then she reflected thus: "As the worst of all enmities is the enmity between a wife and a concubine, and the stepmother will be sure to seek for a means of kiliing the child, what ought my husband, what ought I to do? As I shall not be able to keep it alive, I had better give it to her."

After taking counsel with her husband, who agreed with her in the matter, she said to the wife, "O sister, I give you my son; take him." The wife thought, "As she who has a son ranks as the mistress of the house, I will bring him up."

After she had taken charge of the boy the father died. A dispute arose between the two women as to the possession of the house, each of them asserting that it belonged to her. They had recourse to the king. He ordered his ministers to go to the house and to make inquiries as to the ownership of the son. They investigated the matter, but the day came to an end before they had brought it to a satisfactory conclusion. In the evening they returned to their homes. Viśākhā again questioned Mṛgadhara, who told her everything. Viśākhā said, "What need is there of investigation? Speak to the two women thus: 'As we do not know to which of you two the boy belongs, let her who is the strongest take the boy.' When each of them has taken hold of one of the boy's hands, and he begins to cry out on account of the pain, the real mother will let go, being full of compassion for him, and knowing that if her child remains alive she will be able to see it again; but the other, who has no compassion for him, will not let go. Then beat her with a switch, and she will thereupon confess the truth as to the whole matter. That is the proper test."

Mṛgadhara told this to the ministers, and so forth, as is written above, down to the words, "The king said, 'The Champā maiden is wise.'"

Told by the Constable

From the Arabic

KNOW ye that when I entered the service of this Emir, I had a great repute and every low fellow and lewd feared me most of all mankind, and when I rode through the city, each and every of the folk would point at me with their fingers and sign at me with their eyes. It happened one day, as I sat in the palace of the Prefecture, back-propped against a wall, considering in myself, suddenly there fell somewhat in my lap, and behold, it was a purse sealed and tied. So I hent it in hand and lo! it had in it an hundred dirhams, but I found not who threw it and I said, "Lauded be the Lord, the King of the Kingdoms!" Another day, as I sat in the same way, somewhat fell on me and startled me, and lookye, 'twas a purse like the first: I took it and hiding the matter, made as though I slept, albeit sleep was not with me. One day as I thus shammed sleep, I suddenly sensed in my lap a hand, and in it a purse of the finest; so I seized the hand and behold, 'twas that of a fair woman. Quoth I to her, "O my lady, who art thou?" and quoth she, "Rise and come away from here, that I may make myself known to thee." Presently I rose up and following her, walked on, without tarrying, till we stopped at the door of a high-builded house, whereupon I asked her,

"O my lady, who art thou? Indeed, thou hast done me kindness, and what is the reason of this?" She answered, "By Allah, O Captain Mu'in, I am a woman on whom love and longing are sore for desire of the daughter of the Kazi Amin al-Hukm. Now there was between me and her what was and fondness for her fell upon my heart and I agreed upon an assignation with her, according to possibility and convenience; but her father Amin al-Hukm took her and went away, and my heart cleaveth to her and yearning and distraction waxed sore upon me for her sake." I said to her, marveling the while at her words, "What wouldst thou have me do?" and said she, "O Captain Mu'in, I would have thee lend me a helping hand." Quoth I, "Where am I and where is the daughter of the Kazi Amin al-Hukm?" and quoth she, "Be assured that I would not have thee intrude upon the Kazi's daughter, but I would fain work for the winning of my wishes. This is my will and my want which may not be wroughten save by thine aid." Then she added, "I mean this night to go with heart enheartened and hire me bracelets and armlets and anklets of price; then will I hie me and sit in the street wherein is the house of Amin al-Hukm; and when 'tis the season of the round and folk are asleep, do thou pass, thou and those who are with thee of the men, and thou wilt see me sitting and on me fine raiment and ornaments and wilt smell on me the odor of Ottars; whereupon do thou question me of my case and I will say: I hail from the Citadel and am of the daughters of the deputies, and I came down into the town for a purpose; but night overtook me all unawares and the Zuwaylah Gate was shut against me and all the other portals and I knew not whither I should wend this night. Presently I saw this street and noting the goodly fashion of its ordinance and its cleanliness, I sheltered me therein against break of day. When I speak these words to thee with complete self-possession, the Chief of the watch will have no ill suspicion of me, but will say: There's no help but that we leave her with one who will take care of her till morning. Thereto do thou rejoin: 'Twere best that she night with Amin al-Hukm and lie with his wives and children until dawn of day. Then straightway knock at the Kazi's door, and thus shall I have secured admission into his house, without inconvenience, and won my wish; and—the Peace!" I said to her, "By Allah, this is an easy matter." So, when the night was blackest, we rose to make our round, followed by men with girded swords, and went about the ways and compassed the city, till we came to the street where was the woman, and it was the middle of the night. Here we smelled mighty rich scents and heard the clink of rings: so I said to my comrades, "Methinks I espy a specter"; and the Captain of the watch cried, "See what it is." Accordingly, I undertook the work and entering the thoroughfare presently came out again and said, "I have found a fair woman and she telleth me that she is from the Citadel and that dark night surprised her and she saw this street and noting its cleanness and goodly fashion of ordinance, knew that it belonged to a great man and that needs must there be in it a guardian to keep watch over it, so she sheltered her therein." Quoth the Captain of the watch to me, "Take her and carry her to thy house"; but quoth I, "I seek refuge with Allah! My house is no strong box and on this woman are trinkets and fine clothing. By Allah, we will not deposit the lady save with Amin al-Hukm, in whose street she hath been since the first starkening of the darkness; therefore do thou leave her with him till the break of day." He rejoined, "Do whatso thou willest." So I rapped at the Kazi's gate and out came a black slave of his slaves, to whom said I, "O my lord, take this woman and let her be with you till day shall dawn, for that the lieutenant of the Emir Alam al-Din hath found her with trinkets and fine apparel on her, sitting at the door of your house, and we feared lest her responsibility be upon you; wherefore I suggested 'twere meetest she night with you." So the chattel opened and took her in with him. Now when the morning morrowed, the first who presented himself before the Emir was the Kazi Amin al-Hukm, leaning on two of his negro slaves; and he was crying out and calling for aid and saying, "O Emir, crafty and perfidious, yesternight thou depositedst with me a woman and broughtest her into my house and home, and she arose in the dark and took from me the moneys of the little orphans my wards, six great bags, each containing a thousand dinars, and made off; but as for me, I will say no syllable to thee except in the Soldan's presence." When the Wali heard these words, he was troubled and rose and sat down in his agitation; then he took the Judge and placing him by his side, soothed him and exhorted him to patience, till he had made an end of talk, when he turned to the officers and questioned them of that. They fixed the affair on me and said, "We know nothing of this matter but from Captain Mu'in al-Din." So the Kazi turned to me and said, "Thou wast of accord to practice upon me with this woman, for she said she came from the Citadel." As for me, I stood, with my head bowed ground-wards, forgetting both Sunnah and Farz, and remained sunk in thought, saying, "How came I to be the dupe of that wily wench?" Then cried the Emir to me, "What aileth thee that thou answerest not?" Thereupon I replied, "O my lord, 'tis a custom among the folk that he who hath a payment to make at a certain date is allowed three days' grace: do thou have patience with me so long, and if, at the end of that time, the culprit be not found, I will be responsible for that which is lost." When the folk heard my speech they all approved it as reasonable and the Wali turned to the Kazi and sware to him that he would do his utmost to recover the stolen moneys adding, "And they shall be restored to thee." Then he went away, whilst I mounted without stay or delay and began to-ing and fro-ing about the world without purpose, and indeed I was become the underling of a woman without honesty or honor; and I went my rounds in this way all that my day and that my night, but happened not upon tidings of her; and thus I did on the morrow. On the third day I said to myself, "Thou art mad or silly"; for I was wandering in quest of a woman who knew me and I knew her not, she being veiled when I met her. Then I went round about the third day till the hour of mid-afternoon prayer, and sore waxed my cark and my care for I kenned that there remained to me of my life but the morrow, when the Chief of Police would send for me. However, as sundown-time came, I passed through one of the main streets, and saw a woman at a window; her door was ajar and she was clapping her hands and casting sidelong glances at me, as who should say, "Come up by the door." So I went up, without fear or suspicion, and when I entered, she rose and clasped me to her breast. I marveled at the matter and quoth she to me, "I am she whom thou depositedst with Amin al-Hukm." Quoth I to her, "O my sister, I have been going round and round in request of thee, for indeed thou hast done a deed which will be chronicled and hast cast me into red death on thine account." She asked me, "Dost thou speak thus to me and thou a captain of men?" and I answered, "How should I not be troubled, seeing that I be in concern for an affair I turn over and over in mind, more by token that I continue my day long going about searching for thee and in the night I watch its stars and planets?" Cried she, "Naught shall betide save weal, and thou shalt get the better of him." So saying, she rose and going to a chest, drew out therefrom six bags full of gold and said to me, "This is what I took from Amin al-Hukm's house. So an thou wilt, restore it; else the whole is lawfully thine; and if thou desire other than this, thou shalt obtain it; for I have moneys in plenty and I had no design herein save to marry thee." Then she arose and opening other chests, brought out therefrom wealth galore and I said to her, "O my sister, I have no wish for all this, nor do I want aught except to be quit of that wherein I am." Quoth she, "I came not forth of the Kazi's house without preparing for thine acquittance." Then said she to me, "When the morrow shall morn and Amin al-Hukm shall come to thee bear with him till he have made an end of his speech, and when he is silent, return him no reply; and if the Wali ask: What aileth thee that thou answerest me not? do thou rejoin: O lord and master know that the two words are not alike, but there is no helper for the conquered one save

Allah Almighty. The Kazi will cry, What is the meaning of thy saying, The two words are not alike? And do thou retort: I deposited with thee a damsel from the palace of the Sultan, and most likely some enemy of hers in thy household hath transgressed against her or she hath been secretly murdered. Verily, there were on her raiment and ornaments worth a thousand ducats, and hadst thou put to the question those who are with thee of slaves and slave-girls, needs must thou have litten on some traces of the crime. When he heareth this from thee, his trouble will redouble and he will be angered and will make oath that thou hast no help for it but to go with him to his house: however, do thou say, That will I not do, for I am the party aggrieved, more especially because I am under suspicion with thee. If he redouble in calling on Allah's aid and conjure thee by the oath of divorce saying, Thou must assuredly come, do thou reply, By Allah, I will not go, unless the Chief also go with me. Then, as soon as thou comest to the house, begin by searching the terrace-roofs; then rummage the closets and cabinets; and if thou find naught, humble thyself before the Kazi and be abject and feign thyself subjected, and after examine well the door, because there is a dark corner there. Then come forward, with heart harder than syenite-stone, and lay hold upon a jar of the jars and raise it from its place. Thou wilt find there under it a mantilla-skirt; bring it out publicly and call the Wali in a loud voice, before those who are present. Then open it and thou wilt find it full of blood, and therein a woman's walking boots and somewhat of linen." When I heard from her these words, I rose to go out and she said to me, "Take these hundred sequins, so they may succor thee; and such is my guest-gift to thee." Accordingly I took them and leaving her door ajar returned to my lodging. Next morning, up came the Judge, with his face like the ox-eye, and asked, "In the name of Allah, where is my debtor and where is my property?" Then he wept and cried out and said to the Wali, "Where is that ill-omened fellow, who aboundeth in robbery and villainy?" Thereupon the Chief turned to me and said, "Why dost thou not answer the Kazi?" and I replied, "O Emir, the two heads are not equal, and I, I have no helper; but, an the right be on my side 'twill appear." At this the Judge grew hotter of temper and cried out, "Woe to thee, O ill-omened wight! How wilt thou make manifest that the right is on thy side?" I replied, "O our lord the Kazi, I deposited with thee and in thy charge a woman whom we found at thy door, and on her raiment and ornaments of price. Now she is gone, even as yesterday is gone; and after this thou turnest upon us and suest me for six thousand gold pieces. By Allah, this is none other than a mighty great wrong, and assuredly some foe of hers in thy household hath transgressed against her!" With this the Judge's wrath redoubled and he swore by the most solemn of oaths that I should go with him and search his house. I replied, "By Allah I will not go, unless the Wali go with us; for, an he be present, he and the officers, thou wilt not dare to work thy wicked will upon me." So the Kazi rose and swore an oath, saying, "By the truth of Him who created mankind, we will not go but with the Emir!" Accordingly we repaired to the Judge's house, accompanied by the Chief, and going up, searched it through, but found naught; whereat fear fell upon me and the Wali turned to me and said, "Fie upon thee, O ill-omened fellow! thou hast put us to shame before the men." All this, and I wept and went round about right and left, with the tears running down my face, till we were about to go forth and drew near the door of the house. I looked at the place which the woman had mentioned and asked, "What is yonder dark place I see?" Then said I to the men, "Pull up this jar with me." They did my bidding and I saw somewhat appearing under the jar and said, "Rummage and look at what is under it." So they searched, and behold, they came upon a woman's mantilla and walking boots stained with blood, which when I espied, I fell down in a fainting-fit. Now when the Wali saw this, he said, "By Allah, the Captain is excused!" Then my comrades came round about me and sprinkled water on my face till I recovered, when I arose and accosting the Kazi (who was covered with confusion), said to him, "Thou seest that suspicion is fallen on thee, and indeed this affair is no light matter, because this woman's family will assuredly not sit down quietly under her loss." Therewith the Kazi's heart quaked and fluttered for that he knew the suspicion had reverted upon him, wherefore his color yellowed and his limbs smote together; and he paid of his own money, after the measure of that he had lost, so we would quench that fire for him. Then we departed from him in peace, whilst I said within myself, "Indeed, the woman falsed me not." After that I tarried till three days had passed, when I went to the Hammam and changing my clothes, betook myself to her home, but found the door shut and covered with dust. So I asked the neighbors of her and they answered, "This house hath been empty of habitants these many days; but three days agone there came a woman with an ass, and at supper-time last night she took her gear and went away." Hereat I turned back, bewildered in my wit, and for many a day after I inquired of the dwellers in that street concerning her, but could happen on no tidings of her. And indeed I wondered at the eloquence of her tongue and the readiness of her talk; and this is the most admirable of all I have seen and of whatso hath betided me.

The Unjust Sentence

From the Chinese

MR. CHU was a native of Yang-ku, and, as a young man, was much given to playing tricks and talking in a loose kind of way. Having lost his wife, he went off to ask a certain old woman to arrange another match for him; and on the way he chanced to fall in with a neighbor's wife who took his fancy very much. So he said in joke to the old woman, "Get me that stylish-looking, handsome lady, and I shall be quite satisfied."

"I'll see what I can do," replied the old woman, also joking, "if you will manage to kill her present husband"; upon which Chu laughed and said he certainly would do so. Now about a month afterwards, the said husband, who had gone out to collect some money due to him, was actually killed in a lonely spot; and the magistrate of the district immediately summoned the neighbors and beadle and held the usual inquest, but was unable to find any clue to the murderer. However, the old woman told the story of her conversation with Chu, and suspicion at once fell upon him. The constables came and arrested him, but he stoutly denied the charge; and the magistrate now began to suspect the wife of the murdered man. Accordingly, she was severely beaten and tortured in several ways until her strength failed her, and she falsely acknowledged her guilt.[1]

[1] Such has doubtless been the occasional result of torture in China; but the singular keenness of the mandarins, as a body, in recognizing the innocent and detecting the guilty,—that is, when their own avaricious interests are not involved,—makes this contingency so rare as to be almost unknown. A good instance came under my own notice at Swatow in 1876. For years a Chinese servant had been employed at the foreign Custom House to carry a certain sum of money every week to the bank, and at length his honesty was above suspicion. On the occasion to which I allude he had been sent as usual with the bag of dollars, but after a short absence he rushed back with a frightful gash on his right arm, evidently inflicted by a heavy chopper, and laying the bone bare. The money was gone. He said he had been invited into a tea-house by a couple of soldiers whom he could point out; that they had tried to wrest the bag from him, and that at length one of them seized a chopper and inflicted so severe a wound on his arm, that in his agony he dropped the money, and the soldiers made off with it. The latter were promptly arrested and confronted with their accuser; but, with almost indecent haste, the police magistrate dismissed the case against them, and declared that he believed the man had made away with the money and inflicted the wound on himself. And so it turned out to be, under overwhelming evidence. This servant of proved fidelity had given way to a rash hope of making a little money at the gaming table; had hurried into one of these hells and lost everything in three stakes; had wounded himself on the right arm (he was a left-handed man), and had concocted the story of the soldiers, all within

Chu was then examined, and he said, "This delicate woman could not bear the agony of your tortures; what she has stated is untrue; and, even should her wrong escape the notice of the Gods, for her to die in this way with a stain upon her name is more than I can endure. I will tell the whole truth. I killed the husband that I might secure the wife: she knew nothing at all about it." And when the magistrate asked for some proof, Chu said his bloody clothes would be evidence enough; but when they sent to search his house, no bloody clothes were forthcoming. He was then beaten till he fainted; yet when he came round he still stuck to what he had said. "It is my mother," cried he, "who will not sign the death-warrant of her son. Let me go myself and I will get the clothes." So he was escorted by a guard to his home, and there he explained to his mother that whether she gave up or withheld the clothes it was all the same; that in either case he would have to die, and it was better to die early than late. Thereupon his mother wept bitterly, and going into the bedroom, brought out, after a short delay, the required clothes, which were taken at once to the magistrate's. There was now no doubt as to the truth of Chu's story; and as nothing occurred to change the magistrate's opinion, Chu was thrown into prison to await the day for his execution. Meanwhile, as the magistrate was one day inspecting his jail, suddenly a man appeared in the hall, who glared at him fiercely and roared out, "Dull-headed fool! unfit to be the guardian of the people's interests!" whereupon the crowd of servants standing round rushed forward to seize him, but with one sweep of his arms he laid them all flat on the ground. The magistrate was frightened out of his wits, and tried to escape, but the man cried out to him, "I am one of Kuan Ti's lieutenants. If you move an inch you are

the space of about twenty-five minutes. When he saw that he was detected, he confessed everything, without having received a single blow of the bamboo; but up to the moment of his confession the foreign feeling against that police-magistrate was undeniably strong.

—Herbert A. Giles, Translator.

lost." So the magistrate stood there, shaking from head to foot with fear, while his visitor continued, "The murderer is Kung Piao: Chu had nothing to do with it."

The lieutenant then fell down on the ground, and was to all appearance lifeless; however, after a while he recovered, his face having quite changed, and when they asked him his name, lo! it was Kung Piao. Under the application of the bamboo he confessed his guilt. Always an unprincipled man, he had heard that the murdered man was going out to collect money, and thinking he would be sure to bring it back with him, he had killed him, but had found nothing. Then when he learned that Chu had acknowledged the crime as his own doing, he had rejoiced in secret at such a stroke of luck. How he had got into the magistrate's hall he was quite unable to say. The magistrate now called for some explanation of Chu's bloody clothes, which Chu himself was unable to give; but his mother, who was at once sent for, stated that she had cut her own arm to stain them, and when they examined her they found on her left arm the scar of a recent wound. The magistrate was lost in amazement at all this; unfortunately for him the reversal of his sentence cost him his appointment, and he died in poverty, unable to find his way home. As for Chu, the widow of the murdered man married him in the following year, out of gratitude for his noble behavior.

The Scar on the Throat

From the Arabic

THERE was once a king named Sulayman Shah, who was goodly of policy and counsel, and he had a brother who died and left a daughter; so Sulayman Shah reared her with the best of rearing and the girl became a model of reason and perfection, nor was there in her time a more beautiful than she. Now the king had two sons, one of whom he had appointed in his mind to wed her, while the other purposed to take her. The elder son's name was Bahluwan and that of the younger Malik Shah, and the girl was called Shah Khatun. Now one day King Sulayman Shah went in to his brother's daughter and, kissing her head, said to her, "Thou art my daughter and dearer to me than a child, for the love of thy late father who hath found mercy; wherefore I purpose espousing thee to one of my sons and appointing him my heir apparent, so he may be king after me. Look, then, which thou wilt have of my sons, for that thou hast been reared with them and knowest them." The maiden arose and kissing his hand, said to him, "O my lord, I am thine hand-maid and thou art the ruler over me; so whatever liketh thee do that same, inasmuch as thy wish is higher and honorabler and holier than mine, and if thou wouldst have me serve thee as a hand-maid for the rest of my life, 'twere fairer to me than any mate." The king commended her speech, and conferred on her a robe of honor and gave her magnificent gifts; after which, his choice having fallen upon his younger son, Malik Shah, he wedded her with him and made him his heir apparent and bade the folk swear fealty to him. When this reached his brother Bahluwan and he was aware that his younger brother had by favor been preferred over him, his breast was straitened and the affair was sore to him and envy entered into him and hate; but he hid this in his heart, while fire raged therein because of the damsel and the dominion. Meanwhile Shah Khatun went in bridal splendor to the king's son and conceived by him and bare a son, as he were the illuming moon. When Bahluwan saw this betide his brother, envy and jealousy overcame him; so he went in one night to his father's palace and coming to his brother's chamber, saw the nurse sleeping at the door, with the cradle before her and therein his brother's child asleep. Bahluwan stood by him and fell to looking upon his face, whose radiance was as that of the moon, and Satan insinuated himself into his heart, so that he bethought himself and said, "Why be not this babe mine? Verily, I am worthier of him than my brother; yea, and of the damsel and the dominion." Then the idea got the mastery of him and anger drove him, so that he took out a knife and setting it to the child's gullet, cut his throat and would have severed his windpipe. So he left him for dead, and entering his brother's chamber, saw him asleep, with the Princess by his side, and thought to slay her, but said to himself, "I will leave the girl-wife for myself." Then he went up to his brother and cutting his throat, parted head from body, after which he left him and went away. But now the world was straitened upon him and his life was a light matter to him and he sought the lodging of his sire Sulayman Shah, that he might slay him also, but could not get admission to him. So he went forth from the palace and hid himself in the city till the morrow, when he repaired to one of his father's fortalices and therein fortified himself. On this wise it was with him; but as regards the nurse, she presently awoke that she might give the child suck, and seeing the cradle running with blood, cried out; whereupon the sleepers started up and the king was aroused and making for the place, found the child with his throat cut and the bed running over with blood and his father dead with a slit weasand in his sleeping chamber. They examined the child and found life in him and his windpipe whole and they sewed up the place of the wound: then the king sought his son Bahluwan, but found him not and saw that he had fled; so he knew that it was he who had done this deed, and this was grievous to the king and to the people of his realm and to the lady Shah Khatun. Thereupon the king laid out his son Malik Shah and buried him and made him a mighty funeral and they mourned with passing sore mourning; after which he applied himself to rearing the infant. As for Bahluwan, when he fled and fortified himself, his power waxed amain and there remained for him but to make war upon his father, who had cast his fondness upon the child and used to rear him on his knees and supplicate Almighty Allah that he might live, so he might commit the command to him. When he came to five years of age, the king mounted him on horseback and the people of the city rejoiced in him and prayed for him length of life, that he might take vengeance for his father and heal his grandsire's heart. Meanwhile, Bahluwan the rebel addressed himself to pay court to Cæsar, king of the Roum and crave aid of him in debelling his father, and he inclined unto him and gave him a numerous army. His sire the king hearing of this sent to Cæsar, saying, "O glorious king of might illustrious, succor not an evil doer. This is my son and he hath done so and so and cut his brother's throat and that of his brother's son in the cradle." But he told not the king of the Roum that the child had recovered and was alive. When Cæsar heard the truth of the matter, it was grievous to him as grievous could be, and he sent back to Sulayman Shah, saying, "An it be thy wish, O king, I will cut off his head and send it to thee." But he made answer, saying, "I care naught for him: soon and surely the reward of his deed and his crimes shall overtake him, if not to-day, then to-morrow." And from that date he continued to exchange letters and presents with Cæsar. Now the king of the Roum heard tell of the widowed Princess and of the beauty and loveliness wherewith she was endowed, wherefore his heart clave to her and he sent to seek her in wedlock of Sulayman Shah, who could not refuse him. So he arose and going in to Shah Khatun, said to her, "O my daughter, the king of the Roum hath sent to me to seek thee in marriage. What sayest thou?" She wept and replied, "O king, how canst thou find it in thy heart to address me thus? As for me, abideth there husband for me, after the son of my uncle?" Rejoined the king, "O my daughter, 'tis indeed as thou sayest; but here let us look to the issues of affairs. I must now take compt of death, for that I am a man shot in years and fear not save for thee and thy little son; and indeed I have written to the king of the Roum and others of the kings and said, His uncle slew him, and said not that he hath recovered and is living, but concealed his affair. Now the king of the Roum hath sent to demand thee in marriage, and this is no thing to be refused and fain would we have our back strengthened with him." And she was silent and spake not. So King Sulayman Shah made answer to Cæsar with "Hearing and obeying." Then he arose and dispatched her to him, and Cæsar went in to her and found her passing the description wherewith they had described her; wherefore he loved her every day more and more and preferred her over all his women and his affection for Sulayman Shah was increased; but Shah Katun's heart still clave to her child and she could say naught. As for Sulayman Shah's son, the rebel Bahluwan, when he saw that Shah Khatun had married the king of the Roum, this was grievous to him and he despaired of her. Meanwhile, his father Sulayman Shah watched over the child and cherished him and named him Malik Shah, after the name of his sire. When he reached the age of ten, he made the folk do homage to him and appointed him his heir apparent, and after some days, the old king's time for paying the debt of nature drew near and he died. Now a party of the troops had banded themselves together for Bahluwan; so they sent to him, and bringing him privily, went in to the little Malik Shah and seized him and seated his uncle Bahluwan on the throne of kingship. Then they proclaimed him king and did homage to him all, saying, "Verily, we desire thee and deliver to thee the throne of kingship; but we wish of thee that thou slay not thy brother's son, because we are still bounden by the oaths we swore to his sire and his grandsire and the covenants we made with them." So Bahluwan granted this to them and imprisoned the boy in an underground dungeon and straitened him. Presently, the grievous news reached his mother and this was to her a fresh grief; but she could not speak and committed her affair to Allah Almighty, for that she durst not name this to King Cæsar her spouse, lest she should make her uncle King Sulayman Shah a liar. But as regards Buhlawan the Rebel, he abode king in his father's place and his affairs prospered, while young Malik Shah lay in the souterrain four full-told years, till his favor faded and his charms changed. When He (extolled and exalted be He!) willed to relieve him and to bring him forth of the prison, Bahluwan sat one day with his chief Officers and the Lords of his land and discoursed with them of the story of his sire, King Sulayman Shah and what was in his heart. Now there were present certain Wazirs, men of worth, and they said to him, "O king, verily Allah hath been bountiful to thee and hath brought thee to thy wish, so that thou art become king in thy father's palace and hast won whatso thou wishedst. But, as for this youth, there is no guilt in him, because he, from the day of his coming into the world, hath seen neither ease nor pleasure, and indeed his favor is faded and his charms changed. What is his crime that he should merit such pains and penalties? Indeed, others than he were to blame, and hereto Allah hath given thee the victory over them, and there is no fault in this poor lad." Quoth Bahluwan, "Verily, 'tis as ye say; but I fear his machinations and am not safe from his mischief; haply the most part of the folk will incline unto him." They replied, "O king, what is this boy, and what power hath he? An thou fear him, send him to one of the frontiers." And Bahluwan said, "Ye speak sooth; so we will send him as captain of war to reduce one of the outlying stations." Now over against the place in question was a host of enemies, hard of heart, and in this he designed the slaughter of the youth: so he bade bring him forth of the underground dungeon and caused him draw near to him and saw his case. Then he robed him, whereat the folk rejoiced, and bound for him the banners and, giving him a mighty many, dispatched him to the quarter aforesaid, whither all who went or were slain or were taken. Accordingly Malik Shah fared thither with his force and when it was one of the days, behold, the enemy attacked them in the night; whereupon some of his men fled and the rest the enemy captured; and they seized Malik Shah also and cast him into a pit with a company of his men. His fellows mourned over his beauty and loveliness and there he abode a whole twelve-month in the evilest plight. Now at the beginning of every year it was the enemy's wont to bring forth their prisoners and cast them down from the top of the citadel to the bottom; so at the customed time they brought them forth and cast them down, and Malik Shah with them. However, he fell upon the other men and the ground touched him not, for his term was God-guarded. But those who were cast down there were slain upon the spot and their bodies ceased not to lie there till the wild beasts ate them and the winds scattered their bones. Malik Shah abode strown in his place and aswoon, all that day and that night, and when he revived and found himself safe and sound, he thanked Allah the Most High for his safety and, rising, left the place. He gave not over walking, unknowing whither he went and dieting upon the leaves of the trees; and by day he hid himself where he might and fared on at hazard all the night; and thus he did for some days, till he came to a populous part and seeing folk there, accosted them. He acquainted them with his case, giving them to know that he had been prisoned in the fortress and that they had thrown him down, but Almighty Allah had saved him and brought him off alive. The people had ruth on him and gave him to eat and drink and he abode with them several days; then he questioned them of the way that led to the kingdom of his uncle Bahluwan, but told them not that he was his father's brother. So they showed him the road and he ceased not to go barefoot, till he drew near his uncle's capital, naked, and hungry, and indeed his limbs were lean and his color changed. He sat down at the city gate, when behold, up came a company of King Bahluwan's chief officers, who were out a-hunting and wished to water their horses. They lighted down to rest and the youth accosted them saying, "I would ask you of somewhat that ye may acquaint me therewith." Quoth they, "Ask what thou wilt"; and quoth he, "Is King Bahluwan well?" They derided him and replied, "What a fool art thou, O youth! Thou art a stranger and a beggar, and whence art thou that thou shouldst question concerning the king?" Cried he, "In very sooth, he is my uncle"; whereat they marveled and said, "'Twas one catch-question and now 'tis become two." Then said they to him, "O youth, it is as if thou wert Jinn-mad. Whence comest thou to claim kinship with the king? Indeed, we know not that he hath any kith and kin save a nephew, a brother's son, who was prisoned with him, and he dispatched him to wage war upon the infidels, so that they slew him." Said Malik Shah, "I am he and they slew me not, but there befell me this and that." They knew him forthwith and rising to him, kissed his hands and rejoiced in him and said to him, "O our lord, thou art indeed a king and the son of a king, and we desire thee naught but good and we pray for thy continuance. Look how Allah hath rescued thee from this wicked uncle, who sent thee to a place whence none ever came off safe and sound, purposing not in this but thy destruction; and indeed thou fellest upon death from which Allah delivered thee. How, then, wilt thou return and cast thyself again into thine foeman's hand? By Allah, save thyself and return not to him this second time. Haply thou shalt abide upon the face of the earth till it please Almighty Allah to receive thee; but, an thou fall again into his hand, he will not suffer thee to live a single hour." The Prince thanked them and said to them, "Allah reward you with all weal, for indeed ye give me loyal counsel; but whither would ye have me wend?" Quoth they, "To the land of the Roum, the abiding-place of thy mother." "But," quoth he, "my grandfather Sulayman Shah, when the king of the Roum wrote to him demanding my mother in marriage, hid my affair and secreted my secret; and she hath done the same, and I cannot make her a liar." Rejoined they, "Thou sayest sooth, but we desire thine advantage, and even wert thou to take service with the folk, 'twere a means of thy continuance." Then each and every of them brought out to him money and gave him a modicum and clad him and fed him and fared on with him the length of a parasang, till they brought him far from the city, and letting him know that he was safe, departed from him, while he journeyed till he came forth of his uncle's reign and entered the dominion of the Roum. Then he made a village and taking up his abode therein, applied himself to serving one there in earing and seeding and the like. As for his mother, Shah Khatun, great was her longing for her child and she thought of him ever and news of him was cut off from her, so her life was troubled and she forswore sleep and could not make mention of him before King Cæsar her spouse. Now she had a Eunuch who had come with her from the court of her uncle King Sulayman Shah, and he was intelligent, quick-witted, right-reded. So she took him apart one day and said to him, shedding tears the while, "Thou hast been my Eunuch from my childhood to this day; canst thou not therefore get me tidings of my son, seeing that I cannot speak of his matter?" He replied, "O my lady, this is an affair which thou hast concealed from the commencement, and were thy son here, 'twould not be possible for thee to entertain him, lest thine honor be smirched with the king; for they would never credit thee, since the news hath been bruited abroad that thy son was slain by his uncle." Quoth she, "The case is even as thou sayest and thou speakest sooth; but, provided I know that my son is alive, let him be in these parts pasturing sheep and let me not sight him nor he sight me." He asked, "How shall we manage in this matter?" and she answered, "Here be my treasures and my wealth: take all thou wilt and bring me my son or else tidings of him." Then they devised a device between them, which was that they should feign some business in their own country, to wit that she had wealth there buried from the time of her husband, Malik Shah, and that none knew of it but this Eunuch who was with her, so it behooved him to go fetch it. Accordingly she acquainted the king her husband with that and sought his permit for the Eunuch to fare: and the king granted him leave of absence for the journey and charged him devise a device, lest he come to grief. The Eunuch, therefore, disguised himself in merchant's habit and repairing to Bahluwan's city, began to make espial concerning the youth's case; whereupon they told him that he had been prisoned in a souterrain and that his uncle had released him and dispatched him to such a place, where they had slain him. When the Eunuch heard this, the mishap was grievous to him and his breast was straitened and he knew not what to do. It chanced one day of the days that a certain of the horsemen, who had fallen in with the young Malik Shah by the water and clad him and given him spending-money, saw the Eunuch in the city, habited as a merchant, and recognizing him, questioned him of his case and of the cause of his coming. Quoth he, "I came to sell merchandise"; and quoth the horseman, "I will tell thee somewhat, an thou canst keep it secret." Answered the Eunuch, "That I can! What is it?" and the other said, "We met the king's son, Malik Shah, I and sundry of the Arabs who were with me, and saw him by such a water and gave him spending-money and sent him toward the land of the Roum, near his mother, for that we feared for him lest his uncle Bahluwan slay him." Then he told him all that had passed between them, whereat the Eunuch's countenance changed and he said to the cavalier "Thou art safe!" The knight replied, "Thou also art safe though thou come in quest of him." And the Eunuch rejoined, saying, "Truly, that is my errand: there is no rest for his mother, lying down or rising up, and she hath sent me to seek news of him." Quoth the cavalier, "Go in safety, for he is in a quarter of the land of the Roum, even as I said to thee." The Eunuch thanked him and blessed him and mounting, returned upon his road, following the trail, while the knight rode with him to a certain highway, when he said to him, "This is where we left him." Then he took leave of him and returned to his own city, while the Eunuch fared on along the road, inquiring in every village he entered of the youth, by the description which the rider had given him, and he ceased not thus to do till he came to the village wherein was young Malik Shah. So he entered, and dismounting, made inquiry after the Prince, but none gave him news of him; whereat he abode perplexed concerning his affair and made ready to depart. Accordingly he mounted his horse; but, as he passed through the village, he saw a cow bound with a rope and a youth asleep by her side, hending the halter in hand; so he looked at him and passed on and heeded him not in his heart, but presently he halted and said to himself, " An the youth whom I am questing have become the like of this sleeping youth whom I passed but now, how shall I know him? Alas, the length of my travail and travel! How shall I go about in search of a somebody I know not, one whom, if I saw him face to face I should not know? " So saying he turned back, musing anent that sleeping youth, and coming to him, he still sleeping, dismounted from his mare and sat down by his side. He fixed his eyes upon his face and considered him a while and said in himself, " For aught I wot, this youth may be Malik Shah "; then he began hemming and saying, " Hark ye, O youth! " Whereupon the sleeper awoke and sat up; and the Eunuch asked him, " Who be thy father in this village and where be thy dwelling? " The youth sighed and replied, " I am a stranger "; and quoth the Eunuch, " From what land art thou and who is thy sire? " Quoth the other, " I am from such a land," and the Eunuch ceased not to question him and he to answer his queries, till he was certified of him and knew him. So he arose and embraced him and kissed him and wept over his case: he also told him that he was wandering about in search of him and informed him that he was come privily from the king, his mother's husband, and that his mother would be satisfied to weet that he was alive and well, though she saw him not. Then he re-entered the village and buying the Prince a horse, mounted him, and they ceased not going till they came to the frontier of their own country, where there fell robbers upon them by the way and took all that was with them and pinioned them; after which they threw them into a pit hard by the road and went their ways and left them to die there; and indeed they had cast many folk into that pit and they had perished. The Eunuch fell a weeping in the pit and the youth said to him, " What is this weeping and what shall it profit here? " Quoth the Eunuch, " I weep not for fear of death, but of ruth for thee and the cursedness of thy case and because of thy mother's heart and for that which thou hast suffered of horrors and that thy death should be this ignoble death, after the endurance of all manner of dire distresses." But the youth said, "That which hath betided me was writ to me and that which is written none hath power to efface; and if my life-term be advanced, none may defer it." Then the twain passed that night and the following day and the next night and the next day in the hollow, till they were weak with hunger and came nigh upon death and could but groan feebly. Now it fortuned by the decree of Almighty Allah and His destiny, that Cæsar, king of the Greeks, the spouse of Malik Shah's mother Shah Khatun, went forth a-hunting that morning. He flushed a head of game, he and his company, and chased it, till they came up with it by that pit, whereupon one of them lighted down from his horse, to slaughter it, hard by the mouth of the hollow. He heard a sound of low moaning from the sole of the pit; whereat he arose and mounting his horse, waited till the troops were assembled. Then he acquainted the king with this and he bade one of his servants descend into the hollow; so the man climbed down and brought out the youth and the Eunuch in fainting condition. They cut their pinion-bonds and poured wine down their throats, till they came to themselves, when the king looked at the Eunuch and recognizing him, said, "Harkye, Such-an-one!" The Eunuch replied, "Yes, O my lord the king," and prostrated himself to him; whereat the king wondered with exceeding wonder and asked him, "How camest thou to this place and what hath befallen thee?" The Eunuch answered, "I went and took out the treasure and brought it thus far; but the evil eye was behind me and I unknowing. So the thieves took us alone here and seized the money and cast us into this pit that we might die the slow death of hunger, even as they had done with others; but Allah the Most High sent thee, in pity to us." The king marveled, he and his, and praised the Lord for that he had come thither; after which he turned to the Eunuch and said to him, "What is this youth thou hast with thee?" He replied, "O king, this is the son of a nurse who belonged to us and we left him when he was a little one. I saw him to-day and his mother said to me, 'Take him with thee': so this morning I brought him that he might be a servant to the king, for that he is an adroit youth and a clever." Then the king fared on, he and his company, and with them the Eunuch and the youth, who questioned his companion of Bahluwan and his dealing with his subjects, and he replied, saying, "As thy head liveth, O my lord the king, the folk are in sore annoy with him and not one of them wisheth a sight of him, be they high or low." When the king returned to his palace, he went in to his wife Shah Khatun and said to her, "I give thee the glad tidings of thine Eunuch's return"; and he told her what had betided and of the youth whom he had brought with him. When she heard this, her wits fled and she would have screamed, but her reason restrained her, and the king said to her, "What is this? Art thou overcome with grief for the loss of the moneys or for that which hath befallen the Eunuch?" Said she, "Nay, as thy head liveth, O king! but women are weaklings." Then came the Eunuch and going in to her, told her all that had happened to him and also acquainted her with her son's case and with that which he had suffered of distresses and how his uncle had exposed him to slaughter, and he had been taken prisoner and they had cast him into the pit and hurled him from the highmost of the citadel and how Allah had delivered him from these perils, all of them; and whilst he recounted to her all this, she wept. Then she asked him, "When the king saw him and questioned thee of him, what was it thou saidst him?" and he answered, "I said to him: "This is the son of a nurse who belonged to us. We left him a little one and he grew up; so I brought him, that he might be servant to the king." Cried she, "Thou didst well"; and she charged him to serve the Prince with faithful service. As for the king, he redoubled in kindness to the Eunuch and appointed the youth a liberal allowance and the abode going in to and coming out of the king's house and standing in his service, and every day he waxed better with him. As for Shah Khatun, she used to station herself at watch for him at the windows and in the balconies and gaze upon him, and she frying on coals of fire on his account; yet could she not speak. In such condition she abode a long while and indeed yearning for him was killing her; so she stood and watched for him one day at the door of her chamber and straining him to her bosom, bussed him on the breast and kissed him on either cheek. At this moment, behold, out came the major-domo of the king's household and seeing her embracing the youth, started in amazement. Then he asked to whom that chamber belonged and was answered, "To Shah Khatun, wife of the king," whereupon he turned back, quaking as one smitten by a leven-bolt. The king saw him in a tremor and said to him, "Out on thee! what is the matter?" Said he, "O king, what matter can be more grievous than that which I see?" Asked the king, "What seest thou?" and the officer answered, "I see that the youth, who came with the Eunuch, was not brought with him save on account of Shah Khatun; for I passed but now by her chamber door, and she was standing, watching; and when the youth came up, she rose to him and clipped him and kissed him on his cheek." When the king heard this, he bowed his head amazed, perplexed, and sinking into a seat, clutched at his beard and shook it till he came nigh upon plucking it out. Then he arose forthright and laid hands on the youth and clapped him in jail; he also took the Eunuch and cast them both into a souterrain under his palace. After this he went in to Shah Khatun and said to her, "Brava, by Allah, O daughter of nobles. O thou whom kings sought to wed, for the purity of thy repute and the fairness of the fame of thee! How seemly is thy semblance! Now may Allah curse her whose inward contrarieth her outward, after the likeness of thy base favor, whose exterior is handsome and its interior fulsome, face fair and deeds foul! Verily, I mean to make of thee and of yonder ne'er-do-well an example among the lieges, for that thou sentest not thine Eunuch but of intent on his account, so that he took him and brought him into my palace and thou hast trampled my head with him; and this is none other than exceeding boldness; but thou shalt see what

I will do with you all." So saying, he spat in her face and went out from her; while Shah Khatun said nothing, well knowing that, an she spoke at that time, he would not credit her speech. Then she humbled herself in supplication to Allah Almighty and said, "O God the Great, Thou knowest the things by secrecy ensealed and their outwards revealed and their inwards concealed! If an advanced life-term be appointed to me, let it not be deferred, and if a deferred one, let it not be advanced!" On this wise she passed some days, while the king fell into bewilderment and foreswore meat and drink and sleep, and abode knowing not what he should do and saying to himself, "An I slay the Eunuch and the youth, my soul will not be solaced, for they are not to blame, seeing that she sent to fetch him, and my heart careth not to kill them all three. But I will not be hasty in doing them die, for that I fear repentance." Then he left them, so he might look into the affair. Now he had a nurse, a foster-mother, on whose knees he had been reared, and she was a woman of understanding and suspected him, yet dared not question him. So she went in to Shah Khatun and finding her in yet sadder plight than he, asked her what was to do; but she refused to answer. However, the nurse gave not over coaxing and questioning her, till she swore her to concealment. Accordingly, the old woman made oath that she would keep secret all that she should say to her, whereupon the queen to her related her history, first and last, and told her that the youth was her son. With this the old woman prostrated herself before her and said to her, "This is a right easy matter." But the queen replied, "By Allah, O my mother, I prefer my destruction and that of my son to defending myself by a plea which they will not believe; for they will say: She pleadeth this only that she may fend off shame from herself. And naught will profit me save long-suffering." The old woman was moved by her speech and her wisdom and said to her, "Indeed, O my daughter, 'tis as thou sayest, and I hope in Allah that He will show forth the truth. Have patience and I will presently go in to the king and hear his words and machinate somewhat in this matter, Inshallah!" Thereupon the ancient dame arose and going in to the king, found him with his head between his knees in sore pain of sorrow. She sat down by him a while and bespoke him with soft words and said to him, "Indeed, O my son, thou consumest my vitals, for that these many days thou hast not mounted horse, and thou grievest and I know not what aileth thee." He replied, "O my mother, all is due to yonder accursed, of whom I deemed so well and who hath done this and that." Then he related to her the whole story from beginning to end, and she cried to him, "This thy chagrin is on account of a no-better-than-she-should-be!" Quoth he, "I was but considering by what death I should slay them, so the folk may take warning and repent." And quoth she, "O my son, 'ware precipitance, for it gendereth repentance and the slaying of them shall not escape thee. When thou art assured of this affair, do whatso thou willest." He rejoined, "O my mother, there needeth no assurance anent him for whom she dispatched her Eunuch and he fetched him." But she retorted, "There is a thing wherewith we will make her confess, and all that is in her heart shall be discovered to thee." Asked the king, "What is that?" and she answered, "I will bring thee the heart of a hoopoe, which, when she sleepeth, do thou lay upon her bosom and question her of everything thou wouldst know, and she will discover the same unto thee and show forth the truth to thee." The king rejoiced in this and said to his nurse, "Hasten thou and let none know of thee." So she arose and going in to the queen, said to her, "I have done thy business and 'tis as follows: This night the king will come in to thee and do thou seem asleep; and if he ask thee of aught, do thou answer him, as if in thy sleep." The queen thanked her and the old dame went away and fetching the bird's heart, gave it to the king. Hardly was the night come, when he went in to his wife and found her lying back, a-slumbering; so he sat down by her side and laying the hoopoe's heart on her breast, waited awhile, so he might be assured that she slept. Then said he to her, "Shah Khatun, Shah Khatun, is this my reward from thee?" Quoth she, "What offense have I committed?" and quoth he, "What offense can be greater than this? Thou sentest after yonder youth and broughtest him hither, on account of thy wicked desire." Said she, "This youth is my son and a piece of my heart; and of my longing and affection for him, I could not contain myself, but sprang upon him and kissed him." When the king heard this, he was dazed and amazed and said to her, "Hast thou a proof that this youth is thy son? Indeed, I have a letter from thine uncle King Sulayman Shah, informing me that his uncle Bahluwan cut his throat." Said she, "Yes, he did indeed cut his throat, but severed not the windpipe; so my uncle sewed up the wound and reared him, for that his life-term was not come." When the king heard this, he said, "This proof sufficeth me," and rising forthright in the night, bade bring the youth and the Eunuch. Then he examined his stepson's throat with a candle and saw the scar where it had been cut from ear to ear, and indeed the place had healed up and it was like a thread stretched out. Thereupon the king fell down prostrate before Allah, who had delivered the prince from all these perils and from the distresses he had suffered, and rejoiced with joy exceeding because he had delayed and had not made haste to slay him, in which case mighty sore repentance had betided him.

Devasmitá

From the Sanskrit

THERE is a city in the world famous under the name of Támraliptá, and in that city there was a very rich merchant named Dhanadatta. And he, being childless, assembled many Bráhmans and said to them with due respect, "Take such steps as will procure me a son soon." Then those Bráhmans said to him: "This is not at all difficult, for Bráhmans can accomplish all things in this world by means of ceremonies in accordance with the Scriptures. To give you an instance, there was in old times a king who had no sons, and he had a hundred and five wives in his harem. And by means of a sacrifice to procure a son, there was born to him a son named Jantu, who was like the rising of the new moon to the eyes of his wives. Once on a time an ant bit the boy on the thigh as he was crawling about on his knees, so that he was very unhappy and sobbed loudly. Thereupon the whole harem was full of confused lamentation, and the king himself shrieked out 'My son! my son!' like a common man. The boy was soon comforted, the ant having been removed, and the king blamed the misfortune of his only having one son as the cause of all his grief. And he asked the Bráhmans in his affliction if there was any expedient by which he might obtain a large number of children. They answered him, 'O king, there is one expedient open to you; you must slay this son and offer up all his flesh in the fire. By smelling the smell of that sacrifice all thy wives will obtain sons.' When he heard that, the king had the whole ceremony performed as they directed; and he obtained as many sons as he had wives. So we can obtain a son for you also by a burnt-offering." When they had said this to Dhanadatta, the Bráhmans, after a sacrificial fee had been promised them, performed a sacrifice: then a son was born to that merchant. That son was called Guhasena, and he gradually grew up to man's estate. Then his father Dhanadatta began to look out for a wife for him.

Then his father went with that son of his to another country, on the pretense of traffic, but really to get a daughter-in-law. There he asked an excellent merchant of the name of Dharmagupta to give him his daughter named Devasmitá for his son Guhasena. But Dharmagupta, who was tenderly attached to his daughter, did not approve of that connection, reflecting that the city of Támraliptá was very far off. But when Devasmitá beheld that Guhasena, her mind was immediately attracted by his virtues, and she was set on abandoning her relations, and so she made an assignation with him by means of a confidante, and went away from that country at night with her beloved and his father. When they reached Támraliptá they were married, and the minds of the young couple were firmly knit together by the bond of mutual love. Then Guhasena's father died, and he himself was urged by his relations to go to the country of Kaṭáha for the purpose of trafficking; but his wife Devasmitá was too jealous to approve of that expedition, fearing exceedingly that he would be attracted by some other lady. Then, as his wife did not approve of it, and his relations kept inciting him to it, Guhasena, whose mind was firmly set on doing his duty, was bewildered. Then he went and performed a vow in the temple of the god, observing a rigid fast, trusting that the god would show him some way out of his difficulty. And his wife Devasmitá also performed a vow with him; then Śiva was pleased to appear to that couple in a dream; and giving them two red lotuses the god said to them, "Take each of you one of these lotuses in your hand. And if either of you shall be unfaithful during your separation, the lotus in the hand of the other shall fade, but not otherwise." After hearing this, the two woke up, and each beheld in the hand of the other a red lotus, and it seemed as if they had got one another's hearts. Then Guhasena set out, lotus in hand, but Devasmitá remained in the house with her eyes fixed upon her flower. Guhasena for his part quickly reached the country of Kaṭáha, and began to buy and sell jewels there. And four young merchants in that country, seeing that that unfading lotus was ever in his hand, were greatly astonished. Accordingly they got him to their house by an artifice, and made him drink a great deal of wine, and then asked him the history of the lotus, and he being intoxicated told them the whole story. Then those four young merchants, knowing that Guhasena would take a long time to complete his sales and purchases of jewels and other wares, planned together, like rascals as they were, the seduction of his wife out of curiosity, and eager to accomplish it set out quickly for Támraliptá without their departure being noticed.

There they cast about for some instrument, and at last had recourse to a female ascetic of the name of Yogakarandiká, who lived in a sanctuary of Buddha; and they said to her in an affectionate manner, "Reverend madam, if our object is accomplished by your help, we will give you much wealth." She answered them: "No doubt, you young men desire some woman in this city, so tell me all about it, I will procure you the object of your desire, but I have no wish for money; I have a pupil of distinguished ability named Siddhikarí; owing to her kindness I have obtained untold wealth." The young merchants asked, "How have you obtained untold wealth by the assistance of a pupil?" Being asked this question, the female ascetic said, "If you feel any curiosity about the matter, listen, my sons, I will tell you the whole story.

STORY OF THE CUNNING SIDDHIKARÍ

"Long ago a certain merchant came here from the north; while he was dwelling here, my pupil went and obtained, with a treacherous object, the position of a serving-maid in his house, having first altered her appearance, and after she had gained the confidence of that merchant, she stole all his hoard of gold from his house, and went off secretly in the morning twilight. And as she went out from the city moving rapidly through fear, a certain Domba with his drum in his hand, saw her, and pursued her at full speed with the intention of robbing her. When she had reached the foot of a Nyagrodha tree, she saw that he had come up with her, and so the cunning Siddhikarí said this to him in a plaintive manner, "I have had a jealous quarrel with my husband, and I have left his house to die, therefore my good man, make a noose for me to hang myself with." Then the Domba thought, "Let her hang herself, why should I be guilty of her death, especially as she is a woman?" and so he fastened a noose for her to the tree. Then Siddhikarí, feigning ignorance, said to the Domba, "How is the noose slipped round the neck? show me, I entreat you." Then the Domba placed the drum under his feet, and saying, "This is the way we do the trick," he fastened the noose round his own throat; Siddhikarí for her part smashed the drum to atoms with a kick, and that Domba hung till he was dead. At that moment the merchant arrived in search of her, and beheld from a distance Siddhikarí, who had stolen from him untold treasures, at the foot of the tree. She, too, saw him coming, and climbed up the tree without being noticed, and remained there on a bough, having her body concealed by the dense foliage. When the merchant came up with his servants, he saw the Domba hanging by his neck, but Siddhikarí was nowhere to be seen. Immediately one of his servants said, "I wonder whether she has got up this tree," and proceeded to ascend it himself. Then Siddhikarí said, "I have always loved you, and now you have climbed up where I am, so all this wealth is at your disposal, handsome man, come and embrace me." So she embraced the merchant's servant, and as she was kissing his mouth, she bit off the fool's tongue. He, overcome with the pain, fell from that tree spitting blood from his mouth, uttering some indistinct syllables, which sounded like Lalalla. When he saw that, the merchant was terrified, and supposing that his servant had been seized by a demon, he fled from that place, and went to his own house with his attendants. Then Siddhikarí the female ascetic, equally frightened, descended from the top of the tree, and brought home with her all that wealth. Such a person is my pupil, distinguished for her great discernment, and it is in this way, my sons, that I have obtained wealth by her kindness."

When she had said this to the young merchants, the female ascetic showed to them her pupil who happened to come in at that moment, and said to them, "Now, my sons, tell me the real state of affairs—what woman do you desire? I will quickly procure her for you." When they heard that they said, "Procure us an interview with the wife of the merchant Guhasena named Devasmitá." When she heard that, the ascetic undertook to manage that business for them, and she gave those young merchants her own house to reside in. Then she gratified the servants at Guhasena's house with gifts of sweetmeats and other things, and afterwards entered it with her pupil. Then, as she approached the private rooms of Devasmitá, a hound, that was fastened there with a chain, would not let her come near, but opposed her entrance in the most determined way. Then Devasmitá seeing her, of her own accord sent a maid, and had her brought in, thinking to herself, "What can this person be come for?" After she had entered, the wicked ascetic gave Devasmitá her blessing, and, treating the virtuous woman with affected respect, said to her, "I have always had a desire to see you, but to-day I saw you in a dream, therefore I have come to visit you with impatient eagerness; and my mind is afflicted at beholding you separated from your husband, for beauty and youth are wasted when one is deprived of the society of one's beloved." With this and many other speeches of the same kind she tried to gain the confidence of the virtuous woman in a short interview, and then taking leave of her she returned to her own house. On the second day she took with her a piece of meat full of pepper dust, and went again to the house of Devasmitá, and there she gave that piece of meat to the hound at the door, and the hound gobbled it up, pepper and all. Then owing to the pepper dust, the tears flowed in profusion from the animal's eyes, and her nose began to run. And the cunning ascetic immediately went into the apartment of Devasmitá, who received her hospitably, and began to cry. When Devasmitá asked her why she shed tears, she said with affected reluctance: "My friend, look at this hound weeping outside here. This creature recognized me to-day as having been its companion in a former birth, and began to weep; for that reason my tears gushed through pity." When she heard that, and saw that hound outside apparently weeping, Devasmitá thought for a moment to herself, "What can be the meaning of this wonderful sight?" Then the ascetic said to her, "My daughter, in a former birth, I and that hound were the two wives of a certain

Bráhman. And our husband frequently went about to other countries on embassies by order of the king. Now while he was away from home, I lived at my good will and pleasure, and so did not cheat the elements, of which I was composed, and my senses, of their lawful enjoyment. For considerate treatment of the elements and senses is held to be the highest duty. Therefore I have been born in this birth with a recollection of my former existence. But she, in her former life, through ignorance, confined all her attention to the preservation of her character, therefore she has been degraded and born again as one of the canine race, however, she too remembers her former birth." The wise Devasmitá said to herself, "This is a novel conception of duty; no doubt this woman has laid a treacherous snare for me"; and so she said to her, "Reverend lady, for this long time I have been ignorant of this duty, so procure me an interview with some charming man." Then the ascetic said, "There are residing here some young merchants that have come from another country, so I will bring them to you." When she had said this, the ascetic returned home delighted, and Devasmitá of her own accord said to her maids: "No doubt those scoundrelly young merchants, whoever they may be, have seen that unfading lotus in the hand of my husband, and have on some occasion or other, when he was drinking wine, asked him out of curiosity to tell the whole story of it, and have now come here from that island to deceive me, and this wicked ascetic is employed by them. So bring quickly some wine mixed with Datura, and when you have brought it, have a dog's foot of iron made as quickly as possible." When Devasmitá had given these orders, the maids executed them faithfully, and one of the maids, by her orders, dressed herself up to resemble her mistress. The ascetic for her part chose out of the party of four merchants (each of whom in his eagerness said—"Let me go first"—) one individual, and brought him with her. And concealing him in the dress of her pupil, she introduced him in the evening into the house of Devasmitá, and coming out, disappeared. Then that maid, who was disguised as Devasmitá, courteously persuaded the young merchant to drink some of that wine drugged with Datura. That liquor, like his own immodesty, robbed him of his senses, and then the maids took away his clothes and other equipments and left him stark naked; then they branded him on the forehead with the mark of a dog's foot, and during the night took him and pushed him into a ditch full of filth. Then he recovered consciousness in the last watch of the night, and found himself plunged in a ditch, as it were the hell *Avíchi* assigned to him by his sins. Then he got up and washed himself and went to the house of the female ascetic, in a state of misery, feeling with his fingers the mark on his forehead. And when he got there, he told his friends that he had been robbed on the way, in order that he might not be the only person made ridiculous. And the next morning he sat with a cloth wrapped round his branded forehead, giving as an excuse that he had a headache from keeping awake so long, and drinking too much. In the same way the next young merchant was maltreated, when he got to the house of Devasmitá, and when he returned home stripped, he said, "I put on my ornaments there, and as I was coming out I was plundered by robbers." In the morning he also, on the plea of a headache, put a wrapper on to cover his branded forehead.

In the same way all the four young merchants suffered in turns branding and other humiliating treatment, though they concealed the fact. And they went away from the place, without revealing to the female Buddhist ascetic the ill-treatment they had experienced, hoping that she would suffer in a similar way. On the next day the ascetic went with her disciple to the house of Devasmitá, much delighted at having accomplished what she undertook to do. Then Devasmitá received her courteously, and made her drink wine drugged with Datura, offered as a sign of gratitude. When she and her disciple were intoxicated with it, that chaste wife cut off their ears and noses, and flung them also into a filthy pool. And being distressed by the thought that perhaps these young merchants might go and slay her husband, she told the whole circumstance to her mother-in-law. Then her mother-in-law said to her, "My daughter, you have acted nobly, but possibly some misfortune may happen to my son in consequence of what you have done."

So the wise Devasmitá forthwith put on the dress of a merchant. Then she embarked on a ship, on the pretense of a mercantile expedition, and came to the country of Kaṭáha where her husband was. And when she arrived there, she saw that husband of hers, Guhasena, in the midst of a circle of merchants, like consolation in external bodily form. He seeing her afar off in the dress of a man, as it were, drank her in with his eyes, and thought to himself, "Who may this merchant be that looks so like my beloved wife?" So Devasmitá went and represented to the king that she had a petition to make, and asked him to assemble all his subjects. Then the king full of curiosity assembled all the citizens, and said to that lady disguised as a merchant, "What is your petition?" Then Devasmitá said, "There are residing here in your midst four slaves of mine who have escaped, let the king make them over to me." Then the king said to her, "All the citizens are present here, so look at everyone in order to recognize him, and take those slaves of yours." Then she seized upon the four young merchants, whom she had before treated in such a humiliating way in her house, and who had wrappers bound round their heads. Then the merchants, who were there, flew in a passion, and said to her, "These are the sons of distinguished merchants, how then can they be your slaves?" Then she answered them, "If you do not believe what I say, examine their foreheads which I marked with a dog's foot." They consented, and removing the head-wrappers of these four, they all beheld the dog's foot on their foreheads. Then all the merchants were abashed, and the king, being astonished, himself asked Devasmitá what all this meant. She told the whole story, and all the people burst out laughing, and the king said to the lady, "They are your slaves by the best of titles." Then the other merchants paid a large sum of money to that chaste wife, to redeem those four from slavery, and a fine to the king's treasury. Devasmitá received that money, and recovered her husband, and being honored by all good men, returned then to her own city Támraliptá, and she was never afterwards separated from her beloved.

The Sharpers and the Moneylender

From the Arabic

FOUR sharpers once plotted against a Shroff, a man of much wealth, and agreed upon a sleight for securing some of his coins. So one of them took an ass and laying on it a bag, wherein were dirhams, lighted down at the shop of the Shroff and sought of him small change. The man of moneys brought out to him the silver bits and bartered them with him, whilst the sharper was easy with him in the matter of the exchange, so he might gar him long for more gain. As they were thus, up came the other three sharpers and surrounded the donkey; and one of them said, "'Tis he," and another said, "Wait till I look at him." Then he took to considering the ass and stroking him from crest to tail; whilst the third went up to him and handled him and felt him from head to rump, saying, "Yes, 'tis in him." Said another, "No, 'tis not in him"; and they left not doing the like of this for some time. Then they accosted the donkey's owner and chaffered with him and he said, "I will not sell him but for ten thousand dirhams." They offered him a thousand dirhams; but he refused and swore that he would not vend the ass but for that which he had said. They ceased not adding to their offer till the price reached five thousand dirhams, whilst their mate still said, "I'll not vend him save for ten thousand silver pieces." The Shroff advised him to sell, but he would not do this and said to him, "Ho, shaykh! Thou wottest not the case of this donkey. Stick to silver and gold and what pertaineth thereto of exchange and small change; because indeed the virtue of this ass is a mystery to thee. For every craft its crafty men and for every means of livelihood its peculiar people." When the affair was prolonged upon the three sharpers, they went away and sat down aside; then they came up privily to the money-changer and said to him, "An thou can buy him for us, do so, and we will give thee twenty dirhams." Quoth he, "Go away and sit down at a distance from him." So they did as he bade and the Shroff went up to the owner of the ass and ceased not luring him with lucre and saying, "Leave these wights and sell me the donkey, and I will reckon him a present from thee," till he sold him the animal for five thousand and five hundred dirhams. Accordingly the money-changer weighed out to him that sum of his own moneys, and the owner of the ass took the price and delivered the beast to him, saying, "Whatso shall betide, though he abide a deposit upon thy neck, sell him not to yonder cheats for less than ten thousand dirhams, for that they would fain buy him because of a hidden hoard they know, whereto naught can guide them save this donkey. So close thy hand on him and cross me not, or thou shalt repent." With these words he left him and went away, whereupon up came the three other sharpers, the comrades of him of the ass, and said to the Shroff, "God requite thee for us with good, in that thou hast bought him! How can we reward thee?" Quoth he, "I will not sell him but for ten thousand dirhams." When they heard that they returned to the ass and fell again to examining him like buyers and handling him. Then said they to the money-changer, "Indeed we were deceived in him. This is not the ass we sought and he is not worth to us more than ten nusfs." Then they left him and offered to go away, whereat the Shroff was sore chagrined and cried out at their speech, saying, "O folk, ye asked me to buy him for you and now I have bought him, ye say, we were deceived in him, and he is not worth to us more than ten nusfs." They replied, "We thought that in him was whatso we wanted; but, behold, in him is the contrary of that which we wish; and indeed he hath a blemish, for that he is short of back." Then they made long noses at him and went away from him and dispersed. The money-changer deemed they did but play him off, that they might get the donkey at their own price; but, when they walked away from him and he had long awaited their return, he cried out, saying, "Well-away!" and "Ruin!" and "Sorry case I am in!" and shrieked aloud and rent his raiment. So the market-people assembled to him and questioned him of his case; whereupon he acquainted them with his condition and told them what the knaves had said and how they had cozened him and how they had cajoled him into buying an ass worth fifty dirhams for five thousand and five hundred. His friends blamed him and a gathering of the folk laughed at him and admired his folly and over-faith in believing the talk of the sharpers without suspicion, and meddling with that which he understood not and thrusting himself into that whereof he had no sure knowledge.

The Withered Hand

From the Turkish

ONE of the caliphs of the Abassides, named Mutaasid Billah Yansur bi nour Ullah, was a sovereign of great good judgment and careful justice. He one day, in company with his attendants, visited a palace situated on the banks of the Tigris, where he observed an expert fisherman throw his net into the river, and, after hauling it out, found only three or four fish in it. The caliph remarking this, commanded the fisherman to throw it into the water again for his sake, "and let us see," said he, "what my luck will be." The man did as he was ordered, and soon after, hauling his net out, felt something weighty among its meshes. In consequence of the increased weight, the attendants of the caliph had to aid him, and when the net was on shore, they found in it a leather bag, tightly bound round the mouth. In this bag they at first perceived a number of tiles, and finally at its bottom the hand of a tender and young girl, bent and shriveled. The caliph, on seeing the hand, exclaimed, " Poor creature, what work is this, that the servants of God (Mussulmans) should be thus cut to pieces and thrown into the river without our knowledge? We must find the committer of this wicked act." Now with the caliph was one of his cadis (judges), who spoke and said, " Oh! Ameer of the Faithful, give your precious self no trouble about this matter, for, by your favor, we will investigate, and with proper care and circumspection bring it to light."

The caliph at the same time called the governor of the city of Baghdad, and giving the bag into his hands, said, " Go to the bazaar, show it to the sack sewers, and inquire whose work it is; they know each other's work; and if you find the individual who sewed it, bring him to me."

The cadi had the sack shown to the sewers, and an old grave-looking man, on seeing it, exclaimed that it was his own work. " Lately I sold it," added he, " and two others, to one Yahiya Ilha, a native of Damascus, of the family of the Mahides." The cadi on hearing this said, " Come with me to the caliph; fear nothing, he has only a few questions to ask you." So the old man accompanied him into the presence of the caliph, who demanded of him to whom he had sold it. The old man answered as before, adding, " Oh, Prince of the Faithful, he is a man of high rank, but very wicked and tyrannical, and continually does injury and vexation to true believers. Everyone fears him, and none dare complain against him to the caliph. Lately a lady, named Inaan Magennee, purchased a female slave for one thousand dinars who was very fair and beautiful, and, moreover, a poetess. This man supposed her mistress would sell her to him, but receiving the lady's reply that she had already given her her freedom, he sent her word that there was to be a wedding in the house, and requested that the female should be loaned him for the occasion.

The lady, therefore, sent her as a loan for three days, and, after four or five had elapsed, sending to demand her, received for answer that she had already left his house two or three days ago, and notwithstanding the lady's tears and complaints, she could not obtain her slave, nor even hear any news of her.

"The lady, from fear of this man's violence, held her peace, and left the quarter wherein she had resided, for it is said he had already put several of his neighbors to death."

When the old man was done speaking, the caliph seemed greatly rejoiced, and commanded that Yahiya Ilha should forthwith be brought before him. He came, and when he was shown the hand found in the bag his color changed, and he falsely endeavored to exculpate himself. The lady was likewise brought, and so soon as she saw the hand she commenced weeping, and exclaimed, "Yes, indeed, it is the hand of my poor murdered slave." "Speak," said the caliph to the Mahides, "for by my head I swear to know the truth of this affair." So the man acknowledged that he had killed the slave; and the caliph, in consideration of Hasheem,[1] sentenced him to pay to the owner of the slave one thousand pieces of gold for the loss which she had sustained, and one hundred thousand more for the law of retaliation; after which he allowed him three days in which to settle his affairs in the city, and then leave it forever.

On learning this sentence, the public loudly praised the caliph's judgment, and commended his justice and equity.

[1] Beni Hasheem, one of the most ancient Arabian tribes, from which the Prophet descended.—A. T.

The Melancholist and the Sharper

From the Arabic

THERE was once a Richard hight 'Ajlan, the Hasty, who wasted his wealth, and concern and chagrin got the mastery of him, so that he became a Melancholist and lost his wit. There remained with him of his moneys about twenty dinars and he used to beg alms of the folk, and whatso they gave him in charity he would gather together and add to the gold pieces that were left him. Now there was in that town a Sharper, who made his living by roguery, and he knew that the Melancholist had somewhat of money; so he fell to spying upon him and ceased not watching him till he saw him put into an earthen pot that which he had with him of silvers and enter a deserted ruin, where he sat down, and straightway began to dig a hole, wherein he laid the pot and covering it up, smoothed the ground as it had been. Then he went away and the Sharper came and taking what was in the pot, restored it to its former place. Presently 'Ajlan returned, with somewhat to add to his hoard, but found it not; so he bethought him of who had followed him and remembered that he had found that Sharper assiduous in sitting with him and questioning him. So he went in search of him, assured that he had taken the pot, and gave not over looking for him till he saw him sitting; whereupon he went to him and the Sharper saw him. Then the Melancholist stood within earshot and muttered to himself and said, "In the pot are sixty ducats and I have with me other twenty in such a place and to-day I will unite the whole in the pot." When the Sharper heard him say this to himself, muttering and mumbling, repeating and blundering in his speech, he repented him of having taken the sequins and said, "He will presently return to the pot and find it empty; wherefore that for which I am on the lookout will escape me; and meseemeth 'twere best I replace the dinars, so he may see them and leave all which is with him in the pot, and I can take the whole." Now he feared to return to the pot at once, lest the Melancholist should follow him to the place and find nothing and on this wise his arrangements be marred; so he said to him, "O 'Ajlan, I would have thee come to my lodging and eat bread with me." Therefore the Melancholist went with him to his quarters and he seated him there and going to the market, sold somewhat of his clothes and pawned somewhat from his house and bought the best of food. Then he betook himself to the ruin and replacing the money in the pot, buried it again; after which he returned to his lodging and gave the Melancholist to eat and drink, and they went out together. The Sharper walked away and hid himself, lest his guest should see him, while 'Ajlan repaired to his hiding-place and took the pot. Presently the Sharper returned to the ruin, rejoicing in that which he deemed he should get, and dug in the place, but found naught and knew that the Melancholist had outwitted him. So he began buffeting his face for regret, and fell to following the other whitherso he went, to the intent that he might win what was with him, but he failed in this, because the Melancholist knew what was in his mind and was assured that he spied upon him; so he kept watch over himself. Now, had the Sharper considered the consequences of haste and that which is begotten of loss therefrom, he had not done on such wise.

Lakshadatta and Labdhadatta

From the Sanskrit

THERE was on the earth a city named Lakshapura. In it there lived a king named Lakshadatta, chief of generous men. He never knew how to give a petitioner less than a lac of coins, but he gave five lacs to anyone with whom he conversed. As for the man with whom he was pleased, he lifted him out of poverty, for this reason his name was called Lakshadatta. A certain dependent named Labdhadatta stood day and night at his gate, with a piece of leather for his only loin-rag. He had matted hair, and he never left the king's gate for a second, day or night, in cold, rain, or heat, and the king saw him there. And, though he remained there long in misery, the king did not give him anything, though he was generous and compassionate.

Then, one day the king went to a forest to hunt, and his dependent followed him with a staff in his hand. There, while the king seated on an elephant, armed with a bow, and followed by his army, slew tigers, bears, and deer, with showers of arrows, his dependent, going in front of him, alone on foot, slew with his staff many boars and deer. When the king saw his bravery, he thought in his heart, " It is wonderful that this man should be such a hero," but he did not give him anything. And the king, when he had finished his hunting, returned home to his city, to enjoy himself, but that dependent stood at his palace-gate as before. Once on a time, Lakshadatta went out to conquer a neighboring king of the same family, and he had a terrible battle. And in the battle the dependent struck down in front of him many enemies, with blows from the end of his strong staff of acacia wood. And the king, after conquering his enemies, returned to his own city, and though he had seen the valor of his dependent, he gave him nothing. In this condition the dependent Labdhadatta remained, and many years passed over his head, while he supported himself with difficulty.

And when the sixth year had come, king Lakshadatta happened to see him one day, and feeling pity for him, reflected, " Though he has been long afflicted, I have not as yet given him anything, so why should I not give him something in a disguised form, and so find out whether the guilt of this poor man has been effaced, or not, and whether even now Fortune will grant him a sight of her, or not? " Thus reflecting, the king deliberately entered his treasury, taking with him a lemon in his hand. And upon his return therefrom, he held an assembly of all his subjects, having appointed a meeting outside his palace, and there entered the assembly all his citizens, chiefs, and ministers. And when the dependent entered among them, the king said to him with an affectionate voice, "Come here"; then the dependent, on hearing this, was delighted, and coming near, he sat in front of the king. Then the king said to him, "Utter some composition of your own." Then the dependent recited the following Áryá verse—"Fortune ever replenishes the full man, as all the streams replenish the sea, but she never even comes within the range of the eyes of the poor." When the king had heard this, and had made him recite it again, he was pleased, and gave him the lemon which he had carried. And the people said, "This king puts a stop to the poverty of everyone with whom he is pleased; so this dependent is to be pitied, since this very king, though pleased with him, after summoning him politely, has given him nothing but this lemon; a wishing-tree in the case of ill-starred men, often becomes a *palása*-tree." These were the words which all in the assembly said to one another in their despondency, when they saw that, for they did not know the truth.

But the dependent went out, with the lemon in his hand, and when he was in a state of despondency, a mendicant came before him. And that mendicant, named Rájavandin, seeing that the lemon was a fine one, obtained it from that dependent by giving him a garment. And then the mendicant entered the assembly, and gave that fruit to the king, and the king, recognizing it, said to that hermit, "Where, reverend sir, did you procure this lemon?" Then he told the king that the dependent had given it to him. Then the king was grieved and astonished, reflecting that his guilt was not expiated even now. The king Lakshadatta took the lemon, rose up from the assembly, and performed the duties of the day. And the dependent sold the garment, and after he had eaten and drunk, remained at his usual post at the king's gate.

And on the second day the king held a general assembly,

and everybody appeared at it again, citizens and all. And the king, seeing that the dependent had entered the assembly, called him as before, and made him sit near him. And after making him again recite that very same Áryá verse, being pleased, he gave him that very same lemon which he had given him before. And all there thought with astonishment—"Ah! this is the second time that our master is pleased with him without his gaining by it." And the dependent, in despondency, took the lemon in his hand, and thinking that the king's good will had again been barren of results, went out. At that very moment a certain official met him, who was about to enter that assembly, wishing to see the king. He, when he saw that lemon, took a fancy to it, and regarding the omen, procured it from the dependent by giving him a pair of garments. And entering the king's court, he fell at the feet of the sovereign, and first gave him the lemon, and then another present of his own. And when the king recognized the fruit, he asked the official where he got it, and he replied, "From the dependent." And the king, thinking in his heart that Fortune would not even now give the dependent a sight of her, was exceedingly sad. And he rose up from the assembly with that lemon, and the dependent went to the market with the pair of garments he had got. And by selling one garment he procured meat and drink, and tearing the other in half he made two of it. Then on the third day also the king held a general assembly, and all the subjects entered, as before, and when the dependent entered, the king gave him the same lemon again, after calling him and making him recite the Áryá verse. Then all were astonished, and the dependent went out, and gave that lemon to the king's favorite. And she, like a moving creeper of the tree of the king's regard, gave him gold, which was, so to speak, the flower, the harbinger of the fruit. The dependent sold it, and enjoyed himself that day, and the king's mistress went into his presence. And she gave him that lemon, which was large and fine, and he, recognizing it, asked her whence she procured it. Then she said, "The dependent gave it me." Hearing that, the king thought, "Fortune has not yet looked favorably upon him; his merit in a former life must have been slight, since he does not know that my favor is never barren of results." Thus verily the king reflected, and he took that lemon, and put it away safely, and rose up and performed the duties of the day. And on the fourth day the king held an assembly in the same way, and it was filled with all his subjects, feudatories, ministers and all. And the dependent came there again, and again the king made him sit in front of him, and when he bowed before him, the king made him recite the Áryá verse; and gave him the lemon, and when the dependent had half got hold of it, he suddenly let it go, and the lemon fell on the ground and broke in half. And as the joining of the lemon, which kept it together, was broken, there rolled out of it many valuable jewels, illuminating that place of assembly. All the people, when they saw it, said, "Ah! we were deluded and mistaken, as we did not know the real state of the case, but such is the nature of the king's favor." When the king heard that, he said, "By this artifice I endeavored to ascertain, whether Fortune would now look on him or not. But for three days his guilt was not effaced; now it is effaced, and for that reason Fortune has now granted him a sight of herself." After the king had said this, he gave the dependent those jewels, and also villages, elephants, horses and gold, and made him a feudal chief. And he rose up from that assembly, in which the people applauded, and went to bathe; and that dependent too, having obtained his ends, went to his own dwelling.

The Cunning Crone

From the Arabic

THERE came one day an old woman to the stuff-bazar, with a casket of mighty fine workmanship, containing trinkets, and she was accompanied by a young baggage.

The crone sat down at the shop of a draper and giving him to know that the girl was of the household of the Prefect of Police of the city, took of him, on credit, stuffs to the value of a thousand dinars and deposited with him the casket as security. She opened the casket and showed him that which was therein and he found it full of trinkets of price; so he trusted her with the goods and she farewelled him and carrying the stuffs to the girl who was with her, went her way. Then the old woman was absent from him a great while, and when her absence was prolonged, the draper despaired of her; so he went up to the Prefect's house and asked anent the woman of his household who had taken his stuffs on credit; but could obtain no tidings of her nor happen on any trace of her. Then he brought out the casket of jewelry and showed it to experts, who told him that the trinkets were gilt and that their worth was but an hundred dirhams. When he heard this, he was sore concerned thereat and presenting himself before the Deputy of the Sultan made his complaint to him; whereupon the official knew that a sleight had been served upon him and that the sons of Adam had cozened him and conquered him and cribbed his stuffs. Now the magistrate in question was a man of experience and judgment, well versed in affairs; so he said to the draper, "Remove somewhat from thy shop, including the casket, and to-morrow morning break the lock and cry out and come to me and complain that they have plundered all thy shop. Also mind thou call upon Allah for aid and wail aloud and acquaint the people, so that a world of folk may flock to thee and sight the breach of the lock and that which is missing from thy shop: and on this wise display it to everyone who presenteth himself that the news may be noised abroad, and tell them that thy chief concern is for a casket of great value, deposited with thee by a great man of the town and that thou standest in fear of him. But be thou not afraid and still say ever and anon in thy saying: My casket was the casket of Such-an-one, and I fear him and dare not bespeak him; but you, O company and all ye who are present, I call you to witness of this for me. And if there be with thee more than this saying, say it; and the old woman will assuredly come to thee." The draper answered with, "To hear is to obey," and going forth from the Deputy's presence, betook himself to his shop and brought out thence the casket and merchandise making a great display, which he removed to his house. At break of day he arose and going to his shop, broke the lock and shouted and shrieked and called on Allah for aid, till each and every of the folk assembled about him and all who were in the city were present, whereupon he cried out to them, saying even as the Prefect had bidden him; and this was bruited abroad. Then he made for the Prefecture and presenting himself before the Chief of Police, cried out and complained and made a show of distraction. After three days, the old woman came to him and bringing him the thousand dinars, the price of the stuffs, demanded the casket. When he saw her, he seized her and carried her to the Prefect of the city; and when she came before the Kazi, he said to her, "Woe to thee, O Sataness; did not thy first deed suffice thee, but thou must come a second time?" She replied, "I am of those who seek their plunder in the cities, and we foregather every month; and yesterday we foregathered." He asked her, "Canst thou cause me to catch them?" and she answered, "Yes; but, an thou wait till to-morrow, they will have dispersed; so I will deliver them to thee to-night." The Emir said to her, "Go"; and said she, "Send with me one who shall go with me to them and obey me in whatso I shall say to him, and all that I bid him he shall not gainsay and therein conform to my way." Accordingly, he gave her a company of men and she took them and bringing them to a certain door, said to them, "Stand ye here, at this door, and whoso cometh out to you, seize him; and I will come out to you last of all." "Hearing and obeying," answered they and stood at the door, whilst the crone went in. They waited a whole hour, even as the Sultan's deputy had bidden them, but none came out to them and their standing waxed longsome, and when they were weary of waiting, they went up to the door and smote upon it a heavy blow and a violent, so that they came nigh to break the wooden bolt. Then one of them entered and was absent a long while, but found naught; so he returned to his comrades and said to them, "This is the door of a dark passage, leading to such a thoroughfare; and indeed she laughed at you and left you and went away." When they heard his words, they returned to the Emir and acquainted him with the case, whereby he knew that the old woman was a cunning craftmistress and that she had mocked at them and cozened them and put a cheat on them, to save herself. Witness, then, the wiles of this woman and that which she contrived of guile, for all her lack of foresight in presenting herself a second time to the draper and not suspecting that his conduct was but a sleight; yet, when she found herself hard upon calamity, she straightway devised a device for her deliverance.

Judgment of a Solomon

From the Chinese

IN our district there lived two men, named Hu Ch'êng and Fêng Ngan, between whom there existed an old feud. The former, however, was the stronger of the two; and accordingly Fêng disguised his feelings under a specious appearance of friendship, though Hu never placed much faith in his professions. One day they were drinking together, and being both of them rather the worse for liquor, they began to brag of the various exploits they had achieved. "What care I for poverty," cried Hu, "when I can lay a hundred ounces of silver on the table at a moment's notice?" Now Fêng was well aware of the state of Hu's affairs, and did not hesitate to scout such pretensions, until Hu further informed him in perfect seriousness that the day before he had met a merchant traveling with a large sum of money and had tumbled him down a dry well by the wayside; in confirmation of which he produced several hundred ounces of silver, which really belonged to a brother-in-law on whose behalf he was managing some negotiation for the purchase of land. When they separated, Fêng went off and gave information to the magistrate of the place, who summoned Hu to answer to the charge. Hu then told the actual facts of the case, and his brother-in-law and the owner of the land in question corroborated his statement. However, on examining the dry well by letting a man down with a rope round him, lo! there was a headless corpse lying at the bottom. Hu was horrified at this, and called Heaven to witness that he was innocent; whereupon the magistrate ordered him twenty or thirty blows on the mouth for lying in the presence of such irrefragable proof, and cast him into the condemned cell, where he lay loaded with chains. Orders were issued that the corpse was not to be removed, and a notification was made to the people, calling upon the relatives of the deceased to come forward and claim the body. Next day a woman appeared, and said deceased was her husband; that his name was Ho, and that he was proceeding on business with a large sum of money about him when he was killed by Hu. The magistrate observed that possibly the body in the well might not be that of her husband, to which the woman replied that she felt sure it was; and accordingly the corpse was brought up and examined, when the woman's story was found to be correct. She herself did not go near the body, but stood at a little distance making the most doleful lamentation; until at length the magistrate said, "We have got the murderer, but the body is not complete; you go home and wait until the head has been discovered, when life shall be given for life." He then summoned Hu before him, and told him to produce the head by the next day under penalty of severe torture; but Hu only wandered about with the guard sent in charge of him, crying and lamenting his fate, but finding nothing. The instruments of torture were then produced, and preparations were made as if for torturing Hu; however, they were not applied, and finally the magistrate sent him back to prison, saying, "I suppose that in your hurry you didn't notice where you dropped the head." The woman was then brought before him again; and on learning that her relatives consisted only of one uncle, the magistrate remarked, "A young woman like you, left alone in the world, will hardly be able to earn a livelihood. [Here she burst into tears and implored the magistrate's pity.] The punishment of the guilty man has been already decided upon, but until we get the head, the case cannot be closed. As soon as it is closed, the best thing you can do is to marry again. A young woman like yourself should not be in and out of a police-court." The woman thanked the magistrate and retired; and the latter issued a notice to the people, calling upon them to make a search for the head. On the following day, a man named Wang, a fellow villager of the deceased, reported that he had found the missing head; and his report proving to be true, he was rewarded with 1,000 *cash*. The magistrate now summoned the woman's uncle above-mentioned, and told him that the case was complete, but that as it involved such an important matter as the life of a human being, there would necessarily be some delay in closing it for good and all.[1] "Meanwhile," added the magistrate, "your niece is a young woman and has no children; persuade her to marry again and so keep herself out of these troubles, and never mind what people may say." The uncle at first refused to do this; upon which the magistrate was obliged to threaten him until he was ultimately forced to consent. At this, the woman appeared before the magistrate to thank him for what he had done; whereupon the latter gave out that any

[1] There is a widespread belief that human life in China is held at a cheap rate. This may be accounted for by the fact that death is the legal punishment for many crimes not considered capital in the West; and by the severe measures that are always taken in cases of rebellion, when the innocent and guilty are often indiscriminately massacred. In times of tranquillity, however, this is not the case; and the execution of a criminal is surrounded by a number of formalities which go far to prevent the shedding of innocent blood. The *Hsi-yüan-lu* opens with the words, "There is nothing more important than human life."—HERBERT M. GILES, TRANSLATOR.

person who was willing to take the woman to wife was to present himself at his yamên. Immediately afterwards an application was made—by the very man who had found the head. The magistrate then sent for the woman and asked her if she could say who was the real murderer; to which she replied that Hu Chêng had done the deed. "No!" cried the magistrate, "it was not he. It was you and this man here. [Here both began loudly to protest their innocence.] I have long known this; but, fearing to leave the smallest loophole for escape, I have tarried thus long in elucidating the circumstances. How [to the woman], before the corpse was removed from the well, were you so certain that it was your husband's body? *Because you already knew he was dead.* And does a trader who has several hundred ounces of silver about him dress as shabbily as your husband was dressed? And you [to the man], how did you manage to find the head so readily? *Because you were in a hurry to marry the woman.*" The two culprits stood there as pale as death, unable to utter a word in their defense; and on the application of torture both confessed the crime. For this man, the woman's paramour, had killed her husband, curiously enough, about the time of Hu Chêng's braggart joke. Hu was accordingly released, but Fêng suffered the penalty of a false accuser; he was severely bambooed, and banished for three years. The case was thus brought to a close without the wrongful punishment of a single person.

The Sultan and his Three Sons

From the Arabic

THERE was erewhile in the land of Al-Yaman a man which was a Sultan and under him were three Kinglets whom he overruled. He had four children; to wit, three sons and a daughter: he also owned wealth and treasures greater than reed can pen or page may contain; as well as animals such as horses and camels, sheep and black cattle; and he was held in awe by all the sovereigns. But when his reign had lasted for a length of time, Age brought with it ailments and infirmities and he became incapable of faring forth his Palace to the Divan, the hall of audience; whereupon he summoned his three sons to the presence and said to them, "As for me, 'tis my wish to divide among you all my substance ere I die, that ye may be equal in circumstance and live in accordance with whatso I shall command." And they said, "Hearkening and obedience." Then quoth the Sultan, "Let the eldest of you become sovereign after me: let the cadet succeed to my moneys and treasures, and as for the youngest let him inherit my animals of every kind. Suffer none to transgress against other; but each aid each and assist his co-partner." He then caused them to sign a bond and agreement to abide by his bequeathal; and, after delaying a while, he departed to the mercy of Allah. Thereupon his three sons got ready the funeral gear and whatever was suited to his estate for the mortuary obsequies such as cerements and other matters: they washed the corpse and enshrouded it and prayed over it: then, having committed it to the earth they returned to their palaces where the Wazirs and the Lords of the Land and the city-folk in their multitudes, high and low, rich and poor, flocked to condole with them on the loss of their father. And the news of his decease was soon bruited abroad in all the provinces; and deputations from each and every city came to offer condolence to the King's sons. These ceremonies duly ended, the eldest Prince demanded that he should be seated as Sultan on the stead of his sire in accordance with the paternal will and testament; but he could not obtain it from his two brothers as both and each said, "I will become ruler in room of my father." So enmity and disputes for the government now arose among them and it was not to be won by any; but at last quoth the eldest Prince, "Wend we and submit ourselves to the arbitration of a Sultan of the tributary sultans; and let him to whom he shall adjudge the realm take it and reign over it." Quoth they, "'Tis well!" and thereto agreed, as did also the Wazirs; and the three set out without suite seeking a Sultan of the sultans who had been under the hands of their sire, in order that they might take him to arbitrator. And they stinted not faring till the middle way, when behold, they came upon a mead abounding in herbage and in rain-water lying sheeted. So they sat them down to rest and to eat of their victual, when one of the brothers, casting his eye upon the herbage, cried, "Verily a camel hath lately passed this way laden half with Halwa-sweetmeats and half with Hamiz-pickles." "True," cried the second, "and he was blind of an eye." Hardly, however, had they ended their words when lo! the owner of the camel came upon them (for he had overheard their speech and had said to himself, "By Allah, these three fellows have driven off my property, inasmuch as they have described the burden and eke the beast as one-eyed"), and cried out, "Ye three have carried away my camel!" "By Allah we have not seen him," quoth the Princes, "much less have we touched him"; but quoth the man, "By the Almighty, who can have taken him except you? and if you will not deliver him to me, off with us, I and you three, to the Sultan." They replied, "By all manner of means; let us wend to the sovereign." So the four hied forth, the three Princes and the Cameleer, and ceased not faring till they reached the capital of the King. There they took seat without the wall to rest for an hour's time, and presently they arose and pushed into the city and came to the royal Palace. Then they craved leave of the Chamberlains, and one of the Eunuchs caused them enter and signified to the sovereign that the three sons of Such-an-such a Sultan had made act of presence. So he bade them be set before him and the four went in and saluted him, and prayed for him and he returned their salams. He then asked them, "What is it hath brought you hither and what may ye want in the way of inquiry?" Now the first to speak was the Cameleer and he said, "O my lord the Sultan; verily these three men have carried off my camel by proof of their own speech, for they have indeed described him and the burden he bore! And I require of our lord the Sultan that he take from these wights and deliver to me the camel which is mine as proved by their own words." Presently, asked the Sultan, "What say ye to the claims of this man and the camel belonging to him?" Hereto the Princes made answer, "By Allah, O King of the Age, we have not seen the camel, much less have we stolen him." Thereupon the Cameleer exclaimed, "O my lord, I heard yonder one say that the beast was blind of an eye; and the second said that half his load was of sour stuff and the other half was of sweet stuff." They replied, "True, we spake these words"; and the Sultan cried to them, "Ye have purloined the beast by this proof." They rejoined, "No, by Allah, O my lord. We sat us in such a place for repose and refreshment and we remarked that some of the pasture had been grazed down, so we said: This is the grazing of a camel; and he must have been blind of one eye as the grass was eaten only on one side. But as for our saying that the load was half Halwa-sweetmeats and half Hamiz-pickles, we saw on the place where the camel had knelt the flies gathering in great numbers while on the other were none: so the case was clear to us (as flies settle on naught save the sugared) that one of the panniers must have contained sweets and the other sours." Hearing this the Sultan said to the Cameleer, "O man, fare thee forth and look after thy camel; for these signs and tokens prove not the theft of these men, but only the power of their intellect and their penetration." And when the Cameleer heard this, he went his ways. Presently the Sultan cleared a place in the Palace and allotted to it the Princes for their entertainment: he also directed they be supplied with a banquet and the eunuchs did his bidding. But when it was eventide and supper was served up, the trio sat down to it purposing to eat; the cadet tasting a bit of kid exclaimed, "This kid was suckled by a dog"; and the youngest exclaimed, "Assuredly this Sultan must be of ignoble birth." And this was said by the youths what while the sultan had hidden himself in order to hear and to profit by the Princes' words. So he waxed wroth and entered hastily crying, "What be these speeches ye have spoken?" They replied, "Concerning what thou hast heard inquire within and thou wilt find it wholly true." The Sultan then went forth and summoned the head-shepherd and asked him concerning the kid he had butchered. He replied, "By Allah, O my lord, the nanny-goat that bare the kid died and we found none other in milk to suckle him; but I had a dog that had just pupped and her have I made nourish him." The Sultan lastly hent his sword in hand and proceeded to the apartments of the Sultanah-mother and cried, "By Allah, unless thou avert my shame we will cut thee down with this scimiter! Say me whose son am I?" She replied, "By Allah, O my child, indeed falsehood is an excuse, but fact and truth are more saving and superior. Verily thou art the son of a cook! Thy sire could not obtain boy-children and I bare him only a single daughter. But it so fortuned that the kitchener's wife lay in of a boy (to wit, thyself); so we gave my girl-babe to the cook and took thee as a son of the Sultan, dreading for the realm after thy sire's death." The King went forth from his mother in astonishment at the penetration of the youths and, when he had taken seat in his palace, he summoned the trio and as soon as they appeared he asked them: "Which of you was it that said of the kid's meat that the beast was suckled by a dog? What proof had he of this? How did he learn it and whence did his intelligence discover it to him?" Now when the deceased Sultan's second son heard these words, he made answer: "I, O King of the Age, am he who said that say!" The King replied, "'Tis well"; and the Prince resumed, "O my lord, that which showed me the matter of the meat which was to us brought is as follows: I found the fat of the kid all near by the bone, and I knew that the beast had sucked dog's milk; for the flesh of dogs lieth outside and their fat is on their bones, whereas in sheep and goats the fat lieth upon the meat. Such, then, was my proof wherein there is no doubt nor hesitation; and when thou shalt have made question and inquiry thou wilt find this to be fact." Quoth the Sultan, "'Tis well; thou hast spoken truth and whatso thou sayest is soothfast. But which is he who declared that I am ignoble and what was his proof and what sign in me exposed it to him?" Quoth the youngest Prince, "I am he who said it"; and the Sultan rejoined, "There is no help but that thou provide me with a proof." The Prince rejoined, "O my lord, I have evidence that thou art the son of a cook and a base-born, in that thou didst not sit at meat with us and this was mine all-sufficient evidence. Every man hath three properties which he inheriteth at times from his father, at times from his maternal uncle and at times from his mother. From his sire cometh generosity or niggardness; from his uncle courage or cowardice; from his mother modesty or immodesty; and such is the proof of every man." Then quoth to him the Sultan, "Sooth thou speakest; but say me, men who like you know all things thoroughly by evidence and by your powers of penetration, what cause have they to come seeking arbitration at my hand? Beyond yours there be no increase of intelligence. So fare ye forth from me and manage the matter among yourselves, for 'tis made palpable to me by your own words that naught remaineth to you save to speak of mysterious subjects; nor have I the capacity to adjudge between you after that which I have heard from you. In fine an ye possess any document drawn up by your sire before his decease, act according to it and contrary it not." Upon this the Princes went forth from him and made for their own country and city and did as their father had bidden them do on his death-bed. The eldest enthroned himself as Sultan; the cadet assumed possession and management of the moneys and treasures, and the youngest took to himself the camels and the horses and the beeves and the muttons. Then each and every was indeed equal with his co-partner in the gathering of good.

A Tale of a Demon

From the Sanskrit

ON the banks of the Godávarí there is a place named Pratishṭhána. In it there lived of old time a famous king, named Trivikramasena, the son of Vikramasena, equal to Indra in might. Every day, when he was in his hall of audience, a mendicant named Kshántiśíla came to him, to pay him his respects, and presented him with a fruit. And every day the king, as soon as he received the fruit, gave it into the hand of the superintendent of his treasury who was near him. In this way ten years passed, but one day, when the mendicant had left the hall of audience, after giving the fruit to the king, the king gave it to a young pet monkey, that had escaped from the hands of its keepers, and happened to enter there. While the monkey was eating that fruit, it burst open, and there came out of it a splendid priceless jewel. When the king saw that, he took up the jewel, and asked the treasurer the following question, "Where have you put all those fruits which I have been in the habit of handing over to you, after they were given to me by the mendicant?" When the superintendent of the treasury heard that, he was full of fear, and he said to the king, "I used to throw them into the treasury from the window without opening the door; if your Majesty orders me, I will open it and look for them." When the treasurer said this, the king gave him leave to do so, and he went away, and soon returned, and said to the king, "I see that those fruits have all rotted away in the treasury, and I also see that there is a heap of jewels there resplendent with radiant gleams."

When the king heard it, he was pleased, and gave those jewels to the treasurer, and the next day he said to the mendicant, who came as before, "Mendicant, why do you court me every day with great expenditure of wealth? I will not take your fruit to-day until you tell me." When the king said this, the mendicant said to him in private, "I have an incantation to perform which requires the aid of a brave man. I request, hero, that you will assist me in it." When the king heard that, he consented and promised him that he would do so. Then the mendicant was pleased and he went on to say to that king, "Then I shall be waiting for you at nightfall in the approaching black fortnight, in the great cemetery here, under the shade of a *banyan*-tree, and you must come to me there." The king said, "Well! I will do so." And the mendicant Kshántiśíla returned delighted to his own dwelling.

Then the heroic monarch, as soon as he had got into the black fortnight, remembered the request of the mendicant, which he had promised to accomplish for him, and as soon as night came, he enveloped his head in a black cloth, and left the palace unperceived, sword in hand, and went fearlessly to the cemetery. It was obscured by a dense and terrible pall of darkness, and its aspect was rendered awful by the ghastly flames from the burning of the funeral pyres, and it produced horror by the bones, skeletons, and skulls of men that appeared in it. In it were present formidable Bhútas and Vetálas, joyfully engaged in their horrible activity, and it was alive with the loud yells of jackals, so that it seemed like a second mysterious tremendous form of Bhairava. And after he had searched about in it, he found that mendicant under a *banyan*-tree, engaged in making a circle, and he went up to him and said, "Here I am arrived, mendicant; tell me, what can I do for you?"

When the mendicant heard that, and saw the king, he was delighted, and said to him, "King, if I have found favor in your eyes, go alone a long way from here toward the south, and you will find an *asoka*-tree. On it there is a dead man hanging up; go and bring him here; assist me in this matter, hero." As soon as the brave king, who was faithful to his promise, heard this, he said, "I will do so," and went toward the south. And after he had gone some way in that direction, along a path revealed by the light of the flaming pyres, he reached with difficulty in the darkness that *aśoka*-tree; the tree was scorched with the smoke of funeral pyres, and smelled of raw flesh, and looked like a Bhúta, and he saw the corpse hanging on its trunk, as it were on the shoulder of a demon. So he climbed up, and cutting the string which held it, flung it to the ground. And the moment it was flung down, it cried out, as if in pain. Then the king, supposing it was alive, came down and rubbed its body out of compassion; that made the corpse utter a loud demoniac laugh. Then the king knew that it was possessed by a Vetála, and said without flinching, "Why do you laugh? Come, let us go off." And immediately he missed from the ground the corpse possessed by the Vetála, and perceived that it was once more suspended on that very tree. Then he climbed up again and brought it down, for the heart of heroes is a gem more impenetrable than adamant. Then King Trivikramasena threw the corpse possessed by a Vetála over his shoulder, and proceeded to go off with it, in silence. And as he was going along, the Vetála in the corpse that was on his shoulder said to him, "King, I will tell you a story to beguile the way, listen.

STORY OF THE PRINCE, WHO WAS HELPED TO A WIFE BY THE SON OF HIS FATHER'S MINISTER

There is a city (said the demon) named Váránasí, which is the dwelling-place of Śiva, inhabited by holy beings, and thus resembles the plateau of Mount Kailása. The river Ganges, ever full of water, flows near it, and appears as if it were the necklace ever resting on its neck; in that city there lived of old time a king named Pratápamukuta, who consumed the families of his enemies with his valor, as the fire consumes the forest. He had a son named Vajramukuta, who dashed the god of love's pride in his beauty, and his enemies' confidence in their valor. And that prince had a friend, named Buddhiśaríra, whom he valued more than his life, the sagacious son of a minister.

Once on a time that prince was amusing himself with that friend, and his excessive devotion to the chase made him travel a long distance. As he was cutting off the long-maned heads of lions with his arrows, as it were the chowries that represented the glory of their valor, he entered a great forest. It seemed like the chosen home of love, with singing cuckoos for bards, fanned by trees with their clusters of blossoms, waving like chowries. In it he and the minister's son saw a great lake, looking like a second sea, the birthplace of lotuses of various colors; and in that pool of gods there was seen by him a maiden of heavenly appearance, who had come there with her attendants to bathe. She seemed to fill the splendid tank with the flood of her beauty, and with her glances to create in it a new forest of blue lotuses. With her face, that surpassed the moon in beauty, she seemed to put to shame the white lotuses, and she at once captivated with it the heart of that prince. The youth, too, in the same way, took with a glance such complete possession of her eyes, that she did not regard her own attire or even her ornaments. And as he was looking at her with his attendants, and wondering who she was, she made, under pretense of pastime, a sign to tell him her country and other particulars about her. She took a lotus from her garland of flowers, and put it in her ear, and she remained for a long time twisting it into the form of an ornament called *dantapatra* or tooth-leaf, and then she took another lotus and placed it on her head, and she laid her hand significantly upon her heart. The prince did not at that time understand those signs, but his sagacious friend the minister's son did understand them. The maiden soon departed, being led away from that place by her attendants, and when she had reached her own house, she flung herself down on a sofa, but her heart remained with that prince, to justify the sign she had made.

The prince, for his part, when without her, was like a Vidyádhara who has lost his magic knowledge, and, returning to his own city, he fell into a miserable condition. And one day the minister's son questioned him in private, speaking of that beauty as easy to obtain, whereupon he lost his self-command and exclaimed, "How is she to be obtained, when neither her name, nor her village, nor her origin is known? So why do you offer me false comfort?" When the prince said this to the minister's son, he answered, "What! did you not see, what she told you by her signs? By placing the lotus in her ear, she meant to say this, 'I live in the realm of King Karnotpala.' By making it into the tooth-leaf ornament she meant to say, 'Know that I am the daughter of a dentist there.' By lifting up the lotus she let you know her name was Padmávatí; and by placing her hand on her heart she told you that it was yours. Now there is a king named Karnotpala in the country of Kalinga; he has a favorite courtier, a great dentist named Sangrámavardhana, and he has a daughter named Padmávatí, the pearl of the three worlds, whom he values more than his life. All this I knew from the talk of the people, and so I understood her signs, which were meant to tell her country and the other particulars about her."

When that prince had been told all this by the minister's son, he was pleased with that intelligent man, and rejoiced, as he had now got an opportunity of attaining his object, and, after he had deliberated with him, he set out with him from his palace on the pretense of hunting, but really in search of his beloved, and went again in that direction. And on the way he managed to give his retinue the slip by the speed of his swift horse, and he went to the country of Kalinga accompanied by the minister's son only. There they reached the city of King Karnotpala, and searched for and found the palace of that dentist, and the prince and the minister's son entered the house of an old woman, who lived near there, to lodge. The minister's son gave their horses water and fodder, and placed them there in concealment, and then said to that old woman in the presence of the prince, "Do you know, mother, a dentist named Sangrámavardhana?" When the old woman heard that, she said to him courteously, "I know him well; I was his nurse, and he has now made me attend upon his daughter as a duenna; but I never go there at present, as I have been deprived of my clothes, for my wicked son, who is a gambler, takes away my clothes as soon as he sees them." When the minister's son heard this, he was delighted, and he gratified the old woman with the gift of his upper garment and other presents, and went on to say to her, "You are a mother to us, so do what we request you to do in secret; go to that Padmávatí, the daughter of the dentist, and say to her, 'The prince, whom you saw at the lake, has come here, and out of love he has sent me to tell you.'" When the old woman heard this, she consented, being won over by the presents, and went to Padmávatí, and came back in a moment. And when the prince and the minister's son questioned her, she said to them, "I went and told her secretly that you had come. When she heard that, she scolded me, and struck me on both cheeks with her two hands smeared with camphor. So I have come back weeping, distressed at the insult. See here, my children, these marks of her fingers on my face."

When she said this, the prince was despondent, as he despaired of attaining his object, but the sagacious minister's son said to him in private, "Do not despond, for by keeping her own counsel and scolding the old woman, and striking her on the face with her ten fingers white with camphor, she meant to say, 'Wait for these remaining ten moonlight nights of the white fortnight, for they are unfavorable to an interview.'"

After the minister's son had comforted the prince with these words, he went and sold secretly in the market some gold, which he had about him, and made that old woman prepare a splendid meal, and then those two ate it with that old woman. After the minister's son had spent ten days in this fashion, he again sent the old woman to Padmávatí, to see how matters stood. And she, being fond of delicious food, liquor, and other enjoyments of the kind, went again to the dwelling-house of Padmávatí, to please her guests, and returned and said to them, "I went there to-day and remained silent, but she of her own accord taunted me with that crime of having brought your message, and again struck me here on the breast with three fingers dipped in red dye, so I have returned here thus marked by her." When the minister's son heard this, he said, of his own accord, to the prince, "Do not entertain any despondent notions, for by placing the impression of her three fingers marked with red dye on this woman's heart, she meant to say: 'I cannot receive you for three nights.'"

When the minister's son had said this to the prince, he waited till three days had passed, and again sent the old woman to Padmávatí. She went to her palace, and Padmávatí honored her and gave her food, and lovingly entertained her that day with wine and other enjoyments. And in the evening, when the old woman wished to go back to her house, there arose outside a terrible tumult. Then the people were heard exclaiming, "Alas! Alas! a mad elephant has escaped from the post to which he was tied, and is rushing about, trampling men to death." Then Padmávatí said to that old woman, "You must not go by the public road, which is rendered unsafe by the elephant, so we will put you on a seat, with a rope fastened to it to support it, and let you down by this broad window here into the garden of the house; there you must get up a tree and cross this wall, and then let yourself down by another tree and go to your own house." After she had said this, she had the old woman let down from the window by her maid into the garden, by means of that seat with a rope fastened to it. She went by the way pointed out to her, and related the whole story, exactly as it happened, to the prince and the minister's son. Then the minister's son said to the prince, "Your desire is accomplished, for she has shown you by an artifice the way you should take; so go there this very day, as soon as evening sets in, and by this way enter the palace of your beloved."

When the minister's son said this, the prince went with him into the garden, by the way over the wall pointed out by the old woman. There he saw that rope hanging down with the seat, and at the top of it were some maids, who seemed to be looking out for his arrival. So he got on to the seat, and the moment those female servants saw him, they pulled him up with the rope, and he entered the presence of his beloved through the window. When he had entered, the minister's son returned to his lodging. And when the prince entered, he beheld that Padmávatí with a face like a full moon, shedding forth beauty like beams, like the night of the full moon remaining concealed through fear of the black fortnight. As soon as she saw him, she rose up boldly, and welcomed him with affectionate embraces and other endearments natural in one who had waited for him so long. Then the prince married that fair one by the Gándharva form of marriage, and all his wishes being now fulfilled, remained with her in concealment.

And after he had lived with her some days, he said to her one night, " My friend the minister's son came with me and is staying here, and he is now left alone in the house of your duenna; I must go and pay him a visit, fair one, and then I will return to you." When the cunning Padmávatí heard that, she said to her lover, " Come now, my husband, I have a question to ask you; did you guess the meaning of those signs which I made, or was it that friend of yours the minister's son? " When she said this, the prince said to her, " I did not guess anything at all, but that friend of mine, the minister's son, who is distinguished for superhuman insight, guessed it all, and told it to me." When the fair one heard this, she reflected, and said to him, " Then you have acted wrongly in not telling me about him before. Since he is your friend, he is my brother, and I must always honor him before all others with gifts of betel and other luxuries." When she had dismissed him with these words, the prince left the palace at night by the way by which he came, and returned to his friend. And in the course of conversation he told him, that he had told his beloved how he guessed the meaning of the signs which she made. But the minister's son did not approve of this proceeding on his part, considering it imprudent. And so the day dawned on them conversing.

Then, as they were again talking together after the termination of the morning prayer, the confidante of Padmávatí came in with betel and cooked food in her hand. She asked after the health of the minister's son, and after giving him the dainties, in order by an artifice to prevent the prince from eating any of them, she said, in the course of conversation, that her mistress was awaiting his arrival to feast and spend the day with her, and immediately she departed unobserved. Then the minister's son said to the prince, "Now observe, prince, I will show you something wonderful." Thereupon he gave that cooked food to a dog to eat, and the dog, as soon as he had eaten it, fell dead upon the spot. When the prince saw that, he said to the minister's son, "What is the meaning of this marvel?" And he answered him, "The truth is that the lady has found out that I am intelligent, by the fact that I guessed the meaning of her signs, and so she has sent me this poisoned food in order to kill me, for she is deeply in love with you, and thinks that you, prince, will never be exclusively devoted to her while I am alive, but being under my influence, will perhaps leave her, and go to your own city. So give up the idea of being angry with her, persuade the high-spirited woman to leave her relations, and I will invent and tell you an artifice for carrying her off."

When the minister's son had said this, the prince said to him, "You are rightly named Buddhiśaríra as being an incarnation of wisdom"; and at the very moment that he was thus praising him, there was suddenly heard outside a general cry from the sorrowing multitude, "Alas! Alas! the king's infant son is dead." The minister's son was much delighted at hearing this, and he said to the prince, "Repair now to Padmávatí's palace at night, and there make her drink so much, that she shall be senseless and motionless with intoxication, and apparently dead. And when she is asleep, make a mark on her side with a red hot iron spike, and take away all her ornaments, and return by letting yourself down from the window by a rope; and after that I will take steps to make everything turn out prosperously."

When the minister's son had said this, he had a three-pronged spike made, with points like the bristles of a boar, and gave it to the prince. And the prince took in his hand that weapon which resembled the crooked hard hearts of his beloved and of his friend, which were firm as black iron; and saying, "I will do as you direct," went at night to the palace of Padmávatí as before, for princes should never hesitate about following the advice of an excellent minister. There he made his beloved helpless with drink, and marked her on the side with the spike, and took away her ornaments, and then he returned to that friend of his. And he showed him the ornaments, and told him what he had done. Then the minister's son considered his design as good as accomplished.

And the next morning the minister's son went to the cemetery, and promptly disguised himself as an ascetic, and he made the prince assume the guise of a disciple. And he said to him, "Go and take the pearl necklace which is part of this set of ornaments, and pretend to try to sell it in the market, but put a high price on it, that no one may be willing to buy it, and that everyone may see it being carried about, and if the police here should arrest you, say intrepidly, "My spiritual preceptor gave it me to sell."

When the minister's son had sent off the prince on this errand, he went and wandered about in the market-place, publicly showing the necklace. And while he was thus engaged, he was seen and arrested by the police, who were on the lookout for thieves, as information had been given about the robbery of the dentist's daughter. And they immediately took him to the chief magistrate of the town; and he, seeing that he was dressed as an ascetic, said to him courteously, "Reverend sir, where did you get this necklace of pearls which was lost in this city, for the ornaments of the dentist's daughter were stolen during the night?" When the prince, who was disguised as an ascetic, heard this, he said, "My spiritual preceptor gave it me; come and question him." Then the magistrate of the city came to the minister's son, and bowed, and said to him, "Reverend sir, where did you get this pearl necklace that is in the possession of your pupil?" When the cunning fellow heard that, he took him aside, and said, "I am an ascetic, in the habit of wandering perpetually backwards and forwards in the forests. As chance would have it, I arrived here, and as I was in the cemetery at night, I saw a band of witches collected from different quarters. And one of them brought the prince, with the lotus of his heart laid bare, and offered him to Bhairava. And the witch, who possessed great powers of delusion, being drunk, tried to take away my rosary, while I was reciting my prayers, making horrible contortions with her face. And as she carried the attempt too far, I got angry, and heating with a charm the prongs of my trident, I marked her on the side. And then I took this necklace from her neck. And now I must sell this necklace, as it does not suit an ascetic."

When the magistrate heard this, he went and informed the king. When the king heard it, he concluded that that was the pearl necklace which had been lost, and he sent a trustworthy old woman to see if the dentist's daughter was really marked with a trident on the side. The old woman came back and said that the mark could be clearly seen. Then the king made up his mind that she was a witch, and had really destroyed his child. So he went in person to that minister's son, who was personating an ascetic, and asked him how he ought to punish Padmávatí; and by his advice he ordered her to be banished from the city, though her parents lamented over her. And when she was banished, and was left in the forest, though desolate, she did not abandon the body, supposing that it was all an artifice devised by the minister's son. And in the evening the minister's son and the prince, who had abandoned the dress of ascetics, and were mounted on their horses, came upon her lamenting. And they consoled her, and mounted her upon a horse, and took her to their own kingdom. There the prince lived happily with her. But the dentist, supposing that his daughter had been devoured by wild beasts in the forests, died of grief, and his wife followed him.

When the Vetála had said this, he went on to say to the king, "Now I have a doubt about this story, resolve it for me; was the minister's son guilty of the death of this married couple, or the prince, or Padmávatí? Tell me, for you are the chief of sages. And if, king, you do not tell me the truth, though you know it, this head of yours shall certainly split in a hundred pieces."

When the Vetála said this, the king, who discerned the truth, out of fear of being cursed, gave him this answer, "O thou skilled in magic arts, what difficulty is there about it? Why, none of the three was in fault, but the whole of the guilt attaches to King Karnotpala." The Vetála then said, "Why, what did the king do? Those three were instrumental in the matter. Are the crows in fault when the swans eat the rice?" Then the king said, "Indeed no one of the three was in fault, for the minister's son committed no crime, as he was forwarding his master's interests, and Padmávatí and the prince, being burned with the fire of the arrows of the god of Love, and being therefore undiscerning and ignorant, were not to blame, as they were intent on their own object. But the king Karnotpala, as being untaught in treatises of policy, and not investigating by means of spies the true state of affairs even among his own subjects, and not comprehending the tricks of rogues, and inexperienced in interpreting gestures and other external indications, is to be considered guilty, on account of the indiscreet step which he took."

When the Vetála, who was in the corpse, heard this, as the king by giving this correct answer had broken his silence, he immediately left his shoulder, and went somewhere unobserved by the force of his magic power, in order to test his persistence; and the intrepid king at once determined to recover him.

The Jar of Olives and the Boy Kazi

From the Arabic

UNDER the reign of the Caliph Harun al-Rashid there dwelt in the city of Baghdad a certain merchant, 'Ali Khwajah hight, who had a small stock of goods wherewith he bought and sold and made a bare livelihood, abiding alone and without a family in the house of his forbears. Now so it came to pass that each night for three nights together he saw in vision a venerable Shaykh who bespake him thus, "Thou art beholden to make a pilgrimage to Meccah; why abidest thou sunk in heedless slumber and farest not forth as it behoveth thee?" Hearing these words he became sore startled and affrighted, so that he sold shop and goods and all that he had; and, with firm intent to visit the Holy House of Almighty Allah, he let his home on hire and joined a caravan that was journeying to Meccah the Magnified. But ere he left his natal city he placed a thousand gold pieces, which were over and above his need for the journey, within an earthen jar filled up with Asafiri or Sparrow-olives; and, having made fast the mouth thereof, he carried the jar to a merchant-friend of many years' standing and said, "Belike, O my brother, thou hast heard tell that I purpose going with a caravan on pilgrimage to Meccah, the Holy City; so I have brought a jar of olives the which, I pray thee, preserve for me in trust against my return." The merchant at once arose and handing the key of his warehouse to Ali Khwajah said, "Here, take the key and open the store and therein place the jar anywhere thou choosest, and when thou shalt come back thou wilt find it even as thou leftest it." Hereupon Ali Khwajah did his friend's bidding and locking up the door returned the key to its master. Then loading his traveling goods upon a dromedary and mounting a second beast he fared forth with the caravan. They came at length to Meccah the Magnified, and it was the month Zu al-Hijjah wherein myriads of Moslems hie thither on pilgrimage and pray and prostrate before the Ka'abah-temple. And when he had circuited the Holy House, and fulfilled all the rites and ceremonies required of palmers, he set up a shop for sale of merchandise. By chance two merchants passing along that street espied the fine stuffs and goods in Ali Khwajah's booth and approved much of them and praised their beauty and excellence. Presently quoth one to other, "This man bringeth here most rare and costly goods: now in Cairo, the capital of Egypt-land, would he get full value for them, and far more than in the markets of this city." Hearing mention of Cairo, Ali Khwajah conceived a sore longing to visit that famous capital, so he gave up his intent of return Baghdad-ward and purposed wayfaring to Egypt. Accordingly he joined a caravan and arriving thither was well-pleased with the place, both country and city; and selling his merchandise he made great gain therefrom. Then buying other goods and stuffs he purposed to make Damascus; but for one full month he tarried at Cairo and visited her sanctuaries and saintly places, and after leaving her walls he solaced himself with seeing many famous cities distant several days' journey from the capital along the banks of the River Nilus. Presently, bidding adieu to Egypt he arrived at the Sanctified House, Jerusalem, and prayed in the temple of the Banu Isra'il which the Moslems had reëdified. In due time he reached Damascus and observed that the city was well builded and much peopled, and that the fields and meads were well-watered with springs and channels and that the gardens and vergiers were laden with flowers and fruits. Amid such delights Ali Khwajah hardly thought of Baghdad; withal he ceased not to pursue his journey through Aleppo, Mosul, and Shiraz, tarrying some time at all of these towns, especially at Shiraz, till at length after seven years of wayfaring he came back to Baghdad.

For seven long years the Baghdad merchant never once thought of Ali Khwajah or of the trust committed to his charge; till one day as his wife sat at meat with him at the evening meal, their talk by chance was of olives. Quoth she to him, "I would now fain have some that I may eat of them"; and quoth he, "As thou speakest thereof I bethink me of that Ali Khwajah who seven years ago fared on a pilgrimage to Meccah, and ere he went left in trust with me a jar of Sparrow-olives which still cumbereth the storehouse. Who knoweth where he is or what hath betided him? A man who lately returned with the Hajj-caravan brought me word that Ali Khwajah had quitted Meccah the Magnified with intent to journey on to Egypt. Allah Almighty alone knoweth an he be still alive or he be now dead; however, if his olives be in good condition I will go bring some hither that we may taste them: so give me a platter and a lamp that I may fetch thee somewhat of them." His wife, an honest woman and an upright, made answer, "Allah forbid that thou shouldst do a deed so base and break thy word and covenant. Who can tell? Thou art not assured by any of his death; perchance he may come back from Egypt safe and sound to-morrow or the day after; then wilt thou, an thou cannot deliver unharmed to him what he hath left in pledge, be ashamed of this thy broken troth, and we shall be disgraced before man and dishonored in the presence of thy friend. I will not for my part have any hand in such meanness nor will I taste the olives; furthermore, it standeth not to reason that after seven years' keeping they should be fit to eat. I do implore thee to forswear this ill-purpose." On such wise the merchant's wife protested and prayed her husband that he meddle not with Ali Khwajah's olives, and shamed him of his intent so that for the nonce he cast the matter from his mind. However, although the trader refrained that evening from taking Ali Khwajah's olives, yet he kept the design in memory until one day when, of his obstinacy and unfaith, he resolved to carry out his project; and rising up walked toward the store-room dish in hand. By chance he met his wife who said, "I am no partner with thee in this ill-action: in very truth some evil shall befall thee an thou do such deed." He heard her but heeded her not; and, going to the store-room opened the jar and found the olives spoiled and white with mold; but presently he tilted up the jar and pouring some of its contents into the dish, suddenly saw an Ashrafi fall from the vessel together with the fruit. Then, filled with greed, he turned out all that was within into another jar and wondered with exceeding wonder to find the lower half full of golden coins. Presently, putting up the moneys and the olives he closed the vessel and going back said to his wife, "Thou spakest sooth, for I have examined the jar and have found the fruit moldy and foul of smell; wherefore I returned it to its place and left it as it was aforetime." That night the merchant could not sleep a wink for thinking of the gold and how he might lay hands thereon; and when morning morrowed he took out all the Ashrafis and buying some fresh olives in the Bazar filled up the jar with them and closed the mouth and set it in its usual place. Now it came to pass by Allah's mercy that at the end of the month Ali Khwajah returned safe and sound to Baghdad; and he first went to his old friend, to wit, the merchant who, greeting him with feigned joy, fell on his neck, but withal was sore troubled and perplexed at what might happen. After salutations and much rejoicing on either part Ali Khwajah bespake the merchant on business and begged that he might take back his jar of Asafiri-olives which he had placed in charge of his familiar. Quoth the merchant to Ali Khwajah, "O my friend, I wot not where thou didst leave the jar of olives; but here is the key, go down to the store-house and take all that is thine own." So Ali Khwajah did as he was bidden and carrying the jar from the magazine took his leave and hastened home; but, when he opened the vessel and found not the gold coins, he was distracted and overwhelmed with grief and made bitter lamentation. Then he returned to the merchant and said, "O my friend, Allah, the All-present and the All-seeing, be my witness that, when I went on my pilgrimage to Meccah the Magnified, I left a thousand Ashrafis in that jar, and now I find them not. Canst thou tell me aught concerning them? An thou in thy sore need have made use of them, it mattereth not so thou wilt give them back as soon as thou art able."

The merchant, apparently pitying him, said, "O good my friend, thou didst thyself with thine hand set the jar inside the store-room. I wist not that thou hadst aught in it save olives; yet as thou didst leave it, so in like manner didst thou find it and carry it away; and now thou chargest me with theft of Ashrafis. It seemeth strange and passing strange that thou shouldst make such accusation. When thou wentest thou madest no mention of any money in the jar, but saidst that it was full of olives, even as thou hast found it. Hadst thou left gold coins therein, then surely thou wouldst have recovered them." Hereupon Ali Khwajah begged hard with much entreaty, saying, "Those thousand Ashrafis were all I owned, the money earned by years of toil: I do beseech thee have pity on my case and give them back to me." Replied the merchant, waxing wroth with great wrath, "O my friend, a fine fellow thou art to talk of honesty and withal make such false and lying charge. Begone: hie thee hence and come not to my house again; for now I know thee as thou art, a swindler and impostor." Hearing this dispute between Ali Khwajah and the merchant all the people of the quarter came crowding to the shop; and thus it became well known to all, rich and poor, within the city of Baghdad how that one Ali Khwajah had hidden a thousand Ashrafis within a jar of olives and had placed it on trust with a certain merchant; moreover how, after pilgrimaging to Meccah and seven years of travel the poor man had returned, and that the rich man had gainsaid his words anent the gold and was ready to make oath that he had not received any trust of the kind. At length, when naught else availed, Ali Khwajah was constrained to bring the matter before the Kazi, and to claim one thousand Ashrafis of his false friend. The Judge asked, "What witnesses hast thou who may speak for thee?" and the plaintiff answered, "O my lord the Kazi, I feared to tell the matter to any man lest all come to know of my secret. Allah Almighty is my sole testimony. This merchant was my friend and I recked not that he would prove dishonest and unfaithful." Quoth the Judge, "Then must I needs send for the merchant and hear what he saith on oath"; and when the defendant came they made him swear by all he deemed holy, facing Ka'abah-wards with hands uplifted, and he cried, "I swear that I know naught of any Ashrafis belonging to Ali Khwajah." Hereat the Kazi pronounced him innocent and dismissed him from court; and Ali Khwajah went home sad at heart and said to himself, "Alas, what justice is this which hath been meted out to me, that I should lose my money, and my just cause be deemed unjust! It hath been truly said: He loseth the lave who sueth before a knave." On the next day he drew out a statement of his case; and, as the Caliph Harun al-Rashid was on his way to Friday-prayers, he fell down on the ground before him and presented to him the paper. The Commander of the Faithful read the petition and having understood the case deigned give order saying, "To-morrow bring the accuser and the accused to the audience-hall and place the petition before my presence, for I myself will inquire into this matter." That night the Prince of True Believers, as was his wont, donned disguise to walk about the squares of Baghdad and its streets and lanes and, accompanied by Ja'afar the Barmaki and Masrur the Sworder of his vengeance, proceeded to espy what happened in the city. Immediately on issuing forth he came upon an open place in the Bazar when he heard the hubbub of children a-playing and saw at scanty distance some ten or dozen boys making sport among themselves in the moonlight; and he stopped awhile to watch their diversion. Then one among the lads, a goodly and a fair-complexioned, said to the others, "Come now and let us play the game of Kazi: I will be the Judge; let one of you be Ali Khwajah and another the merchant with whom he placed the thousand Ashrafis in pledge before faring on his pilgrimage: so come ye before me and let each one plead his plea." When the Caliph heard the name of Ali Khwajah he minded him of the petition which had been presented to him for justice against the merchant, and bethought him that he would wait and see how the boy would perform the part of Kazi in their game and upon what decision he would decide. So the Prince watched the mock-trial with keen interest saying to himself, "This case hath verily made such stir within the city that even the children know thereof and re-act it in their sports." Presently, he among the lads who took the part of Ali Khwajah the plaintiff and his playmate who represented the merchant of Baghdad accused of theft, advanced and stood before the boy who as the Kazi sat in pomp and dignity. Quoth the Judge, "O Ali Khwajah, what is thy claim against this merchant?" and the complainant preferred his charge in a plea of full detail. Then said the Kazi to the boy who acted merchant, "What answerest thou to this complaint and why didst thou not return the gold pieces?" The accused made reply even as the real defendant had done and denied the charge before the Judge, professing himself ready to take oath thereto. Then said the boy-Kazi, "Ere thou swear on oath that thou hast not taken the money, I would fain see for myself the jar of olives which the plaintiff deposited with thee on trust." Then turning to the boy who represented Ali Khwajah he cried, "Go thou and instantly produce the jar that I may inspect it." And when the vessel was brought the Kazi said to the two contentious, "See now and say me: be this the very jar which thou, the plaintiff, leftest with the defendant?" and both answered that it was one and the same. Then said the self-constituted Judge, "Open now the jar and bring hither some of the contents that I may see the state in which the Asafiri-olives actually are." Then tasting of the fruit, "How is this? I find their flavor is fresh and their state excellent. Surely during the lapse of seven twelve-months the olives would have become moldy and rotten. Bring now before me two oil-merchants of the town that they may pass opinion upon them." Then two other of the boys assumed the parts commanded and coming into court stood before the Kazi, who asked, "Are ye olive-merchants by trade?" They answered, "We are and this hath been our calling for many generations, and in buying and selling olives we earn our daily bread." Then said the Kazi, "Tell me now, how long do olives keep fresh and well-flavored?" and said they, "O my lord, however carefully we keep them, after the third year they change flavor and color and become no longer fit for food, in fact they are good only to be cast away." Thereupon quoth the boy-Kazi, "Examine me now these olives that are in this jar and say me how old are they and what is their condition and savor." The two boys who played the parts of oil-merchants pretended to take some berries from the jar and taste them and presently they said, "O our lord the Kazi, these olives are in fair condition and full-flavored." Quoth the Kazi, "Ye speak falsely, for 'tis seven years since Ali Khwajah put them in the jar as he was about to go a-pilgrimaging"; and quoth they, "Say whatso thou wilt, those olives are of this year's growth, and there is not an oil-merchant in all Baghdad but who will agree with us." Moreover the accused was made to taste and smell the fruits and he could not but admit that it was even so as they had avouched. Then said the boy-Kazi to the boy-defendant, "'Tis clear thou art a rogue and a rascal, and thou hast done a deed wherefor thou richly deservest the gibbet." Hearing this the children frisked about and clapped their hands with glee and gladness, then seizing hold of him who acted as the merchant of Baghdad, they led him off as to execution. The Commander of the Faithful, Harun al-Rashid, was greatly pleased at this acuteness of the boy who had assumed the part of judge in the play, and commanded his Wazir Ja'afar saying, "Mark well the lad who enacted the Kazi in this mock-trial and see that thou produce him on the morrow: he shall try the case in my presence substantially and in real earnest, even as we have heard him deal with it in play. Summon also the Kazi of this city that he may learn the administration of justice from this child. Moreover send word to Ali Khwajah bidding him bring with him the jar of olives, and have also in readiness two oil-merchants of the town." Thus as they walked along the Caliph gave orders to the Wazir and then returned to his palace. So on the morrow Ja'afar the Barmaki went to that quarter of the town where the children had enacted the mock-trial and asked the schoolmaster where his scholars might be, and he answered, "They have all gone away, each to his home." So the Minister visited the houses pointed out to him and ordered the little ones to appear in his presence. Accordingly they were brought before him, when he said to them, "Who among you is he that yesternight acted the part of Kazi in play and passed sentence in the case of Ali Khwajah?" The eldest of them replied, "'Twas I, O my lord the Wazir"; and then he waxed pale, not knowing why the question was put. Cried the Minister, "Come along with me; the Commander of the Faithful hath need of thee." At this the mother of the lad was sore afraid and wept; but Ja'afar comforted her and said, "O my lady, have no fear and trouble not thyself. Thy son will soon return to thee in safety, Inshallah—God willing—and methinks the Sultan will show much favor unto him." The woman's heart was heartened on hearing these words of the Wazir and she joyfully dressed her boy in his best attire and sent him off with the Wazir, who led him by the hand to the Caliph's audience-hall and executed all the other commandments which had been issued by his liege lord. Then the Commander of the Faithful, having taken seat upon the throne of justice, set the boy upon a seat beside him, and as soon as the contending parties appeared before him, that is Ali Khwajah and the merchant of Baghdad, he commanded them to state each man his case in presence of the child who should adjudge the suit. So the two, plaintiff and defendant, recounted their contention before the boy in full detail; and when the accused stoutly denied the charge and was about to swear on oath that what he said was true, with hands uplifted and facing Ka'abah-wards, the child-Kazi prevented him, saying, "Enough! swear not on oath till thou art bidden; and first let the jar of olives be produced in court." Forthwith the jar was brought forward and placed before him; and the lad bade open it; then, tasting one he gave also to two oil-merchants who had been summoned, that they might do likewise and declare how old was the fruit and whether its savor was good or bad. They did his bidding and said, "The flavor of these olives hath not changed and they are of this year's growth." Then said the boy, "Methinks ye are mistaken, for seven years ago Ali Khwajah put the olives into the jar: how then could fruit of this year find their way therein?" But they replied, "'Tis even as we say: an thou believe not our words send straightway for other oil-merchants and make inquiry of them, so shalt thou know if we speak sooth or lies." But when the merchant of Baghdad saw that he could no longer avail to prove his innocence, he confessed everything; to wit, how he had taken out the Ashrafis and filled the jar with fresh olives. Hearing this the boy said to the Prince of True Believers, "O gracious Sovereign, last night in play we tried this cause, but thou alone hast power to apply the penalty. I have adjudged the matter in thy presence and I humbly pray that thou punish this merchant according to the law of the Koran and the custom of the Apostle; and thou decree the restoring of his thousand gold pieces to Ali Khwajah, for that he hath been proved entitled to them."

Another Solomon

From the Chinese

AT T'ai-yüan there lived a middle-aged woman with her widowed daughter-in-law. The former was on terms of too great intimacy with a notably bad character of the neighborhood; and the daughter, who objected very strongly to this, did her best to keep the man from the house. The elder woman accordingly tried to send the other back to her family, but she would not go; and at length things came to such a pass that the mother-in-law actually went to the mandarin of the place and charged her daughter-in-law with the offense she herself was committing. When the mandarin inquired the name of the man concerned, she said she had only seen him in the dark and didn't know who he was, referring him for information to the accused. The latter, on being summoned, gave the man's name, but retorted the charge on her mother-in-law; and when the man was confronted with them, he promptly declared both their stories to be false. The mandarin, however, said there was a *primâ facie* case against him, and ordered him to be severely beaten, whereupon he confessed that it was the daughter-in-law whom he went to visit. This the woman herself flatly denied, even under torture; and on being released, appealed to a higher court, with a very similar result. Thus the case dragged on, until a Mr. Sun, who was well-known for his judicial acumen, was appointed district magistrate at that place. Calling the parties before him, he bade his lictors prepare stones and knives, at which they were much exercised in their minds, the severest tortures allowed by law being merely gyves and fetters. However, everything was got ready, and the next day Mr. Sun proceeded with his investigation. After hearing all that each one of the three had to say, he delivered the following judgment: "The case is a simple one; for although I cannot say which of you two women is the guilty one, there is no doubt about the man, who has evidently been the means of bringing discredit on a virtuous family. Take those stones and knives there and put him to death. I will be responsible." Thereupon the two women began to stone the man, especially the younger one, who seized the biggest stones she could see and threw them at him with all the might of her pent-up anger; while the mother-in-law chose small stones and struck him on non-vital parts.[1] So with the knives: the daughter-in-law would have killed him at the first blow, had not the mandarin stopped her, and said, "Hold! I now know who is the guilty woman." The mother-in-law was then tortured until she confessed, and the case was thus terminated.

[1] The Chinese distinguish sixteen vital spots on the front of the body and six on the back, with thirty-six and twenty non-vital spots in similar positions, respectively. They allow, however, that a severe blow on a non-vital spot might cause death, and *vice versâ*.

Calamity Ahmad and Habzalam Bazazah

From the Arabic

CALIPH HARUN AL RASCHID went in to Kut al Kulub, who rose to him on sighting him and kissed the ground between his hands; when he said to her, "Hath Ala al-Din visited thee?" and she answered, "No, O Commander of the Faithful, I sent to bid him come, but he would not." So the Caliph bade carry her back to the Harim and saying to Ala al-Din, "Do not absent thyself from us," returned to his palace. Accordingly, next morning Ala al-Din mounted and rode to the Divan, where he took his seat as Chief of the Sixty.

Presently the Caliph ordered his treasurer to give the Wazir Ja'afar ten thousand dinars and said, when his order was obeyed, "I charge thee to go down to the bazaar where handmaidens are sold and buy Ala al-Din a slave girl with this sum." Accordingly in obedience to the King, Ja'afar took Ala al-Din and went down with him to the bazaar.

Now as chance would have it that very day, the Emir Khalid, whom the Caliph had made Governor of Baghdad, went down to the market to buy a slave girl for his son, and the cause of his going was that his wife, Khátun by name, had borne him a son called Habzalam Bazazah, and the same was foul of favor and had reached the age of twenty without learning to mount horse; albeit his father was brave and bold, a doughty rider ready to plunge into the Sea of Darkness.[1] And it happened that on a certain night his mother said to his father, "I want to find him a wife." Quoth Khalid, "The fellow is so foul of favor and withal so sordid and beastly that no woman would take him at a gift." And she answered, "We will buy him a slave girl."

So it befell, for the accomplishing of what Allah Al-

[1] Or night. A metaphor for rushing into peril.

mighty had decreed, that on the same day Ja'afar and Ala al-Din, the Governor Khalid and his son went down to the market, and behold, they saw in the hands of a broker a beautiful girl, lovely faced and of perfect shape, and the Wazir said to him, "O broker, ask her owner if he will take a thousand dinars for her." And as the broker passed by the Governor with the slave, Habzalam Bazazah cast at her one glance of the eyes which entailed for himself one thousand sighs; and he fell in love with her and passion got hold of him and he said, "O my father, buy me yonder slave girl."

So the Emir called the broker, who brought the girl to him and asked her her name. She replied, "My name is Jessamine"; and he said to Habzalam Bazazah, "O my son, an she please thee, do thou bid higher for her." Then he asked the broker, "What hath been bidden for her?" and he replied, "A thousand dinars." Said the Governor's son, "She is mine for a thousand pieces of gold and one more," and the broker passed on to Ala al-Din who bid two thousand dinars for her; and as often as the Emir's son bid another dinar, Ala al-Din bid a thousand.

The ugly youth was vexed at this and said, "O broker! who is it that outbiddeth me for the slave girl?" Answered the broker, "It is the Wazir Ja'afar who is minded to buy her for Ala al-din Abu al-Shamat." And Ala al-Din continued till he brought her price up to ten thousand dinars, and her owner was satisfied to sell her for that sum.

Then he took the girl and said to her, "I give thee thy freedom for the love of Almighty Allah"; and forthwith wrote his contract of marriage with her and carried her to his house.

Now when the broker returned, after having received his brokerage, the Emir's son summoned him and said to him, "Where is the girl?" Quoth he, "She was bought for ten thousand dinars by Ala al-Din, who hath set her free and married her." At this the young man was greatly vexed and cast down and, sighing many a sigh, returned home, sick for love of the damsel; and he threw himself on his bed and refused food, for love and longing were sore upon him.

Now when his mother saw him in this plight, she said to him, "Heaven assain thee, O my son! What aileth thee?" And he answered, "Buy me Jessamine, O my mother!" Quoth she, "When the flower seller passeth I will buy thee a basketful of jessamine." Quoth he, "It is not the jessamine one smells, but a slave girl named Jessamine, whom my father would not buy for me." So she said to her husband, "Why and wherefore didst thou not buy him the girl?" and he replied, "What is fit for the lord is not fit for the liege and I have no power to take her: no less a man bought her than Ala al-Din, Chief of the Sixty."

Then the youth's weakness redoubled upon him, till he gave up sleeping and eating, and his mother bound her head with the fillets of mourning. And while in her sadness she sat at home, lamenting over her son, behold came in to her an old woman, known as the mother of Ahmad Kamakim, the arch thief, a knave who would bore through a middle wall and scale the tallest of the tall and steal the very kohl off the eyeball. From his earliest years he had been given to these malpractices, till they made him Captain of the Watch, when he stole a sum of money; and the Chief of Police, coming upon him in the act, carried him to the Caliph, who bade put him to death on the common execution ground. But he implored protection of the Wazir whose intercession the Caliph never rejected; so he pleaded for him with the Commander of the Faithful who said, "How canst thou intercede for this pest of the human race?" Ja'afar answered, "O Commander of the Faithful, do thou imprison him; whoso built the first jail was a sage, seeing that a jail is the grave of the living and a joy for the foe." So the Caliph bade lay him in bilboes and write thereon, "Appointed to remain here until death, and not to be loosed but on the corpse-washer's bench"; and they cast him fettered into limbo.

Now his mother was a frequent visitor to the house of

the Emir Khalid, who was Governor and Chief of Police; and she used to go in to her son in jail and say to him, "Did I not warn thee to turn from thy wicked ways?" And he would always answer her, "Allah decreed this to me; but, O my mother, when thou visitest the Emir's wife, make her intercede for me with her husband." So when the old woman came into the Lady Khatun, she found her bound with the fillets of mourning, and said to her, "Wherefore dost thou mourn?" She replied, "For my son Habzalam Bazazah"; and the old woman exclaimed, "Heaven assain thy son! what hath befallen him?" So the mother told her the whole story, and she said, "What wouldst thou say of him who should achieve such a feat as would save thy son?" Asked the lady, "And what feat wilt thou do?" Quoth the old woman, "I have a son called Ahmad Kamakim, the arch thief, who lieth chained in jail and on his bilboes is written: Appointed to remain till death; so do thou don thy richest clothes and trick thee out with thy finest jewels and present thyself to thy husband with an open face and smiling mien; and say: By Allah, 'tis a strange thing! When a man desireth aught of his wife he dunneth her till she doeth it; but if a wife desire aught of her husband, he will not grant it to her. Then he will say: What dost thou want? and do thou answer: First swear to grant my request. If he swear to thee by his head or by Allah, say to him: Swear to me the oath of divorce and do not yield to him except he do this. And when he hath sworn to thee the oath of divorce, say to him: Thou keepest in prison a man called Ahmad Kamakim, and he hath a poor old mother who hath set upon me and who urgeth me in the matter and who saith, 'Let thy husband intercede for him with the Caliph, that my son may repent and thou gain heavenly guerdon.'" And the Lady Khatun replied, "I hear and obey."

So when her husband came in to his wife, she spoke to him as she had been taught and made him swear the divorce oath and yield to her wishes. When morning dawned, after he had made the Ghusl-ablution and prayed the dawn prayer, he repaired to the prison and said, "O Ahmad Kamakim, O thou arch thief, dost thou repent of thy works?" whereto he replied, "I do indeed repent and turn to Allah and say with heart and tongue: I ask pardon of Allah." So the Governor took him out of jail and carried him to the Court (he being still in bilboes), and approaching the Caliph kissed ground before him.

Quoth the King, "O Emir Khalid, what seekest thou?" whereupon he brought forward Ahmad Kamakim, shuffling and tripping in his fetters, and the Caliph said to him, "What! art thou yet alive, O Kamakim?" He replied, "O Commander of the Faithful, the miserable are long-lived." Quoth the Caliph to the Emir, "Why hast thou brought him hither?" and quoth he, "O Commander of the Faithful, he hath a poor old mother cut off from the world who hath none but this son and she hath had recourse to thy slave, imploring him to intercede with thee to strike off his chains, for he repenteth of his evil courses; and to make him Captain of the Watch as before."

The Caliph asked Ahmad Kamakim, "Dost thou repent of thy sins?" "I do indeed repent me to Allah, O Commander of the Faithful," answered he; whereupon the Caliph called for the blacksmith and made him strike off his irons on the corpse-washer's bench. Moreover, he restored him to his former office and charged him to walk in the ways of godliness and righteousness. So he kissed the Caliph's hands, and, being invested with the uniform of Captain of the Watch, he went forth, whilst they made proclamation of his appointment.

Now for a long time he abode in the exercise of his office, till one day his mother went in to the Governor's wife, who said to her, "Praised be Allah who hath delivered thy son from prison and restored him to health and safety! But why dost thou not bid him contrive some trick to get the girl Jessamine for my son Habzalam Bazazah?" "That will I," answered she and, going out from her, repaired to her son. She found him drunk with wine and said to him, "O my son, no one caused thy release from jail but the wife of the Governor, and she would have thee find some means to slay Ala al-Din Abu al-Shamat and get his slave girl Jessamine for her son Habzalam Bazazah." He answered, "That will be the easiest of things; and I must needs set about it this very night."

Now this was the first night of the new month, and it was the custom of the Caliph to spend that night with the Lady Zubaydah, for the setting free of a slave girl, or a Mameluke, or something of the sort. Moreover, on such occasions he used to doff his royal habit, together with his rosary and dagger-sword and royal signet, and set them all upon a chair in the sitting saloon: and he had also a gold lantern, adorned with three jewels strung on a wire of gold, by which he set great store; and he would commit all these things to the charge of the eunuchs, whilst he went into the Lady Zubaydah's apartment.

So the arch thief Ahmad Kamakim waited till midnight, when Canopus shone bright, and all creatures to sleep were dight, whilst the Creator veiled them with the veil of night. Then he took his drawn sword in his right hand and his grappling hook in his left and, repairing to the Caliph's sitting saloon, planted his scaling ladder and cast his grapnel on to the side of the terrace roof; then, raising the trapdoor, let himself down into the saloon, where he found the eunuchs asleep.

He drugged them with hemp fumes; and, taking the Caliph's dress, dagger, rosary, kerchief, signet ring, and the lantern whereupon were the pearls, returned whence he came and betook himself to the house of Ala al-Din, who had that night celebrated his wedding festivities with Jessamine. So arch thief Ahmad Kamakim climbed over into his saloon and, raising one of the marble slabs from the sunken part of the floor, dug a hole under it and laid the stolen things therein, all save the lantern, which he kept for himself. Then he plastered down the marble slab as it was before, and returning whence he came, went back to his own house, saying, "I will now tackle my drink and set this lantern before me and quaff the cup to its light."

Now as soon as it was dawn of day, the Caliph went out into the sitting chamber; and, seeing the eunuchs drugged with hemp, aroused them. Then he put his hand to the chair and found neither dress nor signet nor rosary nor dagger-sword nor kerchief nor lantern; whereat he was exceeding wroth and, donning the dress of anger, which was a scarlet suit,[1] sat down in the Divan.

So the Wazir Ja'afar came forward and kissing the ground before him, said, "Allah avert all evil from the Commander of the Faithful!" Answered the Caliph, "O Wazir, the evil is passing great!" Ja'afar asked, "What has happened?" So he told him what had occurred; and behold, the Chief of Police appeared with Ahmad Kamakim the robber at his stirrup, when he found the Commander of the Faithful sore enraged.

As soon as the Caliph saw him he said to him, "O Emir Khalid, how goes Baghdad?" And he answered, "Safe and secure." Cried he, "Thou liest!" "How so, O Prince of True Believers?" asked the Emir. So he told him the case and added, "I charge thee to bring me back all the stolen things." Replied the Emir, "O Commander of the Faithful, the vinegar worm is of and in the vinegar, and no stranger can get at this place."[2]

But the Caliph said, "Except thou bring me these things, I will put thee to death." Quoth he, "Ere thou slay me, slay Ahmad Kamakim, for none should know the robber and the traitor but the Captain of the Watch."

Then came forward Ahmad Kamakim and said to the Caliph, "Accept my intercession for the Chief of Police, and I will be responsible to thee for the thief and will track his trail till I find him; but give me two Kazis and two

[1] This till very late years was the custom in Persia, and Fath Ali Shah never appeared in scarlet without ordering some horrible cruelties. In Dar-For wearing a red cashmere turban was a sign of wrath, and sending a blood-red dress to a subject meant that he would be slain.

[2] That is, this robbery was committed in the palace by some one belonging to it.

Assessors, for he who did this thing feareth thee not, nor doth he fear the Governor nor any other." Answered the Caliph, "Thou shalt have what thou wantest; but let search be made first in my palace and then in those of the Wazir and the Chief of the Sixty." Rejoined Ahmad Kamakim, "Thou sayest well, O Commander of the Faithful; belike the man that did this ill deed be one who hath been reared in the King's household or in that of one of his officers." Cried the Caliph, "As my head liveth, whosoever shall have done the deed I will assuredly put him to death, be it mine own son!"

Then Ahmad Kamakim received a written warrant to enter and perforce search the houses; so he went forth, taking in his hand a rod made of bronze and copper, iron and steel, of each three equal parts. He first searched the palace of the Caliph, then that of the Wazir Ja'afar; after which he went the round of the houses of the Chamberlains and the Viceroys till he came to that of Ala al-Din.

Now when the Chief of the Sixty heard the clamor before his house, he left his wife Jessamine and went down and, opening the door, found the Master of Police without in the midst of a tumultuous crowd. So he said, "What is the matter, O Emir Khalid?" Thereupon the Chief told him the case and Ala al-Din said, "Enter my house and search it." The Governor replied, "Pardon, O my lord; thou art a man in whom trust is reposed and Allah forfend that the trusty turn traitor!" Quoth Ala al-Din, "There is no help for it but that my house be searched."

So the Chief of Police entered, attended by the Kazi and his Assessors; whereupon Ahmad Kamakin went straight to the depressed floor of the saloon and came to the slab under which he had buried the stolen goods, and let the rod fall upon it with such violence that the marble broke in sunder, and behold something glittered underneath.

Then said he, "Bismillah; in the name of Allah! Mashallah; whatso Allah willeth! By the blessing of our coming a hoard hath been hit upon; wait while we go down into this hiding place and see what is therein." So the

Kazi and Assessors looked into the hole and finding there the stolen goods, drew up a statement of how they had discovered them in Ala al-Din's house, to which they set their seals. Then they bade seize upon Ala al-Din and took his turban from his head, and officially registered all his moneys and effects which were in the mansion.

Meanwhile, arch thief Ahmad Kamakim laid hands on Jessamine, and committed her to his mother, saying, "Deliver her to Khatun, the Governor's lady." So the old woman took her and carried her to the wife of the Master of Police.

Now as soon as Habzalam Bazazah saw her, health and heart returned to him, and he arose without stay or delay and joyed with exceeding joy and would have drawn near her; but she plucked a dagger from her girdle and said, "Keep off from me, or I will kill thee and kill myself after."

With this the ugly youth's love-longing redoubled and he sickened for yearning and unfulfilled desire; and refusing food returned to his pillow.

Then said his mother to her, "O wretch, how canst thou make me thus to sorrow for my son? Needs must I punish thee with torture; and as for Ala al-Din, he will assuredly be hanged." "And I will die for love of him," answered Jessamine. Then the Governor's wife arose and stripped her of her jewels and silken raiment and, clothing her in sackcloth, sent her down into the kitchen and made her a scullery wench, saying, "The reward for thy constancy shall be to break up firewood and peel onions and set fire under the cooking pots." Quoth she, "I am willing to suffer all manner of hardships and servitude, but I will not suffer the sight of thy son." However, Allah inclined the hearts of the slave girls to her and they used to do her service in the kitchen.

Such was the case with Jessamine; but as regards Ala al-Din, they carried him, together with the stolen goods, to the Divan where the Caliph still sat upon his throne. And behold, the King looked upon his effects and said,

"Where did ye find them?" They replied, "In the very middle of the house belonging to Ala al-Din Abu al-Shamat," whereat the Caliph was filled with wrath and took the things, but found not the lantern among them and said, "O Ala al-Din, where is the lantern?" He answered, "I stole it not; I know naught of it; I never saw it; I can give no information about it!" Said the Caliph, "O traitor, how cometh it that I brought thee near unto me and thou hast cast me out afar, and I trusted in thee and thou betrayest me?" And he commanded to hang him.

So the Chief of Police took him and went down with him into the city, whilst the crier preceded them proclaiming aloud and saying, "This is the reward and the least of the reward he shall receive who doth treason against the Caliphs of True Belief!" And the folk flocked to the place where the gallows stood.

Thus far concerning him; but as regards Ahmad al-Danaf, Ala al-Din's adopted father, he was sitting making merry with his followers in a garden, and carousing and pleasuring when lo! in came one of the water carriers of the Divan and, kissing the hand of Ahmad al-Danaf, said to him, "O Captain Ahmad, O Danaf! thou sittest at thine ease with water flowing at thy feet, and thou knowest not what hath happened." Asked Ahmad, "What is it?" and the other answered, "They have gone down to the gallows with thy son Ala al-Din, adopted by a covenant before Allah!" Quoth Ahmad, "What is the remedy here, O Hasan Shuuman, and what sayest thou of this?"

He replied, "Assuredly Ala al-Din is innocent and this blame hath come to him from some one enemy." Quoth Ahmad, "What counselest thou?" and Hasan said, "We must rescue him, Inshallah!"

Then he went to the jail and said to the jailer, "Give us some one who deserveth death." So he gave him one that was likest of men to Ala al-Din Abu al-Shamat; and they covered his head and carried him to the place of execution between Ahmad al-Danaf and Ali al-Zaybak of Cairo.

Now they had brought Ala al-Din to the gibbet, to hang him, but Ahmad al-Danaf came forward and set his foot on that of the hangman, who said, "Give me room to do my duty." He replied, "O accursed, take this man and hang him in Ala al-Din's stead; for he is innocent and we will ransom him with this fellow, even as Abraham ransomed Isaac with the ram."

So the hangman seized the man and hanged him in lieu of Ala al-Din; whereupon Ahmad and Ali took Ala al-Din and carried him to Ahmad's quarters and, when there, Ala al-Din turned to him and said, "O my sire and chief, Allah requite thee with the best of good!"

Quoth he, "O Ala al-Din, what is this deed thou hast done? The mercy of Allah be on him who said: Whoever trusteth thee betray him not, e'en if thou be a traitor. Now the Caliph set thee in high place about him and styled thee 'Trusty' and 'Faithful'; how then couldst thou deal thus with him and steal his goods?"

"By the Most Great Name, O my father and chief," replied Ala al-Din, "I had no hand in this, nor did I such deed, nor know I who did it." Quoth Ahmad, "Of a surety none did this but a manifest enemy, and whoever doth aught shall be requited for his deed; but, O Ala al-Din, thou canst sojourn no longer in Baghdad, for Kings, O my son, may not pass from one thing to another, and when they go in quest of a man, ah! long is his travail."

"Whither shall I go, O my chief?" asked Ala al-Din; and he answered, "O my son, I will bring thee to Alexandria, for 'tis a blessed place; its threshold is green and its sojourn is agreeable." And Ala al-Din rejoined, "I hear and I obey, O my chief." So Ahmad said to Hasan Shuuman, "Be mindful and, when the Caliph asketh for me, say: He is gone touring about the provinces."

Then, taking Ala al-Din, he went forth of Baghdad and stayed, not going till they came to the outlying vineyards and gardens, where they met two Jews of the Caliph's tax-gatherers, riding on mules. Quoth Ahmad al-Danaf to these, "Give me the blackmail," and quoth they, "Why should we pay thee blackmail?" whereto he replied, "Because I am the watchman of this valley." So they gave him each an hundred gold pieces, after which he slew them and took their mules, one of which he mounted, whilst Ala al-Din bestrode the other.

Then they rode on till they came to the city of Ayas and put up their beasts for the night at the Khan. And when morning dawned, Ala al-Din sold his own mule and committed that of Ahmad to the charge of the doorkeeper of the caravansary, after which they took ship from Ayas port and sailed to Alexandria. Here they landed and walked up to the bazaar and behold, there was a broker crying a shop and a chamber behind it for nine hundred and fifty dinars. Upon this Ala al-Din bid a thousand which the broker accepted, for the premises belonged to the Treasury; and the seller handed over to him the keys, and the buyer opened the shop and found the inner parlor furnished with carpets and cushions. Moreover, he found there a storeroom full of sails and masts, cordage, and seaman's chests, bags of beads and cowrie shells, stirrups, battle axes, maces, knives, scissors, and such matters, for the last owner of the shop had been a dealer in second-hand goods.

So he took his seat in the shop and Ahmad al-Danaf said to him, "O my son, the shop and the room and that which is therein are become thine; so tarry thou here and buy and sell; and repine not at thy lot, for Almighty Allah blesseth trade." After this he abode with him three days and on the fourth he took leave of him, saying, "Abide here till I go back and bring thee the Caliph's pardon and learn who hath played thee this trick." Then he shipped for Ayas, where he took the mule from the inn and, returning to Baghdad met Pestilence Hasan and his followers, to whom said he, "Hath the Caliph asked after me?" and he replied, "No, nor hast thou come to his thought."

So he resumed his service about the Caliph's person and set himself to sniff about for news of Ala al-Din's case, till one day he heard the Caliph say to the Wazir, "See, O Ja'afar, how Ala al-Din dealt with me!" Replied the Minister, "O Commander of the Faithful, thou hast requited him with hanging, and hath he not met with his reward?" Quoth he, "O Wazir, I have a mind to go down and see him hanging"; and the Wazir answered, "Do what thou wilt, O Commander of the Faithful." So the Caliph, accomplained by Ja'afar went down to the place of execution and, raising his eyes, saw the hanged man to be other than Ala al-Din Abu al-Shamat, surnamed the Trusty, and said, "O Wazir, this is not Ala al-Din!" "How knowest thou that it is not he?" asked the Minister, and the Caliph answered, "Ala al-Din was short and this one is tall." Quoth Ja'afar, "Hanging stretcheth." Quoth the Caliph, "Ala al-Din was fair and this one's hair is black." Said Ja'afar, "Knowest thou not, O Commander of the Faithful, that death is followed by blackness?" Then the Caliph bade take down the body from the gallows-tree and they found the names of the two Shaykhs, Abu Bakr and Omar, written on his heels, whereupon cried the Caliph, "O Wazir, Ala al-Din was a Sunnite,[1] and this fellow is a Rejecter, a Shi'ah." He answered, "Glory be to Allah who knoweth the hidden things, while we know not whether this was Ala al-Din or other than he."

Then the Caliph bade bury the body and they buried it; and Ala al-Din was forgotten as though he never had been.

Such was his case; but as regards Habzalam Bazazah, the Emir Khalid's son, he ceased not to languish for love and longing till he died and they joined him to the dust. Now as for the young wife Jessamine, she gave birth to a boy-child like unto the moon; and when her fellow slave girls said to her, "What wilt thou name him?" she an-

[1] A Sunnite is a follower of the orthodox *tradition* (Arabic *sunna*), which was *rejected* by the Shi'ahs (Arabic *sectarian*), the followers of Ali and his martyred sons, Hasan and Hosain, the grandsons of the Prophet.

swered, " Were his father well he had named him; but now I will name him Aslan."

Now it so came to pass that one day after two years, whilst his mother was busied with the service of the kitchen the boy went out and, seeing the stairs, mounted to the guest chamber. And the Emir Khalid who was sitting there took him upon his lap and glorified his Lord for that which he had created and fashioned; then closely eying his face, the Governor saw that he was the likest of all creatures to Ala al-Din Abu al-Shamat. Presently his mother Jessamine sought for him and finding him not, mounted to the guest chamber, where she saw the Emir seated with the child playing in his lap, for Allah had inclined his heart to the boy. And when the child espied his mother, he would have thrown himself upon her; but the Emir held him tight to his bosom and said to Jessamine, " Come hither, O damsel! " So she came to him, when said to her, " Whose son is this? " and she replied, " He is my son." " And who is his father? " asked the Emir; and she answered, " His father was Ala al-Din Abu al-Shamat, but now he is become thy son." Quoth Khalid, " In very sooth Ala al-Din was a traitor." Quoth she, " Allah deliver him from treason! the heavens forfend and forbid that the ' Trusty ' should be a traitor! "

Then said he, " When this boy shall grow up and reach man's estate and say to thee: Who is my father? do thou say to him: Thou art the son of the Emir Khalid, Governor and Chief of Police." And she answered, " I hear and I obey."

Then he adopted the boy and reared him with the goodliest rearing, and engaged for him a professor of law and religious science, and an expert pensman who taught him to read and write; so he read the Koran twice and learned it by heart, and he grew up, saying to the Emir, " O my father! " Moreover, the Governor used to go down with him to the tilting-ground and assemble horsemen and teach the lad the fashion of fight and fray, and the place to plant lance thrust and saber stroke; so that by the time he was fourteen years old he became a valiant wight and accomplished knight and gained the rank of Emir. Now it chanced one day that Aslan fell in with Ahmad Kamakim, the arch thief, and accompanied him as cup companion to the tavern, and behold, Ahmad took out the jeweled lantern he had stolen from the Caliph and, setting it before him, pledged the wine cup to its light, till he became drunken.

So Aslan said to him, "O captain, give me this lantern," but he replied, "I cannot give it to thee." Asked Aslan, "Why not?" and Ahmad answered, "Because lives have been lost for it." "Whose life?" inquired Aslan; and Ahmad rejoined, "There came hither a man who was made Chief of the Sixty; he was named Ala al-Din Abu al-Shamat, and he lost his life through this lantern." Quoth Aslan, "And what was that story, and what brought about his death?" Quoth Ahmad Kamakim, "Thou hadst an elder brother by name Habzalam Bazazah, and when he reached the age of sixteen and was inclined for marriage, thy father would have bought him a slave girl named Jessamine." And he went on to tell him the whole story from first to last of Habzalam Bazazah's illness and what befell Ala al-Din in his innocence. When Aslan heard this, he said in thought, "Haply this slave girl was my mother Jessamine, and my father was none other than Ala al-Din Abu al-Shamat."

So the boy went out from him sorrowful, and met Calamity Ahmad, who at sight of him exclaimed, "Glory be to Him unto whom none is like!" Asked Hasan the Pestilence, "Whereat dost thou marvel, O my chief?" and Ahmad the Calamity replied, "At the make of yonder boy Aslan, for he is the likest of human creatures to Ala al-Din Abu al-Shamat." Then he called the lad and said to him, "O Aslan, what is thy mother's name?" to which he replied, "She is called the damsel Jessamine;" and the other said, "Hark ye, Aslan, be of good cheer and keep thine eyes cool and clear; for thy father was none other than Ala al-Din Abu al-Shamat: but, O my son, go thou in to thy mother and question her of thy father." He said, "Hearkening and obedience," and, going in to his mother, put the question; whereupon quoth she, "Thy sire is the Emir Khalid!" "Not so," rejoined he, "my father was none other than Ala al-Din Abu al-Shamat."

At this the mother wept and said, "Who acquainted thee with this, O my son?" and he answered, "Ahmad al-Danaf, Captain of the Guard." So she told him the whole story, saying, "O my son, the True hath prevailed and the False hath failed: know that Ala al-Din Abu al-Shamat was indeed thy sire, but it was none save the Emir Khalid who reared thee and adopted thee as his son. And now, O my child, when thou seest Ahmad al-Danaf the captain, do thou say to him: I conjure thee, by Allah, O my chief, take my blood revenge on the murderer of my father Ala al-Din Abu al-Shamat!"

So he went out from his mother and betaking himself to Calamity Ahmad, kissed his hand. Quoth the Captain, "What aileth thee, O Aslan?" and quoth he, "Now I know for certain that my father was Ala al-Din Abu al-Shamat, and I would have thee take my blood revenge on his murderer." He asked, "And who was thy father's murderer?" whereto Aslan answered, "Ahmad Kamakim, the arch thief." "Who told thee this?" inquired he, and Aslan rejoined, "I saw in his hand the jeweled lantern which was lost with the rest of the Caliph's gear, and I said to him: Give me this lantern! but he refused, saying: Lives have been lost on account of this, and told me it was he who had broken into the palace and stolen the articles and deposited them in my father's house."

Then said Ahmad al-Danaf, "When thou seest the Emir Khalid don his harness of war say to him: Equip me like thyself and take me with thee. Then do thou go forth and perform some feat of prowess before the Commander of the Faithful, and he will say to thee: Ask a boon of me, O Aslan! And do thou make answer: I ask of thee this boon, that thou take my blood revenge on my father's murderer. If he says: Thy father is yet alive and is the Emir Khalid, the Chief of the Police; answer thou: My father was Ala al-Din Abu al-Shamat, and the Emir Khalid hath a claim upon me only as the foster father who adopted me. Then tell him all that passed between thee and Ahmad Kamakim and say: O Prince of True Believers, order him to be searched and I will bring the lantern forth from his bosom."

Thereupon said Aslan to him, "I hear and obey"; and, returning to the Emir Khalid, found him making ready to repair to the Caliph's court, and said to him, "I would fain have thee arm and harness me like thyself and take me with thee to the Divan." So he equipped him and carried him thither.

Then the Caliph sallied forth of Baghdad with his troops, and they pitched tents and pavilions without the city; whereupon the host divided into two parties, and forming ranks fell to playing Polo, one striking the ball with the mall, and another striking it back to him. Now there was among the troops a spy, who had been hired to slay the Caliph; so he took the ball and smiting it with the bat drove it straight at the Caliph's face, when behold, Aslan fended it off and catching it drove it back at him who smote it, so that it struck him between the shoulders, and he fell to the ground. The Caliph exclaimed, "Allah bless thee, O Aslan!" and they all dismounted and sat on chairs.

Then the Caliph bade them bring the smiter of the ball before him and said, "Who tempted thee to do this thing, and art thou friend or foe?" Quoth he, "I am thy foe and it was my purpose to kill thee." Asked the Caliph, "And wherefor? Art not a Moslem?" Replied the spy, "No! I am a Rejecter."

So the Caliph bade them put him to death, and said to Aslan, "Ask a boon of me." Quoth he, "I ask of thee this boon, that thou take my blood revenge on my father's murderer." He said, "Thy father is alive and there he stands on his two feet." "And who is he?" asked Aslan; and the Caliph answered, "He is the Emir Khalid, Chief of Police." Rejoined Aslan, "O Commander of the Faithful, he is no father of mine, save by right of fosterage; my father was none other than Ala al-Din Abu al-Shamat." "Then thy father was a traitor," cried the Caliph. "Allah forbid, O Commander of the Faithful," rejoined Aslan, "that the 'Trusty' should be a traitor! But how did he betray thee?" Quoth the Caliph, "He stole my habit and what was therewith."

Aslan retorted, "O Commander of the Faithful, Allah forfend that my father should be a traitor! But, O my lord, when thy habit was lost and found, didst thou likewise recover the lantern which was stolen from thee?" Answered the Caliph, "We never got it back;" and Aslan said, "I saw it in the hands of Ahmad Kamakim and begged it of him; but he refused to give it me, saying: Lives have been lost on account of this. Then he told me of the sickness of Habzalam Bazazah, son of the Emir Khalid, by reason of his passion for the damsel Jessamine, and how he himself was released from bonds, and that it was he who stole the habit and the lamp. So do thou, O Commander of the Faithful, take my blood revenge from my father on him who murdered him."

At once the Caliph cried, "Seize ye Ahmad Kamakim!" and they seized him; whereupon he asked, "Where be the Captain Ahmad al-Danaf?" And when he was summoned the Caliph bade him search Kamakim; so he put his hand into the thief's bosom and pulled out the lantern. Said the Caliph, "Come hither, thou traitor: whence hadst thou this lantern?" and Kamakim replied, "I bought it, O Commander of the Faithful!" The Caliph rejoined, "Where didst thou buy it?" Then they beat him till he owned that he had stolen the lantern, the habit, and the rest, and the Caliph said to him, "What moved thee to do this thing, O traitor, and ruin Ala al-Din Abu al-Shamat, the Trusty and Faithful?" Then he bade them lay hands on him and on the Chief of Police, but the Chief said, "O Commander of the Faithful, indeed I am unjustly treated; thou badest me hang him, and I had no knowledge of this trick, for the plot was contrived between the old woman and Ahmad Kamakim and my wife. I crave thine intercession, O Aslan."

So Aslan interceded for him with the Caliph, who said, "What hath Allah done with this youngster's mother?" Answered Khalid, "She is with me," and the Caliph continued, "I command that thou order thy wife to dress her in her own clothes and ornaments and restore her to her former degree, a lady of rank; and do thou remove the seals from Ala al-Din's house and give his son possession of his estate." "I hear and obey," answered Khalid; and, going forth, gave the order to his wife who clad Jessamine in her own apparel, whilst he himself removed the seals from Ala al-Din's house and gave Aslan the keys.

Then said the Caliph, "Ask a boon of me, O Aslan!" and he replied, "I beg of thee the boon to unite me with my father." Whereat the Caliph wept and said, "Most like thy sire was he that was hanged and is dead; but by the life of my forefathers, whoso bringeth me the glad news that he is yet in the bondage of this life, I will give him all he seeketh!" Then came forward Ahmad al-Danaf, and, kissing the ground between his hands, said, "Grant me indemnity, O Commander of the Faithful!" "Thou hast it," answered the Caliph; and Calamity Ahmad said, "I give thee the good news that Ala al-Din Abu al-Shamat, the Trusty, the Faithful is alive and well." Quoth the Caliph, "What is this thou sayest?" Quoth Al-Danaf, "As thy head liveth I say sooth; for I ransomed him with another, of those who deserved death; and carried him to Alexandria where I opened for him a shop and set him up as dealer in second-hand goods."

So they journeyed to Alexandria. They alighted without the city and Ala al-Din hid the women in a cavern, whilst he went into Alexandria and fetched them outer clothing, wherewith he covered them. Then he carried them to his shop and, leaving them in the "ben" [1] walked forth to fetch them the morning meal, and behold, he

[1] As opposed to the "but," or outer room.

met Calamity Ahmad who chanced to be coming from Baghdad. He saw him in the street and received him with open arms, saluting him and welcoming him. Whereupon Ahmad al-Danaf gave him the good news of his son Aslan and how he was now come to the age of twenty: and Ala al-Din, in his turn, told the Captain of the Guard all that had befallen him from first to last, whereat he marveled with exceeding marvel. Then he brought him to his shop and sitting room where they passed the night; and next day he sold his place of business and laid its price with other moneys.

Now Ahmad al-Danaf had told him that the Caliph sought him; but he said, "I am bound first for Cairo, to salute my father and mother and the people of my house." So they all went to Cairo the God-guarded; and here they alighted in the street called Yellow, where stood the house of Shamat al-Din. Then Ala al-Din knocked at the door, and his mother said, "Who is at the door, now that we have lost our beloved for evermore?" He replied, "'Tis I! Ala al-Din!" whereupon they came down and embraced him. Then he sent his wives and baggage into the house, and entering himself with Ahmad al-Danaf, rested there three days, after which he was minded to set out for Baghdad. His father said, "Abide with me, O my son!" but he answered, "I cannot bear to be parted from my child Aslan." So he took his father and mother and set forth for Baghdad.

Now when they came there, Ahmad al-Danaf went in to the Caliph and gave him the glad tidings of Ala al-Din's arrival and told him his story; whereupon the King went forth to greet him, taking the youth Aslan and they met and embraced each other. Then the Commander of the Faithful summoned the arch thief Ahmad Kamakim and said to Ala al-Din, "Up and at thy foe!" So he drew his sword and smote off Ahmad Kamakim's head. Presently the Caliph held festival for Ala al-Din and, summoning the Kazis and witnesses, wrote the contract and married him to the Princess Husn Maryam. Moreover, the Caliph made Aslan Chief of the Sixty and bestowed upon him and his father sumptuous dresses of honor; and they abode in the enjoyment of all joys and joyance of life, till there came to them the Destroyer of delights and the Sunderer of societies.

A Man-hating Maiden

From the Sanskrit

THE ever worthy and famous King Vikramáditoya had a painter named Nagarasvámin, who enjoyed the revenues of a hundred villages, and surpassed Viśvakarman. That painter used every two or three days to paint a picture of a girl, and give it as a present to the king, taking care to exemplify different types of beauty.

Now, once on a time, it happened that that painter had, because a feast was going on, forgotten to paint the required girl for the king. And when the day for giving the present arrived, the painter remembered and was bewildered, saying to himself, "Alas! what can I give to the king?" And at that moment a traveler come from afar suddenly approached him and placed a book in his hand, and went off somewhere quickly. The painter out of curiosity opened the book, and saw within a picture of a girl on canvas. Inasmuch as the girl was of wonderful beauty, no sooner did he see her picture than he took it and gave it to the king, rejoicing that, so far from having no picture to present that day, he had obtained such an exceedingly beautiful one. But the king, as soon as he saw it, was astonished, and said to him, "My good fellow, this is not your painting, this is the painting of Viśvakarman; for how could a mere mortal be skillful enough to paint such beauty?" When the painter heard this, he told the king exactly what had taken place.

Then the king kept ever looking at the picture of the girl, and never took his eyes off it, and one night he saw in a dream a girl exactly like her, but in another land. But as he eagerly rushed to embrace her, who was eager to meet him, the night came to an end, and he was woke up by the watchman. When the king awoke, he was so angry at the interruption of his delightful interview with that maiden, that he banished that watchman from the city. And he said to himself, "To think that a traveler should bring a book, and that in it there should be the painted figure of a girl, and that I should in a dream behold this same girl apparently alive! All this elaborate dispensation of destiny makes me think that she must be a real maiden, but I do not know in what land she lives; how am I to obtain her?"

Full of such reflections, the king took pleasure in nothing, and burned with the fever of love so that his attendants were full of anxiety. And the warder Bhadráyudha asked the afflicted king in private the cause of his grief, whereupon he spoke as follows:

"Listen, I will tell you, my friend. So much at any rate you know, that that painter gave me the picture of a girl. And I fell asleep thinking on her, and I remember that in my dream I crossed the sea, and reached and entered a very beautiful city. There I saw many armed maidens in front of me, and they, as soon as they saw me, raised a tumultuous cry of 'Kill, kill.' Then a certain female ascetic came and with great precipitation made me enter her house, and briefly said to me this, 'My son, here is the man-hating princess Malayavatí come this way, diverting herself as she pleases. And the moment she sees a man, she makes these maidens of hers kill him: so I brought you in here to save your life.'

"When the female ascetic had said this, she immediately made me put on female attire; and I submitted to that, knowing that it was not lawful to slay those maidens. But, when the princess entered into the house with her maidens, I looked at her, and lo! she was the very lady that had been shown me in a picture. And I said to myself, 'Fortunate am I in that, after first seeing this lady in a picture, I now behold her again in flesh and blood, dear as my life.'

" In the meanwhile the princess, at the head of her maidens, said to that female ascetic, ' We saw some male enter here.' The ascetic showed me, and answered, ' I know of no male; here is my sister's daughter, who is with me as a guest.' Then the princess seeing me, although I was disguised as a woman, forgot her dislike of men, and was at once overcome by love. She remained for a moment, with every hair on her body erect, motionless as if in thought, being, so to speak, nailed to the spot at once with arrows by Love, who had spied his opportunity. And in a moment the princess said to the ascetic, ' Then, noble lady, why should not your sister's daughter be my guest also? Let her come to my palace; I will send her back duly honored.' Saying this, she took me by the hand, and led me away to her palace. And I remember, I discerned her intention, and consented, and went there, and that sly old female ascetic gave me leave to depart.

" Then I remained there with that princess, who was diverting herself with the amusement of marrying her maidens to one another, and so forth. Her eyes were fixed on me, and she would not let me out of her sight for an instant, and no occupation pleased her in which I did not take part. Then those maidens, I remember, made the princess a bride, and me her husband, and married us in sport. And when we had been married, we entered at night the bridal chamber, and the princess fearlessly threw her arms round my neck. And then I told her who I was, and embraced her, and delighted at having attained her object, she looked at me and then remained a long time with her eyes bashfully fixed on the ground. And at that moment that villain of a watchman woke me up. So, Bhadráyudha, the upshot of the whole matter is that I can no longer live without that Malayavatí, whom I have seen in a picture and in a dream."

When the king said this, the warder Bhadráyudha perceived that it was a true dream, and he consoled the monarch, and said to him, " If the king remembers it all exactly, let him draw that city on a piece of canvas in order that some expedient may be devised in this matter." The moment the king heard this suggestion of Bhadráyudha's, he proceeded to draw that splendid city on a piece of canvas, and all the scene that took place there. Then the warder at once took the drawing, and had a new monastery made, and hung it up there on the wall. And he directed that in relief-houses attached to the monastery, a quantity of food, with pairs of garments and gold, should be given to bards coming from distant countries. And he gave this order to the dwellers in the monastery, "If anyone comes here, who knows the city represented here in a picture, let me be informed of it."

In the meanwhile the fierce elephant of the rainy season with irresistible loud deep thunder-roar and long *ketaka* tusks came down upon the forest of the heats, a forest the breezes of which were scented with the perfume of the jasmine, in which travelers sat down on the ground in the shade, and trumpet-flowers bloomed. At that time the forest-fire of separation of that king Vikramáditya began to burn more fiercely, fanned by the eastern breeze. Then the following cries were heard among the ladies of his court, "Háralatá, bring ice! Chitrángí, sprinkle him with sandal-wood juice! Patralekhá, make a bed cool with lotus-leaves! Kandarpasená, fan him with plantain-leaves!" And in course of time the cloudy season terrible with lightning passed away for that king, but the fever of love burning with the sorrow of separation did not pass away.

Then the autumn with her open lotus-face, and smile of unclosed flowers, came, vocal with the cries of swans, seeming to utter this command, "Let travelers advance on their journey; let pleasant tidings be brought about absent dear ones; happy may their merry meetings be!" On a certain day in that season a bard, who had come from a distance, of the name of Sanvarasiddhi, having heard the fame of that monastery, built by the warder, entered it to get food. After he had been fed, and presented with a pair of garments, he saw that painting on the wall of the monastery. When the bard had carefully scanned the city delineated there he was astonished, and said, "I wonder who can have drawn this city? For I alone have seen it, I am certain, and no other; and here it is drawn by some second person." When the inhabitants of the monastery heard that, they told Bhadráyudha; then he came in person, and took that bard to the king. The king said to Sanvarasiddhi, "Have you really seen that city?" Then Sanvarasiddhi gave him the following answer:

"When I was wandering about the world, I crossed the sea that separates the isles, and beheld that great city Malayapura. In that city there dwells a king of the name of Malayasinha, and he has a matchless daughter, named Malayavatí, who used to abhor males. But one night she somehow or other saw in a dream a great hero in a convent. The moment she saw him, that evil spirit of detestation of the male sex fled from her mind, as if terrified. Then she took him to her palace, and in her dream married him, and entered with him the bridal chamber. And at that moment the night came to an end, and an attendant in her room woke her up. Then she banished that servant in her anger, and thinking upon that dear one, whom she had seen in her dream, seeing no way of escape owing to the blazing fire of separation, utterly overpowered by love, she never rose from her couch except to fall back upon it again with relaxed limbs. She was dumb, as if possessed by a demon, as if stunned by a blow, for when her attendants questioned her, she gave them no answer.

"Then her father and mother came to hear of it, and questioned her; and at last she was, with exceeding difficulty, persuaded to tell them what happened to her in the dream, by the mouth of a confidential female friend. Then her father comforted her, but she made a solemn vow that, if she did not obtain her beloved in six months, she would enter the fire. And already five months are past; who knows what will become of her? This is the story that I heard about her in that city."

When Sanvarasiddhi had told this story, which tallied so well with the king's own dream, the king was pleased at knowing the certainty of the matter, and Bhadráyudha said to him, "The business is as good as effected, for that king and his country own your paramount supremacy. So let us go there before the sixth month has passed away." When the warder had said this, King Vikramáditya made him inform Sanvarasiddhi of all the circumstances connected with the matter, and honored him with a present of much wealth, and bade him show him the way, and then he seemed to bequeath his own burning heat to the rays of the sun, his paleness to the clouds, and his thinness to the waters of the rivers, and having become free from sorrow, set out at once, escorted by a small force, for the dwelling-place of his beloved.

In course of time, as he advanced, he crossed the sea, and reached that city, and there he saw the people in front of it engaged in loud lamentation, and when he questioned them, he received this answer, " The Princess Malayavatí here, as the period of six months is at an end, and she has not obtained her beloved, is preparing to enter the fire." Then the king went to the place where the pyre had been made ready.

When the people saw him, they made way for him, and then the princess beheld that unexpected nectar-rain to her eyes. And she said to her ladies-in-waiting, " Here is that beloved come who married me in a dream, so tell my father quickly." They went and told this to her father, and then that king, delivered from his grief, and filled with joy, submissively approached the sovereign. At that moment the bard Sanvarasiddhi, who knew his time, lifted up his arm, and chanted aloud this strain, " Hail thou that with the flame of thy valor hast consumed the forest of the army of demons and Mlechchhas! Hail king, lord of the seven-sea-girt earth-bride! Hail thou that hast imposed thy exceedingly heavy yoke on the bowed heads of all kings, conquered by thee! Hail, Vishamaśíla, hail Vikramáditya, ocean of valor!"

When the bard said this, King Malayasinha knew that it was Vikramáditya himself that had come, and embraced his feet. And after he had welcomed him, he entered his palace with him, and his daughter Malayavatí, thus delivered from death. And that king gave that daughter of his to King Vikramáditya, thinking himself fortunate in having obtained such a son-in-law. And King Vikramáditya, when he saw in his arms, in flesh and blood, that Malayavatí, whom he had previously seen in a picture and in a dream, considered it a wonderful fruit of the wishing-tree of Siva's favor. Then Vikramáditya took with him his wife Malayavatí, like an incarnation of bliss, and crossed the sea resembling his long regretful separation, and being submissively waited upon at every step by kings, with various presents in their hands, returned to his own city Ujjayiní. And on beholding there that might of his, that satisfied freely every kind of curiosity, what people were not astonished, what people did not rejoice, what people did not make high festival?

Told by the Constable

From the Arabic

YE must know that a company, among whom was a friend of mine, once invited me to an entertainment; so I went with him, and when we came into his house and sat down on his couch, he said to me, "This is a blessed day and a day of gladness, and who is he that liveth to see the like of this day? I desire that thou practice with us and disapprove not our proceedings, for that thou hast been accustomed to fall in with those who offer this." I consented thereto and their talk happened upon the like of this subject. Presently, my friend, who had invited me, arose from among them and said to them, "Listen to me and I will acquaint you with an adventure which happened to me. There was a certain person who used to visit me in my shop, and I knew him not nor he knew me, nor ever in his life had he seen me; but he was wont, whenever he wanted a dirham or two, by way of loan, to come to me and ask me, without acquaintance or introduction between me and him, and I would give him what he required. I told none of him, and matters abode thus between us a long while till he began a-borrowing at a time ten or twenty dirhams, more or less. One day, as I stood in my shop, behold, a woman suddenly came up to me and stopped before me; and she was a presence as she were the full moon rising from among the constellations, and the place was a-light by her light. When I saw her, I fixed my eyes on her and stared in her face; and she fell to bespeaking me with soft voice. When I heard her words and the sweetness of her speech, I was drawn to her; and as soon as she saw that I longed for her, she did her errand and promising me a meeting, went away, leaving my thoughts occupied with her and fire a-flame in my heart. Accordingly I abode, perplexed and pondering my affair, the fire still burning in my heart, till the third day, when she came again and I could hardly credit her coming. When I saw her, I talked with her and cajoled her and courted her and craved her favor with speech and invited her to my house; but, hearing all this, she only answered, "I will not go up into anyone's house." Quoth I, "I will go with thee," and quoth she, "Arise and come with me." So I rose and putting into my sleeve a kerchief, wherein was a fair sum of silver and a considerable, followed the woman, who forewent me and ceased not walking till she brought me to a lane and to a door, which she bade me unlock. I refused and she opened it and led me into the vestibule. As soon as I had entered, she bolted the entrance door from within and said to me, "Sit here till I go in to the slave-girls and cause them enter a place whence they shall not see me." "'Tis well," answered I and sat down: whereupon she entered and was absent from me an eye-twinkling, after which she returned to me, without a veil, and straightway said, "Arise and enter in the name of Allah." So I arose and went in after her and we gave not over going till we reached a saloon. When I examined the place, I found it neither handsome nor pleasant, but desolate and dreadful without symmetry or cleanliness; indeed, it was loathsome to look upon and there was in it a foul smell. After this inspection I seated myself amiddlemost the saloon, misdoubting; and lo and behold! as I sat, there came down on me from the daïs a body of seven naked men, without other clothing than leather belts about their waists. One of them walked up to me and took my turban, while another seized my kerchief that was in my sleeve, with my money, and a third stripped me of my clothes; after which a fourth came and bound my hands behind my back with his belt. Then they all took me up, pinioned as I was, and casting me down, fell a-haling me toward a sink-hole that was there and were about to cut my throat, when suddenly there came a violent knocking at the door. As they heard the raps, they were afraid and their minds were diverted from me by affright; so the woman went out and presently returning, said to them, "Fear not; no harm shall betide you this day. 'Tis only your comrade who hath brought you your dinner." With this the new-comer entered, bringing with him a roasted lamb; and when he came in to them, he asked, "What is to do with you, that ye have tucked up sleeves and bag-trousers?" Replied they, "This is a head of game we've caught." As he heard these words, he came up to me and peering in my face, cried out and said, "By Allah, this is my brother, the son of my mother and father! Allah! Allah!" Then he loosed me from my pinion-bonds and bussed my head, and behold it was my friend who used to borrow silver of me. When I kissed his head, he kissed mine and said, "O my brother, be not affrighted"; and he called for my clothes and coin and restored all to me nor was aught missing. Also, he brought me a porcelain bowl full of sherbet of sugar, with lemons therein, and gave me to drink; and the company came and seated me at a table. So I ate with them and he said to me, "O my lord and my brother, now have bread and salt passed between us and thou hast discovered our secret and our case; but secrets with the noble are safe." I replied, "As I am a lawfully-begotten child and a well-born, I will not name aught of this nor denounce you!" They assured themselves of me by an oath; then they brought me out and I went my way, very hardly crediting but that I was of the dead. I lay ill in my house a whole month; after which I went to the Hammam and coming out, opened my shop and sat selling and buying as was my wont, but saw no more of that man or that woman till, one day, there stopped before my shop a young Turkoman, as he were the full moon; and he was a sheep-merchant and had with him a leathern bag, wherein was money, the price of sheep he had sold. He was followed by the woman, and when he stopped over against my shop, she stood by his side and cajoled him, and indeed he inclined to her with great inclination. As for me, I was dying of solicitude for him and began casting furtive glances at him and winked at him, till he chanced to look round and saw me signing to him; whereupon the woman gazed at me and made a signal with her hand and went away. The Turkoman followed her and I deemed him dead without a doubt; wherefore I feared with exceeding fear and shut my shop. Then I journeyed for a year's space and returning, opened my shop; whereupon, behold, the woman as she walked by came up to me and said, "This is none other than a great absence." I replied, "I have been on a journey"; and she asked, "Why didst thou wink at the Turkoman?" I answered, "Allah forfend! I did not wink at him." Quoth she, "Beware lest thou thwart me"; and went away. Awhile after this a familiar of mine invited me to his house and when I came to him, we ate and drank and chatted. Then he asked me, "O my friend, hath there befallen thee aught of sore trouble in the length of thy life?" Answered I, "Tell me first, hath there befallen thee aught?" He rejoined: Know that one day I espied a fair woman; so I followed her and sued her to come home with me. Quoth she, I will not enter anyone's house but my own; so come thou to my home, an thou wilt, and be it on such a day. Accordingly, on the appointed day her messenger came to me, proposing to carry me to her; and when he announced his purpose I arose and went with him, till we arrived at a goodly house and a great door. He opened the door and I entered, whereupon he bolted it behind me and would have gone in; but I feared with exceeding fear and foregoing him to the second door, whereby he would have had me enter, bolted it and cried out at him, saying, "By Allah, an thou open not to me, I will slay thee; for I am none of those whom thou canst readily cozen." "What deemest thou of cozening?" "Verily, I am startled by the loneliness of the house and the lack of any keeper at its door; for I see none appear." "O my lord, this is a private door." "Private or public, open to me." So he opened to me and I went out and had gone but a little way from the door when I met a woman, who said to me, "A long life was fore-ordained to thee; else hadst thou never come forth of yonder house." I asked, "How so?" and she answered, "Inquire of thy friend Such-an-one" (naming thee), "and he will acquaint thee with strange things." So, Allah upon thee, O my friend, tell me what befell thee of wondrous and marvelous, for I have told thee what befell me." "O my brother, I am bound by a solemn oath." "O my friend, false thine oath and tell me." "Indeed, I dread the issue of this." But he urged me till I told him all, whereat he marveled. Then I went away from him and abode a long while, without further news. One day, I met another of my friends who said to me, "A neighbor of mine hath invited me to hear singers," but I said: "I will not foregather with anyone." However, he prevailed upon me; so we repaired to the place and found there a person, who came to meet us and said, "Bismillah!" Then he pulled out a key and opened the door, whereupon we entered and he locked the door after us. Quoth I, "We are the first of the folk; but where be the singers' voices?" He replied, "They're within the house: this is but a private door; so be not amazed at the absence of the folk." My friend said to me, "Behold, we are two, and what can they dare to do with us?" Then he brought us into the house, and when we entered the saloon, we found it desolate exceedingly and dreadful of aspect. Quoth my friend, "We are fallen into a trap; but there is no Majesty and there is no Might save in Allah, the

Glorious, the Great!" And quoth I, "May God never requite thee for me with good!" Then we sat down on the edge of the daïs and suddenly I espied a closet beside me; so I peered into it and my friend asked me, "What seest thou?" I answered, "I see there wealth in store and corpses of murdered men galore. Look." So he looked and cried, "By Allah, we are down among the dead!" and we fell a-weeping, I and he. As we were thus, behold, four men came in upon us, by the door at which we had entered, and they were naked, wearing only leather belts about their waists, and made for my friend. He ran at them and dealing one of them a blow with his sword-pommel, knocked him down, whereupon the other three rushed upon him. I seized the opportunity to escape while they were occupied with him, and espying a door by my side, slipped into it and found myself in an underground room, without issue, even a window. So I made sure of death, and said, "There is no Majesty and there is no Might save in Allah, the Glorious, the Great!" Then I looked at the top of the vault and saw in it a range of glaze and colored lunettes; so I clambered up for dear life, till I reached the lunettes, and I out of my wits for fear. I made shift to remove the glass and scrambling out through the setting, found behind them a wall which I bestrode. Thence I saw folk walking in the street; so I cast myself down to the ground and Allah Almighty preserved me, and when I reached the face of earth, unhurt, the folk flocked round me and I acquainted them with my adventure. Now as Destiny decreed, the Chief of Police was passing through the market-street; so the people told him what was to do and he made for the door and bade raise it off its hinges. We entered with a rush and found the thieves, as they had thrown my friend down and cut his throat; for they occupied not themselves with me, but said, "Whither shall yonder fellow wend? Verily, he is in our grasp." So the Wali hent them with the hand and questioned them of their case, and they confessed against the woman and against their associates in Cairo. Then he took them and went forth, after he had locked up the house and sealed it; and I accompanied him till he came without the first house. He found the door bolted from within; so he bade raise it and we entered and found another door. This also he caused pull up, enjoining his men to silence till the doors should be lifted, and we entered and found the band occupied with new game, whom the woman had just brought in and whose throat they were about to cut. The Chief released the man and gave him back whatso the thieves had taken from him; and he laid hands on the woman and the rest and took forth of the house a mint of money, with which they found the purse of the Turkoman sheep-merchant. They at once nailed up the thieves against the house-wall, while, as for the woman, they wrapped her in one of her mantillas and nailing her to a board, set her upon a camel and went round about the town with her. Thus Allah razed their dwelling-places and did away from me that which I feared from them. All this befell while I looked on, and I saw not my friend who had saved me from them the first time, whereat I wondered to the utterest of wonderment. However, some days afterward, he came up to me, and indeed he had renounced the world and donned a Fakir's dress; and he saluted me and went away. Then he again began to pay me frequent visits and I entered into conversation with him and questioned him of the band and how he came to escape, he alone of them all. He replied, "I left them from the day on which Allah the Most High delivered thee from them, for that they would not obey my say; so I swore I would no longer consort with them." Quoth I, "By Allah, I marvel at thee, for that assuredly thou wast the cause of my preservation!" Quoth he, "The world is full of this sort; and we beseech the Almighty to send us safety, for that these wretches practice upon men with every kind of malpractice."

The Clever Thief

From the Tibetan

IN olden times there lived in a hill-town a householder, who married a wife of his own caste. When a son was born unto him, he said to his wife, "Goodwife, now that there is born unto us a causer of debts and diminisher of means, I will take merchandise and go to sea." She replied, "Do so, lord." So he went to sea with his merchandise, and there he died.

After his wife had got over her mourning, she continued to live, partly supported by her handiwork, and partly by her relatives. Not far from her dwelt a weaver who was skilled in his art, and who by means of adroitness succeeded in everything. Seeing that he, by means of his art, had become well to do, she came to the conclusion that weaving was better than going to sea, for when a man did the latter, he needlessly exposed himself to misfortune. So she said to the weaver, "O brother, teach this nephew of yours to weave." He replied, "As that is right, I will do so." The youth became his apprentice, and in a short time learned the art of weaving, for he was sharp and quick.

As the weaver wore fine clothes, took good baths, and partook of delicate food, the youth said to him one day, "Uncle, how is it that although you and I are occupied in exactly the same kind of work, yet you have fine clothes, good baths, and delicate food, but I never have a chance of such things?" The weaver replied, "Nephew, I carry on two kinds of work. By day I practice weaving, but by night thieving."

"If that be so, uncle, I too will practice thieving."

"Nephew, you cannot commit a theft."

"Uncle, I can."

The weaver thought he would test him a little, so he took him to the market-place, purchased a hare there, and gave it to him, saying, "Nephew, I shall take a bath and then return home. Meanwhile, go on roasting this hare." While he was taking his bath, the youth hastily roasted the hare and ate up one of its legs. When the weaver returned from his bath, he said, "Nephew, have you roasted the hare?"

"Yes!"

"Let's see it, then."

When the youth had brought the hare, and the weaver saw that it only had three legs, he said, "Nephew, where is the fourth leg gone?"

"Uncle, it is true that hares have four legs, but if the fourth leg is not there, it cannot have gone anywhere."

The weaver thought, "Although I have long been a thief, yet this lad is a still greater thief." And he went with the youth and the three-legged hare into a drinking-house and called for liquor. When they had both drunk, the weaver said, "Nephew, the score must be paid by a trick."

"Uncle, he who has drunk may play a trick; why should I, who have not drunk, do this thing?"

The weaver saw that the lad was a great swindler, so he determined to carry out a theft along with him.

They betook themselves to housebreaking. Once when they had made a hole into a house, and the weaver was going to pass his head through the opening, the youth said, "Uncle, although you are a thief, yet you do not understand your business. The legs should be put in first, not the head. For if the head should get cut off, its owner would be recognized, and his whole family would be plunged into ruin. Therefore put your feet in first."

When the weaver had done so, attention was called to the fact, and a cry was raised of "Thieves! thieves!" At that cry a great number of people assembled, who seized the weaver by his legs and began to pull him in. The youth, all by himself, could not succeed in pulling him out; but he cut off the weaver's head and got away with it.

The ministers brought the news to the king, saying, "Your Majesty, the thief was himself arrested at the spot where the housebreaking took place; but some one cut off his head and went away with it." The king said, "O friends, he who has cut off the head and gone away with it is a great thief. Go and expose the headless trunk at the crossway of the main street. Then place yourselves on one side, and arrest whoever embraces it and wails over it, for that will be the thief." Thereupon those servants of the king exposed the headless trunk at the crossway of the main street, and stationed themselves on one side. Thinking it would be wrong not to embrace his uncle and moan over him, the other thief assumed the appearance of a madman, and took to embracing men, women, carts, horses, bullocks, buffaloes, goats, and dogs. Afterwards, all men thinking he was mad, he pressed the headless trunk to his breast, wailed over it as long as he liked, and then went his way. The king was informed by his men that a madman had pressed the headless trunk to his bosom, and while he held it there had wailed over it, and had then gone away. The king said, "O friends, this man of a surety was the other thief. Ye have acted wrongly in not laying hands upon him. Therefore shall hands be laid upon you."

The other thief said to himself, "If I do not show honor to my uncle, I shall be acting badly." So he assumed the appearance of a carter, and drove a cart up to the spot laden with dry wood. When he arrived there, he upset the cart with its load of dry wood, unyoked the oxen, set the cart on fire, and then went away. The headless trunk was consumed by the flames. The king was informed by his men that the corpse was burned, and they told him all that had taken place. The king said, "O friends, the carter was certainly the thief. Ye have acted wrongly in not laying hands upon him. Therefore shall hands be laid upon you."

The thief said to himself, "I shall not be acting rightly unless I take soul-offerings to the burial-place for my uncle." So he assumed the appearance of a Brahman, and wandered from house to house collecting food. From what he collected he made five oblation-cakes, which he left at the burial-place, and then went his way. The king's men told him that a Brahman had wandered from house to house collecting food, and had then left five oblation-cakes on the spot where the body had been burned, and had then gone away. The king said, " O friends, that was really the thief. Ye have acted wrongly in not laying hands upon him."

The thief thought, " I shall be acting badly if I do not throw my uncle's bones into the Ganges." So he assumed the appearance of a Kāpālika,[1] went to the place where the corpse had been burned, smeared his body with ashes, filled a skull with bones and ashes, flung it into the Ganges, and then went his way. When the king had been told by his men all that had happened, he said, " O friends, this was really the thief. Ye have acted wrongly in not laying hands upon him."

From the "Kah-gyur." One of the oldest of popular tales is the story told by Herodotus (bk. ii. chap. 121) of the treasury of Rhampsinitus, which its builder's two sons are in the habit of robbing, until one of the thieves is caught in the snares set for their feet, whereupon the other, to prevent a discovery, cuts off his brother's head and runs away. The king gives orders to expose the corpse, and to keep watch so as to see whether anyone weeps and wails over it. The surviving son, forced by his mother's threats to look after his brother's burial, comes to the spot provided with skins of wine, makes the watchmen drunk, shaves off the right side of their beards, and carries away the dead body. Thereupon the king's daughter is obliged to yield herself to everyone who will relate to her the cleverest and most scandalous trick he has ever played in his life. The doer of the deed comes and betrays himself. But when the princess tries to seize him, he leaves in her hold, not his own hand, but that of the dead man. At last the king promises his daughter's hand to the doer of this deed, so the thief reveals himself and receives the princess. As a like legend is connected with the treasury of Hyrieus in Orchomenus, where Trophonius cut off the head of his brother Agamedes, and as according to Charax the same story is told also of the treasury of Augeias at Elis, we can easily understand why some commentators, like C. O. Müller, wish to claim the legend for the Greeks, while Buttmann wishes to trace it to the East.—TRANSLATOR.

[1] A skull-carrying Śiva-worshiper.

The King Who Made Mats

From the Persian

IN ancient times there was in the country of Aberbaijan a king who cherished wisdom and administered justice; the tiller of his equity-loving nature kept the garden of his kingdom always clean of the chaff and trash of oppression, and preserved with the light of the torch of high-mindedness and largesses the surface of the breast of those that hoped and solicited, from the darkness of hardship and destitution. By means of his discernment he became acquainted with the worth and station due to men of profession, and always honored the high polish of the speculum of accomplishments and perfections with the throne of dignity and the place of respect.

One day whilst he was sitting in the palace of pomp and splendor, dispensing justice and retribution, and engaged in diving into the depths of the circumstances of the people, two men took hold of the collar of complaint. One of them had no trade, and the other was skillful and accomplished; and although the one who had no trade brought forward arguments and evidences in support of his claim, and it became clear that he was in the right, the king purposely turned the scales in favor of the clever fellow, and ordered the man without a trade to be punished.

The king happened to have a vizier equal to Plato in science, and who always drew upon the leaves of the book of circumstances with the pen of propriety of opinion and prudence of arrangement. Wondering at the decision of the king, he rose from his place and said:

"O thou leader of the caravan of prosperity of realms, by the blows of whose world-conquering scimiter the peace of the breasts of opponents is destroyed, and from the fruits of whose convoy of success the countries of the hearts of the amicable are made populous and flourishing, I have a request to make: first that the skyward-flying Homai[1] of your gracious disposition may pervade the atmosphere of compliance with my solicitation."

The king said, "Explain."

The vizier answered: "I pray that the life of this innocent youth, whose guiltlessness must be visible upon the mirror of your majesty's mind, may be spared for my sake; and that it might be disclosed to me why your majesty pardoned the guilty and condemned the innocent man?"

The king said: "I have absolved him, whom you call guilty, because I have arrived at the certainty that he is unblamable and has the right on his side. I also have reason to believe that this is not the proper time to elucidate the matter, but it will be done as soon as we are alone."

A short time afterwards the tree of the assembly shed the leaves and fruit of its multitude; the lamp of the apartment of privacy was trimmed and made bright, when the king spoke:

"Thou quintessence of acuteness, something happened to me once which plunged me into the sea of astonishment; since that time I made a vow to show favor to a man who has a profession, even if he should be blameworthy otherwise; and to punish and persecute him who has no trade or occupation, even if he should be my own son; so that the high and the low, seeing this, be induced to teach their children trades in conformity with their circumstances; because labor is too simple and gentle a refuge from misfortune and a means to attain prosperity.

"Know thou that when my father was yet walking in the garden of life, and was sitting upon the throne of happiness and government, on a certain day those who were present at the audience were discussing the advantages of trades and accomplishments, and although I had made myself acquainted with several sciences and accomplishments

[1] A bird of happy omen; it is said never to touch the ground, and every head it overshades will wear a crown.

befitting a royal prince, I was anxious to learn yet some other trade. I determined that each of the tradesmen established in the city should display his skill before my eyes in order that I might apply myself to any trade which should captivate my fancy. After having seen them no one pleased me so much as mat-making, because the master of that art had introduced into the specimen which he worked all sorts of pretty figures.

"The instructor was engaged and I was taught. I assisted every day, until I became skillful in this business.

"One day I happened to entertain a desire of making an excursion of pleasure on the sea. I took leave of the king and embarked on board a boat with a number of courtiers. We amused ourselves for two days with fishing, but as all mortals are subject to the vicissitudes of fortune, on the third day a dreadful storm arose, the sea was lashed by it into furious waves, our boat went to pieces, and my companions became food for the palate of the whale of destiny.

"I was floating about on a broken plank with two of my associates for several days, erring like chaff in the ebb and tide of the abyss, and having our throats choked every moment by the gripe of mortal fear; we humbled and turned ourselves to the footstool of the Answerer of prayers, because nobody ever besought Him in vain.

"By this favor the wind drove the broken plank toward the shore, and all three of us, having landed safe and sound, made our way to an oasis which contained various fruits, and aromatic plants numerous beyond conception; we disported ourselves several days in that place, and during the night we took refuge on the trees, for fear of rapacious beasts, until we reached the end of the oasis and entered the desert, through the ups and downs of which we progressed for several days till the guide of our destinies led us into the city of Bagdad.

"I possessed several rings of great value, and went to the bazaar in the company of my friends in order to purchase food; having sold a ring, we entered the shop of a cook who had displayed a variety of dishes, and in whose service a handsome boy was busying himself; we handed to him a few dirhams to obtain some victuals. He cast a glance at us and said:

"'Young men, nobility and greatness shine from your foreheads. In this city it is considered disgraceful that youths like yourselves should be eating their food in the bazaar; in the neighborhood there is a very beautiful room, to which people like you are accustomed to resort. Do me the favor to adjourn to that place, that I may send there something worthy of you.'

"He sent his boy with us, whom we followed; after a short time we arrived at the house, stepped into the porch and entered the mansion, which we found to be very neat and variously ornamented. We wished to remain there.

"The boy, however, opened the door of another apartment and affirmed it to be a very pleasant place; I entered it with my companions, and we were beginning to amuse ourselves by contemplating the exquisite and wonderful paintings that ornamented its walls, when the boy said, 'I am going to bring you your meal.' As soon as he was gone the floor of the house began to move as if a great earthquake had happened. We wished to take to our heels, but the pavement separated, and all three of us were precipitated into a subterranean well which was dark like the graves of infidels, and black like their hearts.

"We lost all hope and were ready to die; we said: 'This time our adverse fortune has let fly the arrow of a strange event, and we have fallen into an uncommon place of destruction, so that the signification of our rescue will become as a word without meaning, like the name of the fabulous bird Unka.'

"That cook happened to be a Jew and an enemy of Mohammedans; it was his habit from a long time to make use of those compliments in order to decoy Mussulman foreigners to that house, whom he threw into that well, roasted their flesh, and sold it to other Mussulmans.

"Our necks were pledged in this affair and we were

in apprehension what turn it would take when the same youth descended into the depth of the well, having a sword in his hand, and was about to murder us, when we said to him: 'Friend! What advantage is going to accrue to you from killing us, unhappy wretches! If gain be your object, we know the trade of mat-making which is very profitable in this town; bring the tools necessary for that occupation to this place, and we will make a mat every day.' The wretch hastened away and informed his master of our intention; they provided us with the required materials; we made a mat, for which they threw down to us every day a loaf of barley bread.

"We were continuing in this state for some time, and were despairing of our condition, when a stratagem occurred to me; I finished a mat with all possible care and ornaments, and wove into its borders the description of my circumstances in the Arabic language. This happened during the reign of Harun Alraschid, so I said if this carpet were to be offered to the Khalif a considerable sum might be gained.

"The greediness of the Jew having become an obstacle to his circumspection and to his regard of consequences, he carried the mat to the palace of the Khalif, who highly approved of it. But after he had examined it more minutely he discovered the explanation round its borders, and having by the perusal of it arrived at the state of things, he asked the Jew where he got the mat from, and whose work it was? He answered: 'I have a friend in Busra who sent it to me.' The Khalif said: 'Wait a little, that I may present thee with a reward worthy of it.'

"Having called for a servant he whispered something into his ear; the servant left, and having delivered me and my companions from the well, carried me to Harun. As soon as the Jew perceived us he began to tremble; the Khalif asked: 'Who are these?' The Jew struck with his hand the ring of the door of negation and said: 'I do not know.' The Khalif ordered the instruments of torture to be brought forward; when the Jew heard this he confessed everything. Harun commanded the Jew to be suspended upon the tree of punishment, and the poison of perdition to be poured into the throat of his existence.

"My prudent plan was highly approved of; I was sent to the bath and presented with rich clothes; the Khalif asked me about my adventures, which I related to him from beginning to end; and as the long service of my father had laid the Khalif under obligations to him, and as the Khalif knew that I was the apple of the eye of that monarch, he was the more kind to me and said: 'Be of good cheer! Please God, we will help you to go to your country.' After having entertained me for several days he presented me with nearly ten strings of camels and all sorts of articles which are necessary or useful to Grandees, and dispatched me with fifty men and a letter to my father, to my own country.

"When I arrived in my own capital the corpse of my father was just being carried out of the city. After having mourned over the death of my father I established myself upon the throne of dominion. Although my peace was for some time in jeopardy from the misfortune just mentioned, nevertheless it is by the help of a trade that I was saved. I have perfect confidence in skillful men and I have decided always to honor men that have a profession, and to despise those that have none."

The Bráhman Who Lost His Treasure

From the Sanskrit

THERE is a city named Śrávastí, and in it there lived in old time a king of the name of Prasenajit, and one day a strange Bráhman arrived in that city. A merchant, thinking he was virtuous, because he lived on rice in the husk, provided him a lodging there in the house of a Bráhman. There he was loaded by him every day with presents of unhusked rice and other gifts, and gradually by other great merchants also, who came to hear his story. In this way the miserly fellow gradually accumulated a thousand *dínárs*, and, going to the forest, he dug a hole and buried it in the ground, and he went every day and examined the spot. Now one day he saw that the hole, in which he had hidden his gold, had been re-opened, and that all the gold had gone. When he saw that hole empty, his soul was smitten, and not only was there a void in his heart, but the whole universe seemed to him to be void also. And then he came crying to the Bráhman, in whose house he lived, and when questioned, he told him his whole story: and he made up his mind to go to a holy bathing-place, and starve himself to death. Then the merchant, who supplied him with food, hearing of it, came there with others, and said to him, "Bráhman, why do you long to die for the loss of your wealth? Wealth, like an unseasonable cloud, suddenly comes and goes." Though plied by him with these and similar arguments, he would not abandon his fixed determination to commit suicide, for wealth is dearer to the miser than life itself. But when the Bráhman was going to the holy place to commit suicide, the king Prasenajit himself, having heard of it, came to him and asked him, "Bráhman, do you know of any mark by which you can recognize the place where you buried your *dínárs*?" When the Bráhman heard that, he said, "There is a small tree in the wood there, I buried that wealth at its foot." When the king heard that, he said, "I will find that wealth and give it back to you, or I will give it you from my own treasury, do not commit suicide, Bráhman." After saying this, and so diverting the Bráhman from his intention of committing suicide, the king intrusted him to the care of the merchant, and retired to his palace. There he pretended to have a headache, and sending out the door-keeper, he summoned all the physicians in the city by proclamation with beat of drum. And he took aside every single one of them and questioned him privately in the following words: "What patients have you here, and how many, and what medicine have you prescribed for each?" And they thereupon, one by one, answered all the king's questions. Then one among the physicians, when his turn came to be questioned, said this, "The merchant Mátṛidatta has been out of sorts, O king, and this is the second day, that I have prescribed for him *nágabalá*." When the king heard that, he sent for the merchant, and said to him, "Tell me, who fetched you the *nágabalá*?" The merchant said, "My servant, your highness." When the king got this answer from the merchant, he quickly summoned the servant and said to him, "Give up that treasure belonging to a Bráhman, consisting of a store of *dínárs*, which you found when you were digging at the foot of a tree for *nágabalá*." When the king said this to him, the servant was frightened and confessed immediately, and bringing those *dínárs* left them there. So the king for his part summoned the Bráhman and gave him, who had been fasting in the meanwhile, his *dínárs*, lost and found again, like a second soul external to his body.

The Duel of the Two Sharpers

From the Arabic

THERE was once, in the city of Baghdad, a man hight Al-Marwazi who was a sharper and ruined the folk with his rogueries and he was renowned in all quarters for knavery. He went out one day, carrying a load of small pebbles, and swore to himself that he would not return to his lodging till he had sold it at the price of raisins. Now there was in another city a second sharper, hight Al-Razi one of its worst, who went out the same day, bearing a load of round stones, anent which he too had sworn to himself that he would not sell it but at the price of sun-dried figs. So the twain fared on with that which was by them and ceased not going till they met in one of the khans, and one complained to other of what he had suffered on travel in quest of gain and of the little demand for his wares. Now each of them had it in mind to cheat his fellow; so the man of Marw said to the man of Rayy, "Wilt thou sell me that?" He said, "Yes," and the other continued, "And wilt thou buy that which is with me?" The man of Rayy consented; so they agreed upon this and each of them sold to his mate that which was with him in exchange for the other's; after which they bade farewell and both fared forth. As soon as the twain were out of sight, they examined their loads, to see what was therein, and one of them found that he had a load of small pebbles and the other that he had a load of round stones; whereupon each of them turned back in quest of his fellow. They met again in the khan and laughing at each other canceled their bargain; then they agreed to enter into partnership and that all they had of money and other good should be in common, share and share alike. Then quoth Al-Razi to Al-Marwazi, "Come with me to my city, for that 'tis nearer than thine." So he went with him, and when he arrived at his quarters, he said to his wife and household and neighbors, "This is my brother, who hath been absent in the land of Khorasan and is come back." And he abode with him in all honor for a space of three days. On the fourth day, Al-Razi said to him, "Know, O my brother, that I purpose to do something." The other asked, "What is it?" and the first answered, "I mean to feign myself dead and do thou go to the bazar and hire two porters and a bier. Then take me up and go about the streets and markets with my body and collect alms on my account.[1] Accordingly the Marw man repaired to the market and, fetching that which he sought, returned to the Rayy man's house, where he found his fellow cast down in the entrance-passage, with his beard tied and his eyes shut, and his complexion was paled and his limbs were loose. So he deemed him really dead and shook him but he spoke not; then he took a knife

[1] Moslems are bound to see True Believers decently buried, and the poor often beg alms for the funeral.

and pricked his feet, but he budged not. Presently said Al-Razi, "What is this, O fool?" and said Al-Marwazi, "I deemed thou wast dead in very deed." Al-Razi cried, "Get thee to business, and leave funning." So he took him up and went with him to the market and collected alms for him that day till eventide, when he bore him back to his abode and waited till the morrow. Next morning, he again took up the bier and walked round with it as before, in quest of charity. Presently, the Chief of Police, who was of those who had given him alms on the previous day, met him; so he was angered and fell on the porters and beat them and took the dead body, saying, "I will bury him and win reward in Heaven." So his followers took him up and carrying him to the Police-officer, fetched grave-diggers, who dug him a grave. Then they brought him a shroud and perfumes and fetched an old man of the quarter, to wash him; so the Shaykh recited over him the appointed prayers and laying him on the bench, washed him and shrouded him. When the dead man found himself alone, he sprang up, as he were a Satan; and, donning the corpse-washer's dress, took the cups and water-can and wrapped them up in the napkins; then he clapped his shroud under his armpit and went out. The doorkeepers thought that he was the washer and asked him, "Hast thou made an end of the washing, so we may acquaint the Emir?" The sharper answered, "Yes," and made off to his abode, where he found the Marw man a-wooing his wife and saying to her, "By thy life, thou wilt never again look upon his face for the best reason that by this time he is buried: I myself escaped not from them but after toil and trouble, and if he speak, they will do him to death." Quoth she, "And what wouldst thou have of me?" and quoth he, "Be mine, for I am better than thy husband." Now when the Rayy man heard this, he rushed in upon them, and when Al-Marwazi saw him, he wondered at him and said to him, "How didst thou make thine escape?" Accordingly he told him the trick he had played and they abode talking of that which they had collected from the folk, and indeed they had gotten great store of money. Then said the man of Marw, "In very sooth, mine absence hath been prolonged and lief would I return to my own land." Al-Razi said, "As thou willest"; and the other rejoined, "Let us divide the moneys we have made and do thou go with me to my home, so I may show thee my tricks and my works." Replied the man of Rayy, "Come to-morrow, and we will divide the coin." So the Marw man went away and the other turned to his wife and said to her, "We have collected us great plenty of money, and the dog would fain take the half of it; but such thing shall never be, for my mind hath been changed against him, since I heard him making love to thee; now, therefore, I propose to play him a trick and enjoy all the money; and do thou not oppose me." She replied, "'Tis well;" and he said to her, "To-morrow, at peep o' day I will feign myself dead, and do thou cry aloud and tear thy hair, whereupon the folk will flock to me. Then lay me out and bury me; and, when the folk are gone away from the grave, dig down to me and take me; and fear not for me, as I can abide without harm two days in the tomb-niche." Whereto she made answer, "Do e'en whatso thou wilt." Accordingly, when it was the dawn-hour, she bound his beard and spreading a veil over him, shrieked aloud, whereupon the people of the quarter flocked to her, men and women. Presently, up came Al-Marwazi, for the division of the money, and hearing the keening asked, "What may be the news?" Quoth they, "Thy brother is dead"; and quoth he in himself, "The accursed fellow cozeneth me, so he may get all the coin for himself, but I will presently do with him what shall soon re-quicken him." Then he tore the bosom of his robe and bared his head, weeping and saying, "Alas, my brother, ah! Alas, my chief, ah! Alas, my lord, ah!" And he went in to the men, who rose and condoled with him. Then he accosted the Rayy man's wife and said to her, "How came his death to occur?" Said she, "I know nothing except that, when I arose in the morning, I found him dead." Moreover, he questioned her of the money which was with her, but she cried, "I have no knowledge of this and no tidings." So he sat down at his fellow-sharper's head, and said to him, "Know, O Razi, that I will not leave thee till after ten days with their nights, wherein I will wake and sleep by thy grave. So rise and don't be a fool." But he answered him not, and the man of Marw drew his knife and fell to sticking it into the other's hands and feet, purposing to make him move; but he stirred not and he presently grew weary of this and determined that the sharper was really dead. However, he still had his suspicions and said to himself, "This fellow is falsing me, so he may enjoy all the money." Therewith he began to prepare the body for burial and bought for it perfumes and whatso was needed. Then they brought him to the washing-place and Al-Marwazi came to him; and, heating water till it boiled and bubbled and a third of it was evaporated, fell to pouring it on his skin, so that it turned bright red and lively blue and was blistered; but he abode still motionless. Presently they wrapped him in the shroud and set him on the bier, which they took up and bearing him to the burial-place, placed him in the grave-niche and filled in the earth; after which the folk dispersed. But the Marw man and the widow abode by the tomb, weeping, and ceased not sitting till sundown, when the woman said to him, "Come, let us hie us home, for this weeping will not profit us, nor will it restore the dead." He replied to her, "By Allah, I will not budge hence till I have slept and waked by this tomb ten days with their nights!" When she heard this his speech, she feared lest he should keep his word and his oath, and so her husband perish; but she said in her mind, "This one dissembleth: an I leave him and return to my house, he will tarry by him a little while and go away." And Al-Marwazi said to her, "Arise, thou, and hie thee home." So she arose and repaired to her house, while the man of Marw abode in his place till the night was half spent, when he said to himself, "How long? Yet how can I let this knavish dog die and lose the money? Better I open the tomb on him and bring him forth and take my due of him by dint of grievous beating and torment." Accordingly, he dug him up and pulled him forth of the grave; after which he betook himself to a garden hard by the burial-ground and cut thence staves and palm-fronds. Then he tied the dead man's legs and laid on to him with the staff and beat him a grievous beating; but the body never budged. When the time grew longsome on him, his shoulders became a-weary and he feared lest some one of the watch passing on his round should surprise and seize him. So he took up Al-Razi and carrying him forth of the cemetery, stayed not till he came to the Magians' mortuary-place and casting him down in a Tower of Silence, rained heavy blows upon him till his shoulders failed him, but the other stirred not. Then he seated him by his side and rested; after which he rose and renewed the beating upon him; and thus he did till the end of the night, but without making him move. Now, as Destiny decreed, a band of robbers whose wont it was, when they had stolen anything, to resort to that place and there divide their loot, came thither in early-dawn, according to their custom; they numbered ten and they had with them much wealth which they were carrying. When they approached the Tower of Silence, they heard a noise of blows within it and their captain cried, "This is a Magian whom the Angels are tormenting." So they entered the cemetery and as soon as they arrived over against him, the man of Marw feared lest they should be the watchmen come upon him, therefore he fled and stood among the tombs. The robbers advanced to the place and finding the man of Rayy bound by the feet and by him some seventy sticks, wondered at this with exceeding wonder and said, "Allah confound thee! This was a miscreant, a man of many crimes; for earth hath rejected him from her womb, and by my life, he is yet fresh! This is his first night in the tomb and the Angels were tormenting him but now; so whoso of you hath a sin upon his soul, let him beat him, by way of offering to Almighty Allah." The robbers said, "We be sinners one and all"; so each of them went up to the corpse and dealt it about an hundred blows, one saying the while, "This is for my father!" and another laid on to him crying, "This is for my grandfather!" whilst a third muttered, "This is for my brother!" and a fourth exclaimed, "This is for my mother!" And they gave not taking turns at him and beating him till they were weary, whilst Al-Marwazi stood laughing and saying in himself, "'Tis not I alone who have entered into default against him. There is no Majesty and there is no Might save in Allah, the Glorious, the Great!" Then the robbers applied themselves to sharing their loot wherein was a sword which caused them to fall out anent the man who should take it. Quoth the Captain, "'Tis my rede that we make proof of it; so, an it be a fine blade, we shall know its worth, and if it be worthless we shall know that"; whereto they said, "Try it on this corpse, for it is fresh." So the Captain took the sword and drawing it, brandished and made a false cut with it; but, when the man of Rayy saw this, he felt sure of death and said in his mind, "I have borne the washing-slab and the boiling water and the pricking with the knife-point and the grave-niche and its straitness and all this, trusting in Allah that I might be delivered from death, and indeed I have been delivered; but the sword I may not suffer, seeing that one stroke of it will make me a dead man." So saying, he sprang to his feet and seizing a thigh-bone of one departed, shouted at the top of his voice, "O ye dead ones, take them to yourselves!" And he smote one of them, whilst his mate of Marw smote another and they cried out at them and buffeted them on their neck-napes: whereupon the robbers left that which was with them of loot and ran away; and indeed their wits took flight for terror and they ceased not running till they came forth of the Magians' mortuary-ground and left it a parasang's length behind them, when they halted, trembling and affrighted for the muchness of that which had befallen them of fear and awe of the dead. As for Al-Razi and Al-Marwazi, they made peace each with other and sat down to share the spoil. Quoth the man of Marw, "I will not give thee a dirham of this money, till thou pay me my due of the moneys that be in thy house." And quoth the man of Rayy, "I will do naught of the kind, nor will I withdraw this from aught of my due." So they fell out thereupon and disputed each with other and either of the twain went saying to his fellow, "I will not give thee a dirham!" Wherefore words ran high between them and the brawl was prolonged. Meanwhile, when the robbers halted, one of them said to the others, "Let us go back and see"; and the Captain said, "This thing is impossible of the dead; never heard we that they came to life in such way. Return we and take our moneys, for that the dead have no need of money." And they were divided in opinion as to returning: but presently one said, "Indeed, our weapons are gone and we may not prevail against them and will not draw near the place: only let one of us go look at it, and if he hear no sound of them, let him suggest to us what we shall do." At this they agreed that they should send a man of them and assigned him for such mission two parts of the plunder. Accordingly he returned to the burial-ground and gave not over going till he stood at the door of the Tower of Silence, when he heard the words of Al-Marwazi to his fellow, "I will not give thee a single dirham of the money!" The other said the same and they were occupied with brawling and abuse and talk. So the robber returned in haste to his mates, who said, "What is behind thee?" Quoth he, "Get you gone and run for your lives, O fools, and save yourselves: much people of the dead are come to life and between them are words and brawls." Hereat the robbers fled, whilst the two sharpers returned to the man of Rayy's house and made peace and added the robbers' spoil to the moneys they had gained and lived a length of time.

The Lady and the Kazi

From the Persian

DURING the reign of Sultan Mahomed Subaktaghin in Ghaznin, a man was traveling from Aderbaijan to Hindustan; when he arrived in Ghaznin, he was much pleased with the climate, so he decided to settle there; and as he had great experience in commerce, he went to the bazaar and became a broker and was very successful in business.

He intended to marry, and fortune being propitious to him, he entered into a matrimonial alliance with a virtuous and handsome young woman; by degrees his business also became more and more flourishing, and having accumulated much wealth, he was numbered among the richest merchants.

He wished to extend his transactions to Hindustan and sent goods to that country; but as he had no connections or intimate friends in Ghaznin who might take charge of his wife till his return, this thought troubled him greatly, and as he considered it the first duty of a respectable man to be on his guard on this subject, and not to hazard his reputation and honor, he determined not to start on his journey till he had provided an asylum for his spouse.

Now since the Kazi of the city was a man noted for his piety, virtue, and honor, he said to himself: "I cannot do better than intrust the keeping of my wife to so godly and honest a man, who is a magistrate and a churchman, and enjoys the esteem of the rich and the poor; let her remain in his house till I return from my journey."

He hastened to make his obeisance to the Kazi and said: "O President of the judgment seat of truth and piety, by whose talented and searching disposition the explanations of religious and secular questions are flowing, and by whose essentially holy authority and intelligence the commendatory and prohibitory laws are corroborated, may your righteous opinion always remain the guide of those who seek to walk in the strait way of piety. I, your humble servant, am an inhabitant of this city, and it is my intention to undertake a journey to Hindustan; I have a young wife, the leaves of whose modesty and virtue are bound up in the splendid volume of her natural excellence; but as I have nobody who might protect and take care of her, and also because she might fall under the obloquy of false tongues, I flatter myself that she might find a refuge under the guardianship of your lordship."

The Kazi placed the seal of acquiescence upon this request and said that he would take care of her. That man furnished his wife with all the necessary expenses for one year, delivered her to the Kazi, and started on his journey.

The lady spent her whole time in the house of the Kazi in prayer and devotion, and nearly a whole year had elapsed without the breeze of a single profane glance having blown on the vernal abode of her face, and without her having ever heard the bird of a voice in the foliage of her ears; till one day the Kazi unexpectedly made his appearance and looked at her, when he perceived her Leila-like beauty sitting within the black mansion of her musked ringlets, and her sweet tenderness mounted upon the palfrey [1] of attractiveness and melancholy, the Kazi's intellect became troubled, and Ferhad-like [2] he began to dig the Bistún of his soul, which was melting and burning in the censer of distraction.

He was anxious to make overtures against her virtue, but being aware of her whole nature and chastity, he durst not attempt it; nevertheless, when the wife of the Kazi one day absented herself to visit the public baths and had left the lady alone to take care of the house, he was so completely dominated by his unlawful passion that he threw skyward the turban of concupiscence and said:

[1] In the text, "Gulgún," the name of the horse which Lady Shirin rides, in the poem of "Ferhad and Shirin."

[2] Ferhad dug in the mountain Bistún and sculptured Shirin's likeness.

"The desired game for which I looked in the skies,
Has now on earth fallen into the net of my good fortune."

The Kazi locked the door and commenced his stratagem by complimenting her modesty; and continued to address her in the following strain:

"Virtuous lady! The reputation of my honesty and piety has spread in the world and penetrated all corners, neither could the charms of the paradisaical Houris seduce my righteous disposition from the road of firm determination, or impel me to transgress the laws of purity; then why do you avoid me so much? If the absence of intelligence and of the knowledge of the true state of things keep your face veiled with the curtain of bashfulness, my obedience to the laws of God, and my fear of eternal punishment at the day of resurrection, prohibit me from allowing the fire of sensuality to be kindled within me.

"I would not disturb your peace even with the sinful glance of my eye.

"Be of good cheer and throw aside the veil of apprehension from your face, because there is no danger of sinning; and although it is against the law of God and the Prophet to exact services from guests, yet since you belong to the house and I am dependent on your kindness, I would request you to procure me some food, for I am hungry."

The woman placed the prohibitory veil of bashfulness on her face, and waited upon the Kazi with all due modesty; she put the meal before him and retired to a corner; the Kazi had provided himself with a drug which deprives of his senses anyone who tastes it, and said to the woman: "You know that three kinds of persons will be rejected from the mercy of God on the day of resurrection, and will be subjected to endless tortures; firstly, he who eats alone; secondly, he who sleeps alone; and thirdly, he who travels alone; and till now it has never happened to me that I did any of these three things; since I am now eating alone and anyone who does this has the devil for his companion, and to whomsoever this happens, his faith will be endangered; why should you not, in order to free me from the snares of the devil, defile your hands by partaking of this meal?"

He did not cease to invite her till she sat down near the table and helped herself to some food. The Kazi took this opportunity to throw some of the medicine into the plate; after the unfortunate woman had swallowed a few morsels she felt herself fainting, and wanting to get up from the table, her feet refused to bear her, and she fell senseless to the ground.

The Kazi quickly gathered up the articles that were on the table and meditated worse things; when he suddenly heard noises on the outside; this greatly disturbed him, and he was much embarrassed where to conceal the woman so that nobody might discover the circumstance.

Now the Kazi happened to keep his money and valuables in a subterranean room which was situated exactly under the apartment in which he was. Nobody knew anything about this place except himself; he opened the trapdoor, thrust the woman into it and again covered the floor with the carpet; then he went out and saw that his family had returned from the bath.

The Kazi said: "Why did you all leave the house empty?" They answered: "We have left the wife of the merchant to take care of the place." The Kazi said: "It is two hours since I arrived at home and have seen no one; why do you trust such a person? She may have taken away something." They were all astonished and said that she was not such a woman, and wondered what had become of her.

While this talk was going on the husband of that woman, having just returned from his journey to Hindustan, came at that moment to the house of the Kazi to inquire for his wife. The Kazi said: "It is some time since your wife has left the house without giving us notice or asking permission."

The merchant said: "O Kazi! This is not the time to

crack jokes; deliver to me my wife." The Kazi swore an oath and affirmed that he was in earnest. The merchant said: " I am too well acquainted with the nature and disposition of my wife ever to believe her to be capable of such a trick; there must be something else the matter."

The Kazi got angry and replied: " It is I who must be offended, you foolish man; why do you talk nonsense and uselessly insult us? Go and see where your wife is!"— As the merchant was greatly attached to his spouse, and the smoke of distress was beginning to ascend from the oven of his brains, he tore the collar of patience and hastened to make his complaint to the Sultan, and prostrating himself upon the carpet of supplication he said:

" Oh, exalted and happy monarch,
May felicity be the servant of your palace.
The Kazi of the city has done me injustice,
Greater than the blast of a tornado of the west.
If it be permitted I shall explain
The injustice of that mean-spirited wretch."

The Sultan said: " Bring forward your complaint that I may become acquainted with it." The merchant said: " I am a native of Aderbaijan, and it was the fame of the justice and protection which the poor obtain at the hands of your majesty that induced me to settle in this country, and it is some time since I dwelt under the shadow of your majesty's protection. I had a beautiful and modest wife, and intending to travel to Hindustan, I committed her one year ago to the charge of the Kazi. Now I have again returned, but he, being deceived by his covetousness, refuses to give up to me my wife."

The Sultan ordered the Kazi to be brought into his presence, but the latter, suspecting what would happen, suborned by the promise of money several vagabonds to testify, when called upon, that they had seen the merchant's wife absent herself from the Kazi's house three months ago.

When the Kazi arrived, the Sultan asked him what kind of a complaint the merchant had against him.

The Kazi said: "May the torch of your majesty's welfare be luminous, and the castle of opposition ruinous! This man has intrusted his wife to me and it is nearly three months since she went out of my house without giving any notice, and up to this time she has not come back; we have been unable to discover any traces of her."

The merchant answered: "This is contrary to the nature of my wife, and I do not believe it." The Sultan said: "Who are the witnesses?"

The Kazi answered that several neighbors and householders of the vicinity were acquainted with the fact, and wrote down their names; at a sign of the Sultan to a Chamberlain, these witnesses were brought in, and they confirmed the assertion of the Kazi.

Then the Sultan said to the merchant: "As the Kazi has established his assertion by witnesses, your complaint falls to the ground." Upon this the merchant retired disappointed.

The Sultan was in the habit of perambulating the bazaars and streets of the city occasionally, in disguise, to mix among the people, and thus discover what they thought of him. That night he left his palace according to his wont and walked about.

He happened to pass near the door of a shop where boys were playing the game of "The King and his Vizier." One of the children was made king, and said to the others: "I am king and you are all under my authority; you must not seek to evade my commands." Another boy said: "If you give unjust judgments like Sultan Mahomed we shall soon depose you." The other asked: "What injustice has Sultan Mahomed done?"

He answered: "To-day the affair of a merchant came before the Sultan. This merchant had confided his wife to the keeping of the Kazi, and he hid her in his own house; the Sultan called for witnesses, when the Kazi gained his cause by bringing into court witnesses whom he had previously bribed. It is a great pity that people should have the administration of justice in their hands who are unable to distinguish between right and wrong; had I been in the place of the Sultan I would very quickly have discovered the truth or falsehood of the witnesses of the Kazi."

When the Sultan had heard the conversation of these children he sighed and returned to his palace in great agitation of mind; next morning as soon as it was daylight he sent somebody to fetch the boy. The boy came and the Sultan received him in a very friendly way, saying: "This day you shall be my Lieutenant the whole day from morning till evening, and I intend to allow you to sit in judgment and to act entirely according to your own will." Then the Sultan whispered to a Chamberlain to invite the merchant again to state his complaint against the Kazi.

The merchant came and did so; the witnesses were again called for, whom the Kazi again brought into court. The Kazi wished to take a seat, but the boy said: "Ho, Master Kazi! It is a long time since the leading strings of judicial power, and the power of tying and untying the knotty points of law, have been in your hands; why do you seem to be so ignorant of legal customs? You have been brought into this court as a party in a lawsuit and not as an assessor; it is the rule that you should stand below on an equality with your accuser, till the court breaks up, and then you should obey whatever its decision might be."

The Kazi went and placed himself near the merchant; then the merchant proffered his complaint, and the Kazi again affirmed that the woman had abandoned the house three months ago.

The boy said: "Have you any witnesses?" The Kazi beckoned to his followers and said: "These are the witnesses."

The boy called one of the witnesses and asked him in a subdued voice whether he had seen the woman? He said: "Yes." Then he inquired further what signs there were on her person, stature, or face? The man became embarrassed and said: "She has a mole on her forehead, one of her teeth is wanting, she is of a fresh complexion, tall and slender."

The boy asked: "What time of day was it when she went away from the house of the Kazi?" He answered: "Morning." The boy said: "Remain in this place."

Then he called for another witness of whom he also asked the description, and got the following answer: "She is of low stature, lean, her cheeks are white and red, she has a mole near the lips, and she left the house in the afternoon."

Having placed this individual in another corner, he called for a third witness whose evidence contradicted both the others, and gradually he examined all of them, and found them disagreeing in everything.

The Sultan was sitting by the side of the boy and heard all; when the hearing of the witnesses was completed, the boy said: "You God-forgetting wretches, why do you give false evidence? Let the instruments of torture be brought forward that we may find out the truth." As soon as they heard the name of torture mentioned, they all offered to say the truth, and acknowledged themselves to be a set of poor fellows whom the Kazi had bribed with a sum of money and had instructed what to say; they also confessed that they knew nothing whatever about the woman.

The boy called the Kazi, and asked him what he had to say in this business; the Kazi commenced to tremble all over his body, and said: "The truth is as I have stated it." The boy said: "Our Kazi is a bold man, and his haughtiness hinders him from acknowledging the truth; the instruments of punishment ought to be made use of."

When the Kazi heard this, the fear of torture greatly distressed him, and he confessed the truth. Upon this the boy kissed the floor of good manners with the lips of obedience, and said: "The remainder of this affair is to be settled by the Sultan." The Sultan was much pleased with the acuteness and intelligence of the boy, and ordered the Kazi to be beheaded and all his property to be given to the wife of that merchant. The boy was treated kindly and educated, until by degrees he won the whole confidence of the Sultan and became one of his greater favorites.

Mahaushadha

From the Tibetan

ONE day the king went into the park with his wives, and enjoyed himself there together with them. One of them took off a string of pearls worth a hundred thousand pieces of money and hung it on a spray of an aśoka tree. While sporting with the king she forgot about it and left it there. At midnight, after she had gone back to the palace with the king, she remembered that she had left her necklace in the forest. Meanwhile it had been carried off to the top of a tree by a female monkey.

The king ordered his men to hasten to the forest and bring back the necklace. They went there, but they did not find it. Now a beggar had gone there in search of the remnants of the food of which other men had made a meal. As he came forth from the forest after partaking of such food, the king's men arrested him. As no one else was to be seen there, they called on him to render up the necklace. Although he protested that he had not taken it, had not even seen it, yet he was beaten with fists and stakes, and then thrown into prison.

Tormented by hunger, he reflected that, unless he contrived some cunning way of escape he would die there of starvation. So he said to the jailer that he had, it was true, taken the pearl necklace, but that he had given it to such and such a young merchant. Him also the king's men summoned, and the two men were set fast connected by wooden fetters.

The merchant used to receive from home dainty food. While he was partaking of it the beggar asked him for some. But the merchant reviled him, saying, "It is all very well for you to accuse me of theft in order that I may nourish you with my food. I will give you none of it." And having thus spoken, he ate it all up.

After this, when the merchant wished to change his place, and said, "Let us stand up and move," the beggar replied, "I will not listen to your words; I shall not get up." Then said the merchant, "Henceforward will I behave so that you will be contented." Thus with friendly words and with an oath he won over the beggar, and was able to do as he wished.

The next day the merchant sent home orders to provide in future food enough for two persons. Thereat the beggar was highly pleased, and he reflected that in former times he used to wander about the whole city without being able to find the means of filling his belly, but now food and drink in plenty were at hand.

While they so enjoyed themselves a further desire arose within them. They thought that in order to have still more pleasure they must call in a lute-player. So the beggar accused a lute-player also of having taken the string of pearls. Then the king's men cast him also into the prison.

After some time the others besought the beggar to find some means whereby they might become free, saying that in that case he should want for nothing. He promised to do so, and bethought himself that no one could be of use except Mahaushadha. So he told the king's men that Mahaushadha's son had likewise taken part in the affair, and they sent for him also.

When Mahaushadha heard that his son had been imprisoned, he felt that he must certainly go to the palace, for if he did not do so his son would fret himself. On arriving there, he asked the king what offense his son had committed. The king replied that he had been imprisoned on the testimony of the beggar with respect to the stolen pearl necklace. When Mahaushadha had become fully acquainted with the contrivance of the captives, he said to the king, "The theft has not been committed by any of these people. Let them all go free on my word." So they were released.

After this he went out to the park, and came to the spot, to the very tree, where they had been before. When he looked closely at the tree, he perceived a female monkey sitting at the top of it. Then he felt sure that this animal had taken the string of pearls, and that it must be enticed to come down by some artifice. So he asked the king to go there with his wife, and when there, to hang a necklace round her neck. When that was done, the monkey, as it sat on the tree-top, hung the pearl necklace round its neck. Then Mahaushadha told the king's wife to dance. When she did so, the monkey on the tree-top also began to dance; but still the string of pearls did not fall from off its neck. In order to bring that about, Mahaushadha asked the king to make his wife, as she danced, hang down her head. Then the monkey also began to dance about with its head hanging down, whereupon the string of pearls fell down from off its neck. Full of joy, the king embraced Mahaushadha and bestowed much property upon him.

Avicenna and the Observant Young Man

From the Turkish

WHEN Aboo Sinna [1] was in Ispahan, in the three hundred and ninety-eighth year of the Hedjreh, that powerful person, Alai ed Dowlet Aboo Jaafer Delimee was its governor. At that time distinctions and marks of regard were bestowed on Aboo Sinna without ceasing. One day the Sultan took from his waist a rich and valuable belt, and bestowed it upon that excellent Sheik. This the latter afterwards gave to one of the Sultan's own attendants. The Sultan, observing it on the individual, inquired how

[1] Avicenna, the foremost Arabic physician and philosopher, who lived 980–1037.

he came by it. The man replied that he had received it from the Sheik as a present. The Sultan was greatly displeased and rebuked the attendant severely for having accepted it; at the same time he swore to take the Sheik's life for caring so little for his gifts. But one of the Sheik's friends giving him information of what had occurred, he acted on the proverb which says, "Separate from him whom you cannot withstand," and forthwith departed from that country in disguise. On coming to another city and dismounting at a caravanserai, he walked to the market-place in search of provisions. Whilst thus engaged, he observed a youth of talent and science, around whom a crowd of people were collected asking him for remedies. The youth in turn showed to each one the remedies for his complaint, and the means of recovery from his malady. Presently a woman made her appearance, bearing a white vase in her hand, which she showed to him. The youth said that the vase belonged to a Jew; which the woman confirmed. Afterwards he said that she had eaten that day half an egg and some curds; and this the woman also avowed. The young man next asked if the woman did not then reside in a filthy part of the city; and the woman answered affirmatively. Aboo Sinna, observing the youth's superior talents, was astonished at his language and the remedies which he prescribed. The young man's eyes happened to meet those of Aboo Sinna; and making him a secret sign of recognition, he addressed the Sheik with deference and said, "You are he who has received that divine science, and are that unequaled and most perfectly excellent person, the Reis Aboo Ali bin Sinna, who fled from Ispahan through fear of the Sultan Alai ed Dowlet, and are come to this place with the intention of residing here." Then feeling kindly towards the Sheik, he left all his business, kissed the Sheik's feet, took his hand in his, and led him to his own house. After receiving from the young man all the usual attentions of a servant, the Sheik asked him whence he had drawn his conclusions, and how he knew that the vase belonged to a Jew. The youth replied, " I observed the old woman's tunic, and knew from its marks that she was a Jewess; and I judged that the vase also belonged to one of the same people. Her dress was soiled with eggs and with curdled milk; and I knew that she must have eaten of both these things. Moreover, knowing that the Jew quarter at this time is a filthy place, I remarked that it was unclean." " But," said the Sheik, " how did you become acquainted with me and my profession?" The youth said in reply, " Knowing the envy of Alai ed Dowlet, the circumstance of your having fled from him is a proof of the renown of your excellence, and that your sagacity and mental powers must be as bright as the sun in the heavens. I have heard too of the good qualities with which you are gifted, and I beheld on your noble front the characteristics of those traits, which beamed upon me like the midday sun; from all of which I felt assured that you were the celebrated physician Aboo Sinna. I likewise knew that the Sultan could not bear to be separated from you for a moment, and therefore was convinced that you must have left him by your own desire and against his will." The young man next bent the knee of politeness before the Sheik, and thanked God for allowing him to meet with such a man. The Sheik then said, " What have you to ask of me? Tell me your wishes, and, as far as my destiny permits, I will endeavor to promote them." The intelligent youth replied, " It is impossible that you should remain separated from the Sultan; and what I ask from you is, that when you again appear before him, you will relate the occurrence which you have witnessed, and obtain me a place in his service, even as one of his most humble attendants."

Some days after this, a man came to the Sheik on the part of the Sultan, who begged his pardon for the past, and invited him to return to his palace. The Sheik took the youth with him, and on reaching the Sultan, related what he had witnessed respecting him; wherefore the Sultan forthwith appointed him to be one of his own pages.

PART III

Ancient Latin and Greek Mystery Stories

HERODOTUS (484-424 B.C.)

LUCIUS APULEIUS (2ND CENTURY A.D.)

PLINY THE ELDER (1ST CENTURY A.D.)

Herodotus

The Thief Versus King Rhampsinitus

KING RHAMPSINITUS was possessed, they said, of great riches in silver—indeed to such an amount, that none of the princes, his successors, surpassed or even equaled his wealth. For the better custody of this money, he proposed to build a vast chamber of hewn stone, one side of which was to form a part of the outer wall of his palace. The builder, therefore, having designs upon the treasures, contrived, as he was making the building, to insert in this wall a stone, which could easily be removed from its place by two men, or even one. So the chamber was finished, and the king's money stored away in it.

Time passed, and the builder fell sick; when finding his end approaching, he called for his two sons, and related to them the contrivance he had made in the king's treasure-chamber, telling them it was for their sakes he had done it, so that they might always live in affluence. Then he gave them clear directions concerning the mode of removing the stone, and communicated the measurements, bidding them carefully keep the secret, whereby they would be Comptrollers of the Royal Exchequer so long as they lived. Then the father died, and the sons were not slow in setting to work; they went by night to the palace, found the stone in the wall of the building, and having removed it with ease, plundered the treasury of a round sum.

When the king next paid a visit to the apartment he was astonished to see that the money was sunk in some of the vessels wherein it was stored away. Whom to accuse, however, he knew not, as the seals were all perfect, and the fastenings of the room secure. Still each time that he repeated his visits, he found that more money was gone. The thieves in truth never stopped, but plundered the treasury ever more and more.

At last the king determined to have some traps made, and set near the vessels which contained his wealth. This was done, and when the thieves came, as usual, to the treasure chamber, and one of them entering through the aperture, made straight for the jars, suddenly he found himself caught in one of the traps. Perceiving that he was lost, he instantly called his brother, and telling him what had happened, entreated him to enter as quickly as possible and cut off his head, that when his body should be discovered it might not be recognized, which would have the effect of bringing ruin upon both. The other thief thought the advice good, and was persuaded to follow it; then, fitting the stone into its place, he went home, taking with him his brother's head.

When day dawned, the king came into the room, and marveled greatly to see the body of the thief in the trap without a head, while the building was still whole, and neither entrance nor exit was to be seen anywhere. In this perplexity he commanded the body of the dead man to be hung up outside the palace wall, and set a guard to watch it, with orders that if any persons were seen weeping or lamenting near the place, they should be seized and brought before him. When the mother heard of this exposure of the corpse of her son, she took it sorely to heart, and spoke to her surviving child, bidding him devise some plan or other to get back the body, and threatening that if he did not exert himself she would go herself to the king and denounce him as the robber.

The son said all he could to persuade her to let the matter rest, but in vain: she still continued to trouble him, until at last he yielded to her importunity, and contrived as follows: Filling some skins with wine, he loaded them on donkeys, which he drove before him till he came to the place where the guards were watching the dead body, when pulling two or three of the skins towards him, he untied some of the necks which dangled by the asses' sides. The wine poured freely out, whereupon he began to beat his head and shout with all his might, seeming not to know which of the donkeys he should turn to first.

When the guards saw the wine running, delighted to profit by the occasion, they rushed one and all into the road, each with some vessel or other, and caught the liquor as it was spilling. The driver pretended anger, and loaded them with abuse; whereon they did their best to pacify him, until at last he appeared to soften, and recover his good humor, drove his asses aside out of the road, and set to work to re-arrange their burthens; meanwhile, as he talked and chatted with the guards, one of them began to rally him, and make him laugh, whereupon he gave them one of the skins as a gift. They now made up their minds to sit down and have a drinking-bout where they were, so they begged him to remain and drink with them. Then the man let himself be persuaded, and stayed.

As the drinking went on, they grew very friendly together, so presently he gave them another skin, upon which they drank so copiously that they were all overcome with liquor, and growing drowsy, lay down, and fell asleep on the spot. The thief waited till it was the dead of the night, and then took down the body of his brother; after which, in mockery, he shaved off the right side of all the soldiers' beards, and so left them. Laying his brother's body upon the asses, he carried it home to his mother, having thus accomplished the thing that she had required of him.

When it came to the king's ears that the thief's body was stolen away, he was sorely vexed. Wishing, therefore, whatever it might cost, to catch the man who had contrived the trick, he had recourse (the priest said) to an expedient which I can scarcely credit. He announced that he would bestow his own daughter upon the man who would narrate to her the best story of the cleverest and wickedest thing done by himself. If anyone in reply told her the story of the thief, she was to lay hold of him, and not allow him to get away.

The daughter did as her father willed, whereon the

thief, who was well aware of the king's motive, felt a desire to outdo him in craft and cunning. Accordingly he contrived the following plan: He procured the corpse of a man lately dead, and cutting off one of the arms at the shoulder, put it under his dress, and so went to the king's daughter. When she put the question to him as she had done to all the rest, he replied that the wickedest thing he had ever done was cutting off the head of his brother when he was caught in a trap in the king's treasury, and the cleverest was making the guards drunk and carrying off the body. As he spoke, the princess caught at him, but the thief took advantage of the darkness to hold out to her the hand of the corpse. Imagining it to be his own hand, she seized and held it fast; while the thief, leaving it in her grasp, made his escape by the door.

The king, when word was brought him of this fresh success, amazed at the sagacity and boldness of the man, sent messengers to all the towns in his dominions to proclaim a free pardon for the thief, and to promise him a rich reward, if he came and made himself known. The thief took the king at his word, and came boldly into his presence; whereupon Rhampsinitus, greatly admiring him, and looking on him as the most knowing of men, gave him his daughter in marriage. "The Egyptians," he said, "excelled all the rest of the world in wisdom, and this man excelled all other Egyptians."

The Oracle—Its Test by Croesus *

CRŒSUS learnt that Cyrus, the son of Cambyses, had destroyed the empire of Astyages, the son of Cyaxares;

* That practical ability flourished and was not unrewarded, even in the sixth century before Christ, is plain from the good business methods of Crœsus, King of most of Asia Minor, in testing the different Oracles of his time. No wonder Crœsus was the magnate of the day!

That the "barbarians," the Persians invading Greece under the mighty Xerxes, were not always remarkable for bravery, is evident and that the Persians were becoming daily more powerful. This led him to consider with himself whether it were possible to check the growing power of that people before it came to a head. With this design he resolved to make instant trial of the several oracles in Greece, and of the one in Libya. So he sent his messengers in different directions, some to Delphi, some to Abæ in Phocis, and some to Dodona; others to the oracle of Amphiaraüs; others to that of Trophonius; others, again, to Branchidæ in Milesia. These were the Greek oracles which he consulted. To Libya he sent another embassy to consult the oracle of Ammon. These messengers were sent to test the knowledge of the oracles, that, if they were found really to return true answers, he might send a second time, and inquire if he ought to attack the Persians.

The messengers who were dispatched to make trial of the oracles were given the following instructions: they were to keep count of the days from the time of their leaving Sardis, and, reckoning from that date, on the hundredth day they were to consult the oracles, and to inquire of them what Crœsus, the son of Alyattes, king of Lydia, was doing at that moment. The answers given them were to be taken down in writing, and brought back to him. None of the replies remain on record except that of the oracle at Delphi. There, the moment that the Lydians entered the sanctuary,

from the tale which follows this—"How the Oracle Defended Itself." A little later these same barbarians were overwhelmed by the Greeks at the famous naval conflict of Salamis, and Herodotus tells of Xerxes' cry that "My men have behaved like women."

Is there any more to be read from these chronicles of two thousand years ago? Was the immense power of the ancient Oracle, especially that at Delphi, based simply on the ignorance and credulity of the public? Again and again this Oracle swayed the destiny of the two greatest nations in the world—the Greeks and the Persians—and played no small part in the public and private affairs of the Greeks, the most highly civilized people then in existence.

Some explanation follows in the third selection.—Editor.

and before they put their questions, the Pythoness thus answered them in hexameter verse:

"I can count the sands, and I can measure the ocean;
I have ears for the silent, and know what the dumb man meaneth;
Lo! on my sense there striketh the smell of a shell-covered tortoise,
Boiling now on the fire, with the flesh of a lamb, in a caldron,—
Brass is the vessel below, and brass the cover above it."

These words the Lydians wrote down at the mouth of the Pythoness as she prophesied, and then set off on their return to Sardis. When all the messengers had come back with the answers which they had received, Crœsus undid the rolls, and read what was written in each. Only one approved itself to him, that of the Delphic oracle. This he had no sooner heard than he instantly made an act of adoration, and accepted it as true, declaring that the Delphic was the only really oracular shrine, the only one that had discovered in what way he was in fact employed. For on the departure of his messengers he had set himself to think what was most impossible for anyone to conceive of his doing, and then, waiting till the day agreed on came, he acted as he had determined. He took a tortoise and a lamb, and cutting them in pieces with his own hands, boiled them both together in a brazen caldron, covered over with a lid which was also of brass.

Such, then, was the answer returned to Crœsus from Delphi. What the answer was which the Lydians who went to the shrine of Amphiaraüs and performed the customary rites, obtained of the oracle there, I have it not in my power to mention, for there is no record of it. All that is known is, that Crœsus believed himself to have found there also an oracle which spoke the truth.

The Oracle—Its Repulse of the Persians

After passing Parapotami, the barbarians marched to Panopeis; and now the army separated into two bodies, whereof one, which was the more numerous and stronger of the two, marched, under Xerxes himself, towards Athens, entering Bœotia by the country of the Orchomenians. The Bœotians had one and all embraced the cause of the Medes; and their towns were in the possession of Macedonian garrisons, whom Alexander had sent there, to make it manifest to Xerxes that the Bœotians were on the Median side. Such, then, was the road followed by one division of the barbarians.

The other division took guides, and proceeded towards the temple of Delphi, keeping Mount Parnassus on their right hand. They too laid waste such parts of Phocis as they passed through, burning the city of the Panopeans, together with those of the Daulians and of the Æolidæ. This body had been detached from the rest of the army and made to march in this direction, for the purpose of plundering the Delphian temple and conveying to King Xerxes the riches which were there laid up. For Xerxes, as I am informed, was better acquainted with what there was worthy of note at Delphi, than even with what he had left in his own house; so many of those about him were continually describing the treasures—more especially the offerings made by Crœsus, the son of Alyattes.

Now when the Delphians heard what danger they were in, great fear fell on them. In their terror they consulted the oracle concerning the holy treasures, and inquired if they should bury them in the ground, or carry them away to some other country. The god, in reply, bade them leave the treasures untouched—"He was able," he said, "without help to protect his own." So the Delphians, when they received this answer, began to think about saving themselves. And first of all they sent their women and children across the gulf into Achæa; after which the greater number of them climbed up into the tops of Parnassus, and placed their goods for safety in the Corycian cave; while some effected their escape to Amphissa in Locris. In this way all the Delphians quitted the city, except sixty men, and the Prophet.

When the barbarian assailants drew near and were in sight of the place, the Prophet, who was named Aceratus, beheld, in front of the temple, a portion of the sacred armor, which it was not lawful for any mortal hand to touch, lying upon the ground, removed from the inner shrine where it was wont to hang. Then went he and told the prodigy to the Delphians who had remained behind. Meanwhile the enemy pressed forward briskly, and had reached the shrine of Minerva Pronaia, when they were overtaken by other prodigies still more wonderful than the first. Truly it was marvel enough, when warlike harness was seen lying outside the temple, removed there by no power but its own; what followed, however, exceeded in strangeness all prodigies that had ever been seen before. The barbarians had just reached in their advance the chapel of Minerva Pronaia, when a storm of thunder burst suddenly over their heads—at the same time two crags split off from Mount Parnassus, and rolled down upon them with a loud noise, crushing vast numbers beneath their weight—while from the temple of Minerva there went up the war-cry and the shout of victory.

All these things together struck terror into the barbarians, who forthwith turned and fled. The Delphians, seeing this, came down from their hiding places, and smote them with a great slaughter, from which such as escaped fled straight into Bœotia. These men, on their return, declared (as I am told) that besides the marvels mentioned above, they witnessed also other supernatural sights. Two armed warriors, they said, of a stature more than human, pursued after their flying ranks, pressing them close and slaying them.

These men, the Delphians maintain, were two Heroes belonging to the place—by name Phylacus and Autonoüs,

—each of whom has a sacred precinct near the temple; one, that of Phylacus, hard by the road which runs above the temple of Pronaia; the other, that of Autonoüs, near the Castilian spring, at the foot of the peak called Hyampeia. The blocks of stone which fell from Parnassus might still be seen in my day; they lay in the precinct of Pronaia, where they stopped, after rolling through the host of the barbarians. Thus was this body of men forced to retire from the temple.

The Oracle—Behind the Scenes

STUDENTS of antiquity show that the oracles were the powerful organs of "tainted news" in olden times. The "prophecies" usually represented tricks of the priests to aid their political schemes—to impress the superstitious popular mind as nothing else at that day could have done.

Regarding the tale from Herodotus just preceding—the oracle's defense of itself—Rawlinson, the translator, says:

"It is difficult to say how much of this account is, so far as the facts go, true—how much is exaggeration. We may, however, readily conceive that the priests arranged a plan of defense both on this occasion, and on the subsequent attack of the Gauls, B. C. 279, in which they aimed at inspiring their assailants with superstitious fear, and their own side with religious trust and confidence. The fragments of rock may have been carefully prepared beforehand, and have been precipitated by the hands of those who are said to have taken refuge in the peaks—a mode of defense constantly practiced by the inhabitants of mountainous countries. The sound which they made in falling may have been taken for thunder. The prodigy of the armor would require nothing but the hands of a single priest, and would be intended to indicate that the god was going out to the battle. The war-cry from Minerva's temple might be the voice of another priest, and would have been at once the signal and encouragement of an attack. Even the heroes may have been personated by two men of unusual stature, though if this portion of the tale originated with the Persians, it may have been a mere excuse offered to Xerxes, which the Delphic priests turned to their own advantage."

What really lay behind the first tale from Herodotus is thus sketched by *Smith's Dictionary of Antiquities:*

"In treating of the oracle in its public aspect, the idea that it had any extraordinary prophetic power, or second sight, must be laid aside; not that there are not some things in the history that may puzzle us as regards this, especially the first oracle given to Crœsus; but the second oracle to Crœsus, being plainly an evasion, demolishes the effect of the first oracle."

This "second oracle" was to the effect that Crœsus "would destroy a great empire." On the strength of it, he later attacked the Persians under Cyrus—but was forced to surrender his capital of Sardis, and lose his whole kingdom. Of course, the oracle took the ground that Crœsus' own empire had been the subject of its prophecy!

Also regarding the second tale, and the broader meaning of the oracle in general, Smith has this to say: "The miraculous defense of Delphi against the Persians is one of the best attested of heathen miracles; the similar defense against the Gauls has less evidence: but in the first case a natural explanation is open to us; the second is more frankly legendary.

"The real good which the oracle did, and especially in the earlier days, lay in the courage which it imparted through the supernatural blessing of which it was believed to be (and perhaps was) the minister. Sincerity of intention, and the belief in a presiding divine power, were elements of value which, on the whole, it impressed strongly on society.

"Whether we can rely or not on the statements that it supported the great legislators, Lycurgus and Solon, it unquestionably directed and encouraged the colonizing spirit of the Greeks. The most remarkable instance of this is the case of Cyrene, the foundation of which appears to have been entirely due to the Delphic oracle. 'King Apollo sends thee,' are the words of the oracle to Battus. There is, indeed, some likelihood in the supposition that the Delphic oracle had, through its numerous correspondents, real information of the state of foreign countries, such as a private individual could not possess (this is one explanation of the successful reply to Crœsus); if so, force would be added to its spiritual encouragement.

"Undoubtedly, however, the most important act of the Delphic oracle, as regards the internal affairs of the Greek states, was the command which it issued to Sparta to liberate Athens from the despot Hippias; a command issued to an unwilling but dutiful agent, and successfully carried out (510 B. C.). Few deeds in the world's history have been more fruitful of great consequences; but it was too great a service to be rewarded with gratitude. The Athenians declared that the Pythia had been bribed, and falsely attributed their own liberation to Harmodius and Aristogeiton.

"In the romantic history of the Persian war, few things are more interesting than the clash of sentiment between the fiery and resolute Athenians and the timid but clear-sighted oracle. The counsel that was hammered out, as it were, between these two contending (but not hostile) forces —the counsel that the Athenians should betake themselves to their 'wooden walls'—was in fact the very best that could have been given; though, had it failed, the oracle would have no doubt sheltered itself under the ambiguity of the term."

Lucius Apuleius

The Adventure of the Three Robbers

The great satire of Lucius Apuleius, the work through which his name lives after the lapse of nearly eighteen centuries, is "The Golden Ass," a romance from which the following passage has been selected and translated for these Mystery Stories. Lucius, the personage who tells the story, is regarded in some quarters as a portrayal of the author himself. The purpose of "The Golden Ass" was to satirize false priests and other contemporary frauds. But interspersed are many episodes of adventure and strange situations, one of which is here given.

AS Telephron reached the point of his story, his fellow revelers, befuddled with their wine, renewed the boisterous uproar. And while the old topers were clamoring for the customary libation to laughter, Byrrhæna explained to me that the morrow was a day religiously observed by her city from its cradle up; a day on which they alone among mortals propitiated that most sacred god, Laughter, with hilarious and joyful rites. "The fact that you are here," she added, "will make it all the merrier. And I do wish that you would contribute something amusing out of your own cleverness, in honor of the god, to help us duly worship such an important divinity."

"Surely," said I, "what you ask shall be done. And, by Jove! I hope I shall hit upon something good enough to make this mighty god of yours reveal his presence."

Hereupon, my slave reminding me what hour of night it was, I speedily got upon my feet, although none too steadily after my potations, and, having duly taken leave of Byrrhæna, guided my zigzag steps upon the homeward way. But at the very first corner we turned, a sudden gust of wind blew out the solitary torch on which we depended, and left us, plunged in the unforeseen blackness of night, to stumble wearily and painfully to our abode, bruising our feet on every stone in the road.

But when at last, holding each other up, we drew near our goal, there ahead of us were three others, of big and brawny build, expending the full energy of their strength upon our doorposts. And far from being in the least dismayed by our arrival, they seemed only fired to a greater zeal and made assault more fiercely. Quite naturally, it seemed clear to us both, and especially to me, that they were robbers, and of the most dangerous sort. So I forthwith drew the blade which I carry hidden under my cloak for such emergencies, and threw myself, undismayed, into the midst of these highwaymen. One after another, as they successively tried to withstand me, I ran them through, until finally all three lay stretched at my feet, riddled with many a gaping wound, through which they yielded up their breath. By this time Fotis, the maid, had been aroused by the din of battle, and still panting and perspiring freely I slipped in through the opening door, and, as weary as though I had fought with the three-formed Geryon instead of those pugnacious thieves, I yielded myself at one and the same moment to bed and to slumber.

Soon rosy-fingered Dawn, shaking the purple reins, was guiding her steeds across the path of heaven; and, snatched from my untroubled rest, night gave me back to day. Dismay seized my soul at the recollection of my deeds of the past evening. I sat there, crouching on my bed, with my interlaced fingers hugging my knees, and freely gave way to my distress; I already saw in fancy the court, the jury, the verdict, the executioner. How could I hope to find any judge so mild, so benevolent as to pronounce me innocent, soiled as I was with a triple murder, stained with the blood of so many citizens? Was this the glorious climax of my travels that the Chaldean, Diophanes, had so confidently predicted for me? Again and again I went over the whole matter bewailing my hard lot.

Hereupon there came a pounding at our doors and a steadily growing clamor on the threshold. No sooner was admission given than, with an impetuous rush, the whole house was filled with magistrates, police, and the motley crowd that followed. Two officers, by order of the magistrates, promptly laid hands upon me, and started to drag me off, though resistance was the last thing I should have thought of. By the time we had reached the first cross street the entire city was already trailing at our heels in an astonishingly dense mass. And I marched gloomily along with my head hanging down to the very earth—I might even say to the lower regions below the earth.

At length after having made the circuit of every city square, in exactly the way that the victims are led around before a sacrifice meant to ward off evil omens, I was brought into the forum and made to confront the tribunal of justice. The magistrates had taken their seats upon the raised platform, the court crier had commanded silence, when suddenly everyone present, as if with one voice, protested that in so vast a gathering there was danger from the dense crowding, and demanded that a case of such importance should be tried instead in the public theater. No sooner said than the entire populace streamed onward, helter-skelter, and in a marvelously short time had packed the whole auditorium till every aisle and gallery was one solid mass. Many swarmed up the columns, others dangled from the statues, while a few there were that perched, half out of sight, on window ledges and cornices; but all in their amazing eagerness seemed quite careless how far they risked their lives. After the manner of a sacrifice I was led by the public officials down the middle of the stage, and was left standing in the midst of the orchestra. Once more the voice of the court crier boomed forth, calling for the prosecutor, whereupon a certain old man arose, and having first taken a small vase, the bottom of which ended in a narrow funnel, and having filled it with water, which escaping drop by drop should mark the length of his speech, addressed the populace as follows:

"This is no trivial case, most honored citizens, but one which directly concerns the peace of our entire city, and one which will be handed down as a weighty precedent. Wherefore, your individual and common interests equally demand that you should sustain the dignity of the State, and not permit this brutal murderer to escape the penalty of the wholesale butchery that resulted from his bloody deeds. And do not think that I am influenced by any private motives, or giving vent to personal animosity. For I am in command of the night watch, and up to this time I think there is no one who will question my watchful diligence. Accordingly I will state the case and faithfully set forth the events of last night.

"It was about the hour of the third watch, and I was making my round of the entire city, going from door to door with scrupulous vigilance, when suddenly I beheld this bloodthirsty young man, sword in hand, spreading carnage around him; already, no less than three victims of his savagery lay writhing at his feet, gasping forth their breath in a pool of blood. Stricken, as well he might be, with the guilt of so great a crime, the fellow fled, and, slipping into one of the houses under cover of the darkness, lay hidden the rest of the night. But, thanks to the gods who permit no sinner to go unpunished, I forestalled him at daybreak, before he could make his escape by secret ways, and have brought him here for trial before your sacred tribunal of justice. The prisoner at the bar is a threefold murderer; he was taken in the very act; and, furthermore, he is a foreigner. Accordingly, it is your plain duty to return a verdict of guilty against this man from a strange land for a crime which you would severely punish even in the case of one of your own citizens."

Having thus spoken, the remorseless prosecutor suspended his vindictive utterance, and the court crier straightway ordered me to begin my defense, if I had any to make. At first I could not sufficiently control my voice to speak, although less overcome, alas, by the harshness of the accusation than by my own guilty conscience. But at last, miraculously inspired with courage, I made answer as follows:

" I realize how hard it is for a man accused of murder, and confronted with the bodies of three of your citizens, to persuade so large a multitude of his innocence, even though he tells the exact truth and voluntarily admits the facts. But if in mercy you will give me an attentive hearing, I shall easily make clear to you that far from deserving to be put on trial for my life, I have wrongfully incurred the heavy stigma of such a crime as the chance result of justifiable indignation.

" I was making my way home from a dinner party at a rather late hour, after drinking pretty freely, I won't attempt to deny—for that was the head and front of my offense—when, lo and behold! before the very doors of my abode, before the home of the good Milo, your fellow-citizen, I beheld a number of villainous thieves trying to effect an entrance and already prying the doors off from the twisted hinges. All the locks and bolts, so carefully closed for the night, had been wrenched away, and the thieves were planning the slaughter of the inmates. Finally, one of them, bigger and more active than the rest, urged them to action with these words:

" 'Come on, boys! Show the stuff you are made of, and strike for all you are worth while they are asleep! No quarter now, no faint-hearted weakening! Let death go through the house with drawn sword! If you find any in bed, slit their throats before they wake; if any try to resist, cut them down. Our only chance of getting away safe and sound is to leave no one else safe and sound in the whole house.'

" I confess, citizens, that I was badly frightened, both on account of my hosts and myself; and believing that I was doing the duty of a good citizen, I drew the sword which always accompanies me in readiness for such dangers, and started in to drive away or lay low those desperate robbers. But the barbarous and inhuman villains, far from being frightened away, had the audacity to stand against me, although they saw that I was armed. Their serried ranks opposed me. Next, the leader and standard-bearer of the band, assailing me with brawny strength, seized me with both hands by the hair, and bending me backward, prepared to beat out my brains with a paving stone; but while he was still shouting for one, with an unerring stroke I luckily ran him through and stretched him at my feet. Before long a second stroke, aimed between the shoulders, finished off another of them, as he clung tooth and nail to my legs; while the third one, as he rashly advanced, I stabbed full in the chest.

"Since I had fought on the side of law and order, in defense of public safety and my host's home, I felt myself not only without blame but deserving of public praise. I have never before been charged with even the slightest infringement of the law; I enjoy a high reputation among my own people, and all my life have valued a clear conscience above all material possessions. Nor can I understand why I should suffer this prosecution for having taken a just vengeance upon those worthless thieves, since no one can show that there had ever before been any enmity between us, or for that matter that I had ever had any previous acquaintance with the thieves. You have not even established any motive for which I may be supposed to have committed so great a crime."

At this point my emotion again overcame me, and with my hands extended in entreaty, I turned from one to another, beseeching them to spare me in the name of common humanity, for the sake of all that they held dear. I thought by this time they must be moved to pity, thrilled with sympathy for my wretchedness; accordingly I called to witness the Eye of Justice and the Light of Day, and intrusted my case to the providence of God, when lifting up my eyes I discovered that the whole assembly was convulsed with laughter, not excepting my own kind host and relative, Milo, who was shaking with merriment. "So much for friendship!" I thought to myself, "so much for gratitude! In protecting my host, I have become a murderer, on trial for my life; while he, far from raising a finger to help me, makes a mock of my misery."

At this moment a woman clad in black rushed down the center of the stage, weeping and wailing and clasping a small child to her breast. An older woman, covered with rags and similarly shaken with sobs, followed her, both of them waving olive branches as they passed around the bier on which lay the covered bodies of the slain, and lifted up their voices in mournful outcry: "For the sake of common humanity," they wailed, "by all the universal laws of justice, be moved to pity by the undeserved death of these young men! Give to a lonely wife and mother the comfort of vengeance! Come to the aid of this unhappy child left fatherless in his tender years, and offer up the blood of the assassin at the shrine of law and order."

Hereupon the presiding magistrate arose and addressed the people:

"The crime for which the prisoner will later pay the full penalty, not even he attempts to deny. But still another duty remains to be performed, and that is to find out who were his accomplices in this wicked deed; since it does not seem likely that one man alone could have overcome three others so young and strong as these. We must apply torture to extract the truth; and since the slave who accompanied him has made his escape, there is no other alternative left us than to wring the names of his companions from the prisoner himself, in order that we may effectually relieve the public of all apprehension of danger from this desperate gang."

Immediately, in accordance with the Greek usage, fire and the wheel were brought forth, together with all the other instruments of torture. Now indeed my distress was not only increased but multiplied when I saw that I was fated to perish piecemeal. But at this point the old woman, whose noisy lamentations had become a nuisance, broke out with this demand:

"Honored citizens, before you proceed to torture the prisoner, on account of the dear ones whom he has taken from me, will you not permit the bodies of the deceased to be uncovered in order that the sight of their youth and beauty may fire you with a righteous anger and a severity proportioned to the crime?"

These words were received with applause, and straightway the magistrate commanded that I myself should with my own hand draw off the covering from the bodies lying on the bier. In spite of my struggles and desperate determination not to look again upon the consequences of my last night's deed, the court attendants promptly dragged me forward, in obedience to the judge's order, and bending my arm by main force from its place at my side stretched it out above the three corpses. Conquered in the struggle, I yielded to necessity, and much against my will drew down the covering and exposed the bodies.

Great heavens, what a sight! What a miracle! What a transformation in my whole destiny! I had already begun to look upon myself as a vassal of Proserpine, a bondsman of Hades, and now I could only gasp in impotent amazement at the suddenness of the change; words fail me to express fittingly the astounding metamorphosis. For the bodies of my butchered victims were nothing more nor less than three inflated bladders, whose sides still bore the scars of numerous punctures, which, as I recalled my battle of the previous night, were situated at the very points where I had inflicted gaping wounds upon my adversaries. Hereupon the hilarity, which up to this point had been fairly held in check, swept through the crowd like a conflagration. Some gave themselves up helplessly to an unrestrained extravagance of merriment; others did their best to control themselves, holding their aching sides with both hands. And having all laughed until they could laugh no more, they passed out of the theater, their backward glances still centered upon me.

From the moment that I had drawn down that funeral pall I stood fixed as if frozen into stone, as powerless to move as anyone of the theater's statues or columns. Nor did I come out of my stupor until Milo, my host, himself approached and clapping me on the shoulder, drew me away with gentle violence, my tears now flowing freely and sobs choking my voice. He led me back to the house by a roundabout way through the least frequented streets, doing his best meanwhile to soothe my nerves and heal my wounded feelings. But nothing he could say availed to lessen my bitter indignation at having been made so undeservedly ridiculous. But all at once the magistrates themselves, still wearing their insignia of office, arrived at the house and made personal amends in the following words:

"We are well aware, Master Lucius, both of your own high merit and that of your family, for the renown of your name extends throughout the land. Accordingly, you must understand that the treatment which you so keenly resent was in no sense intended as an insult. Therefore, banish your present gloomy mood and dismiss all anger from your mind. For the festival, which we solemnly celebrate with each returning year in honor of the God of Laughter, must always depend upon novelty for its success. And so our god, who owes you so great a debt to-day, decrees that his favoring presence shall follow you wherever you go, and that your cheerful countenance shall everywhere be a signal for hilarity. The whole city, out of gratitude, bestows upon you exceptional honors, enrolling your name as one of its patrons, and decreeing that your likeness in bronze shall be erected as a perpetual memorial of to-day."

Pliny, the Younger

Letter to Sura

OUR leisure furnishes me with the opportunity of learning from you, and you with that of instructing me. Accordingly, I particularly wish to know whether you think there exist such things as phantoms, possessing an appearance peculiar to themselves, and a certain supernatural power, or that mere empty delusions receive a shape from our fears. For my part, I am led to believe in their existence, especially by what I hear happened to Curtius Rufus. While still in humble circumstances and obscure, he was a hanger-on in the suite of the Governor of Africa. While pacing the colonnade one afternoon, there appeared to him a female form of superhuman size and beauty. She informed the terrified man that she was "Africa," and had come to foretell future events; for that he would go to Rome, would fill offices of state there, and would even return to that same province with the highest powers, and die in it. All which things were fulfilled. Moreover, as he touched at Carthage, and was disembarking from his ship, the same form is said to have presented itself to him on the shore. It is certain that, being seized with illness, and auguring the future from the past and misfortune from his previous prosperity, he himself abandoned all hope of life, though none of those about him despaired.

Is not the following story again still more appalling and not less marvelous? I will relate it as it was received by me:

There was at Athens a mansion, spacious and commodious, but of evil repute and dangerous to health. In the dead of night there was a noise as of iron, and, if you listened more closely, a clanking of chains was heard, first of all from a distance, and afterwards hard by. Presently a specter used to appear, an ancient man sinking with emaciation and squalor, with a long beard and bristly hair, wearing shackles on his legs and fetters on his hands, and shaking them. Hence the inmates, by reason of their fears, passed miserable and horrible nights in sleeplessness. This want of sleep was followed by disease, and, their terrors increasing, by death. For in the daytime as well, though the apparition had departed, yet a reminiscence of it flitted before their eyes, and their dread outlived its cause. The mansion was accordingly deserted, and, condemned to solitude, was entirely abandoned to the dreadful ghost. However, it was advertised, on the chance of some one, ignorant of the fearful curse attached to it, being willing to buy or to rent it. Athenodorus, the philosopher, came to Athens and read the advertisement. When he had been informed of the terms, which were so low as to appear suspicious, he made inquiries, and learned the whole of the particulars. Yet none the less on that account, nay, all the more readily, did he rent the house. As evening began to draw on, he ordered a sofa to be set for himself in the front part of the house, and called for his notebooks, writing implements, and a light. The whole of his servants he dismissed to the interior apartments, and for himself applied his soul, eyes, and hand to composition, that his mind might not, from want of occupation, picture to itself the phantoms of which he had heard, or any empty terrors. At the commencement there was the universal silence of night. Soon the shaking of irons and the clanking of chains was heard, yet he never raised his eyes nor slackened his pen, but hardened his soul and deadened his ears by its help. The noise grew and approached: now it seemed to be heard at the door, and next inside the door. He looked round, beheld and recognized the figure he had been told of. It was standing and signaling to him with its finger, as though inviting him. He, in reply, made a sign with his hand that it should wait a moment, and applied himself afresh to his tablets and pen. Upon this the figure kept rattling its chains over his head as he wrote. On looking round again, he saw it making the same signal as before, and without delay took up a light and followed it. It moved with a slow step, as though oppressed by its chains, and, after turning into the courtyard of the house, vanished suddenly and left his company. On being thus left to himself, he marked the spot with some grass and leaves which he plucked. Next day he applied to the magistrates, and urged them to have the spot in question dug up. There were found there some bones attached to and intermingled with fetters; the body to which they had belonged, rotted away by time and the soil, had abandoned them thus naked and corroded to the chains. They were collected and interred at the public expense, and the house was ever afterwards free from the spirit, which had obtained due sepulture.

The above story I believe on the strength of those who affirm it. What follows I am myself in a position to affirm to others. I have a freedman, who is not without some knowledge of letters. A younger brother of his was sleeping with him in the same bed. The latter dreamed he saw some one sitting on the couch, who approached a pair of scissors to his head, and even cut the hair from the crown of it. When day dawned he was found to be cropped round the crown, and his locks were discovered lying about. A very short time afterwards a fresh occurrence of the same kind confirmed the truth of the former one. A lad of mine was sleeping, in company with several others, in the pages' apartment. There came through the windows (so he tells the story) two figures in white tunics, who cut his hair as he lay, and departed the way they came. In his case, too, daylight exhibited him shorn, and his locks scattered around. Nothing remarkable followed, except, perhaps, this, that I was not brought under accusation, as I should have been, if Domitian (in whose reign these events happened) had lived longer. For in his desk was found an information against me which had been presented by Carus; from which circumstance it may be conjectured—inasmuch as it is the custom of accused persons to let their hair grow—that the cutting off of my slaves' hair was a sign of the danger which threatened me being averted.

I beg, then, that you will apply your great learning to this subject. The matter is one which deserves long and deep consideration on your part; nor am I, for my part, undeserving of having the fruits of your wisdom imparted to me. You may even argue on both sides (as your way is), provided you argue more forcibly on one side than the other, so as not to dismiss me in suspense and anxiety, when the very cause of my consulting you has been to have my doubts put an end to.